CHALICE OF DARKNESS

CHALICE OF DARKNESS

Sarah Rayne

**SEVERN
HOUSE**

First world edition published in Great Britain and the USA in 2023
by Severn House, an imprint of Canongate Books Ltd,
14 High Street, Edinburgh EH1 1TE.

Trade paperback edition first published in Great Britain and the USA in 2023
by Severn House, an imprint of Canongate Books Ltd.

severnhouse.com

British Library Cataloguing-in-Publication Data
A CIP catalogue record for this title is available from the British Library.

ISBN-13: 978-1-4483-0640-4 (cased)
ISBN-13: 978-1-4483-0644-2 (trade paper)
ISBN-13: 978-1-4483-0643-5 (e-book)

Typeset by Palimpsest Book Production Ltd.,
Falkirk, Stirlingshire, Scotland.

ONE

Augustus Pocket sat in a corner of the bare stage and hoped that this was not going to be the day when the Fitzglens in general, and Mr Jack Fitzglen in particular, embarked on a course of action that would end in their downfall. After his years as dresser to Mr Jack, Gus supposed he ought to be accustomed to the family's ways, but he was not. Every time one of them came up with a new scheme, Gus imagined them all being locked up in some bleak cell, in company with half the old lags in London.

'They're society burglars, the Fitzglens,' old Todworthy Inkling had said to Gus when Gus first went to work for the family. 'They might bound around the stage, declaiming Shakespeare, and put on lavish concerts for the King, and dine with the wealthy, but they're criminals, every last one of them. Burglars – thieves, robbers, filchers, screwsmen. They're very good at what they do, though – and,' he said, with one of his sly winks, 'they only steal from the rich. And even though they're criminals, they're extremely charming.'

Mr Jack was being extremely charming now. He was standing at the centre of the stage, his eyes alight with enthusiasm.

'I've asked you here tonight because I've worked out our next filch,' he was saying. 'And it's going to involve something so famous and so priceless that it'll be the talk of London for years to come.'

A sharp voice said, 'I hope you aren't about to announce that we're going to lift something like the Star of India, because it would be an impossibility, and I'll have nothing to do with it.'

This was Miss Daphnis, of course – the majestic Daphnis Fitzglen who in her youth had been admired by the King when he was Prince of Wales, and who, even now, could sweep on to a stage and inspect the front row of the stalls through a lorgnette, with a stare that silenced even the most chattersome of audiences.

'Don't talk rot, Daphnis,' said Mr Rudraige, who would never be left out of any argument that was brewing. 'Jack won't be planning anything so outrageous.'

'And so risky,' murmured Mr Byron Fitzglen, who had draped himself on a chaise longue that had been left on the stage after the week's performance. 'But I'm all agog to hear Jack's plan.'

'Never mind agog, get to the point, Jack, because it's Sunday night, let's remember – the one night we're usually free to go about our lawful occasions—'

'Or unlawful,' murmured a sardonic voice from the chaise longue.

'—and when I had your note I was about to set off for the Thespis Club, and they've just had a consignment of Tuke Holdsworth,' said Mr Rudraige, glaring at Byron.

Mr Jack abandoned his centre-stage stance and sat down at the table. 'Aunt Daphnis,' he said, 'of course I haven't got the Star of India in mind, and Rudraige, I'll be brief so you can go along to drink your port at the Thespis.' He leaned forward. His hair, which ladies said was like amber silk or honey with the sun on it, had tumbled over his forehead. 'We're going to mount a marvellous, lavish production,' he said. 'It will be so extravagant and splendid it will be anticipated for weeks ahead of its opening, and we'll be booked up for months. But on opening night . . .'

'Yes?' said several voices.

'On opening night, making a surprising and dramatic appearance of its own, will be something immeasurably rare and famous. Something about which there's always been a great deal of rumour and speculation – about which legends have been spun. When the Amaranth's curtain rises, there it will be.'

'Is it something you want us to filch beforehand, Jack, because we can hardly do that, then display it to half of London on our own stage,' said a dubious voice from the other end of the table.

'Well said, Ambrose,' nodded Miss Daphnis. 'Jack?'

'We won't be filching anything,' said Mr Jack. 'At least – we won't be *seen* to be filching anything. We're going to reclaim something that vanished fifteen years ago.'

'What? What are we going to reclaim?'

The smile that was both mischievous and beckoning showed briefly, then Mr Jack said, 'The Talisman Chalice.'

Jack Fitzglen thought there were times when an audience's reaction disappointed you. Times when you worked and rehearsed until you were drained, and when you almost sweated blood to get a response from your audience – only to find that they sat in stony silence, not laughing or crying or displaying any trace of emotion, so that you wondered why on earth you were in the theatre at all.

But this was not one of those times. The shocked silence that descended on the little group of people on the Amaranth's stage was all he could have wished.

He thought it would be either his Uncle Rudraige or Daphnis who would speak first, and in the end it was Rudraige. Of course it would be, thought Jack, with an inward and affectionate smile.

Rudraige said, 'That sounds like an extremely far-fetched scheme.'

'It sounds like an impossibility,' put in Byron. 'Apart from anything else, nobody's ever known what happened to the Talisman Chalice, have they?'

'It was supposed to have been stolen,' said Daphnis, 'although nobody ever found out who had stolen it – or if anyone did find out, it was all kept very secret. Fifteen years ago, wasn't it, Rudraige?'

'It was. You and Jack were too young to be really aware of it at the time, Byron, but I remember it very well.'

'It was going to be part of a display the Victoria & Albert Museum were mounting—'

'To celebrate Edward VII's fiftieth birthday,' said Rudraige, eagerly. 'The museum had arranged a special glass case for it, and then, when it came to it, the chalice was nowhere to be found. The V&A were horrified and all kinds of wild accusations flew around. All the newspapers reported it. "Royal treasure stolen", that was what they wrote. And, "One of the oldest items in the monarch's possession". The whole thing caught people's imaginations.'

'And sold a lot of newspapers in the process,' remarked Daphnis, tartly.

'Well, yes.'

'I always thought the chalice didn't really exist,' said a rather worried voice that had not spoken yet. 'My mother said the stories about it were just twopence-coloured tales cooked up by the newspapers.'

'It does exist, Cecily,' said Jack, turning to her.

'Yes, and weren't ballads even written about it?' asked Byron.

'They were.' Rudraige frowned in an effort of memory. 'Daphnis, wasn't there one supposed to be about its history – what was it called—?'

'"The Lament of the Luck-filled Vessel",' said Daphnis. 'I remember it very well. "There's a fortune's gone a-begging/ And the luck's gone out the door—" I don't recall any more of the words, though.'

'Nor do I, but it was a good song,' said Rudraige, rumty-tumming a tune on the table top with his fingertips.

Jack said, 'It's true that nobody ever knew what happened to the chalice.' He looked round at them. 'Until now,' he said.

There was another of the abrupt silences, then Ambrose said, 'You've never found it, Jack? Or found out who pilfered it?'

'Of course he hasn't. He's teasing us.'

'I'm not teasing you, and I haven't found it yet, and I have no idea who might have pilfered it. But I think I might have discovered where it is,' said Jack. By this time even Byron had forgotten about being a languid poet and was sitting up straight so as not to miss anything.

Jack reached into a pocket, and produced a large envelope. 'This is a letter to my father,' he said, pleased that his voice sounded perfectly normal, because he did not want to show any emotion about this. 'I found it in the old costume room – I was looking for ideas for something dazzling and unusual that we might use as a focus for our next piece.'

'Or that we might profitably filch,' murmured Ambrose.

'Well, that, too. And I found this.'

Before anyone could ask questions, he read the letter out.

"'My dear Aiden – and I hope I may call you that.

"I send you with this letter two photographs which show me with both the items you arranged to be brought to me last month. You may be sure they will be kept safely.

"The photographs have been taken discreetly and in secrecy, and, of course, are not known about here. However, I think they are excellent reproductions, and I am sending them partly as a mark of my gratitude, but also because it will mean that somewhere beyond this house proof of my ownership will exist. Perhaps one day I will be glad of that. If it is ever possible for the sender to be told how much I treasure his gift and how much it meant to me, I would be most grateful.

"Thank you so very much for what you have done. It pains me to now write this, but I know you will understand when I say that *on no account must you come to Vallow and certainly never to Vallow Hall.* I wish it could be otherwise, but you and I both know it can not.

"With my very warmest good wishes, Maude."'

'It's dated December 1891,' said Jack. 'With it were these photographs.'

He placed them on the table, and they all leaned forward. Byron abandoned the chaise longue and came over to the table. Jack sat back, watching them, curious to know if the photographs affected them in the way they had affected him. At first glance the images were not so very remarkable; two of them showed a young lady with dark hair coiled smoothly into the nape of her neck, wearing a gown that Jack thought was the style of the Nineties. In one photograph she was holding some kind of document – it was impossible to read the writing on it, but there was the impression of ornate script and of ribbon sewn down the left-hand side, as in a legal document. In the other photograph more of the room was visible, as if the photographer had moved his equipment back a little way. It might be any drawing room in any large house, although it looked more like a study, or even a library.

But the third photograph was different. It showed a piecrust table, and on it was a large, stemmed bowl, elaborately shaped, almost with folds, suggesting the petals of a rose. Even in the black and white and grey image it was obvious that the bowl was glass, and that it was tinted. Tiny figures were discernible, as if several scenes were depicted, and it was as if an illuminated medieval manuscript had been cast in glass, or as if a stained-glass window had been re-shaped. Jack again regretted the absence of colour, because in reality the chalice would glow with richness – crimson and violet and jade . . .

He said, 'I'm taking it that the lady in those two photographs is the writer of the letter.'

'Maude,' said Byron, softly.

'Yes. And that,' said Jack, touching the third photograph with a fingertip, 'is the lost Talisman Chalice.'

'The curious thing,' said Rudraige, after the photographs had been passed round and studied, and the letter read by everyone, 'is that on the night of the fire in this theatre, your father went back inside, Jack. None of us ever knew why.'

'But now you think it might have been to get this letter and the photographs?' Why his father had gone back into the burning Amaranth that day was a question that had always lain uncomfortably at the deepest part of Jack's mind. It was not a question he had ever asked until now, because he had never dared allow the memory of his father's death into the light.

But Rudraige said, 'I don't know. But I do think he tried to get up to the costume room.'

'Have any of you heard of Vallow?' asked Jack. 'Or Maude?' As they shook their heads, he said, 'Well, no matter. Because what we're going to do is find the chalice, take it back, and make it the centrepiece of a play here at the Amaranth.' He grinned. 'Can't you just visualize the interest that will create? Most of London will be queuing up for seats.'

'It'd solve the problem of the dry rot,' observed Rudraige, sepulchrally.

'Has the Amaranth got dry rot? My father always said you could never get rid of dry rot. Not once it had got hold of a building.'

'Cecily, the Amaranth's had dry rot ever since anyone can remember. It's positively rampant, but of course it can be got rid of.'

'Always supposing you can afford to do so,' said Ambrose, who had been jotting down figures and apparently trying to add them up.

'Jack, what do you know about the Talisman Chalice?' demanded Daphnis.

'Not very much,' said Jack. 'But I think Byron might know more. Byron?'

'Well, I do know a little,' said Byron, clearly pleased at being deferred to. 'And one of the things I do recall is a superstition that it carries good fortune with it – almost as if it's contained inside the chalice itself.'

'Like a soup tureen,' murmured Cecily.

'But there's a dark side,' Byron went on. 'The legend is that the good fortune is only for the rightful owners, and that if it's taken from them, the luck is poured away, and very ill luck indeed fills it up instead, and spills out on to the – well, the wrongful owner. I think that's what the words of that ballad meant, Rudraige. That line about "A fortune's gone a-begging" was actually "*Fortune's* gone a-begging".'

'Gone a-begging, because the chalice had been stolen from the rightful owners,' said Jack, thoughtfully.

'But who are the rightful owners?' asked Cecily.

Byron glanced at Jack, who nodded, as if to say: *go on.* 'They've had several names over the centuries,' said Byron. 'But when they first acquired the chalice, they were called—'

'Yes?' said several voices, as Byron, who knew, as all the Fitzglens did, the effect of a well-judged pause, broke off. Then he said, 'At the start of the chalice's history they were called Plantagenet.' He looked across at Jack, as if handing the conversation back to him.

Jack said, 'And now, of course, we know them by the name of Saxe-Coburg-Gotha.'

For a moment he thought he had miscalculated. I've over-reached, he thought. Gus always said I would, one day. He glanced at Gus, who was sitting quietly in his chair, and saw him give a small nod of encouragement. This was reassuring, because Gus's instinct was seldom wrong.

Daphnis said, very sharply, 'You're talking about the British royal family? Our own royal family?'

'Yes, he is,' said Byron. 'They're supposed to have acquired the chalice somewhere in the thirteen hundreds. I don't know how or from where, although I should be able to find out. As for the superstition – I wouldn't think the present incumbents of the throne give it much credence. They're far too down to earth.'

'I agree. But,' said Jack, 'around fifteen years ago—'

'In 1891,' murmured Byron, glancing at Maude's letter.

'Perhaps. Around that time, somebody in that family either lost the chalice, or it was stolen.'

'And the theft covered up.' This was Daphnis.

'You know, I wouldn't be surprised if old Edward didn't quietly lift it to bestow on one of his lady friends,' observed Rudraige. '"A little mark of affectionate gratitude, my dear",' he said, and such was his stagecraft that for a moment it was the now-ageing Edward VII who sat there. 'In fact now I think back, I believe that old ballad about fortune going a-begging was supposed to have been written after Edward got drunk one night in company with a crowd of actors and actresses, and related the legend to them.'

'And somebody took notes and wrote the song?' asked Cecily.

'I shouldn't be surprised. I even have a feeling that one of the Gilfillan lot was among the company that night.'

'Oh, they get everywhere, those Gilfillans,' said Ambrose. 'I wouldn't put anything past them. They're always spying on us and trying to get in with their own version of a play ahead of us.' He glanced over his shoulder, as if he expected to see Gilfillans lurking in the wings.

'But,' said Cecily, 'the chalice might simply have been broken by a housemaid who never admitted it – and they simply put out the theft theory to cover it up. I remember we used to have a Sèvres dish and a housemaid was dusting it one day, and—'

'Cecily, if this photograph can be believed, the chalice wasn't smashed by a housemaid brandishing a feather duster,' said Daphnis.

'But look here, Jack, supposing you can find the chalice,' said Rudraige, 'how will you explain it turning up on our stage?' He fixed Jack with the brow-frowning expression that caused audiences to shiver with fearful delight and theatre critics to write how Rudraige Fitzglen could convey villainous menace better than anyone in the English theatre.

'Yes, have you got a plan for that?' demanded Daphnis.

'Of course he'll have a plan,' said Byron.

'The plan is that one of us has an admirer,' said Jack. 'But it's someone who has never let his name be known, but who has nurtured his – or, of course, her – passion for years in utter secrecy. But who's now sent a gift hinting that it has a mysterious history—'

'And expressing the hope it can be used in a play?' asked Byron. 'Oh, I like that.'

'And the gift is the Talisman Chalice,' said Ambrose, thoughtfully.

'Who's going to have the admirer?' demanded Daphnis. 'I wouldn't mind it being me. Someone from my past, we could make it. I was not unsought in my youth,' she added.

'I could write the letter from him,' offered Byron.

'Yes, it's very much your province, Byron.' Jack had hoped Byron would offer, and he was pleased.

'It'd have to prove we hadn't stolen the chalice, but that shouldn't be difficult.' Byron sat up enthusiastically, then remembered about being a poet, and relapsed into semi-languor. 'Of course, I'm quite busy at the moment with the family history and my epic poem, and you can't just switch off the muse—'

'Oh God,' said several voices.

'You'll be very glad when that history's finished, and bound in vellum,' said Byron, indignantly. 'I've already dealt with that uncle on Aunt Daphnis's side who was involved in the disappearance of the Fabergé egg from the Russian imperial court. *And*,' he said, 'I'm on the track of the founder of this family – Highwayman Harry who romped around holding up carriages in the seventeen hundreds.'

'Angels and ministers of grace defend me,' said Rudraige. 'Jack, if Byron ever finishes his opus, for pity's sake make sure it doesn't see the light of day until we're all safely dead. Otherwise we'll all be hailed off to the clink.'

'Yes, but Byron will make a good job of creating a letter to go with the chalice,' said Jack. 'He's forged much more difficult things in his time.'

'Such as when we spruced up that silver coffee pot, and Byron wrote a letter making it seem as if it was a gift from David Garrick to Peg Woffington.' Ambrose nodded. 'He wrote how Garrick was looking forward to drinking coffee out of it with her.'

'Todworthy Inkling got an excellent price for us on the strength of that,' said Jack.

'We had new curtains for the royal box out of it,' put in Cecily.

'I suppose,' said Ambrose, suddenly, 'that it is the real thing, is it, that chalice in the photograph? It isn't a copy?'

'You can't tell from a photograph,' said Byron. 'But I should think it'd be quite difficult to fake convincingly.'

'Then assuming we're agreed that it's the genuine article,' said Rudraige, 'and that its whereabouts can be tracked down, who is going to be the one to actually carry out the filch?'

They glanced at one another. It's that story about the luck going a-begging and ill luck spilling out if the chalice falls into wrongful hands, thought Jack, watching them. They don't like that. If I'm honest, I don't like it, either.

But he smiled round the table, and said, lightly, 'Since this is my idea, I suppose I'd better be the one to carry it out.' And felt, as if it was tangible, the relief go through them.

After everyone had left, Jack looked again at the photograph and re-read Maude's letter. Why had she warned his father never to go to Vallow? Had Aiden been engaged on some filch of his own, and narrowly escaped being caught and had to flee? But that explanation did not seem to fit with the contents of Maude's letter.

If Jack went to this unknown place called Vallow all these years later, what would he find? The Talisman Chalice itself?

Maude? But Maude might have left the country long since, married, gone on safari, died . . .

He stared at the photograph. Maude, whoever you are – or were – I don't think you could be called beautiful and certainly not pretty, he thought. But I suspect most people would take a second look at you and probably a third.

For a fleeting moment he touched in his mind the memory of his mother, who had died when he was born, but who was still spoken of with affection by the family. But the woman in these photographs bore no resemblance to the figure in the silver-framed images that were all he had of his mother. And although he would not have ruled out his father having had one or two lovers since his wife's death, Maude's letter was not couched in lover's terms.

And it was important to remember that it was only in novels or rather pretentious plays that valuable objects were discovered in dusty corners, with mysterious letters from enigmatic ladies folded alongside them . . .

He already knew that he was going to Vallow Hall. He had no idea yet where it was, and he had certainly never heard of Vallow. But he would find it. Even if it turned out to be at the ends of the earth – if it was in some far-flung corner of the Empire, or buried in the undergrowth of the Amazon rainforests or in a remote Tibetan valley – he would go there.

TWO

Vallow Hall was not in a far-flung corner of the Empire or an Amazonian rainforest or a lost valley in Tibet. It was in Northumberland, and it was close to the Scottish border.

'The village is called Vallow as well,' said Jack, studying various maps with Byron after that evening's performance. 'It looks like the tiniest of places. But it's a fair journey from London to Northumberland.'

'Perfectly reachable by rail, though. And once you're there,' said Byron, 'I think you should appear as a gentleman of some substance. Unless you're thinking of using the tramp ploy, but I hope you aren't, because it doesn't really suit you, the tramp ploy. What do you think, Gus?'

'You can play any role there is, Mr Jack,' said Gus, who was ironing shirts in a corner of Jack's dressing room. 'But I'd have to say that being a tramp doesn't come naturally to you.'

'Gus is right. I thought,' said Byron, 'that you could recently have come into an inheritance, and be searching for a country residence to purchase. A great-uncle can have died and left you a modest fortune. That'll mean you can wander around looking at houses and no one will find it peculiar. Actually, of course, you'll be looking for the chalice and investigating Vallow Hall.'

'And Maude,' said Jack.

'And Maude. I thought you might call yourself Joseph Glennon – what do you think? It's near enough to your own name not to feel too strange, but sufficiently unlike it for anyone to guess who you really are.'

Jack tried it out with several different emphases. 'I like it,' he said at last. 'And I think Joseph Glennon is quiet and somewhat diffident and a bit naïve.'

'Academic and slightly overwhelmed by his sudden good fortune,' agreed Byron.

'I'll wear rimless spectacles,' said Jack. 'There's bound to be some in the costume store. They'd look very professorial. And if we don't travel up there until next week I can probably grow a scholarly looking beard. In fact it had better be a week from now anyway, because Ambrose needs rehearsal if he's taking over my part in this current piece. Will the two of you keep an eye on things while I'm away? Some of those younger cousins – Rudraige's side of the family – get a bit unruly at times.'

'Not to mention Rudraige himself,' murmured Byron. 'Now look, I've made notes of a couple of properties in the area that don't seem to be occupied. You could enquire about them. Ambrose has made a sketch map as well, so you can see what's where. This is starting to turn into a quest, isn't it?' he said, hopefully.

'No, it isn't,' said Jack at once. 'It's not a quest, it's a filch. Don't get carried away with quests and parfit gentil knights and journeys to find holy grails.'

'All journeys should be regarded as adventures,' said Byron. 'Think of the great romantic journeys of history – Marco Polo and Christopher Columbus. And all those marvellous journeys in fiction. Would Anna Karenina have had such an extraordinary relationship with Vronsky if they hadn't been shut into a railway carriage for several chapters of the book? Tolstoy knew what he was about, didn't he? And those ancient maps – travellers on the brink of unexplored lands, writing, "Here be dragons" on the maps for the uncharted areas.'

'Byron, I'm only going as far as Northumberland.'

'Your trouble, Jack, is that you've got no romance in your soul,' said Byron, severely. 'Vallow Hall will be your main target of course – just here on the map, d'you see? And then across a field and a bit of woodland is Chauntry School – it sounds as if it'll have an emphasis on music for the pupils. There seems to be a schoolhouse in its grounds that's empty.'

'It looks a bit close to the school,' said Jack, studying Ambrose's sketch. 'Joseph Glennon mightn't want noise from rugby matches or cartloads of visitors on parents' days. What was the other house you found?'

'It's called Bastle House. I don't know what a bastle is, but it's even nearer to the Scottish border than Vallow Hall.'

'It looks very remote,' said Jack, studying Ambrose's map and the strangely named Bastle House. 'I think Mr Glennon might prefer the schoolhouse. I'd better see what's in the war chest if I'm to look prosperous enough to buy country houses. Gus, d'you happen to know what we've got in there?'

'There're still a few things from that last filch in St John's Wood,' said Gus.

'Good. I'll take them along to Tod Inkling tomorrow.'

Gus spent most of the day packing for the journey to Vallow, and wondering what kind of people they would be meeting. Still, Mr Jack was as much at ease with the lowliest match seller in Sloat Alley outside the Amaranth's stage door, or the barmaids in The Punchbowl near the theatre, as he was with the grand ladies and gentlemen who came to watch the plays and who often invited Mr Jack to supper or to posh luncheons in their houses in Belgravia or Fitzroy Square. The fact that Mr Jack – often accompanied by Mr Byron or Mr Ambrose – then visited some of those houses a few nights later with a very different purpose was neither here nor there, and in Mr Jack's favour it had to be said that he only ever took from the rich. Also, he was very generous. Not many people knew that there was a certain soup kitchen near St Martins Lane or a hostel in Spitalfields that received substantial donations.

But Gus did not like the sound of this chalice, even though he did not really believe in superstitions and hoary old stories. People in Pedlar's Yard, where he grew up, had not paid much attention to such things, not unless it might form a useful part of a story to spin when you were on the flimp. Gus's pa had been able to spin a very good story if it looked like being profitable.

Mr Byron was going to find out as much as he could about the chalice, which probably meant he would be browsing in the British Museum and also the Victoria & Albert. Gus could not help with that at all – he would not have known what to do in such places – but there might be one thing he could help with. Mr Rudraige and Miss Daphnis had mentioned a song supposed to be about the chalice. They had even sung the first line – about fortune going a-begging, and a luck-filled bowl. The words had stuck in Gus's mind, and considering them now he thought: supposing that song tells more about this chalice and its history? A lot of those old music hall songs told far more than people realized. They were about the strivings and the struggles of ordinary folk such as Gus had grown up with. They were about poverty and being thrown out of your house because you couldn't pay the rent, or about going up to the workhouse after you had been together for forty years. Sometimes there were even clues inside them about crimes.

Clues.

Gus reached for his cap and the woollen scarf knitted by Miss Cecily as a Christmas gift last year – she had made quite a ceremony of presenting it, even winding it around his neck to make sure it fitted. Then he made his way across Covent Garden, and into the maze of side streets and alleys, until he reached the cobbled alley with the stone arch overhead, and the jutting bow windows of eight or ten shops beyond it.

Mr Todworthy Inkling's premises were at the far end. It was a very wide-reaching trade that Mr Inkling followed; as well as dealing in jewellery and silverware (it was usually better not to enquire too deeply into the histories of some of those items), he carried on a perfectly respectable business in old, and often rare and valuable, books. Within this section was a collection of what Gus had learned to call theatrical memorabilia, and it was this he wanted to investigate.

Mr Inkling, enjoying a glass of malmsey by way of an appetizer to his supper – which he would take in any one of the several taverns on his doorstep – was pleased to see Gus. He was, he said, always very happy to welcome anyone associated with the Fitzglens.

'Mr Jack, of course, brings me the best quality items – he was here only yesterday as a matter of fact, as I daresay you know. Several very nice pieces he brought. A real gentleman, Mr Jack, but then all the family are quality. Miss Daphnis can be a bit of a tartar, and Mr Rudraige has the way of rampaging around the shop and cursing – my word, he knows some splendid

Shakespearean curses, Mr Rudraige, I could make your ears curl. But we generally reach an amicable compromise.'

He rearranged the crimson velvet smoking cap, without which he was never seen, poured Gus a glass of malmsey, and, in answer to Gus's question, said certainly he had a collection of theatrical odds and ends. Something of a mishmash it was, but you picked up what you could.

He topped up his own wine glass, then took Gus along to a small section near the back of the shop, where there were shelves on which were stacked a variety of books, papers, old theatre programmes, and posters.

'A lot is from the music halls,' he said, waving a hand towards the shelves. 'Those cellar places – the Coal Hole, and the Cyder Cellars. My word, they saw some life. You could get away with just about anything on those stages – well, I'm saying stages, but often they weren't much more than platforms, or a bit of a dais at one end of the room. What exactly are you looking for?'

'Street ballads,' said Gus, draining the malmsey, and seeing with slight alarm that it was promptly refilled to the brim because Mr Inkling did not believe in being miserly with his drink.

He was wary about providing any more details on his search, because if Tod thought there might be money to be made he would pounce. So he just said that one of the family had mentioned an old song recently, and he had thought it would be nice if he could find a copy of it. The title, he thought, was 'The Lament of the Luck-filled Vessel'.

'And I think it'd be about fifteen years old. The early Nineties. But if it was a street song, it mightn't have been written down at all.'

'You can but look. The shelves over here will be the likeliest.'

He reached down a stack of tattered playbills and programmes and deposited them on Gus's lap. Fortunately, he then went off to another part of the shop, which meant Gus was able to pour most of the malmsey into a handy plant pot. If he had drunk any more of it, he thought he would not have been able to make much sense of anything useful.

Many of the faded playbills and posters bore names that
would have been recognizable twenty and thirty years ago,
but which nobody today was likely to recognize. Gus found
it sad to know that so many hopeful performers and entertainers
had had just those brief days of their small fame, then vanished.
But it was interesting to delve into this fragment of the theatre
world's past, and he went carefully through everything. And
then suddenly there it was. Little more than a fragment –
tattered and brown with age, and looking as if the edges might
have been chewed by rodents. Most of the page had been torn
away, but at the top was the title: 'The Lament of the Luck-
filled Vessel'. And there was the line that Mr Rudraige and
Miss Daphnis had chanted.

'Fortune's gone a-begging, and the luck's gone out the door.'

It was printed on the page, as clear as it could be. But
under it were three more lines that certainly had not been
chanted.

Gus picked up the magazine, haggled over the cost, since
Mr Inkling's day would have been ruined had he not done so,
managed to decline a fourth glass of malmsey, and made a
slightly unsteady way back to Mr Jack's rooms.

By nine o'clock that evening everything was ready for the
journey to Vallow. Gus was about to show Mr Jack the song
sheet when Mr Byron appeared at the door, dressed in one of
his swirling capes and clutching a large envelope.

'I was going to come to King's Cross in the morning to see
you off,' he said. 'But I thought I might miss you in all that
exhausting bustle and noise, so I'm here now.'

'To stage a dramatic farewell in case I don't come back a
free man?' asked Jack.

'To bring you this.' Mr Byron handed over the envelope.

'What—?'

'It's a draft for the first act of our play about the Talisman
Chalice. Mainly a synopsis, but I've jotted down possibilities
for scenes. It might give you some reading material for the
journey.'

'That's very industrious of you,' said Jack.

'For the last four nights,' said Mr Byron, impressively, 'I've been sitting up until the small hours over this. I work best by candlelight, of course. All the great poets did. At such times the shadows are my companions and—'

'Weren't the gas jets working? Or hadn't you paid the bill?'

'—and if I could track down a human skull to have on my library desk,' said Byron, loftily, 'I should be completely at one with the Muse.'

'I suppose by "library" you mean the lumber room at the head of the stairs in your rooms, do you?' said Jack. 'I remember the last time I tried to get in there we had to move two trunks and Great Uncle Benjamin's sea chest before we could open the door.'

'If you don't want to read what I've written—'

'Of course I want to read it.'

'I expect we'll find the chalice's story is all a lot of romanticizing or embroidering of what facts there actually are,' said Byron. 'But I did find the exact line about the ill luck. It tells that, "If the chalice falls into the hands of someone who has no right to it, then that person is dragged into a darkness from which he or she can never emerge." I can't find who originally said it, but it seems to date from around the fourteen hundreds.'

'Whenever it dates from, we could make use of it, couldn't we?' said Jack. 'It'd give a really dark feel to the piece. We could knock Stevenson's manic Jekyll and Hyde creation – and that sinister hypnotist du Maurier conjured up—'

'Svengali.'

'That's the one. We can knock them into a cocked hat.'

'I must say,' said Byron, 'that if the chalice does date back to the Plantagenets I'd have expected the present royal family to look after it a bit better. It'd be a considerable treasure – you wouldn't think they'd risk losing it or letting it be pilfered.'

'Or pawned if one of them happened to be a bit broke,' said Jack, straight-faced.

'Oh, wouldn't that make a good comedy piece,' said Byron, momentarily diverted. 'Old Queen Victoria marching into Tod Inkling's shop and waving the chalice at him, demanding a few thousand and threatening him with her brolly. But you know, that warning about ill luck – that seems quite persistent. You remember Rudraige and Aunt Daphnis singing that snatch of song?'

'"There's a fortune gone a-begging/And the luck's gone out the door . . ."' said Jack, nodding. 'And you thought the actual line was, "Fortune's gone a-begging".'

Gus thought this was as good a cue line as any ever given on the stage of the Amaranth, so he said, 'Mr Byron's right. That was the line.' Then, as they both turned to look at him, he said, 'I found part of the song earlier today.'

'Where on earth—? No, don't tell me. Tod Inkling,' said Jack. 'You'd find just about everything in the world inside that shop. It didn't occur to me to have a look when I was there to fence the St John's Wood stuff. Gus, you're a marvel.'

It was a good feeling to lay the tattered fragment of the song sheet on the table by the fire, and to see Mr Jack and Mr Byron study it with close attention.

'As you'll see,' said Gus, 'the title's clear enough. "The Lament of the Luck-filled Vessel". And somebody's scribbled at the top to say it was performed in 1893 in one of those cellar places in Maiden Lane – mind you, they'd have anything on stage in those places.'

'They would indeed. I remember some of my father's stories, when I was very small. And,' said Jack, leaning over to trace the words with a fingertip, 'there are three more lines from the one Rudraige and Daphnis remembered.' Very softly, he read out the whole verse.

> Fortune's gone a-begging, and the luck's gone out
>   the door
> And the fences are a-cheering and the King ain't
>   safe no more
> For rum-dubbers picked the locks when no one
>   was around
> And they'll all be at the Tuck-up Fair/If the
>   Talisman don't return.

'It's got to have been written around the time the chalice vanished,' said Byron. 'The dates fit, near enough, and that line about "The King ain't safe no more" would mean the King wasn't thought safe because the chalice had been stolen. The luck had been poured away.'

'But who stole it?' demanded Jack. 'Who could have got near to it? And do we know what a Tuck-up Fair is, by the way?'

'The gallows,' said Byron, darkly.

'Oh, yes, of course it must be. Gus, that must have been quite a search you embarked on.'

Gus did not say he would have scoured the entire city and taken apart buildings to find the song in its entirety – or that he might still do so when they got back to London.

'Did Tod Inkling see this, Gus?' asked Mr Byron suddenly. 'Because if he thinks there's money to be made anywhere—'

'I know that. I didn't let it seem to be very important.'

'Good man. Jack, I'll wend my way homewards.' Mr Byron paused in front of a small mirror to make sure his hair was in its customary careful disarray. 'I'll keep working and delving, and I'll be very interested to hear what you think of my first couple of scenes. But for the moment, it's goodbye, Godspeed and good luck.'

He allowed himself to be ushered out of the door and into the big, carpeted hall, which Mr Jack's rooms shared with four other sets of gentlemen. It was as well they were all currently away, because once out there, Mr Byron launched into a speech that appeared to have something to do with a journey to an undiscovered country from whose bourn no traveller returned. Gus did not recognize it, but Mr Jack laughed, and said this was just about the most gruesome fare-well speech anyone could deliver, and if Byron had to quote *Hamlet*, he might at least find lines that didn't concentrate on death.

Mr Byron waved his hat, and ran lightly down the stairs to the street door. As Mr Jack closed the door, he said, 'I'll save Byron's draft for the journey tomorrow. Are we all packed and ready, Gus?'

'I think so. I've packed your dinner jacket, as well, Mr Jack, in case you're asked to dine with any of the local families while we're at Vallow.'

They looked at one another. 'Such as the mysterious Maude's family?' said Jack. 'She's probably no longer there after all these years, of course, you do realize that?'

'Very likely not,' agreed Gus. 'But I've packed the jacket anyway.'

After Gus had gone to bed Jack took out the photographs of Maude, and studied the one showing her holding the legal-looking document. A will? Title Deeds to a property?

Byron had mentioned two properties in Vallow that the mythical Joseph Glennon might inspect with a view to purchasing. A schoolhouse, he had said. Chauntry Schoolhouse. And a place called Bastle House near the Scottish border.

There was no reason to wonder if the unreadable lettering on the blurred parchment in Maude's photograph might read *Bastle House*. But since Joseph Glennon was supposed to be looking for a country residence to purchase, if Bastle House really was empty, it should at least be looked at. There was no reason in the world to feel apprehensive about it.

Maude Vallow had been frightened of Bastle House since she had first seen it.

She would always remember that first glimpse – she had only been at Vallow Hall for a week, still trying to get used to being married, still cautiously exploring the house and finding out about its history. But the moment she saw Bastle House from an upstairs window she had felt as if something dark and smothering had fallen around her.

It stood by itself on a high ridge of land, jutting up against the sky like a single rotting tooth, and local people said it was a real landmark, although they wondered why vagrants never broke into it, because it had been empty ever since anyone could remember. It was generally felt, though, that whoever owned the old place – speculation about that varied considerably – had made it secure enough to keep out vagrants.

Maude tried to think that Bastle House would be perfectly ordinary inside. A faded dictionary in Saul's study had an entry explaining that the word *bastle* derived from the French *bastille*, meaning, in essence, a fortification or a defence. That seemed to explain the house's appearance. It had narrow windows set deeply into the thick stone walls – even from the bedroom window they looked like slitted eyes, as if the house was constantly watching the surrounding countryside for potential intruders. Maude did not know if the house stood in Northumberland and was therefore an English stronghold against the Scots, or whether it was just over the border in Scotland, and consequently a Scottish defence against the English.

But whatever it was, and whichever country it stood in, even seen from here it had a stern, dour look, as if it would stand no nonsense from Plantagenet kings plotting to conquer Scotland, or, of course, from rioting Scots storming and pillaging their way down into England in order to restore dispossessed Stuart kings to England's throne.

She often went quietly up to that particular bedroom, always waiting until no one was around. Once there, she would curl into the deep windowsills, and stare across the treetops trying to understand why Bastle House made her feel like this.

She wondered if one day she would go out to it. It was the wildest idea in the world, and probably living in the gloom of Vallow Hall was affecting her mind. But sometimes you felt compelled to revisit a nightmare to make sure it was not real, or you had to deliberately open a book at a page with the frightening drawing – like the wolf lying in bed waiting for Red Riding Hood – so you could assure yourself it could not hurt you.

One day she might go along Candle Lane and over the stile, and along the woodland path and confront Bastle House. It was only a house. It could not hurt her.

Vallow Hall could not hurt her either. At first, Maude had thought it resembled a house in a novel – not any particular novel, but one of the dark, mysterious dwellings you read about. She had thought it was a house she could explore, and whose history she could uncover, but all there was to uncover was that it was cold and damp and unfriendly. Spiteful little winds found their way down the twisty old chimneys, so that sour smoke drifted out leaving a sooty film on the mirrors, and marks on the walls as if invisible hands had groped along them when nobody was around. If Maude had been a heroine from a novel, she would have uncovered all kinds of secrets and mysteries about the house.

But heroines in novels would not have let themselves come to Vallow Hall in the first place, because they would not have given way to Maude's overbearing Aunt Hilda, and submitted meekly to marriage to a humourless man with skin like a shrivelled walnut shell. A man who got into Maude's bed every Saturday night, and prodded gruntingly at the parts of her body she had thought were meant to be entirely private, then fumbled under his nightshirt for what seemed an age, eventually getting angrily out of her bed and stumping off to his own room. Maude was not at all sure what actually happened in a bed after people were married, but she thought there was more to it than these grunting fumblings and proddings.

Heroines in novels, when faced with this kind of situation, generally took a lover and ran happily off with him. But Maude had no idea how to go about taking a lover, even if there were any likely candidates in Vallow, which there were not, and she could not imagine where they could run off to anyway. She certainly could not run back to Aunt Hilda, who, from Maude's seventeenth birthday onwards, had scoured the county to find a husband – any husband – for a niece whom she had grudgingly taken into her house because of it being her duty.

Sometimes Maude imagined packing a small bag, and walking down to the tall iron gates and on to Candle Lane, and then all the way to the railway station. Vallow Halt was only a couple of miles from the Hall, and once there she would simply wait for a train to arrive and get into it. The trouble was that Saul or one of the servants – most likely the sour-faced Agnes who was not quite a housekeeper but a bit more than a maid – would appear on the platform, and haul her back to Vallow.

Even as she wove these half-plans she did not think she would ever have the courage to put them into action. She thought she was destined to remain at Vallow Hall for the rest of her life.

THREE

S aul Vallow had not wanted to marry Maude. He had not actually wanted to marry anyone. But it could not be avoided: Vallow Hall was in severe need of renovation – the roof leaked in four separate places and Mrs Cheesely, the cook, said the sound of rain dripping into the enamel buckets and saucepans placed at judicious intervals was enough to drive a body demented, never mind spoil a person's hand with pastry. As if that were not enough, the wretched kitchen maid Lily put her foot through a rotting board in a stairway and then hobbled around with it bandaged for several days, which Saul considered nothing but attention-seeking.

He might, of course, have raised a mortgage on the Hall, which would have provided him with funds for the leaking roof and the rotting floorboards, but would have meant the bank and his solicitor knowing the Vallow coffers were empty. The bank was an impersonal body, based in Alnwick, but the solicitor, one Ernest Meazle, was local, and local people gossiped. Saul was not having half the county knowing that he had had to resort to such means.

And then Maude had been put in his way by the pushy Hilda Grout. Normally, Saul would not have paid this any heed, but Maude was quite a considerable heiress.

He took a long time to make the decision, but when finally he approached Hilda Grout, she accepted his request for Maude's hand with alacrity. Of course she did. Saul was Vallow of Vallow Hall – a person of standing and substance in the county. During the preparations for the wedding, and throughout the ceremony itself, he reminded himself that Maude had only just reached her eighteenth birthday, and that she had clearly led a very sheltered life. It was unlikely that she knew what to expect on the wedding night.

She did not. She stared at him with wide, scared eyes from the depths of the deep old four-poster in Vallow Hall's master bedroom, clutching the embroidered nightgown around her. When Saul climbed in, pulling up his nightshirt with optimism (because you never knew what you might find yourself capable of), she lay back, her fists clenched in fear.

It was as well that she was so very innocent, because despite Saul's determined efforts, what he had not been able to achieve as a young man, he certainly could not achieve twenty years on. However, he reserved the second Saturday of each month for regular attempts. He did not note it in his diary, of course, but it coincided with the vicar's monthly meeting to check the church accounts for which Saul acted as unofficial treasurer, so that acted as a good reminder.

After a little while, he thought it advisable to limit, as far as possible, Maude's socializing. He did not want her making unguarded remarks to acquaintances, or hearing exchanges of confidences between married women that might provide her with precise knowledge of marriage beds and what happened in them – to the extent that she realized none of it had happened in her own marriage bed. It was not very likely that ladies would discuss such matters, but Saul had occasionally been present when a certain bawdy flavour had crept into gentlemen-only conversations. He had put most of the tales down to boasting or, at best, exaggeration, and he could not imagine ladies talking in that way. Even so, he was not taking any risks.

He made no objection to the charity work she undertook with the church – in fact people might have looked askance if the mistress of Vallow Hall had not made some contribution to that. Nor was there any reason for concern about her occasional modest involvement with Chauntry School and its concerts. She would certainly not hear any descriptive stories about marriage beds among the church helpers, and as far as Saul had ever noticed, Chauntry's precentor was one of those vague academics, whose life was entirely bound up with the school and his work.

However, when Maude broached the possibility of holding one or two modest musical soirées, Saul had to say he did not care for the idea. He would not, he said, forbid her from playing the piano in the music room – the room that had been created by a long-ago mistress of the Hall – and he supposed the instrument ought to be kept in use. But he could not be doing with a constant drone of dreary tunes – he did not care who had composed them, he said. Agnes must make sure the room was kept locked, and only opened once a week for a couple of hours. Lily might as well go in to dust and sweep it at the same time.

In the autumn following the wedding an invitation arrived to spend a weekend at Hymbre House.

Saul told Maude she need not attend.

'I shall have to accept, though. They're important people in the county, Sir John and Lady Hymbre, and I don't want to offend them. He's chairman of the Bench, and her brother has a position at court – a very minor position, I think, but even so . . . It will be very formal and probably extremely tiresome – not at all what you would like, so you had better write a polite note declining. You can say your health is poor.'

Maude smiled, then before he could stop her, she went to his study to find notepaper and pen, and wrote a polite acceptance for them both. Before Saul could find out, she gave the note to Lily to post.

'And it's important, so I'd like it to be taken to the post office right away, please.'

Lily, scenting intrigue, which she loved, and always ready to take the opportunity to further her erratic romance with the poulterer's boy in the village anyway, went off at once, concealing the note in her shawl as if it contained State secrets.

When, later in the day, Saul asked if Maude had written to Lady Hymbre, she said she was afraid she must have misunderstood him, because she had sent an acceptance for both of them. His eyes snapped with annoyance, but then he shrugged and said, 'Very well, but you had better remain at my side all the time, so I can guide you through it – particularly the formal dinner.'

'Thank you,' said Maude, in an expressionless voice, and went off to her bedroom to look through her wardrobe, because spending a weekend with important people, one of whom had a brother in court circles – never mind how minor – was a

very big event in her life, in fact it would probably be a very
big event in anybody's life.

She could wear the green, velvet-trimmed travelling two-
piece for the train journey, and for the formal dinner at which
Saul thought she would not know how to behave (did he think
she would drink from the finger bowls, for goodness' sake!),
the champagne lace gown with the wide, décolleté neckline,
and the ivory silk roses. There was a hair ornament shaped
like a silk rose to go with it. She had never worn the gown,
but it had been part of her trousseau, because Aunt Hilda had
said she must have one or two gowns for formal evening
gatherings; she was not sending Maude into marriage without
the proper clothes. Perhaps there might be events to which
Hilda herself might be invited, she had said.

So far there had not been any events to which Maude had
wanted to invite her aunt, in fact there had not been any events
at Vallow Hall at all, formal or otherwise, and the gown had
hung in a dust sheet in her wardrobe. But it was elegant and
dignified and Maude hoped it was not vain to believe it was
also becoming.

The elegant and dignified champagne lace seemed as if it was
very becoming indeed. Lady Hymbre complimented Maude
on how well she looked, and several of the gentlemen cast
what Maude thought could be admiring glances her way. This
was gratifying, because she was not used to being looked at
admiringly.

At dinner that night she sat next to a young man who looked
at her with more admiration than any of the others. Maude
thought there had been introductions earlier, but Saul had been
droning on to her about Hymbre House and its history, and
she had not heard the introductions properly. There were place
cards at the table, but there was an elaborate table centre partly
masking the one at the young man's place, and she could
hardly lean over to read it. So she said that she hoped it was
not impolite, but she had not caught the introduction, and that
she was Maude Vallow.

He smiled – he had rather a slow smile, as if his mind
had to make itself up as to whether smiling was the correct

thing to do – then he said, very nicely, 'I think as it's you, and as you are very beautiful indeed, you should call me Eddy.' He looked at her, almost as if to see how she received this, and when she smiled, he said, 'You know, there are going to be parlour games after dinner, and I'm very bad at parlour games.'

'Oh, so am I,' said Maude, never having actually participated in a parlour game.

'Then shall we go into the conservatory, just the two of us, and I can get to know you a little better?' he said.

'Will Lady Hymbre mind?' said Maude, casting a doubtful glance at their hostess, who was seated imposingly at the foot of the table, and who seemed to be watching Maude and the young man called Eddy very fixedly.

'I'm sure she won't,' he said. 'But to put your mind at rest, my dear, I'll have a word with her.'

It seemed that Lady Hymbre did not in the least mind two of her guests taking themselves off to the conservatory while everyone else tried to guess the book titles that were being acted out in Charades, or making up wild stories in Consequences, some of which were making the younger female guests shriek with mirth.

As she slipped out of the room Maude had a moment of nervousness, but there was surely no reason not to talk for a while with another guest, and the young man was courteous and gentlemanly. Saul was deep in earnest discussion with two of the older men and he did not even look round. Lady Hymbre did, though, and she smiled and gave a half-nod, and looked at Maude very approvingly.

The conservatory was warm and shadowy, and there was a heavy, heady scent of flowers. Eddy indicated a small silver tray bearing a decanter of wine and two tall-stemmed glasses set on a low table.

'I thought we deserved a glass of champagne. To go with your gown, Maude.'

This was entirely charming, and Maude, who was not very used to champagne – who was not really used to it at all – sipped with enjoyment, and then drank a second glass, because it seemed impolite to refuse. Her companion's fingers brushed hers when he handed her the glass, and she wondered if she might be partaking in a flirtation – she had read about flirtations in conservatories. If so, it was all very polite and well-mannered, and providing she did not stay here too long – and certainly providing she did not have any more champagne – there was nothing wrong about it.

He was very easy to talk to; he listened to everything she said, and smiled and nodded and asked her questions about her life and where she lived. He did not say much about himself, other than that he had recently come back from travelling, and had seen some interesting sights in other countries. He was not what Maude would have called handsome precisely, having a rather heavy jaw so that you might describe him as a bit jowly, but he had nice dark hair, and eyes which somehow had a sleepy look. Slumbrous might be the word.

But when she got up to go back to the drawing room, the room tilted slightly and she gasped and put out a hand to steady herself.

Eddy had stood up at the same time, and he put out a hand to her. 'Have I made you a bit squiffy, Maude?' he said. 'I'm sorry. Perhaps you oughtn't to go back to the drawing room. Perhaps I had better help you up to your bedroom.'

'I could go up on my own.'

'Oh, no,' he said, very gently, smiling down at her. 'I'm coming with you, Maude.'

Lady Hymbre had allotted to Maude and Saul two adjoining bedrooms. The inter-connecting door was closed, and the room where Maude's things had been laid out was warm and comfortable. Her nightgown was on the bed, ready for her, and there was a fire in the hearth. Somebody – presumably one of the maids – had lit the gas jets earlier, turning them very low, so that the room was filled with a soft light.

But the bedroom was as unsteady as the conservatory had been, and Maude was relieved to be helped to the bed, where she could sit down.

The young man hesitated then, and looked down at her. 'Would you like me to fetch your husband?' he said, and for some really strange reason Maude had the impression he was not asking that exact question, but that his words had a different meaning altogether, which he expected her to understand.

But she said, at once, 'Oh, no, you mustn't fetch Saul,' and he seemed to relax, and came to sit by her on the bed, taking her hand, and then putting up his other hand to her hair.

Maude had no idea how to respond, but it was nice to have something to cling on to while she was still feeling so peculiar, and it was surprisingly comfortable to feel him stroking her hair, and then unclipping the hair ornament so that her hair fell from its pinnings and tumbled about her shoulders.

'Oh, beautiful,' he said in a different voice, and began to twine her loose hair between his fingers. 'I'm so very pleased we met tonight, Maude.'

His hands were still caressing her hair, and now they were on her shoulders as well and her shoulders were bare because of the gown being low-cut. And then somehow – Maude had no idea how it had happened – the fastenings of her gown were being loosened, and it was being slipped down, so that her silk chemise was visible.

He said, in a whisper close to her ear, 'This is all right, isn't it, Maude? This is what we meant?'

'Oh, yes,' said Maude, not knowing what else to say.

His hands were sliding under her gown, and he was breathing fast as if he had been running. 'And – you'll forgive me asking – but you are quite prepared, are you?'

'Oh, yes,' said Maude again, having no idea what he meant, but not wanting to appear stupid or ignorant or naïve.

He thrust his hands deeper under her gown, and began to move against her, and it was a little like the way Saul moved on those Saturday nights, but in a curious way it was nothing like that at all, because Eddy was doing so with more assurance. There was a moment when he seemed to draw back from her slightly, and Maude drew in a shaky breath of relief, because clearly he was now going back to his own room or perhaps back to the drawing room, and it was over.

But it was not over. There was the sense of him fumbling at something low down, and then the sound of a belt being unclasped – and buttons unfastening? But Maude was still unsteady from the champagne, and she could not be sure she was entirely understanding what was happening.

And then, shockingly, there was the feel of his bare skin against her legs – his thighs, a brush of hair – and the blurred sensation cleared slightly, because it was suddenly obvious that he was going to do to her what Saul did, and it would be horrible and embarrassing, and she would have to see him tomorrow morning at the breakfast table knowing this had happened between them . . . And Saul might come in at any moment and catch them . . .

Here came the prodding now, just as she had known it would. Dreadful. Maude thought about shouting for help, but it was not very likely that anyone would hear her, and if anyone did hear and come running it would be even more embarrassing. So she shut her eyes and waited for it to stop, because it would only last for a few minutes, it only ever did . . .

It did not, though. And it was starting to be very different from what Saul did. This was stronger, somehow more assured and – this was the really surprising thing – it was as if he was enjoying it and wanting to take her into the enjoyment with him. For a remarkable moment Maude felt as if the two of them were sharing something private and special and good.

And then suddenly he was pushing at her with more force, and something hard and very insistent was being forced upwards and right inside her body. Maude gasped and her eyes flew open and met those of the man above her. He was smiling down at her, and she thought he said something about was this all right, because for him this was marvellous. She had no idea how to reply, but it did not seem to matter, because he was moving faster and faster, and this was not like anything she had ever had done to her before, and then without warning there was a deep secret pain, and she cried out with it. And then – the most astonishing thing of all – there was a brief extraordinary moment of soaring pleasure. Like a firework exploding against a night sky – like a shooting star. Then Eddy gasped and cried out, and slumped half on to his side, one arm still about her.

After a few moments Maude managed to half sit up, and to push aside her gown which was crumpled. In doing so she became aware of a sticky wetness between her legs, and when she looked down, there was blood on the sheet beneath her.

It was the most embarrassing situation she had ever known. Eddy sat up and looked at her, and then looked at the blood, and in a voice of shock, said, 'My dear girl, I had no idea you were a virgin . . . Your husband— My God, if I had known, I would never have . . .'

Maude was crying. She said, 'I don't understand – I don't know what to do—'

He was pulling his clothes together; Maude did not want to watch as he buttoned his trousers and tucked in his shirt, so she went on staring at the bloodied sheet. But he said, 'I think you should ring for one of the maids – can you tell some story about . . .' He frowned, then said, 'About this being the week for your head to ache?'

It took a moment to realize what he meant, then Maude understood, and the colour flamed in her cheeks, because you did not, ever, refer to that uncomfortable week you had once a month. You might have to mention it to a maid in your house, but never ever to anyone else and above all never to a man.

So, not looking at him, she said in a mumble, 'Yes, I'll do that. Please will you go now?'

'I will. But I shall make sure you're all right, Maude,' he said. 'I shall make it my business to know. And if there's any trouble . . .' A pause, then he said, 'I should want to know.'

'How could I be in touch with you?' Maude had no idea what he meant by trouble, but she asked the question anyway.

He said, slowly, 'A message could be got to me through one of two gentlemen. Connor O'Kane, who was here with me tonight – you didn't meet him – no? He helped arrange the music entertainment after luncheon. I can give you an address for him.' He reached into his jacket for a small pocket book, scribbled a few lines on it and gave the page to her. 'Or there's a man called Aiden Fitzglen at the Amaranth Theatre in London,' he said. 'His theatre has held concerts, recitals for . . .' He broke off, frowning, as if he had said more than he had intended, then leaned over, dropped a kiss on the top of her head and went quietly out of the room.

In the end it was quite easy. Maude had an awkward conversation with the housemaid, who whisked the sheet away and brought a fresh one, and Saul, when he finally came upstairs, went into the adjoining room and clambered into bed without even coming in to say goodnight.

And it turned out that ladies staying at Hymbre House were always served breakfast in bed, and by the time Maude got downstairs there was no sign of Eddy and people were leaving. It meant there was a bustle of departures, and farewells and thanks, and Maude and Saul were swept up in it, and they were on the train back to Vallow almost before Maude had time to think.

'A pleasant enough weekend,' Saul said, sitting in the corner seat in their railway carriage, and unfolding a newspaper. 'But not an experience I want to repeat.'

Maude did not answer, partly because he would not expect it, but mainly because she could not think what to say. She had no idea how she felt, but she could not stop remembering what the man called Eddy had said before he left the bedroom.

'If there's any trouble,' he had said, and then he had given her the names of two gentlemen. Connor O'Kane with a London address, and Aiden Fitzglen who was somehow part of a big London theatre. She would not, of course, ever be in touch with either of them, and it would not be necessary anyway, but if she needed to do so, she thought she would rather it was Mr O'Kane than the other man. A London theatre sounded very grand and imposing.

FOUR

One of the things that fascinated Gus about Mr Jack was the way in which he could immerse himself in any part he was playing. It did not matter if he was not on a stage with an audience to watch, either. This morning, for instance, on the platform at King's Cross, he was playing the part of the hesitant, scholarly Mr Joseph Glennon. The small neat beard he had grown over the last week gave him the appearance of having just come from one of the universities, and his general air was one of bewilderment at having to cope with the noisy bustle of the platforms. The beard made him look older, too – mid or even late thirties – and he had drawn his shoulders forward slightly in what he said was a scholar's stoop. Gus watched him hesitantly summon a couple of porters and hold an anxious conversation with them about the stowing of his luggage. Could it be put in the guard's van? Oh, it could. He was most grateful to them, and here was a coin or two for their trouble.

They travelled first class – Mr Jack said he was not having Gus sent off to third.

'Wooden benches, the windows glued shut, and very likely folk being sick on the floor from the jolting of the carriages,' he said, as they got on board and found seats.

When the train finally pulled out of the station, Mr Jack reached for the notes Mr Byron had brought last evening.

'Can you listen to these, Gus? Byron did say it's only a rough draft, but reading it will give me a better sense of it. Also, between us we might spot some idea for the actual filch.'

'I'd like to hear it,' said Gus, at once.

'Good man. We've got the carriage to ourselves – I don't think there are many stops, so no one's likely to come in. And we don't change trains for at least three hours, if not longer.'

As he picked up the first page, Gus saw that he was already so deeply inside the character of Mr Joseph Glennon he was

even patting his pockets for his spectacles, which were plain
glass. He smiled slightly, then sat back in the comfortable
first-class seat, and listened.

'The chalice's legend,' Byron wrote, 'really does seem to go
all the way back to the Plantagenets – in fact it seems to have
begun with no less a person than Richard II. It was made for
the founders of an Essex monastery, and there are plenty of
descriptions. The colours of the glass are described as violet and
magenta, lapis lazuli blue and gentian, as well as amethyst,
and – take particular note of this one, Jack – amaranthine
purple, "so that the chalice should echo the Greek term for
unfading or immortal". It's as if this is meant, isn't it?'

'It's why my great-great-grandfather called our theatre the
Amaranth,' said Mr Jack, glancing across to Gus. 'That's what
Byron means, of course. The name was meant to indicate that
the family's place in theatrical history would be everlasting
– would never fade.'

'I remember Mr Rudraige telling me that.' Gus was pleased
that he could proffer this knowledge.

'According to the legend,' wrote Byron, 'the monks handed
down a somewhat discreditable story about Richard II – that
during a royal progress and a visit to the monastery, he stole
the chalice. I don't know why a King of England would steal
something like that – I haven't been able to find any suggestion of a motive – but I'd imagine that Richard simply saw
the thing, liked it, and decided it would look better in a royal
apartment than in a backwater monastery. You can't say they
weren't acquisitive, never mind arrogant, those Plantagenets.

'I'll try to find out more about that monastery, although it's
doubtful if it exists now, and it's the kind of search that could
take years – or where you could open an old ledger tomorrow
and find exactly what you want.

'I'm thinking the curtain can rise to show Richard alone in
a shadowy cloister – we can get Bill the Chip to create some
stone-looking arches, I expect. I think there might be a few
flats left from when we did that Schiller play about Mary,
Queen of Scots. I'm sure we kept the flats, although the piece
didn't do very well, as I recall.'

'It played to an audience of thirty on the first night, and we took it off after a week,' said Jack, adjusting Joseph Glennon's spectacles.

'Richard will tiptoe across the stage, constantly glancing over his shoulder – although *not*, I should say, in the manner of French farce – and with a sack slung on his back. From the shadows he'll lift something from an alcove – something that the audience won't be able to see, because we want the chalice to make a really grand appearance later. So Richard will secrete it in a bag, before exiting the stage. And there we have the first set of "wrongful hands", and Richard's first downward steps into his fate. Because soon after that royal visit, he was deposed and thrown into prison in the bowels of Pontefract Castle. The throne was taken by Henry Bolingbroke – Henry IV.'

'And,' said Jack, turning the page, 'what do you bet Byron's going to suggest the next scene is Richard in the dungeon, bewailing his fate.'

'I think,' Byron wrote on the next page, 'that we ought then to have a dungeon scene, with Richard languishing in chains and a stone cell, mourning the loss of his throne, and ascribing it to his having filched a sacred communion chalice from a monastery – and how, because of it, he believes his line is now cursed.'

'Told you,' said Mr Jack. 'Still, to open a play showing a King of England committing the theft of a sacred object, then having him announcing that he's cursed, and that the curse might be passed on to his descendants – that should make the audience sit up and take notice. What do you think?'

'I think audiences will love it,' said Gus. He listened to the next scene, then said, 'I like those gaolers and turnkeys Mr Byron has put in there – comic relief, is it called? All that swigging of ale and quarrelling. Although that part where one accuses the other of filching his wife, and of – how did he put it?'

'Swiving her up against the wall of the latrines, and saying it was a pity he was scarcely better equipped than if he had a three-inch cattle prod in his breeches,' said Jack, grinning.

'Might that have to be censored a bit?' asked Gus, doubtfully.

'If we don't want the Lord Chancellor to come down on us like a ton of bricks it'll certainly have to be censored. We'll probably have to cut it out for the matinee anyway.'

Gus thought they would most likely have to cut the lines out for all performances, because he was not at all sure if it was respectful to the monarchy – past or present – to show a King of England held prisoner by drunken men talking about swiving.

'The turnkeys should exit singing a drunken, bawdy song,' Byron had written. 'My imagination doesn't stretch to actually writing that, but I daresay Uncle Rudraige could come up with something.'

'If Rudraige can't, nobody can,' said Jack.

He put down the pages, leaned back against the padded seat, then looked at the turnip-faced watch, which he had borrowed from Rudraige and which they had thought was nicely in character for the scholarly Mr Glennon.

'It's half past twelve. Let's see what the Great Northern Railway can offer in the way of lunch. There's still two hours before we change trains.'

The Northern Railway's lunch was very good indeed. 'And very substantial,' said Mr Jack – and Gus enjoyed it, although when later they changed trains to a smaller and bouncier local one and the track twisted and turned like a corkscrew, he rather regretted the large helping of treacle pudding.

As the train went along Jack's mind was on their destination – Vallow Hall. Would the chalice really be there? And would the mysterious Maude be there, as well?

They were travelling through open countryside with trees and woodlands and bits of low wall, dotted here and there with lonely looking farmhouses. It was not yet dark, but there was a thickening of the light. Jack glanced at Gus who was sitting in the other corner of the carriage, and thought he was a bit pale. But it had been a long journey, and this train in particular was enough to shake anyone up. He reached into a pocket for the small hip flask he generally carried with him, and passed it over.

'If you're feeling a bit stirred up by the train, a tot of brandy should settle things.'

'One way or the other,' replied Gus, drinking a small measure of the brandy gratefully.

Joseph Glennon's turnip watch showed it to be close to three o'clock. It had been mad to make this journey in the bleak month of November – it would be dark by the time they reached Vallow. Ambrose, planning the journey, had found a local pub that offered 'comfortable accommodation for travellers'. It was called the Mercian Arms and Joseph Glennon and his manservant were booked in for three nights. Jack was just thinking that they would at least get there in time for dinner when the train rounded a sharp curve in the track, and he was confronted with a view across fields. On the far horizon was a rearing outline, standing on top of a high ridge of land, clear and stark against the sky—

'Ticket, sir?'

The guard's voice startled him, but he produced his ticket, and saw the guard looking out of the window. The house was receding in the distance, but it was still in view. Jack said, 'That's a strange-looking old place.'

'That's Bastle House,' said the guard, clipping the ticket, and clearly pleased to be able to impart local information to a visitor to this part of the world. 'Bit of a landmark, it is. Gloomy old place. Been empty for many a long year. One of the old border fortifications, so they tell. Ugly as sin, though.'

'It is ugly,' said Jack, absently, still staring out of the window at the crouching outline. A faint apprehension brushed his mind, but then the train chugged around the rest of the curve, and Bastle House vanished from view.

It was a matter of mild curiosity to the regular patrons of the Mercian Arms that an academic gentleman from London was staying in Vallow for a few days. Looking for a country house to buy, so Ned Nithercott said, and Ned would know if anyone would, for he'd driven the gentleman and his manservant from Vallow Halt. The Halt was not one of your big grand railway stations such as you heard about, with cabs and omnibuses and very likely carriages all waiting for travellers, but Ned, who acted as postie for the area, on account of his wife keeping the local post office, always trundled the dogcart along to the

Halt when a train – any train – was expected. Folk who had travelled any distance on one of those jolting contraptions were entitled to be transported to their destination, along with any luggage they might have with them.

The gentleman – whose name turned out to be Mr Joseph Glennon – had been interested in the area, asking Ned about this house or that one as they passed them on the way, and whether any of them might be available for purchase. The manservant or whatever he was had not said anything at all; in fact he'd slumped against the side of the cart, one hand on his stomach, his handkerchief clapped to his mouth. Ned had been quite worried for the fate of his cart, although it was not surprising if the poor man had had his innards scrambled up all the way from London in a railway train. Ned had had to direct him to the outside privy at the side of the Mercian Arms the moment the cart pulled up. Later, Mrs Gurning, the landlady, had taken up a bowl of what she called good strengthening broth, this being a sovereign remedy for the digestion, although Ned said personally he would not touch a mouthful, it being stewed with more onions than any broth had a right to contain.

It was noticed, by the regulars in the public bar, that while Mr Glennon was quietly taking his evening meal in the coffee room, Mrs Gurning took the opportunity to go upstairs to the manservant's room, to see if he was needing anything else. It would have been uncharitable to remark that her cheeks were slightly flushed when she came back downstairs to the bar, but it was well known that the Widow Gurning was never backward when it came to ministering to the needs of a single gentleman.

The following morning Jack and Gus were presented with breakfast plates heaped with food, which included something Mrs Gurning explained was black pudding – a fine northern delicacy, sure to set them both up a treat.

'And a letter's come for you, Mr Glennon. Brought along by Ned Nithercott first thing. Early delivery of letters we get. Will there be anything else, sir?'

'I think this is a very elegant sufficiency, thank you,' said

Jack, as Gus surveyed his plate with dismay, and Mrs Gurning bustled happily away to inform the kitchens that you could always tell Quality when they came to stay.

'Uncle Rudraige's writing,' said Jack, slitting open the envelope with the butter knife. 'Pass the marmalade, Gus, and I'll read it out between mouthfuls of crunching toast.'

> My dear Jack,
>   I thought you might appreciate a note on your first morning.
>   There's no need to worry about things while you're away, because I'll be keeping a firm hand on the reins.

'Heaven preserve us,' said Jack, reaching for a second slice of toast.

> Byron and I had a discussion about our proposed piece in The Punchbowl after the matinee yesterday, and it sounds as if there will need to be a fair number of settings showing the chalice's story down the centuries, so I've had a word with Bill the Chip about that. (As you know, your father always had a very high opinion of his skills as carpenter.) I told Bill we would finally have to construct a revolve on the Amaranth's stage. You'll know the principle of a revolve, of course – it's more or less a massive turntable that sits on top of the main stage, with runners or wheels under it. You can set up two or even three scenes beforehand, and when they're needed, the revolve is simply pulled around until the next scene is facing the auditorium. It does away with that frantic scramble to change scenes during intervals, and it will avoid some of the near-disasters we've had over the years. You're too young to remember the night when an entire painted flat representing Elsinore crashed down on to somebody's foot, and a series of violent oaths rent the entire theatre while Hamlet was soliloquizing in front of the drop curtain. I remember it vividly, because it so happened I was the one playing Hamlet that night (I was a touch slimmer in those days). I lost the entire thread of the speech as a result, and the front row of the stalls

jeered, although I always suspected the Gilfillans of being behind that.

However, Bill the Chip is dubious about a revolve. He says Irving never had one at the Lyceum and said what was good enough for Irving is good enough for the Fitzglens. But faint heart never won fair revolve, Jack, and I shall talk Bill round. And it's high time we stirred up the theatre world a bit. Those Gilfillans have been romping around London as if they're the reincarnation of David Garrick and Shakespeare's entire Globe company rolled into one, and they need putting in their place. Somebody told me they actually put House Full boards outside their theatre *for an entire week.* Of course their auditorium is quite small, so it'd become full very quickly indeed. A few of them were in The Punchbowl last night – celebrating the final night of their run of *Othello*, seemingly. Miss Viola Gilfillan was with them. She had quite good notices for her Desdemona – Daphnis says the *Evening Standard* praised it to the skies, and referred to Viola's 'meaningful pauses'.

'Meaningful pauses rubbish,' said Jack, at once. '*Punch* said they were outright dries – she had to take three prompts. Did I tell you that, Gus?'

'I don't think you did,' said Gus, who would not for worlds have said Mr Jack had told him twice.

'Daphnis cut out an article from the *Standard* about Viola,' Mr Rudraige went on. 'She thought you might like to see it, so I'm sending it with this letter.'

When Jack unfolded the cutting it showed a very good head-and-shoulders photograph of Viola Gilfillan in Desdemona's costume. The heading was 'Miss Viola Gilfillan after her wonderfully successful performance in the Gilfillan production of Shakespeare's great tragedy'.

Gus said, a bit hesitantly, that it was a good likeness.

'It's touched up, of course,' said Mr Jack, staring at it. 'And the article mentions her copper-coloured hair – that'll be touched up as well, I expect. And she'd insist on the light being exactly right and as flattering as possible.'

But he went on looking at the photograph, and Gus had poured himself a second cup of coffee before he finally read the article out.

'It says, "Miss Gilfillan modestly accepted all the congratulations showered on her for her splendid performance. Asked by the Standard's reporter whether London audiences would ever have the pleasure of seeing her play Juliet, Miss Gilfillan treated him to her famous slightly crooked smile, and said she would have to be sure of having her perfect Romeo.

"'There is an actor I have in my mind for that," she admitted. "His colouring would be complimentary to mine – a fair-haired Romeo to a Titian-haired Juliet. But it is not likely that the actor in question would ever agree to appear on the Gilfillan stage." Pressed for more, she quoted the famous line from *Romeo and Juliet* about the 'Two families, alike in dignity . . . From ancient grudge break to new mutiny . . .' and would not be drawn further. The *Standard* leaves its readers to draw their own conclusions."'

'What utter nonsense,' said Mr Jack, scowling and looking more like a villain from a melodrama intent on murder, than a mild academic engaged in a blameless search for a country house. 'She said that deliberately to annoy me. You do realize that?'

'Yes,' said Gus, not daring to meet his master's eyes.

'Rudraige thinks so, too,' said Mr Jack, picking up the letter again to read what Mr Rudraige had written. 'Listen.'

> Obviously Viola aimed that at you, but I have to say that her comment about a fair-haired Romeo is quite true – it would undoubtedly make for a striking look. Especially with those dark eyes of yours, Jack – you inherited those from your father, of course. But we all know you would never agree to be Viola Gilfillan's Romeo, and even if you did, you would act her off the stage on the first night, dear boy. Still, you know, this isn't the first time those Gilfillans have attempted to lure one of our family on to their stage. That old villain, Furnival Gilfillan, once took your Aunt Daphnis out to supper at Rule's and suggested she appear as his Portia on the Gilfillans' stage. Daphnis

refused – but not until she had enjoyed a very lavish, very expensive supper at Furnival's expense.

Anyway, Daphnis sends her good wishes for a successful outcome to your filch, Jack, and Cecily says it will be chilly in those northern climes, so be sure to wear warm undergarments. Ambrose is concerned about you eating anything you don't recognize, since there's no knowing what unfamiliar local dishes might do to the digestion. He reminded us all that he is a martyr to his digestion, and actually he did have a bout of hiccups halfway through Act Three yesterday, although I managed to cover it up by booming out my own lines and one or two of Ambrose's as well, so everything was perfectly all right.

Your ever-loving Uncle Rudraige.

Mr Jack replaced the letter and the cutting in the envelope, said it was to be hoped Rudraige did not get carried away and start an Amaranth revolution, then consulted the turnip watch and said they would explore the village. Gus, relieved to have got away from the Gilfillans in general and Miss Viola Gilfillan in particular, agreed.

'I noticed a solicitor's office when the cart brought us here from the station last night,' said Jack, getting up from the table. 'There was a brass plate saying E. Meazle. I think Joseph Glennon might call on E. Meazle to enquire about houses for sale, don't you?'

'Establishing the character,' nodded Gus. 'A good idea.'

'What do I wear for a visit to a solicitor, do you think? Bearing in mind that I'm a hopeful, rather naïve seeker of a country house to purchase?'

'The greatcoat,' said Gus, as they went up to the bedrooms. 'Mr Glennon would be a bit nervous about the cold and careful of his health.'

'So he would. And the muffler to go with it? Yes, of course. Cecely knitted it for me as a Christmas present, and she'd never forgive me if I didn't make use of it.'

'She knitted one for me, as well.'

'So I heard. And,' said Jack, with a sly grin, 'bedsocks to go with it.'

'Bedsocks are very useful in winter,' said Gus, defensively. 'It was very kind of her. You know, I think it looks as if it might rain, so we'll take the big umbrella as well.'

As well as the muffler and the umbrella, Mr Jack took the silver-topped walking cane, which Mr Rudraige had lifted from a Gilfillan gentleman who had been occupying the Amaranth's stage box during Miss Daphnis's portrayal of Lady Macbeth some years previously. The Gilfillan in question had apparently spent the entire play ogling the stage, then had observed, very loudly in the crush bar afterwards, that Daphnis Fitzglen's declaiming of the famous "Give me the knife" line had sounded more like a cook preparing to chop vegetables for stew than a villainous heroine seducing her lord into a murder most foul.

The story was that Rudraige had felt such an insult should not go unpunished, and had considered that liberating the cane had been a fair way to redress the balance.

FIVE

The morning was cold and sharp, but sunlight lay across the cobblestones of the village square, and Jack found it all attractive. He thought local markets – even small fairs – might be held here, and that all the locals would attend. There was a traditional green with several wooden benches, a stone monument commemorating something, and several shops, bow-fronted and looking as if they might date back to the middle of the last century, or even earlier. High-waisted gowns and poke bonnets, thought Jack, pleased with these images.

There was a wooden notice board on stilts, giving details of church services and events, and a poster advertising a choral concert at Chauntry School that evening. This struck a friendly note; everyone was please to come along and bring their friends – there was only a small charge for seats – and there would be some Schubert *lieder* to enjoy, and a selection of folk songs indigenous to the area, including 'Bobby Shafto's Gone to Sea', and Chauntry's own arrangement of the famous old legend, 'The Lambton Worm'. As usual, the traditional favourite, 'Blaydon Races' would be performed, in which everyone was welcome to join, although please to refrain from too enthusiastic stamping of feet to the chorus, because after last Christmas it had been necessary to re-lay the entire floor of the concert hall.

Jack smiled at this, then said, 'Gus, if you were planning to come to live in a place, you'd be interested in its activities and its residents, wouldn't you? And Byron mentioned an empty schoolhouse in the grounds of Chauntry itself, so the concert would give us a good opportunity to investigate. I'm inclined to think we'll go along.'

'I suppose we'd better.'

'I think so. We'll ask at the pub about tickets and how to get out there. For now, we'll see what the local solicitor has to offer.'

But once inside the small offices, with the legend over its door proclaiming it to be *Solicitors, Conveyancers, Notaries Public, Wills and Probate*, Jack thought it was as well he was not genuinely looking for a house to buy. Gus was consigned to wait in a dismal outer office, and Mr Joseph Glennon was shown into the office of Mr E. Meazle himself. Mr Meazle was seated behind a high desk, and regarded his unexpected visitor with disapproval. He wore an old-fashioned high wing collar from which a thin chicken neck protruded, and Jack committed his appearance to memory in case the Amaranth should ever revive Tom Taylor's play *A Nice Firm*, with its tumbled scenes in a legal office, and picturesque untidiness of law papers and japanned deed boxes and cobwebs.

In response to Jack's explanation about searching for a property, Mr Meazle did not think he could be of any help.

'I'm sorry to hear that,' said Jack, in a crestfallen tone. 'You see, I don't know this part of the world, other than to pass through it on the train. En route to Scotland, generally.' He considered throwing in Balmoral at this point, but thought Mr Meazle was unlikely to believe that Joseph Glennon moved in such exalted circles. He said, 'But I've always felt it was a place where I'd like to live some day, and I thought a local solicitor might be the very person to know of any likely houses available. And, of course, to help with the legal side of a purchase. I've lately come into a very unexpected legacy, and I've got it in mind to lead a quiet rural life.' He ventured a timid smile. 'Someone at the pub – I'm staying at the Mercian Arms, you know – mentioned a Vallow Hall as being one of the large houses hereabouts. Do you know it? I thought I might call and introduce myself, and see if the owners know of any likely properties.'

'There is a Vallow Hall,' said Meazle. 'The Vallow family have lived there for generations. But the present owner doesn't see visitors – he's virtually a recluse.'

'Ah. An elderly gentleman?' asked Jack. 'Or in ill health?'

'He won't be so very old, although I have no idea as to his health. He was once quite active in the area – a justice of the peace – on several local committees. He was on the board of governors of St Botolph's Orphanage, as well, in fact I believe they wanted him to administer an education programme they were setting up. But it was at the time he was giving up most of his public duties, so he declined. It was some considerable way for him to travel with any frequency, too – St Botolph's is on the other side of Alnwick. The education programme was formed, though, and I believe it's very well thought of. But Mr Vallow plays virtually no part in local life these days.'

'Still, I might try calling on him. I'm grateful for your time. Good-day to you.'

Walking back across the village square, Jack relayed the conversation to Gus, who listened, then said, 'So a recluse lives at Vallow Hall.'

'Yes, and I wonder how long he's been a recluse – and why he became one in the first place, because if it started fifteen years ago . . .' Jack frowned, then said, 'Have we got Ambrose's sketch map with us? Ah, thanks.'

He unfolded the map, remembering to don the spectacles in case anyone might be watching, and studied it. To an onlooker this would be quite natural – Mr Glennon studying the layout of the village where he was hoping to buy a property.

Ambrose had taken trouble over the map, and had added approximate distances between salient points. Vallow Hall was clearly shown, with the approach to it along Candle Lane. The name conjured up bobbing carriage lights and the old tradition of link boys carrying lanterns to light the way. Byron had added a few touches of his own, including a little drawing of how he thought Vallow Hall might look. Typically, he had got carried away and had drawn in gothic arches and gargoyles, so that Vallow Hall looked as if it might make a good setting for a play about any one of a dozen dark old houses from the gloomiest gothic fiction.

'What we need to do,' said Jack, folding up the map, and looking about him, 'is find Candle Lane. According to the map, it leads directly off this square, so . . . Yes, there it is by the saddler's shop. And if Ambrose's calculations can be trusted – and I should think they can – Vallow Hall is within reasonably easy walking distance.'

*   *   *

As they crossed the square and turned into Candle Lane, Jack was aware of a thrum of excitement. Vallow Hall, he thought. In a very short time I'm going to see it. I'm going to walk up to its front door and request admittance. The chalice might be in there or it might not. But I could find out a bit more about Maude.

He had expected Candle Lane to be wreathed in mystery and heavy with secrets, but it was an ordinary country lane – there would be hundreds like it the length and breadth of the land – the ground rutted from carts, the hedges on each side thrusting forward. In the autumn there would be blackberries, which the local children would pick. For a moment Jack almost wished he really was Joseph Glennon, hoping to live out here, intending to pursue a peaceful rural existence. Then he remembered the Amaranth and the thrill of a first night, and the acclaim and applause of audiences. Hard on the heels of that he remembered how it felt to enter some rich luxurious house without being caught, and to delicately and judiciously remove pieces of jewellery or silver. The vision of a rural idyll ceased to hold any attraction.

They reached a high greystone wall, and Jack stepped back to look up at it.

'The wall enclosing the house,' he said. 'Eight feet high, but no more. And we packed the silk ladder with the grappling hooks, didn't we?'

'We haven't brought it this morning, but it's at the bottom of the luggage,' confirmed Gus. 'There're gates farther along, though. They might be open.'

The gates were tall and had elaborate iron scrollwork. When Jack reached for the latch it lifted smoothly, and the left-hand gate swung inwards. As they stepped through, he paused to examine the latch more closely.

'Simple mechanism,' he said. 'Easily dealt with if I come back and the gates are locked.'

They walked along a wide curving carriageway fringed with thick shrubbery, then rounded a final curve. And there was the house. Jack stood still for a moment, studying it. It was built of the same dour grey stone as the wall that enclosed it, and it had a brooding air, as if there might be secrets inside it, and as if it hugged the secrets to itself and frowned on any intruders. Trees had been allowed to grow up around it; their branches would tap on the upper windows, like skeletal fingers. It was not quite a Bronte-esque Wuthering Heights, or Austen's Northanger Abbey, but Jack thought Byron had not been far off the mark with those gothic touches. As they got closer, though, this impression faded a little, and perhaps after all it was nothing more than a rather sad old country house that must once have seen better days.

He said, 'Let's see if we can get ourselves invited in. The main door's more like a church porch, isn't it? Will there be a doorkeeper who we'll have to ask to raise a portcullis, do you think? Or an oubliette we'll have to step around, or . . .? Oh, no, there's a bell rope. Very mundane.'

When he pulled the twisted iron rope there was a second or two of silence, and then the sound of the bell clanging inside the house. It was a mournful sound, and Jack felt something akin to fear scrape across his skin. To counteract this, he said to Gus, 'Ideally we should now hear dragging footsteps, and a leering face peering through a tiny chink in the door.'

'Mr Jack, do hush, or they'll hear you— And someone's coming.'

The footsteps approaching the door were brisk and sharp, although the door was only opened halfway. A rather harsh female voice said, 'Yes?'

Against the dimness of the hall Jack made out a tall, well-built lady with large features but a thin mouth. She was wearing a high-necked gown – there was an impression of whalebone and no-nonsense. She might be some kind of house-keeper, although the house's condition did not suggest it had much of a household staff. Possibly she was a dependent relative assigned to answer the door if no one else was available.

He took this all in, then with an ingenuous smile said, 'Good morning to you. I'm Joseph Glennon, and this is my manser-vant, Mr Augustus Pocket.'

'Well?' There was a quick backward glance over the lady's shoulder, either as if she had been engaged on some vital task and wanted to get back to it, or as if she was looking to see if anyone was in earshot.

'I apologize for calling without an introduction, but I'm in Vallow for a few days, looking for a country house to buy in the area,' said Jack. He spread his hands in a rueful gesture. 'I don't know this part of the world, so I thought I'd approach one or two local landowners, to see if they might know of any possible properties. Is the master – or the mistress – of the house at home and perhaps available to have a word with me?'

This had sounded quite good, quite believable when he had worked it out earlier, but in the face of the woman's stony stare it lost some of its credibility.

She said, 'I don't know of any houses for sale. I can't help you.'

As she made to shut the door, Jack took a step forward, and she paused and looked coldly at him. But before he could say anything else a door on the left of the hall opened, and a man's voice called out, 'Cousin Hilda, I heard voices – are there visitors? I wasn't informed of any.'

A figure walked across the hall towards them. It would be absurd to think the hall's dimness clung to it like strings of ancient cobwebs, and it would be nothing more than the uncertain light in the house, probably coupled with Jack's too-lively imagination. But the really curious thing – the unsettling thing – was that as the man came into the light and the illusion of cobweb strands dissolved, a sense of extreme fear scraped across Jack's mind. It was so strong that he thought he might actually have flinched.

And yet the man was ordinary, if not especially appealing. He looked to be in his fifties, but he had a slight stoop. Strands of sparse hair like dried straw were combed over balding sections of his narrow head, and his eyes had a slightly hooded appearance. Jack tried not to think that coupled with the hunched-over shoulders they gave him a slightly predatory look.

'It's only someone looking for a house to buy,' said Cousin Hilda. 'I've told him there aren't any.'

The dismissive tone of this annoyed Jack so much that he nearly forgot Joseph Glennon's mild personality, but Gus nudged him with a foot, and he managed to say, 'Good morning, sir. As the lady has said, I'm engaged in a search for a house to buy hereabouts. I've had a word with the local solicitor, and I'm calling on several of the local people to introduce myself. Everyone has been very friendly, so I thought it would be acceptable to come out here. Would you be Mr Vallow?' He might easily be Brigadier Vallow or Sir Somebody Vallow, or even a Lordship, but you had to start somewhere.

The man said, 'I'm Saul Vallow.' His voice grated on Jack – there was a dissonance that made him think of a cracked piece of china. But he said, 'How do you do, sir. I'm Joseph Glennon.'

'Joseph Glennon.' It came out as if the man was trying to see how it sounded. It would be absurd to think there was a suspicious note in his voice – even a note of disbelief. He did not take Jack's proffered hand; he just studied him with an intensity that was disconcerting. Then he said, 'Miss Grout is right to say there are no properties available to buy here-abouts. I'm sorry we cannot be of any help. Good-day to you.'

Jack said, 'I should apologize for having taken up your time.' He stepped back as if preparing to go, then turned back just as Hilda Grout was starting to close the door.

'There was one house I wondered about,' he said. 'I saw it from the train on the way here. A strange old place it looked. It was over the fields.' He made a vague half-pointing gesture, not indicating any specific area, since Mr Glennon had no sense of direction. 'Someone said it was probably Bastle House I saw, and that it had been empty for years. Do you know it?'

Bastle House. The name dropped into the dim old hall like a stone plummeting into a dark pond, and Jack had the impression that shock went through Saul Vallow. At his side, Miss Grout drew in a sharp breath and made an involuntary move-ment with one hand, as if pushing something away. He glanced at her, then said to Saul Vallow, 'Have I got the name right?'

'There is a house with that name. You could well have seen it from the train.'

'Would you know who owns it? Or how I might trace the owner? If it's been empty for a while, he might be interested in an offer.'

'I don't believe anyone knows who owns it,' said Vallow. 'I'd forgotten about it, as a matter of fact. It's something of a – a blight on the countryside.'

'Something to ignore as much as possible,' put in Cousin Hilda. 'An appalling place.'

'And probably dangerous,' said Saul Vallow. 'It would certainly need a great deal of money spending on it.' His tone indicated that he did not think Joseph Glennon's means would be anywhere near enough to fund such work.

'I might take a look at it anyway,' said Jack. 'Thank you very much again. Good-day to you both.'

He was aware of Gus giving a small, respectful nod, but neither Vallow nor Miss Grout said anything in the way of farewell, and they were scarcely out of the deep old porch before there was the sound of the door closing, and of a key turning in the lock.

Vallow Hall retreated into its brooding silence and its secrets.

As they retraced their steps along Candle Lane and came into the village square, Gus said, 'You didn't like him, did you, Mr Jack? Mr Saul Vallow?'

Jack said, 'No.' The strange fear brushed his mind again, and he had to make an effort to push it away. He said, 'And it's a curious thing, Gus, but I was relieved when he didn't take my hand. I'm going to get a look inside that house, though. One way or another.'

'When?'

Jack thought for a moment, then said, 'Not tonight, I don't think. It'd be too soon after our visit. If anything went wrong – if old Vallow even only half-suspected someone was lurking around he might connect it to the unexpected visit of Mr Joseph Glennon. Also, tonight is the Chauntry School concert, so there could be people out and about until quite late. But we've still got the afternoon ahead of us, and we could go out to Bastle House. Empty houses are ideal to hide secrets. And that reaction from Saul Vallow and the Grout female when I asked about that place—'

'They didn't like it,' said Gus, at once. 'And they fell over themselves to tell you how unsuitable it would be for you.'

They crossed the square, and as they went into the Mercian Arms, Jack said, 'It's just on mid-day. Let's see if we can get an early lunch, and then work out how we can get to Bastle House. It doesn't look so very far on Ambrose's map.'

Mrs Gurning greeted them, appeared keen to help Gus divest himself of his scarf, and expressed herself as delighted to provide luncheon for them.

'There's cold roast beef and home-made horseradish, and a pot of soup that's been simmering on the stove this last two hours. I daresay Mr Pocket will be glad of that, for you need feeding up to my mind, Mr Pocket, what with you being so poorly last evening.'

'That sounds excellent,' said Jack. 'And is it possible to hire a conveyance this afternoon? So that I can see a bit more of the area and look at likely houses?'

'Well, Ned Nithercott can usually oblige,' said Mrs Gurning. 'Him as brought you from the station in his cart yesterday. But I don't know as he'd be able to do so today, on account of the concert up to Chauntry this evening. Lot of to-ing and fro-ing there always is for a Chauntry concert. Things being delivered up to the school – always a real good supper they lay on – and then folk arriving at the station. Parents, come to see their sons sing on the stage, and having to be collected from their trains. Ned takes them back and forth. Quite run off his feet he is, if you can believe what he says. But it's quite an event for Vallow, a Chauntry concert, and a grand evening.'

Jack said, 'I saw the poster about it in the square. I thought I might go along.'

'Oh, you'd enjoy it,' said Mrs Gurning at once. 'And we've got tickets at the bar – I have an arrangement with the house-keeper at Chauntry about that. Folk often buy tickets here, what with us being in the centre of Vallow. I can let you have two – I daresay Mr Pocket is as partial to a bit of good music as the next man.'

'He is indeed. We'll certainly have two tickets,' said Jack, and Mrs Gurning beamed.

'Only one and sixpence each they are. Proceeds go to the

church – for Poor Relief and St Botolph's – part workhouse, part orphanage, that is, and everyone's always pleased to donate, and Chauntry's very keen on helping the orphans. But I'll find out when Ned might be available to take you out and about. Probably tomorrow, it'd be. Oh, and another letter came for you while you were out. Late morning post. I kept it behind the bar until you came in.' She brought the letter over to their table, holding it up and examining it from all angles.

'Thank you,' said Jack, taking the envelope, which bore Byron's distinctive scrawl.

'And these are the tickets for the Chauntry concert. I'll put the three shillings on your bill, shall I? Now, some folks go along in their own traps, but Ned will be bringing his cart to the market square at seven o'clock, and the school sends down its own wagonette as well – big lumbering thing it is, but it takes upwards of a dozen people. They make two or three journeys if they have to.'

'That all sounds excellent. Thank you.'

As Mrs Gurning took herself off, Jack said, 'Let's have lunch, then go up to my room to read Byron's letter. We'll decide whether to see if we can walk out to Bastle House after that. I don't know about you, Gus, but after coping with Meazles and Vallows I'm ravenous.'

'I'm hoping to catch the ten o'clock post with this,' wrote Byron, after Jack had unfolded the letter, and perched on the window ledge to read it to Gus. 'I'm scribbling at a frantic rate, so I hope it will be readable. But I must say, Jack, that over these last two or three days I've become so absorbed in delving into the past that I'm beginning to find the present slightly disconcerting. I'm assuming you've read H G Wells' *The Time Machine*? I'm starting to wonder if I might have stepped inside a similar contraption without realizing it.

'What I've discovered is that after Richard II's death, his possessions – such as they were by that time – were scattered far and wide, so there's no knowing what became of most of them. However – and it's a fairly important "however" – in a very dull book about him there's a reference to some of his things being taken to Ludlow Castle in Shropshire. I suppose whatever had been retrieved might have been regarded as Plantagenet relics or even heirlooms, so they'd be gathered up and kept. There's the remains of an inventory – it doesn't seem to mention the chalice as such, but it does say that a certain item "would better have been left in the dungeon, rather than carried forth to Ludlow Castle, there to spread its dragging darkness". So I think we could make a reasonable assumption that the chalice did go to Ludlow.

'But what I didn't know is that some years later two young boys were brought to that castle. One was eleven or twelve years old, and his brother was slightly younger – around nine.

'They lived and studied there, and it sounds as if some kind of librarian or under-chaplain acted as tutor, so I shall do my best to trace him. He isn't named anywhere – at least not anywhere I've found yet – which is annoying of him, but he's described as "a scholarly gentleman, much given to recording his work".

'But if I can't name him, I can name those two boys. They were the never-to-be-crowned Edward V of England and his younger brother, Richard, Duke of York. The boys who were to go down in history as the Princes in the Tower.'

Jack was staring at the letter. 'The Princes in the Tower,' he said, half to himself. 'The sons of Edward IV who vanished. My God, I hadn't expected that.'

'Nor had I. But even I've heard of the Princes in the Tower,' said Gus.

'In 1483,' Byron went on, 'those boys were taken to the Tower of London – in the belief that it was in preparation for young Edward's coronation. No one has ever known what became of them after that, but to this day it's believed they were murdered – with the murderer generally believed to have been Richard III, probably the most famous Wicked Uncle of all time. A good many people have questioned Richard's guilt, though, and the truth has never really been known. Probably it never will be.

'It's impossible to connect the chalice to the princes – even to know if they would have been aware of its presence in Ludlow Castle. I've looked the place up, and it's a vast sprawling Norman fortification, so it was probably possible to live there for years without going into every part of it.

'But I shall continue to pursue all possible lines of research, and I'll send everything I find to you with the speed of a winged Mercury – and that's a very appropriate emblem, since as well as being able to dart between underworlds and over-worlds and find ways around the boundaries of life and death, Mercury is also supposed to be the protector of travellers, thieves, merchants and orators. I should think the Fitzglen clan *en masse* would fall into any or all of those categories.

'Good luck with *The Quest*.

'Byron.'

SIX

After the astonishing night with the young man called Eddy, as December wore on Vallow Hall seemed to Maude to be even bleaker than ever. She took to wearing her warmest gowns and making sure to put a wool shawl around her shoulders before going downstairs for the day, and tried not to count how many weeks there were until the warmer weather came.

It was particularly cold on the day the morning post brought two letters, one addressed to Saul, the other to Maude. Saul read his over breakfast, frowning, and then looking complacent.

'An unexpected meeting in Alnwick,' he said. 'All the JPs in the county are invited. It's on Friday, which is only two days' notice, but I think I should attend.'

He would attend, of course. He liked being a Justice of the Peace and regarded with respect and treated with deference, although he usually set off for Alnwick complaining about having to be away from Vallow for an entire day, and grumbling about the inconvenient train times. When he returned, it was always with an air of satisfaction, because he was pleased at having been able to exert authority and consign people to prison or levy fines which they would not be able to pay.

'The meeting is at ten o'clock, though – very thoughtless of them. They know I have a journey of at least three quarters of an hour from Vallow,' he said. 'I shall have a word to say about that, although I don't know who I'll be speaking to, because I can't make out the signature on the letter. Still, they've had the courtesy to send train tickets and they're offering luncheon as well, which they've never done before. There may be a new treasurer or secretary. But the return train ticket is for a three o'clock train, which means I shan't be back until after four.'

'You could get an earlier train if the luncheon ends in time,' suggested Maude.

'No I could not, not when tickets have been bought and paid for by somebody.' His mouth formed into a thin mean shape. 'And what is your letter about, my dear?'

Maude wondered if there were households and marriages where ladies were allowed to have letters without their contents being questioned. But she seldom received a letter, so it was worthy of notice. It was not anything private, anyway.

She said, 'It's a note from Chauntry. I must have mentioned finding some Schubert songs, and they've asked if I could take one or two along for the pupils to practise for their end-of-term concert. It's to be on the day before Christmas Eve, so they'd like the music before the weekend. As a matter of fact they say Friday would be a particularly convenient day, so I could go along while you're in Alnwick.'

Almost from the beginning he had not liked her going anywhere or meeting local people more than necessary, but Maude did not think he would object to this. She suspected he wanted to remain in favour with Chauntry School in case there was ever a vacancy on their board of governors.

And after a moment, he said, 'I suppose that would be all right, although I should have thought they would send someone to collect the music, rather than expect you to take it to them.'

'I don't mind. It's a nice walk anyway, and it isn't very far.'

'It won't be too much for you, will it? The walk?'

'Oh, no. I've walked there a number of times, and they're sure to ask me in. They usually offer a cup of coffee, too.'

'You look pale,' he said. 'And you haven't eaten any breakfast, I notice.'

'I'm not very hungry. I had a cup of tea in bed.'

He was not really interested in whether she ate breakfast or not, and he had only said it because Agnes was in the room, waiting by the sideboard in case any more kedgeree or scrambled eggs needed to be spooned out for the master. He liked the servants to see him as a thoughtful and considerate husband. Maude sometimes imagined little scenes in which she had a furious row with Saul in front of them, shouting that he was

mean and selfish and boring, and describing the horrible proddings and red-faced gropings in bed and how he only ever had
a soft floppiness between his thighs, while other men—

But this was a thought that could not be allowed to take
substance. In any case, Maude would never dare to speak like
that to Saul, not in front of the servants and not in private, either.
She could never let anyone know that after that night at Hymbre
House she was now aware of what was supposed to happen
in a bed and what was supposed to happen physically to a
man. At the time she had been startled and nearly panic-
stricken, but it was starting to feel like a good memory –
something she would cherish. And Eddy had been kind
afterwards – gentle and concerned about the blood between
her thighs, and also tactful, suggesting she should tell the
Hymbre House servants that it was – how had he put it? That
it was the week for her head to ache. It had been a very deli-
cate way of putting it.

When Maude came to think about it, she had not had a
week when her head had ached since that night. It did not
matter, though, and it was rather a relief not to have to bother
with it.

After Saul set off for Vallow Halt and his journey to Alnwick
early on Friday, Maude asked Agnes to unlock the music room.

'I need to collect some music scores for the school. There's
no need to lock it again, because I might need to return some
of the music. So leave it open until I get back.'

She found the Schubert songs easily enough, and fortunately
they were in a small cupboard, so she did not have to ask
Agnes to drag out the tapestry-lidded box that stood under the
piano. There were four she could take. *Lieder*, they were called,
of course: poetry set to music. She must remember to use the
term when she saw the precentor at Chauntry later on. People
said he had founded the music department when he was a
young man, and had built up the school's reputation over the
years. Maude did not know him very well, but she had been
to the school three or four times, and they often exchanged a
few words after church on Sundays, which would be when
the Schubert songs must have been mentioned.

She wrapped her thickest cloak around her and set off. It was very cold, but that would probably help to clear her head. She felt quite muzzy in the mornings these days – even to the point of feeling a bit sick sometimes. This was not something to mention to anyone, however. Aunt Hilda had always been very strict about not discussing bodily ailments, which was indelicate and could embarrass people. So Maude had not mentioned the vague sick feeling to anyone, and had got into the way of moving slowly when she got out of bed until the sensation passed, which it generally did by the middle of the morning. She managed to avoid actually eating any breakfast, which also helped. It was a pity she could not avoid Saul's fortnightly fumblings in her bed too, because if anything was likely to make a person sick it was that.

The young man at Hymbre House had not made her feel sick, and he certainly had not fumbled. Walking along the damp gardens, with moisture dripping from the branches of the trees, she smiled. She would probably never see him again, but the memory was still a good one. And what they had done – what he had done to her – was clearly the act of love about which poets waxed lyrical and over which lovers sighed and vowed to count the world well lost. It was nice to think she could now have her own dream. It was a very slight one, but it was better than not having any dream at all.

Chauntry School stood in its own grounds, and it was a nice old building, greystone with ivy covering parts of the walls. Behind it were the fields where the boys played cricket. Saul sometimes grumbled that from the morning room he could hear them shouting, but Maude had never heard them and even if she had she would not have minded.

Usually when she plied the old-fashioned door knocker the caretaker answered it. He was a sprightly old gentleman who had lived in Vallow all his life, and been at Chauntry ever since anyone could remember. It was said that after a few drinks in the taproom of the Mercian Arms he would relate all kinds of colourful tales about the various families of Vallow and the surrounding districts. Lily, Vallow Hall's kitchen maid, had told Maude that no one really believed the stories, but everyone liked listening to them.

Today, though, a complete stranger opened the door, and said, making it a statement and almost an identification, 'Maude Vallow. I'm so glad you've come. I hoped you'd manage it. Come along in.'

Before Maude could explain about bringing the music, and ask how the man knew who she was, he said, 'I saw you at Hymbre House a few weeks ago. We were both guests of Lady Hymbre, although I was more in the nature of the entertainment after dinner and we didn't actually speak. I'm Connor O'Kane.'

Connor O'Kane. Memory went back to Eddy saying if there should be any trouble after their encounter she could get a message to him by way of two gentlemen. One of those gentlemen had been called Aiden Fitzglen and he had been something to do with a London theatre, which had sounded a bit daunting. But the other name had been Connor O'Kane, and seeing him now Maude recognized him from that weekend. He had had a violinist accompanying him, and they had played for the guests, for about half an hour – Chopin it had been. She had enjoyed it very much.

'So I think,' the young man was saying, 'that we could regard that as an introduction, and you can quite safely come into the library with me.'

He smiled, and led her into the library. Maude had been in here before, and she always thought it was a welcoming room. There was a comforting scent of old leather and the feeling that it was a place where people would relax and read and talk. A fire burned in the hearth, and Connor O'Kane gestured to her to sit near to it.

'And now, Maude,' he said, 'I have a confession to make. I've got you here under false pretences. This isn't because of music scores – although I'm sure the school will be pleased to have whatever you've brought. But it's something quite different. I have something here for you that a mutual friend asked me to bring and to deliver into your hands.'

'A mutual friend?'

'Yes.' Connor O'Kane paused, then said, 'His Highness, Prince Albert Victor, Duke of Clarence and Avondale.'

For a moment the words made no sense, then, as Maude

stared at him, he said, 'He's the eldest son of the Prince of Wales. You knew him just as Eddy.'

Maude felt as if she had fallen into a deep well. The warm room receded, and although she thought she tried to say something, no words came.

As if from a distance, she heard Mr O'Kane saying in a concerned voice, 'I'm sorry, I assumed you knew who he was—'

'No . . . I had no idea—'

'Sit down. And stay here – I'll get someone to bring you a cup of tea, or even a glass of brandy.'

Maude managed to say, 'A cup of tea,' because however restorative brandy might be, she could not go back to Vallow Hall smelling of it.

There was a murmur of voices from the hall, and Maude tried to get her mind into place again. She felt weak and trembly, and she had no idea what she should do. She wondered, vaguely, how she would manage to get back to Vallow Hall, because she did not think she could even stand up, never mind walk back along Candle Lane. But when Mr O'Kane returned it was almost as if he had sensed this concern, because he said, 'In a little while – when we've had our talk – I'll get one of the men here to take you back to the Hall. Your husband won't miss you for a few hours – he'll be in Alnwick by now. He won't be back until lunchtime at the very earliest.'

'How do you know he's in Alnwick?'

'Because I'm the one who sent him the letter summoning him to a meeting there,' said Mr O'Kane, and the smile came again. 'There's no meeting, I'm afraid. I faked the whole thing. Shocking, isn't it? I found out all the details about your husband beforehand, of course – his position as a JP and so on. Occasionally I – or someone else – has to do this kind of thing for His Highness.'

'Why?'

'Usually to help him out of a difficult situation if he gets himself into one. He's . . .' There was a slight pause as if he were trying to find the right words. 'He isn't perhaps the most discerning of men,' he said, carefully. 'He sometimes misjudges what would be sensible or advisable behaviour, or doesn't realize that he might be going into a situation that could turn out to be awkward, or to give people a wrong impression. There've been a few rather discreditable stories about him recently – stories of how he's visited slightly questionable places and made unwise friendships . . .' He frowned, then said, 'But I'd stake my life that he's never done anything cruel or hurtful, and he's often misunderstood. He has a very kind side and a great sense of responsibility. That's his upbringing, of course.'

His upbringing. His upbringing to fit him for one day becoming King of England.

'I'm here today on his behalf and with the best of motives on his side,' said Mr O'Kane. 'I do want you to know that. The prince wants you to know it, too.'

The prince . . . The room tilted again, and Maude had to grasp the arms of the chair to remain sitting upright. She could not fit that title, that grandeur, into the image she had of the young man called Eddy who had been kind and tactful. And even loving – she would believe he had been that for that brief time they had been together.

'He asked me to work out the details of a plan for you,' said Mr O'Kane. 'He wants to be sure you'll be all right, you see. It's the kind of man he is, under all the ceremony and pomp. And that's why I'm here now.'

There was a soft tap at the door and a tray of tea was brought in and set down on the table near the hearth. Maude thought it was one of the younger masters, but he only smiled and she was glad to remember that she had seen him a few times on her visits here. It made this wildly bizarre situation feel a bit more normal, although probably the world would never seem entirely normal again.

After the man had gone, Connor O'Kane said, 'Chauntry seemed a good place for us to meet. You know the precentor a little, so I didn't think your husband would find it strange if a note was sent about some music for the pupils.' He poured the tea and handed her a cup. 'In fact the precentor is my cousin. Dr Declan Kendal.'

'Oh!' said Maude, staring at him. 'Yes, I can see a resemblance. I thought there was something about you I recognized.'

'Declan's always been regarded as the scholar of the family,' said her companion. 'He came to Chauntry straight from Oxford, and he's lived in a kind of ivory tower ever since.' He smiled, and unexpectedly it was the rare smile of the mild-mannered academic precentor, but with a touch of flamboyance. 'I'm the one who goes out into the world and entertains people with music,' he said. 'And occasionally consorts with minor royalty. My cousin teaches it and doesn't really know much about the world beyond the groves of academe.'

'Yes, I see.' Maude drank the tea gratefully, as Connor O'Kane produced from a corner of the room an oak box, plain, but smooth with age, the grain of the wood satiny and beautiful. On one side was an indentation, oval in shape, as if something had been fixed to the box's side, but had broken off it. He placed the box on a low table in front of her chair, and next to it put a thick oilskin package.

'The box contains something extremely valuable,' he said. 'I admit I was a bit startled when the prince put his plan to me, and I did ask whether this was something he ought to be giving away. But he was insistent, and once his mind's made up there's no changing it. He said that in any case, it was something that belonged to him as much as it belonged to anyone else in his family, and that he was entirely prepared for a few stories to circulate when its disappearance was known. That prospect didn't seem to worry him in the least – he said there had always been speculation about it anyway, so one more set of stories wouldn't matter.'

'Stories?' said Maude, a bit nervously.

'Yes, but whatever is said or speculated, you can be sure none of it will involve you,' said Connor O'Kane, at once.

'Thank you.' Maude thought she could trust Connor O'Kane on this point.

'The prince didn't tell me how he actually managed to get at the thing without anyone knowing, and I didn't feel I could ask him. There are,' said Connor, with a sudden grin, 'boundaries that you don't cross.'

'Yes, of course.'

'He'd have seen it as a bit of an adventure,' he said. 'A rather exciting deception.'

Remembering how Eddy had spirited her away from the guests at Hymbre House, and had seemed to enjoy doing so, Maude could believe this.

'And I think he would like you to keep what's in this box as a memento,' said Connor, tapping the oak lid lightly. 'It needn't raise difficult questions for you, need it? Perhaps you could say it's a legacy from a relative or even make out that you found it packed away somewhere at Vallow Hall itself?'

Maude was by this time strongly curious. She said, 'But what exactly is it?'

'See for yourself,' he said. 'It isn't locked.'

Maude set down her teacup and reached for the box. There were no hinges on the lid, but beneath its rim was a narrow groove, and the lid lifted smoothly and easily. Beneath were layers of soft muslin. She removed them cautiously, and, as what lay beneath came into view, she gasped, and sat very still. It was surely only a coincidence that in that moment a shaft of late-morning sunlight came in through the latticed windows of the old library and that a log broke in the fire sending flames upwards. Firelight and sunlight mingled, lighting what lay inside the box to jewel colours. The thought – *it doesn't like being in the dark* – went through her mind.

'It's a bowl,' said Connor, softly. 'A chalice, if we're to be accurate. Stemmed, and with the glass engraved – coloured and etched, and very beautiful, as you can see. It's certainly extremely old. I don't know its history, because the prince didn't seem to know it, but I think originally it came from a religious house. It's been in his family for a very long time indeed.'

'I've never seen anything so lovely,' said Maude, softly. The chalice fitted the box very neatly. She carefully lifted it out, and set it on the low table. The sunshine and the firelight fell directly across it, bringing to life the tiny figures engraved into the glass. Some of them had a religious look as if they might be bishops or cardinals engaged in some sacred cere-mony; others wore circlets as crowns and held swords aloft, as if poised for battle. Still others were clearly Eastern figures, with exotic costumes and headwear.

The colours were glowing blues and deep reds and rich amber, and around the rim the glass had been formed into thin layers, resembling the petals of a rose. Maude turned it this way and that to see the details more clearly. It was possible to trace with a fingertip the outlines of the engravings – the figures and the swords and religious cups – and to feel and appreciate the silkiness of the glass itself.

'It's one of the most beautiful things I've ever seen,' she said at last, but with the words a coldness seemed to brush across her mind. It was almost as if candles had been snuffed or gas jets turned down, draining all light and warmth. That was absurd – sunshine was still streaming in through the old windows of the room, causing the scents of polish from the nice old furniture to drift across the room, and the fire was crackling in the grate. The chalice, still held between her cupped hands, was lit to glowing life. But she had an extraordinary sense that a darkness was creeping closer. When she set the chalice on the table the feeling vanished, though.

Connor O'Kane handed her the oilskin package. 'This is the other part of the prince's gift.'

Inside the package was a document made up of two or three thick pages sewn down the left-hand side with narrow green tape. Attached to the top of the page was a small card, with an engraved name, and a crest. Across it was written in rather sprawling writing:

'*For a very lovely lady and for the memory of our night together at Hymbre House which will always remain with me. E.*'

Maude stared at this, then picked up the document. The lettering was elaborate, but it was easy enough to read it. Two names jumped out at her immediately.

Albert Victor Christian Edward Saxe-Coburg-Gotha, the Duke of Clarence and Avondale. And beneath it, Maude's own name.

'It's all couched in legal terms,' Connor O'Kane was saying, 'and there's no punctuation, because legal documents don't permit that. But I think it's clear enough.'

It was perfectly clear, and the part that was clearest of all was the sentence that said:

> To be conveyed absolutely and in perpetuity into the sole ownership of Maude Vallow unconditionally for her use as she sees fit all that piece and parcel of ground with the messuage dwellinghouse and other buildings delineated in red on the plan herein and known as *The Bastle House* in the County of Northumberland.

Bastle House. The dark nightmare house. The black crouching lodestar she could see from Vallow's topmost rooms, and that she had always known she would one day approach and enter.

And now she was its owner.

SEVEN

After what felt like a long time, Maude said, 'This is real, I suppose? It isn't a – false thing?'

'It's real, and it's also legal,' said Connor, at once. 'The prince acted through an intermediary – his name didn't appear in the initial transaction and neither did yours. He wanted to find a property in the area that might be available, and when this house was suggested one of his aides acted as the initial buyer. Then, once the purchase had gone through, the ownership was transferred from the aide to the prince, and now he's transferred that ownership to you. Conveyed it, is the legal term.'

'I can't possibly accept it,' said Maude firmly, putting the document back on the low table.

'That would be a great pity,' said Connor. 'The prince very much wants you to accept. The English aristocracy have a great respect for property – an inbuilt belief in its value and in what it represents.' He gave a slightly rueful grin. 'And when you think how many houses that family have . . . It was my cousin who suggested Bastle House might be available, and it seemed a good idea. Declan said it had been empty ever since anyone could remember, and that if the owner could be traced, it might be available. It wasn't difficult to find the owner through Land Registries and such things. Declan did most of that locally – no one really takes any notice of a gentle scholarly music teacher looking through records and archives.'

'He found the owner?'

'Yes. It turned out to be an elderly semi-recluse living in the wilds of Scotland – I have the impression that he was the last of his family, and it sounded as if he was quite glad to get rid of the place. And so the sale – all the sales – went through. From the reclusive gentleman to the prince's aide, from the aide to the prince himself, and now from him to you.'

Maude said slowly, 'And since there'll have been a limitless amount of money and the best legal people available, it would have been a smooth transaction.'

'D'you know, you sounded almost cynical for a moment there. I think you might have hidden depths, Maude Vallow.'

He smiled, then said, 'But yes, it was a smooth transaction. Thankfully the Married Women's Property Act meant the house could be conveyed into your name alone – that you could own it in your own right – although we had to find a few loopholes in the law to get round the problem of what's called uninherited property. It's a fairly new law, but it worked in our favour. The prince wanted to make sure the house would remain yours without—'

'Without any possibility of my husband taking it away from me?'

'Yes. And without him needing to know anything about it, of course. If you read the entire Deed you'll see it's full of "absolutelys" and "unconditionallys" and "in perpetuities". But it's as water-tight as it can be, I should think. If legal advisers to the future King of England couldn't find ways to arrange it as His Highness wanted – well, there's no hope for the entire legal profession. You'll see that it was witnessed by a man called Aiden Fitzglen. It's more usual to have two witnesses, but we decided that Declan and I should be kept out of it. He's known locally, and I'm known to have a bit of a connection with the prince, so either of our names might have raised questions or created a link.'

'Who is Aiden Fitzglen?'

'A friend of mine in the theatre world – a very gifted actor-manager. He's staged one or two events for the prince at his theatre, so the prince knows him slightly through that. In fact Aiden came up with all kinds of useful suggestions,' said Connor. 'He thought up a great many possibilities for what might happen and what needed to be guarded against and planned for. That was his stage background, of course – it was almost as if he was writing the script for a play. It's very much thanks to him that we put this whole plan together.'

'I'd like him to know I'm grateful.' She would be able to thank the precentor – Declan Kendal – herself, but the unknown Mr Fitzglen was a different matter. 'Could you tell him that?'

'Certainly. I could perhaps even let him have a note if you wrote one.'

'Yes – yes, I think I'd like to do that.'

'You do understand,' said Connor, slowly, 'that we can't risk any of this ever coming out? There must never be any hint of what happened between you and the prince.'

'I understand. I'm being paid off, aren't I? I . . . I spent a night with a member of the royal family, and this is to ensure I keep quiet about it. That I don't create any scandals.'

They looked at one another. 'It is important that it doesn't come out,' he said, at last. 'But I think there's a bit more to it. I think the prince genuinely felt something very strong and very deep for you – even though it was a brief encounter. I think your memory will stay with him for a very long time, and I think he wants to be sure you'll be looked after – especially if there are any – well, any consequences.'

Maude thought about this, then said, 'Mr O'Kane—'

'Couldn't you call me Connor?' he said. 'You know my cousin, and you and I seem to have come a long way in the last hour and shared a fair number of secrets. Secrets have the way of sweeping etiquette aside.'

Maude smiled. 'All right then, Connor, I don't want any of this to become known any more than the prince does. My husband – I can't risk him ever finding out. Not through you or your cousin – or Mr Fitzglen in London.'

'Your husband won't find out from any of us. You can trust all of us, I promise that.' He saw her glance at the Deeds to Bastle House, and said, 'And you don't need to do anything about that, if you don't want to. You don't even need to go inside the place. See it as a secret investment, if you can. In a year or two you could arrange a sale – it could be done discreetly. Property always appreciates in value, and land is there for all time – it doesn't get up and walk away. The money from a sale could be deposited very quietly and discreetly in an account in your name. I or one of the aides could arrange all that for you. You can always get in touch with me through my cousin Declan.'

'Thank you.'

'It would mean you were entirely independent,' said Connor.

'You must, though, keep the Title Deeds – this document – somewhere safe. Can you do that? You'd need to produce them if you did sell the place.'

Somewhere safe. Such as a room that was kept locked and only opened for an hour once a week so that the mistress could play an out-of-tune piano?

Maude said slowly, 'There is somewhere I could keep them.'

'Good. And now the keys,' he said, reaching into a pocket, and handing them to her. 'There's symbolism in this, isn't there? The keys of a house.'

As her hand closed around the bunch of heavy keys Maude thought: so now it really is mine, that old house. *Mine.* It's been given to me by a future King of England – given as a bribe to keep silent about going to bed with him. No, I won't think that. Connor O'Kane said there was more to it – that Eddy had had a certain feeling for me, and I'll believe that. She brought her mind back to Connor, who was saying something about a photograph.

'The prince would like a photograph of you, perhaps with the chalice as a small memento of his own. Would you agree to that? Declan could take one while you're here. They have a camera for various events with the pupils, and he's got quite interested in the process. He's surprisingly good.'

It was nice to think of Eddy – Prince Albert Victor Christian Edward – wanting this. Maude smiled. 'Yes, I'll do that.'

She was pleased and reassured all over again to see the precentor – she was able to think of him as Dr Kendal now. Declan. And it was interesting to be part of the unfamiliar and complicated process for taking a photograph.

'We're starting to take photographs of the boys at the end of term, and of the plays and concerts and prize-givings,' said Declan Kendal. 'And it means we've got a permanent record of the events, and parents often order copies.'

'My cousin might be unworldly, but not so much that he objects to turning a few coins for the school's coffers,' said Connor, and smiled affectionately at the precentor.

'The school's finances can always use a little help,' said Dr Kendal, apparently unconcerned. 'Mrs Vallow, could you sit at this table near the window? The light should be right, and we can put the chalice on the table itself . . . Yes, exactly like that. You look very elegant.'

There were clickings and brief flares of light, and then there was a photograph of her with the parchment document.

'Proof positive of ownership,' said Connor. 'And something for His Highness to keep under his pillow.' Maude was not sure how to take this, but he grinned as he said it.

'The plates will be processed in Alnwick,' said Dr Kendal. 'I'll deal with that myself, and no one else will know about them. All that the people in the Alnwick shop will see will be a lady seated at a table in a book room. Entirely ordinary and conventional. Connor will arrange for His Highness to have copies, but if you'd like copies for yourself . . .'

'I think I would.' As Dr Kendal had said, there was nothing at all remarkable about a photograph of Maude seated at a table, with bookshelves and a window. It could easily have been Aunt Hilda's house, in fact. And the photographs would be her own extra and private memento of Eddy.

'I'll request additional ones,' said Dr Kendal. 'And I'll send you a note when they're ready – a real note this time, perhaps arranging for you to collect the Schubert scores you brought this morning.' He glanced at Connor. 'Is everything dealt with?'

'I think so. Maude, it's been a pleasure – and a memorable experience to meet you.'

'For me as well.' Maude did not suppose she would ever see Connor O'Kane again, but it was nice to think she had got to know Chauntry's precentor a little better. It seemed that there was something about sharing a secret that created a particular kind of friendship. As Connor had said, it had the way of sweeping etiquette away.

Dr Kendal said, 'I'll arrange for you to return to the Hall. The wagonette can take you.'

'I can walk—'

'No, don't do that. I know it isn't far, but you'll have the chalice with you, and the box might be noticed. People might talk – quite innocently, but things get round. Let's make sure to keep it just between the three of us.'

They both went out, and Maude was grateful to have a few minutes alone. *Alone with that document that makes me the owner of Bastle House*, she thought. Alone with the chalice. Eddy's gifts. It should have been a good feeling – a safe feeling to think of them in such a way, but as soon as she lifted the chalice to replace it in the box, the sensation of a cold darkness came at her again. She had to force herself to swathe the chalice in its muslin layers and place it in the box. There was just room for the oilskin package, and also for the keys.

Connor and the precentor were in the hall, talking in low voices. It was wrong to listen to someone else's conversation – Aunt Hilda had always said listeners seldom heard good of themselves – but the door to the hall had not been completely shut. Maude could not help hearing Connor say, 'I haven't told Maude Vallow about the manuscript. I don't want you to do so, either.'

'Yes, there's the manuscript, isn't there?' said Declan, slowly. 'I think you're right that she doesn't need to know anything about it, though.'

'I don't really know anything about it myself. I imagine it's some kind of provenance for the chalice – that's what the prince seemed to think, although I don't believe he knows all that much about it. The chalice's disappearance will be discovered sooner or later, of course, and I suppose there'll be a few stories and rumours. They'll die down after a while, though, and probably it'll eventually be regarded as a "lost" treasure – unless Eddy admits to his family what he's done. Although,' said Connor, thoughtfully, 'I shouldn't think that's very likely. If the chalice were ever to be genuinely lost or destroyed, though—'

'The manuscript could be evidence that it once existed?'

'Exactly. I do know it's absurd, but I'd like to think there'd be some proof of it somewhere.'

'I thought I was supposed to be the romantic of the family,' said Declan, and Maude heard the sudden amusement in his voice.

'So you are. But this is . . . Well, anyway, Declan, I'd like to think of that manuscript being kept somewhere separate.

Somewhere safe, though. In the hands of someone I can trust.'
A pause. 'Could that be done?'

Declan Kendal did not immediately answer, then he said,
slowly, 'It could.'

'Ah. I thought so. Thank you.'

'I do agree that we don't tell Maude about it,' said Declan.
'There's no need – she's got enough to contend with as it is
– the chalice and the Deeds to that house.' He paused, then
said, 'What about the superstition, though? Shall you tell her
about that?'

'Certainly not,' said Connor, quite sharply. 'There's no
reason for her to know.'

'I think I agree with you about that, too. It would only
worry her – also frighten her, perhaps. I have the impression
she doesn't have a very happy life. Saul Vallow's a cold man
– God knows what he'd do if he found out about any of this.'

'He won't find out. We'll all make sure. I think Maude will
make sure, as well.'

'Did the prince believe that old superstition – that warning?
How is it worded? Something about wrongful owners of the
chalice being dragged into a darkness?' said Declan.

'He just said it was a story that had developed over the
years – layers added by each generation,' said Connor. 'But
he said even if there was anything in it, the chalice was his
to give to anyone he chose. That he's the rightful owner, so
the "darkness" of the legend couldn't affect him.'

'What about Maude Vallow, though? Is she now the rightful
owner? Because if she isn't—'

'Declan, that story is a medieval superstition,' said Connor.

'But do you believe it, Con?'

'No, of course I don't. I think you might, though,' said
Connor, slowly. 'I noticed you were careful to position the
chalice in the strongest light you could find.'

'That was to get the best image possible for the photograph.'

'Was it?'

Maude leaned forward to hear the reply, but at that moment
the main outer door was opened, and someone was calling
that the cart was at the door. Whatever reply Dr Kendal made
was lost.

But the snatch of overheard conversation was still with her as the school's wagonette took her back to Vallow Hall. There was a manuscript that those two thought she needn't know about. What manuscript? Why wasn't she to know about it?

It was that mention of a superstition that had stayed with her – that reference to a darkness of some kind being part of the chalice. Maude shivered slightly, remembering how she had felt when she cupped her hands around the chalice. Because that was exactly what she had felt. A darkness, creeping closer to her.

Saul Vallow thought anyone who knew him would describe him as a temperate man, but travelling back to Vallow Hall this afternoon he was in a very bad temper indeed. He was, in fact, fuming to think that some pettifogging jackanapes in some office had been so inefficient as to summon him on a fool's errand.

He had presented himself at the court offices, expecting to see fellow magistrates, anticipating a pleasant luncheon, and he had been greeted with blank astonishment and incomprehension.

Minions had been sent scurrying hither and yon while he was kept waiting in a draughty room, and finally it had been admitted that no one could be found who owned to sending the letter summoning him to a meeting that did not exist. A council official – Saul had no idea who the man was – had taken him along to the Alnwick Arms and had given him quite a tolerable luncheon by way of apology.

But he was aggrieved all over again to find that when he eventually got back to the Hall, Maude was not on hand to welcome him home and ask about his day. Agnes was there, though, and clearly she had been on the watch for him. She helped him off with his coat and scarf, and clicked her tongue in annoyance to hear that the meeting had all been some kind of hoax.

'It makes you wonder who sent the letter, doesn't it, sir? The mistress is upstairs, although she was in the music room until about ten minutes ago – went straight in there as soon as she got back. No she wasn't playing the piano, that I do know, it being something you hear all the way down in the kitchens. Is there anything else, sir? Because I need to give Mrs Cheesely a hand with dinner – Lily's more concerned with watching from the window for the poulterer's boy. I'd have thought she'd look a bit higher than a common beak-hunter, that Lily, what with being brought up in a strict chapel family, as she's always reminding us.'

As Saul washed and changed before dinner it occurred to him that it was odd that Maude had been in the music room all afternoon without actually playing any music. He frowned at his reflection in the mirror, combing his hair over the thin patches. His father had lost most of his hair while quite a young man, but Saul was wearing a good deal better. You might say that he presented quite a dapper figure. Not that he was vain.

The more he thought about what Agnes had said, the odder it seemed, and once downstairs he went along to the music room. It was probably coincidence that Agnes appeared at the same time. Saul did not expect her to follow him into the music room, but she did so, closing the door, and standing just inside the room, her eyes darting back and forth.

Whatever Maude's reasons for spending a silent afternoon in here, the room looked exactly as usual, not that Saul came in here very often, in fact hardly ever. But the cushions were plumped up, the two wing chairs were on each side of the tall windows, and the piano lid was closed.

'Always smells musty in here, don't it?' said Agnes from behind him. 'A bit damp on this side of the house. I'll light the gas, shall I?'

'There's no need,' began Saul, but Agnes was already lighting two of the jets, and closing the curtains at the two windows. She turned back, and looked round the room. 'Something's different,' she said, suddenly.

'Is it?' Saul would not have known if the entire music room had been rearranged, or half the furniture taken away.

'Yes, but I don't know what . . . Yes I do. It's what the mistress always calls the music chest. That big box thing under the piano, with cloth on the lid.'

'Tapestry,' said Saul, looking at the box, seeing nothing wrong with it.

'It's been moved,' said Agnes. 'Dragged out from under the piano. It's always kept there, well away from the sunlight so's it won't fade. But it's been pulled out then put back – see those marks across the carpet? The mistress must have moved it. No one else comes in here – only me and Lily to clean the room once a week, and we pull it out then, so as to sweep into the corners. Afterwards we use the carpet beater to bring the pile of the carpet back up. I make sure it's properly done every week. I know what's due to a gentleman's house, you see.'

Her eyes darted slyly to him. Saul ignored her, but he could see what she meant about the carpet. Had Maude dragged the tapestry box out? But why would she go to such trouble? If she had wanted it moving – if she needed to get some of the old music out – she would have called Agnes or Lily. But if she had wanted to put something inside it that she did not want anyone to find . . . It was a ridiculous thought, but he heard himself say, 'Agnes, pull the box out so I can open it. You can manage that, can't you?'

'I think so. And we don't want anyone seeing what we're doing, do we?'

Again, her tone was shutting the two of them into something secret, and Saul said, sharply, 'There'll be nothing to be found.'

He sat down to watch her crawl under the piano, and drag the box out.

'It's rucked up the carpet again, but I'll get Lily to beat the carpet tomorrow, sir. It's not the day for it to be done, but still.'

'Thank you, Agnes.' Any other servant would have heard the dismissal note in his voice and left, but Agnes stood watching as he opened the music chest.

At first, in the flickering light from the gas jets, Saul thought there was going to be nothing remarkable inside – only a stack of old music scores, some of them tattered, all of them covered in the squiggles and symbols that only people like that pretentious music teacher at Chauntry could understand. Well, and Maude, too, of course; Saul was a fair man and he would allow that Maude could read these incomprehensible markings, and play music from them.

He took a few of the pieces out, reading the titles as he did so, thinking how fanciful most of them were, and noticing that some were not even written in English, for heaven's sake. There were one or two books as well – biographies of famous composers, he thought. His grandmother had liked reading them, and Maude liked them, as well.

But halfway down was something that was neither music nor books, and it was something that was very strange to find in such a place.

A legal document. Four pages of thick parchment, sewn with fanciful green ribbon or tape down the left-hand side. The writing on the parchment was the usual over-elaborate script that lawyers liked to use, to make themselves seem important and justify charging exorbitant fees. Saul lifted the document out, and sat down beneath one of the gas jets to read it. He was scarcely aware of his surroundings any longer, and he was certainly no longer aware of Agnes.

He read the document three times, not because he did not understand it, but because he found it difficult to believe what it said. It was for the conveyance of a property, and in the clearest legal terms imaginable – always supposing you could ever describe legal language as clear – it set down that the property called Bastle House passed from the ownership of Albert Victor Christian Edward, Duke of Clarence and Avondale, into the sole and absolute ownership of Maude Vallow.

The document had been witnessed. There was the name, in somewhat extravagant writing. Aiden Fitzglen. The name meant nothing to Saul.

Lying in the corner of the music chest was a set of keys – big, heavy keys, strung on to a metal ring. They were not labelled, but they did not need to be, because they had been placed next to the legal document, and they could only be the keys to Bastle House itself.

And there was something else. Clipped to the first page of the Title Deeds was a small card, like a gentleman's visiting card. It had a tiny engraved shield at the top, with, on the left, a lion, and on the right what Saul thought was a unicorn. At the top, arrogantly embossed, was a crown. Beneath the crown and the shield was a name, in thick bold black letters.

Albert Victor Christian Edward Saxe-Coburg-Gotha.
Under that was written:
'*For a very lovely lady and for the memory of our night together at Hymbre House which will always remain with me.*'
The initial *E* was clearly inscribed beneath it.

EIGHT

S aul stared at the parchment sheets and the card for a very long time. His mind was filled with a whirling confusion, but gradually, rather like the pieces of a child's kaleidoscope, the facts began to fall into place. As they did so, he understood what had happened.

Maude – his own wife – had behaved in the worst possible way that night at Hymbre House. She had lifted her skirts and opened her legs for a man she had only just met. She had let him perform on her the act that Saul, her lawful husband, had never managed to do. While he had been enjoying an innocent game of cards with a few gentlemen, his wife had been in bed with another man. And the man in question was not just anybody – he was a member of the reigning royal family, in fact he was the eldest son of the Prince of Wales. He was Queen Victoria's grandson, and the heir to the throne.

Saul had not been introduced to the prince that night, and when he looked back he remembered that the young man had been surrounded by other guests for most of the evening, so he had had no idea of his identity. It had all been very casual – he had heard it said that royalty sometimes liked a little anonymity, presumably so that they could pursue their immoral adventures.

That debauched young man had pursued an immoral adventure that night, that was for sure. The adventure had resulted in him deflowering Saul's wife – there were no other words for it. Saul would take his Bible oath that Maude had been a virgin until that night. Clearly the prince had seduced her, and moreover had had the bad manners to do it in a house where he was a guest. Saul would not even have put it past Lady Hymbre to have arranged the entire thing, to curry favour with royalty. A sick anger came up into his throat again.

As he turned the thick parchment pages over, he suddenly remembered Agnes's presence. She was sitting in a chair next to him, leaning forward to look at the document, and clearly she had been reading it with him.

'Oh, sir,' she said, softly. 'That man – the prince – seduced the mistress, didn't he? And this . . .' She indicated the document. 'This is the bribe to make sure she'll keep quiet about it. It's what royalty do. Pay off their women.'

'There may be a perfectly innocent explanation,' said Saul, coldly. 'But there's no call for you to concern yourself with it, Agnes.' He stood up, indicating that the matter was at an end, but she did not move, and her next words came like a blow.

She said, 'Sir, there's something you ought to know.' Her eyes were glittering. 'The mistress,' she said, 'I think she's going to have a child.'

The silence came down again. As Saul stared at her, trying to find a suitable response, she said, 'She's been sick most mornings. She's tried to keep it from everyone, but you can't hide being sick, can you? Nor you can't do it silently, neither.'

'There could be any number of reasons—'

'But there's something else,' said Agnes. 'I don't want to embarrass you, sir, although between us two I don't think we need to worry about that, do we? There's an – an omission from the mistress's routine.' And, as he stared at her, not understanding, she said, 'There's something that should be happening, but isn't.'

'Agnes, I don't know what you—'

'Every month,' said Agnes, very deliberately.

Saul felt hot colour rush to his face, then he said, 'Ah. Yes, I see.'

'And, of course,' said Agnes, softly, 'the child will be his, won't it? The prince's. Because we both know it can't be yours. We both know you can't do it, don't we, sir?' She leaned closer. 'Neither of us has ever forgotten, have we?'

Saul had not forgotten, and he never would forget. Blackmail was an ugly word, but it was what Agnes had used to get herself into Vallow Hall.

It had been his own fault. If he had not listened, as a younger man, to other men bragging of their conquests after a few drinks . . . If he had not become resentful at being well over thirty without having done that particular act . . . Not that he would have boasted about it if he had, but still . . .

The end had been that he had visited a house with a certain reputation. It had been in Berwick-on-Tweed, which Saul had thought was sufficiently far from Vallow for him to be unrecognized. Obviously he had not given his name, but the girl to whose bedroom he was shown had given hers. She said she was called Angelique, and there had been some joke about how angels could sometimes behave as devils. Saul was not so naïve as to think she was really called Angelique, but he had gone along with the game. It was a game that turned out to be horribly embarrassing, although Angelique had been sympathetic, saying ever such a lot of gentlemen had this problem, that he wouldn't believe how often it happened. Nerves. Embarrassment. Supposing they tried this to get him going . . .? Or perhaps this . . .?

Saul had been startled at how adroit and how knowledgeable she was. But no amount of adroitness and knowledge had been any good. His manhood had remained stubbornly and embarrassingly flaccid, and in the end they had to accept defeat. It had all been perfectly amicable, and he had paid in full, of course. Despite his care there was a possibility that he had been recognized – not by Angelique necessarily, but by someone seeing him going into the house or coming out of it. He was not risking a story going round Berwick – perhaps even getting back to Vallow – that Saul Vallow had visited a house of ill repute, and that as well as not being able to get his flag even half-mast, he had left without paying for the house's services. If he were to be completely honest, he had not been able to get even as far as a quarter-mast or anywhere near it.

It had not mattered. It was not a very important part of life, and he could perfectly well do without it. Nor would anyone ever know what had happened.

It was only a couple of years afterwards that his father died, and Saul succeeded to the ownership of Vallow Hall, and with it to the various important positions his father had occupied in the county. He became a Justice of the Peace, a magistrate. He was invited to take his father's place on a number of committees – including a seat on the Board of Guardians for St Botolph's Orphanage. He diligently attended all the meetings and court sessions, although he did not often go to St Botolph's, because it meant travelling half across the county, and the Guardians were not what Saul would call generous when it came to expenses. Also, it was extremely tedious work. St Botolph's was a bleak old building, half workhouse, half orphanage, and most people in the area tried to pretend it did not exist, because poverty and parentless children – bastards, if you wanted to be plain – were shameful and best ignored. But it sounded well for people to know he was involved in the administration.

The rather squalid incident in the Berwick house almost completely faded from Saul's memory. On the rare occasion that he did remember it, he could reassure himself that he would not encounter that girl again.

He encountered her two weeks after the announcement of his engagement to Maude. She came blatantly up to Vallow Hall, requested an interview, and asked to be given a job as parlour maid.

Saul did not immediately realize who she was, because she looked very different from the lady who had tried to rouse his interest in the Berwick-on-Tweed bedroom. It had been at least five years ago – probably a bit more – but the woman looked a good deal older. Of course, that bedroom had been dimly lit, and she had painted her face and had her hair hanging round her shoulders. Now it was pinned severely back from her face, and the face itself, without powder and rouge, was sallow and thin-lipped.

She gave her name as Agnes. Agnes Scroop. But then she came nearer and smiled. In a soft voice, she said, 'But you'll more likely remember me as Angelique.' Then she smiled. 'It's been some time, hasn't it, sir? But I've followed what's been happening to you. I did that with a number of my gentlemen – you never know when old friends might come in useful. You're by way of being an old friend, aren't you?

And now you're Squire of Vallow Hall, and I hear you're about to marry quite a wealthy young lady. You'll be glad of that, I daresay.' This was accompanied with a disparaging look round the room, taking in the dingy curtains and the worn rug, and the damp patch under the window where a gutter leaked with disastrous persistence.

Saul said, as coldly as he could, 'You must be mad if you think I'd allow someone with your past into this house.'

'I've left all that behind. I never talk about it – not unless I feel someone needs to know about it. Your new young wife might be someone I'd talk to, though. She should know about her husband's abilities. More to the point, about his lack of them.'

There was a sudden silence. The woman had not quite said, 'If you don't employ me, I'll make sure your bride-to-be knows you're as impotent as a mule – and you'll lose the money she's bringing to Vallow,' but Saul knew it was what she meant.

But then she surprised him. In a different voice, she said, 'I'd always be on your side, sir. Anything that was needed – anything that might help – you could rely on me. There might come a time when you'd be glad of that.'

Saul had known, of course, that Agnes Scroop would not do anything without payment, any more than her alter ego, Angelique, would have done. But the thought darted across his mind that you never knew what strange tools you might one day be glad of. In the end, he had agreed to her coming to work at Vallow Hall. He let the respectable Agnes Scroop, who once had been Angelique from a disreputable house in Berwick-on-Tweed, take up a post as parlour maid. It was the price he was being forced to pay for her silence, but he could not see any way round it. By the time Maude came to the house, Agnes was an established part of the household, and Maude accepted her without question.

After Agnes left the music room, Saul sat for a long time with the gas flares burning lower, the Title Deeds to Bastle House still in his hands.

His mind was in a tumbling confusion, but within that

confusion was a burning hatred for this profligate young man who thrust his undisciplined manhood into any light-minded woman who would lie down for him. Maude had lain down for him. She had met him only a couple of hours earlier, but she had still done that. Had she enjoyed it? With that thought came a fierce desire to punish her – to throw her out of his house there and then, without a penny to her name and her reputation in tatters.

It could not be done, of course. It would create a scandal of a magnitude that would never be forgotten. As for actual divorce, Saul had an idea that an Act of Parliament was necessary, and when he thought that the name of the Queen's grandson would be dragged into the proceedings as an adulterous party, he shuddered. There was also his own lack of ability in the marital bed, which might have to be disclosed. That was certainly not something he was going to risk.

In addition to Maude herself, three people knew what had happened at Hymbre House that night. One was the prince himself, although Saul did not think he would give much attention to what, for him, would have been a very light and casual encounter. Afterwards he had presumably told people to sort out the purchase of Bastle House on his behalf, which would be payment to ensure Maude's silence. He had probably signed a few documents, then forgotten the entire thing. But what about that unknown man who had witnessed the document? It seemed a fair bet that he would have known or guessed the truth. Aiden Fitzglen's name did not mean anything to Saul, and he had no idea whether it would be possible to trace him.

But he would give his mind to that later, because there was a third person who did not need tracing – and it was a person who knew what had happened, and who represented much more of an immediate threat. Agnes. Agnes would certainly be looking to see how she could turn this situation to her own advantage. Once a blackmailer, always a blackmailer.

After some time, Saul replaced the document in the music chest, careful to leave it and the keys exactly as he had found them, since Maude must not suspect he had discovered any of this. Then he rang for Agnes.

When she appeared, he said, without preamble, 'Agnes, it's clear to both of us that the mistress – that there was a relationship between her and the prince.'

'At Hymbre House.' Agnes nodded.

'Yes. But that wasn't normal behaviour – not for the mistress. Betraying her marriage vows with a complete stranger – a man she had only just met—'

'You think she was forced? That he raped her?'

'I didn't mean that.' Saul paused though, considering this idea, but seeing at once that it would open up even more trouble than a divorce. Also, if people believed Maude had been raped, they might feel sorry for her, which was the last thing Saul wanted. The thought of the palace's reaction to such an accusation was not to be even considered.

Choosing his words with care, he said, 'It's such abnormal behaviour that I'm wondering . . . Agnes, have you noticed anything strange about the mistress's behaviour lately? Anything to suggest there could be times when she isn't – isn't entirely sane?'

Agnes looked at him for a moment, then said, slowly, 'You think she could be going mad?'

Mad. The word lay on the air, clear as a curse.

Saul said, 'I did mean that. There have been one or two disquieting signs – signs that perhaps only a husband would notice. A servant might do so, as well, though.'

He waited. The plan that had come to him was still shadowy and unformed, and he was feeling his way along it very warily indeed. If Agnes did not accept this first tentative approach . . .

But she said, slowly, 'It's odd, sir, but I was only saying to Mrs Cheesely and Lily this week that the mistress hasn't been herself lately. She's had an odd look in her eyes. And very strange things she says sometimes, too.'

'Ah.' A pause, then Saul said briskly, 'I don't think we need to do anything yet, Agnes, but between us we need to watch her, closely.'

'I can do that. It would mean extra work, like.'

Damn the woman, she did not miss a single opportunity. But Saul said, 'There could be a suitable increase to your wages.'

'Whatever you think, sir,' she said. Her tone was demure, but her eyes were glittering.

'Have a word with Mrs Cheesely about it. Lily, too. But be discreet. Say only that I'm a little concerned about the mistress's health – about her emotional state. No more than that.'

'I could do that,' she said. 'And once they know about the child, they'll likely be sympathetic.'

The child. After Agnes had gone, Saul finally confronted this aspect. He supposed that someone who had lived the life Agnes had done could be trusted to know about such things. But assuming she was right, what should he do? He could certainly pass the child off as his own, and it would be accepted without question – only he, Agnes and Maude herself knew Saul could not have fathered a child on anyone. But what about the child? What if it discovered the truth about its parentage? What might it do in the years ahead?

It was absurd to think in terms of a claim to the throne, of course – it was centuries since there had been pretenders or anything of that kind in this country. But there were other claims that might be made by a greedy, acquisitive young man – or young woman. Claims that might be urged by others in the know.

'He's your father,' such people might say – people such as the sly, greedy Agnes Scroop. People such as the unknown Aiden Fitzglen, even? 'You deserve something from him,' they might say.

It could result in a truly dreadful scandal. Newspaper reports – shameful headlines about a King's bastard growing up in a remote Northumberland village – speculation as to the relationship and to Maude Vallow's morals. Saul flinched from the possibilities. Was there anything he could do about it?

His mind came full circle – back to the knowledge that there were three people who might pose a danger in the future.

Maude herself, and two other people who knew the truth, and who might reveal it – make use of it – at any time in the future.

The as yet unknown Aiden Fitzglen.

And Agnes.

NINE

It was almost three weeks after Maude had been to Chauntry School that Mrs Cheesely appeared at the breakfast table. She was scarlet-faced with annoyance, and she stood in the doorway and said she was sorry to interrupt breakfast, madam and sir, but she had come to tell them that it seemed as how Agnes had upped and gone, with scarcely an apology.

'Gone?' said Maude, startled, and Saul looked up from his perusal of the morning newspaper. 'Where has she gone, Mrs Cheesely?'

'Something about family illness,' said Mrs Cheesely, with a sniff indicative of disbelief. 'A note was left in my kitchen, ma'am. It seems Agnes had one of those telegraph messages – not that I'd trust the things, nothing but wires and whisperings being sent across the country without folk knowing about it, downright unnatural to my mind. Nor I can't tell you when it came, for I didn't hear anyone bring it to the kitchen door, on account of me and Lily going up early last night. The note might have come before dinner, though, for I don't recall seeing Agnes around after that. Or it could even have been later, when she was making what she always called a last round of the house. She had the way of doing that, madam – coming quietly down the stairs to see that doors and windows were all properly locked and suchlike.'

'I didn't know Agnes had any family,' said Maude, not acknowledging that she knew about Agnes's stealthy walk round the house late at night or that Agnes always pushed Maude's bedroom door open very slightly, and peered inside.

Mrs Cheesely said Agnes had never talked much about herself, and they none of them had known anything about her.

'But there it was, ma'am, all wrote down in the note, and not the smallest suggestion as to when she might be back – or even if she'll be coming back at all. I will say though,' added Mrs Cheesely, as one prepared to be fair even if the effort choked her, 'that whatever time of day or night Agnes did go, she went quietly, not disturbing anyone. Neither Lily nor me heard her. Aren't you eating that kedgeree, madam? I made it special.'

'Just a cup of tea this morning,' said Maude. 'And I'm sure we'll hear soon from Agnes. But if she's likely to be away for any length of time, we can get a girl up from the village to help out. I expect Mr Vallow will like to invite one or two neighbours in for Christmas, so if Agnes isn't back then, you might need a bit of help.' She had already planned suggesting they ask Dr Kendal, perhaps for sherry after the Christmas morning service at the church. And a few other neighbours too, of course.

From behind his newspaper Saul remarked that he did not think they would be entertaining very much. 'You aren't really up to it, my dear.' He got up from the table. 'You remember I'm in court this morning? I don't like leaving you on your own, with Agnes not here, but I can't let them down.'

'Of course I'll be all right.'

Maude was guiltily aware of relief that Agnes had been called away, which was dreadful if Agnes really had gone to help with family illness. But coupled with Saul's commitment in Alnwick, she might now have the opportunity she had been waiting for.

Ever since she had brought the chalice from Chauntry School, Maude had been having quite bad nightmares. It was ridiculous to associate them with the chalice, but she could not stop remembering that brief conversation between Declan Kendal and Connor O'Kane. A darkness, they had said. A darkness that would drag down any wrongful owners of the chalice. And Maude, cupping the exquisitely beautiful chalice between her hands, had felt as if something dark and menacing was crawling silently towards her.

When she got back to the Hall that day, she had hidden the chalice in the attics, amongst the miscellany of broken-down furniture and junk that no one had bothered to dispose of. There were several ancient trunks, one containing some moth-eaten curtains. Maude had wrapped these around the chalice and its box, and placed it at the bottom of the trunk, with the other curtains covering it. If anyone found it, it would be assumed that some long-ago Vallow had acquired it, and it had been tidied away up here.

But the nightmares had started that same night – dreadful suffocating dreams, in which people died with the chalice watching like a single gloating eye. If the chalice were no longer in the Hall, would those dreams stop? Until today it had been practically impossible to do anything about moving the chalice to another place – Agnes had always seemed to be sneaking around, watching everything Maude did.

But today was suddenly different. Today Agnes was not here, and Saul would be in Alnwick. He would take the nine thirty train, as he always did, and return by the two or the three thirty. And once he had gone, Maude would be able to get the chalice away. She did not have to think where she would take it – there was only one place.

Recently Bastle House had got into the dreams, so that she thought she walked along the meadow path and climbed over the old stile, and stared across at the house. By now she even knew what it would be like inside – a couple of the books in Saul's study had descriptions of bastle houses, and even illustrations of them. They almost all had a single large room running across the entire front and width of the building, and a deep stone chimney breast with recesses for storing logs in winter. There would be a scullery partly sunk into the foundations, with a trapdoor opening on to the deep fortified cellar, which would also have a padlocked door on to the outside. That was where prisoners had been kept in the days when there was border fighting, and the bastles had been constructed so that there could be no escape for prisoners thrown down there.

Saul bustled off to Alnwick, and Maude waited until she heard the village clock chime ten o'clock. Then, having already seen Lily, wearing a rather flamboyant bonnet, run eagerly out of the kitchen door, she took matches and candles from the store room. They would not be missed and Bastle House was unlikely to have any gas, so the rooms would be dark.

She took the chalice from its hiding place, and placed it, still in its box and wrapped in the curtain, in the portmanteau

which had been part of the set of luggage bestowed on her by
Aunt Hilda at her marriage. Aunt Hilda had not given her
much by way of wedding gifts, saying that Maude's marriage
was going to leave her less comfortably off. But there had
been some jewellery which had belonged to someone in the
family – pearls and matching pearl earrings which Maude had
worn on her wedding day – and the set of luggage. The portmanteau was large enough for the chalice and small enough
not to attract attention. If Maude did meet anyone on the way
she would make some vague reference to a donation of clothes
for the needier of the villagers, or even use the music ploy
again. With this last thought came the memory of Chauntry
School, and a brief, unexpected reassurance in remembering
that there was someone there who knew all about this.

There was an old lantern in the attics, as well. Maude thought
it was what was called a bullseye lantern – it had bulgy glass
sides and a flap that could be opened so that a burning candle
inside would shine out. It would be easier than lighting single
candles, so she put it in the portmanteau, then collected a
warm cloak from her bedroom and went downstairs. The hall
was deserted, and Maude went across to the main door and
outside. She deliberately walked slowly down the carriageway,
pausing to examine some shrubs as if this was a perfectly
ordinary day and she was going on a perfectly ordinary errand
into the village. Her heart was pounding, but she reached the
tall gates without anyone appearing, and went out into Candle
Lane.

Saul was extremely pleased with the way his plan was
working out.

Once he had made sure about Agnes keeping watch on
Maude he had written to Maude's aunt. He had couched his
letter in very careful terms, and Miss Grout had replied
promptly. Her letter was exactly what Saul had hoped.

'I am sorry to hear that Maude's mental state is causing
you concern,' wrote Hilda Grout. 'In reply to your (most tact-
fully phrased) question, I cannot say there was ever any actual
mental instability in that side of the family. I hope you know
that if there had been I would have made you aware of it. I

do know, though, that Maude's mother was much given to extravagant moods, which I always believed could have been a precursor to something more sinister.

'As to your invitation to come to Vallow Hall without Maude knowing, I would be very willing to do so. My present situation, living with my elderly cousin, is not proving very satisfactory, and, of course, Maude's inheritance went with her when she married, so my means are slender. A prolonged stay in your lovely house would be most welcome – especially if it transpires that Maude needs a degree of control. I believe I could be of help with that. There are certain things that have to be nipped in the bud if they are not to end in actual restraint becoming necessary. We will hope that does not happen.

'I do feel it will be necessary for you to have an older woman on hand over the coming months, especially if difficult decisions lie ahead.'

It was signed with respectful affection.

'Dear Miss Grout,' wrote Saul, in his reply. 'Since my original letter, matters appear to have taken a more distressing turn. You indicated that you would be prepared to come to Vallow, and I wonder if you could now do so immediately. If you are able to travel here this coming Friday I will ensure that you are met at Vallow Halt. I do not care to write any details in this letter, but I shall be able to explain it all to you when you arrive.

'There is a train which reaches the Halt at eleven o'clock. If convenient, I will arrange for a seat for you. It is a most reliable service, and I know from my own small travels that the first-class carriages on this line are comfortable.

'With kind regards, I am yours, affectionately and hopefully, Saul Vallow.'

He was not worried that Miss Grout would refuse. His only real concern was that Maude would not go out to Bastle House on the day. If she did not, Hilda Grout could be absorbed into the household in such a way that Maude could not protest, but it would mean bringing Agnes back to Vallow Hall, and starting all over again with a new plan. But Saul did not think Maude would be able to resist the opportunity he had contrived.

He did not think she had yet seen the house given to her, and she would be curious about it. Anyone would.

He was right. As soon as she thought he would be safely on the train, the whoring little bitch went out. Saul, waiting in the concealment of the thick shrubbery that grew against Vallow's walls, thought she looked quite jaunty as she went along towards the meadow path and the old stile. It was obvious that she had no idea she was walking into a trap.

As Maude went along Candle Lane it was a sharp, cold day and mist was clinging to the trees.

She was apprehensive, but she was also very curious. She was finally going to see the house that had fascinated her since she came to Vallow Hall – the dark, lonely old place that had started to creep into her dreams. She would be confronting those dreams today – and the chalice would be left in a place where its malevolence could not reach her.

But this was such an absurd thought to have in the bright wintry morning, that she thought, instead, how Bastle House was Eddy's gift to her, and how Declan Kendal and Connor O'Kane – also the unknown Aiden Fitzglen who had witnessed the document – had worked together to make her the owner. That felt friendly and reassuring – almost as if they were walking alongside her this morning.

She approached the stile, grateful that she had seen no one so far, and climbed over it. Aunt Hilda would have been shocked at such an unseemly display of petticoats, but Maude did not see that a brief flurry of petticoats was so very shocking, and in any case Aunt Hilda was miles away. Older people in Vallow called this the Styl, from an almost-forgotten Scottish word. Maude liked this; she liked finding links to the past, and hearing old words and names still being used.

Here was the narrow woodland path that fringed the little wood on her right. She kept to the shelter of the trees in case anyone did happen to be around. It was not a very long walk, and now, ahead of her, was Bastle House itself, stark and forbidding against the sky. Seen close to, it had a very slight sense of distortion, as if the walls had not been built at exactly the right angle. Or, thought Maude, slowing her steps and staring at it, as if something deep inside it might have slipped at some time in the past, wrenching it out of true. And then she thought that perhaps this was a memory from the night-mares, because houses were not built with that distortion.

There were no windows near the ground – Maude thought this would be to make it difficult for enemies to break in – but there were several about a third of the way up – narrow, watchful windows. At the centre was a door, approached by a short flight of stone steps. That's the main way in, thought Maude, but to be sure she walked all the way round. The ground was uneven, and here and there were hoofmarks where cattle must have wandered out here, or perhaps huddled close to the walls for shelter from the weather. Weeds had grown up, hiding parts of the walls. But they did not hide the door that was set low into the thick walls – so low that it was partly below the level of the ground, meaning you would have to kneel down and almost crawl to get through it. That will lead into the bastle itself, thought Maude, repressing a shiver. But in the same moment she heard, from across the fields, the distant chimes of the church clock – eleven o'clock – and the normality of this pulled her back into the ordinary world.

She went back to the front of the house and up the stone steps to the main door. The steps were worn in the centre – that would be from all the people who must have gone up and down them over the years – perhaps over the centuries. She glanced about her to make sure no one was around, then reached into the portmanteau for the keys.

As she slid the largest of the keys into the lock she was expecting it to resist, but it did not. The lock scraped a bit, but then it turned perfectly smoothly.

Maude took a deep breath and pushed the door open.

TEN

As the door swung inwards, Maude had the impression that something deep within the old house stirred, as if shadows that had been lying quietly in the corners had looked up. That would just be the sudden ingress of light and air from outside disturbing the dimness, though. Or would it? Supposing tramps or vagrants had got in, and were hiding in those shadows, watching her? But surely there would have been signs of anyone having broken in – damage to windows or doors – and there were no such signs at all.

She lit one of the candles, and wedged it inside the lantern. It sent a warm glow across the darkness, and there in front of her was the room she had known she would see. Exactly as Saul's books had described. A long room stretching across the entire width of the house, with a wide old hearth and a stone chimney breast that went up to the ceiling and had little recesses on each side. There was a long table at the centre, incredibly still covered with a crimson chenille cloth, with chairs drawn up to it. A tall dresser stood against the wall. Thick dust lay everywhere, as if something had draped a veil over the entire house.

Maude set the lantern on the dresser, then lit two more candles from it and placed one on the table and the other on the dresser. The oak of the dresser was slightly faded on one side from where sunlight came in through one of the narrow windows, and Connor O'Kane's words to Dr Kendal when they were photographing the chalice in Chauntry School came unexpectedly to her.

'I noticed you particularly positioned the chalice in the strongest light you could find,' Connor had said.

She opened the portmanteau, took the chalice from its box, and placed it on the dresser, where it would stand in the gentle sunshine. And now could she go home? No, of course she could not. To banish the nightmares altogether, she needed to

look into all the rooms. In any case, this was her house. She
would look at it properly.

Two doors opened off this room, one on each side of the
fireplace. The left-hand one showed an inner, much smaller
sitting room, and the room on the right had a big range, and
a deep old sink, with a grisly looking copper cauldron
crouching in a corner. Shallow stone steps led deeper down
into the bowels of the house. Maude looked at them, then took
a firmer hold on the lantern, and went cautiously down. The
shadows seemed to press in more closely, but she reminded
herself that she was descending to a lower level, and that there
were no windows, so she was going down into a darkness –
no, she would not think that, it sounded like the words of the
legend Declan Kendal had quoted. Something about being
dragged into a darkness, it had been.

At the foot of the steps was a kind of half-cellar. In one
corner was an ancient pump, and there was a smell of stagnant
water. Maude thought if ever she did – or was able to – sell
this house, or even – wild idea – live in it herself, an entire
army of workmen would be needed to make it habitable. Eddy,
did you give me an asset or a liability, she wondered, which
was an ungrateful thought to entertain.

She moved the lantern around slowly, praying not to see or
hear any small scuttling movements in the corners, because
there would almost certainly be rats in a place like this, but
as long as she did not actually see any . . .

There were scuttlings, though – as if now that the old house
had been disturbed, its very timbers and stones were waking
and wanting to inspect this intruder. Maude stood still,
listening, but thinking that if anything moved it was only
timbers expanding in the air caused by the opening of doors.
She moved the lantern again, and saw at last what she had
known would be here. The trapdoor. The lid of the bastle itself.

That's where the real darkness is, thought Maude. She
tilted the light slightly, and its glow picked up something
lying near to the trapdoor's edge – something very small, but
something that caught the light. Maude took a step nearer,
but her senses were already tumbling and the shadows seemed
to be crawling towards her, like goblin fingers reaching out.

She did not need to bend down to pick up this tiny object that shone amidst the dust and she did not even need to wonder what it was – she knew already, because it, and its fellow, normally lay in her own jewellery box on her dressing table.

The object that lay on the dusty floor was one of the pearl earrings Aunt Hilda had given her on the occasion of her betrothal to Saul, and which Maude had worn on her wedding day.

As Maude stared at the earring, fear was flooding her mind, because there was only one explanation for its presence here. She must have been to this house before – and to this subterranean room. But when? And why? The memory of the nightmares came at her at once, but they had only been dreams, hadn't they? *Hadn't they . . .?*

Those flashes of familiarity could be explained by her having read the books in Saul's study – the descriptions and illustrations of bastle houses had been very clear. But that did not explain the earring.

Moving slowly, as if afraid of someone hearing, she put the lantern on the ground, where its light fell across the squared shape of the trapdoor. It was not a very large trapdoor – perhaps four feet square – and sunk into it was a thick bar, clearly intended for lifting it. It showed up small marks in the dust and grime around the edges of the bar, as well. Finger marks, thought Maude. Marks your fingertips would leave if you grasped a very dusty surface. Had she knelt on the ground and reached for the trapdoor, and were those finger marks her own?

Her mind shuddered away from lifting the trapdoor, but of their own volition her hands were already reaching for it, grasping the bar. *I'm lifting the lid on the darkness*, thought Maude, fighting a rising panic. *But I don't have to do it, I really don't. Except that I do have to do it, because I must find out why that earring is here.*

At first she thought the trapdoor was stuck, and there was a brief, guilty relief, because after all she was not going to be able to open up this dark vault. Then she pulled on it again, and there was a creaking sound as if ancient bones were struggling into life. The door came up – a couple of inches at first, so that a rim of blackness showed all around the edges, and then suddenly crashed all the way back, clanging loudly on the ground. The sound reverberated through the small room, and echoed through the old house. Tiny clouds of dust billowed upwards, clouding her vision, then settled back down.

For a moment there was only the black square of the now-open underground space, then Maude pushed the lantern closer to the open cellar.

Into its smeary light, almost as if it had reared up accusingly, was the face of a woman – the eyes wide and staring, the lips stretched in a dreadful silent scream. One hand was flung upwards, as if it had been clinging to the underside of the trapdoor, and had only been wrenched free by the trapdoor crashing back on to the floor. The other hand was gripping an iron rung jutting out from the wall. Maude saw with sick horror that the hand reaching up was bruised and bloodied, the nails half torn away. She dared to push the lantern a little nearer, using the tip of one foot to do so, and now the light fell deeper into the cellar, showing up iron rungs driven into the wall – like a rough-and-ready ladder. The woman must have climbed up those rungs until she reached the hatch, then she had clung to the topmost rung with one hand, while beating frantically on the underside of the trapdoor with the other. Had she screamed for help as she did so, praying for someone to hear and rescue her? Yes, of course she had. You had only to see those dreadful stretched-wide lips to know that.

And when the trapdoor crashed back, she had still been clutching the underside of the trapdoor so that when Maude opened it, it had pulled her a little way out of the cellar opening. She could not have moved of her own volition, because she was dead. Maude had never seen a dead person, but there could be no doubt. The woman's eyes were fixed in a dreadful stare, and her skin was the cold grey colour and texture of a slab of stone. She had been down there, imprisoned in the underground room, its lid slammed firmly down on her. She had tried to push it up, though – that bruised and torn hand was mute evidence. But it had been no use, and she had died down there, alone in the darkness.

Maude backed away from the yawning square of blackness, wrapping her arms around her body as if to keep in some vestige of warmth, shaking so badly she thought she might fall apart. But she could not take her eyes from what was framed in the open hatch. And even like that – even with that terrible sightless stare and that frozen scream – she recognized the woman.

It was Agnes.

Every nerve in Maude's body was screaming at her to go back up the stone steps at once, to run all the way back to Vallow Hall and pretend this had never happened, because no one would ever know . . .

She could not do it. Her mind was spinning with confusion and terror, and time seemed to have slipped its moorings, but gradually she was aware that the lantern's light had burned down, and the stone room was growing darker. The world had shrunk to this dreadful place, with the fixed dead stare of Agnes from the open cellar, and the sight of Agnes's hand raw and torn from trying to beat her way out.

Overhead the house seemed to be coming alive. The little scuttlings and creaks Maude had heard earlier were forming into recognizable sounds. *Creak-creak . . . Creak-creak . . .* At first she thought she was imagining them, then suddenly she knew she was not. Someone was walking around overhead. Maude cowered back against the wall. Someone was up there. If she went up those steps she would meet whoever it was. There was no other way she could get out of this dreadful room.

The footsteps were in the upper scullery now, and she pressed back against the wall even more, as if by doing so she could be absorbed into it and be invisible. Then the light shifted, and a dark shape appeared at the head of the steps. It stood for a moment, then it began to descend the steps, and Maude saw that it was not just one person – there were two outlines. Two people who had come in here, and who would find her with Agnes's body. And her earring, still lying in the dust.

Then Saul's voice said, 'Maude?' He came all the way down the steps and stood in front of her, looking down at her. Behind him was a thin, bony figure, the lips shut in the familiar rat-trap line. Aunt Hilda.

The stone room, with the flickering lantern light sending macabre shadows writhing across the walls and the deeper shadows reaching out their long fingers, folded completely around her.

Saul saw, the minute he looked down into the cellar, that his plan had succeeded. He was not surprised. He had taken great care with everything, and it had paid off, because here was Maude, in the grisly stone room, the damning earring lying in the light of a lantern for Miss Grout to see.

Maude had apparently fainted, which was rather annoying, since it might mean she would have to be carried back to Vallow Hall. The important thing, though, was that what Saul thought of as the second part of his plan had worked.

The first part had been Agnes, of course. It had been laugh-ably easy to get her out to Bastle House – he had only to tell her he had found out that the mistress was going to meet the prince there on Friday, and she had leapt at the idea of helping to catch them out. She had found it all perfectly plausible – hadn't she seen for herself the document making the mistress owner of Bastle House? When Saul said he needed what was called an independent witness to a meeting between Maude and the prince, Agnes said at once that she would do whatever was needed. Yes, certainly she understood that he could not be the witness himself, being what they called an interested party. The prince deserved to be taught a lesson, the whoring libertine that he was, known in some of the sleaziest of London's clubs.

'I daresay you'll be surprised to hear me speak against such places, sir, what with my past, but I worked alongside a girl who went to work in London – a house in Cleveland Street, it was, and the stories they tell about it – well, it's a scandal and a disgrace for the man who'll one day be King of England to go there.'

Saul had never heard of Cleveland Street, but the meaning was clear enough, and Agnes was prepared to do whatever he asked of her, which was all that mattered.

Bastle House, when he had gone quietly along to look at it earlier in the week, taking the keys from where Maude had hidden them, had turned out to be exactly right for his plan. A strange house it was, one of the old border fortifications. The deep cellar with its sturdy old door on to the scrubland would have seen a few violent incidents. It would soon be seeing one more.

Agnes, keeping their secret appointment in the early hours of Friday morning, thought the underground stone room was a very good hiding place. She would stay upstairs until she saw anyone coming across the fields, she said. Then she would dart down here to hide. She would leave the door ajar, and she would be able to hear everything that was said. She would not mind how long she had to wait. It was a dark old house, but she had brought matches and candles until it should start to get light.

She walked round the stone room, peering into the dim corners, and it was while she was turned away from him that Saul raised the heavy brass candlestick taken surreptitiously from a dresser upstairs, and crunched it down on her skull. She slumped to the ground, her eyes rolling up to show only the whites, and Saul bent over, feeling for a heartbeat. He could find not the smallest flicker of one, although it was difficult to tell through all the corseting and whalebone the woman had under her gown. He sat down on the ground to wait for a short while to be sure, and then felt for the heartbeat again. Nothing. She was dead. He pulled up the trapdoor of the cellar – it did not open easily, but he eventually managed it – and tipped her body into the yawning blackness. It hit the ground with a dull thud, and Saul nodded in satisfaction, then dropped one of the earrings taken from Maude's dressing table into the cellar. In the light from his candle he saw that it had fallen close to Agnes's body. Exactly right.

There was an iron ladder fastened to the wall beneath the trapdoor, but after shining the candlelight on it, Saul was satisfied that even if a prisoner could swarm up those rusting rungs, the trapdoor itself could not be opened from beneath. Not that it mattered, though, because Agnes was dead. He slammed the lid down, and heard it click into place. Then he placed the other earring on the ground near to it.

It was still very early when he got back to the Hall – barely five o'clock. No one was up yet, and he was able to plant in the kitchen the note he had written, supposedly from Agnes, about the sick relative. Then he went up to bed until it should be time to get up.

Hilda Grout, arriving at Vallow Hall, was startled to be told by Saul that they must go out to Bastle House at once – that Maude, poor, witless creature, had apparently gone running off, and they must reach her before she caused some harm, either to herself or to another. Miss Grout paused for long enough only to let Lily take her suitcase up to her bedroom, and to wash her hands after the journey since trains were always so grimy, and then set off with Saul along Candle Lane and the meadow path.

Once inside the house the story told itself. There were the earrings, which Miss Grout recognized as her own wedding gift to Maude – one near the cellar opening, the other down in the cellar itself. There was Agnes's dead body. And there was Maude, huddled into a corner of the dusty cellar, her eyes wide and staring.

Between them Saul and Hilda Grout got Maude up the steps and outside. The keys were in Maude's bag, and Saul locked the door, and made sure windows and doors were all secure, as well.

They wrapped Maude in his topcoat, and between them half-carried her as far as the old stile on the edge of the meadow. Miss Grout remained with her while Saul went back to the Hall to get the gardener to bring the trap as near to the stile as possible. It was a fair walk and he got quite cold without his coat, but it could not be helped.

Lily and Mrs Cheesely were shocked and round-eyed when Maude was carried in, still half-swooning, and seeming hardly to know where she was. In answer to their questions (Oh sir, whatever has happened?), Saul said as far as he could make out, the mistress had gone out for a morning stroll and been overcome by some sort of dizzy spell. They had found her by the stile – and as well that they had, for she seemed to have no memory of anything.

It was clear to Saul that neither Lily nor Mrs Cheesely were in the least suspicious. It was also clear that neither of them cared overmuch for Hilda Grout. This did not matter; Saul did not care overmuch for her himself, but you used what tools were to hand.

He went into the drawing room where Miss Grout was sipping tea. She was deeply shocked by what had happened.

'If I had not seen it with my own eyes, Mr Vallow . . . To think that my own niece was capable of taking the life of another creature. But there was no mistaking what she had done, was there?'

'I'm afraid not,' said Saul, sadly. 'It's dreadfully clear that Maude had killed that poor woman before we got there, and that she was going to slam the trapdoor down.'

'And leave the – the body there, assuming no one would find it for a very long time? That empty old house – I don't suppose anyone goes in there from one year to the next.'

'Exactly so.' It was very gratifying how Hilda Grout was working all this out for herself. Saul hardly needed to lead her along his plan at all.

'But why would she do such a thing, Mr Vallow?' said Miss Grout. 'For I presume that even the insane have some kind of reasoning behind their actions?'

'Maude had developed a deep distrust of Agnes,' said Saul, who had prepared for this question. 'She had begun to believe Agnes was spying on her, although Agnes had never shown her anything but loyalty and kindness. A most trustworthy servant. But these last weeks Maude became convinced that Agnes had some malicious intent towards her. That was when I began to suspect her mind was going – that was when I wrote to you. But now . . .' He broke off, pinching the bridge of his nose with his forefinger and thumb. 'I can't let her suffer the consequences of what she's done, Miss Grout. I can't . . .'

Hilda Grout said, slowly, 'But need there be consequences? I would not, you understand, normally advocate any kind of conspiracy to cover up such an act, but—'

'I would not normally advocate it either,' said Saul. 'As a Justice of the Peace I am sworn to uphold the law and punish the guilty. I take it very seriously. But this is my own wife . . .' Again he broke off, as if overcome by emotion, then said, 'I'm afraid that discovery is almost inevitable. When the owner of Bastle House – whoever he is, wherever he is – returns, he will find Agnes's body. And since Agnes has been a servant here for some time, Vallow Hall will not escape investigation. I should be questioned. I would do my best, but I am not a good liar, Miss Grout. And there was the earring down in the cellar. We had to leave it down there, you remember. Neither of us could have got down there to retrieve it.'

'The earring – I had forgotten about that.' Miss Grout's hand flew to her mouth in consternation.

'Were Maude to be questioned, she would never stand up to it. Her mind is already flawed. They would break her,' said Saul. 'She would have to stand trial.'

'And found guilty?'

'I believe there would be no doubt about that. They would hang her.'

'Or,' said Hilda Grout, 'they would put her in some institution. One of those grim places—'

'Which is as unthinkable as letting her be hanged,' said Saul. He paused, then said, slowly, 'But there may be another solution.'

ELEVEN

Jack enjoyed the short journey to Chauntry School. The showman in him appreciated how the carriageway was lit by lanterns and flares, judiciously placed so that the school's wagonette and the rattletrap that was the Nithercott cart drove through soft pools of radiance, and then through swirling misty shadows cast by the trees. It crossed his mind that whoever was responsible for the organizing of this had almost a theatrical eye for an effect. When they reached the house, double doors at its centre were folded back, with two men both in academic gowns positioned there to direct where coats and cloaks could be left and point the way to the school's concert hall. There would be supper afterwards in the dining room, but everyone was please to feel free to look around the entire ground floor. They were proud of Chauntry, said one of them, and they enjoyed showing it off.

As Jack and Gus took their seats in the assembly hall, Jack noticed that a good many people were in evening dress, and he was glad he had worn a dinner jacket. Gus had thought it a good idea to do so. 'You want to look prosperous, Mr Jack, and you always look so distinguished in evening things. Specially now, with the beard.'

The concert was professionally presented, and Jack thought the performances were of a high standard. One boy of perhaps fourteen or fifteen played particularly well – Jack did not know the music, but the programme stated it to be Frédéric Chopin's *Fantaisie-Impromptu*, and it was a complex piece. He was pleased when the boy received rapturous applause, and as it died away he glanced at his programme, interested to see who the organisers might be. At the top of the first page were the words: *Concert and musical arrangements by Chauntry School precentor, Dr Declan Kendal*. There was a list of letters after Dr Kendal's name, none of which meant much to Jack.

Mr Glennon joined rather hesitantly in the choruses of the

folk songs at the end. He had something of a liking for folk songs and their traditions and he knew the words of most of them. When the audience filtered happily out, heading for the dining room, Jack followed them, collected a glass of wine from a lavishly spread buffet, then said quietly to Gus that he was going to explore.

'But you stay here, and listen for any bits of conversation that might be useful.'

Gus nodded, and Jack wandered out to the big hall. Several doors opened off it, most of them bearing neat lettering, proclaiming them to be the Common Room, Precentor's Study, Library . . .

Library, thought Jack, and he walked casually along the hall, apparently examining various prints and framed sketches that hung on the walls, before going, with a somewhat abstracted air, into the library. Joseph Glennon was interested in libraries – he would like to see what books lined the shelves.

But the instant Jack entered the room it was as if something reared up to strike him across the eyes. He flinched, then forced himself to look about him. It was a long room with a brick chimney breast on one wall, and it was lit by several soft wall lights. They cast small islands of light, and it was a quiet and restful room – a good place for study, and perfectly ordinary and unremarkable.

Except that it was not ordinary and it was not unremarkable, because it was the room from the photograph.

It was unmistakable. The furniture – the fireplace – the bookshelves . . . The big desk in the bay window, with the leather inlay and gold scrollwork around the edges . . . All were instantly recognizable. There were the chairs with tapestry coverings, and the heavy curtains at the bay window in the same distinctive fabric. Most recognizable of all was the piecrust table standing partly in the bay window – the table where the chalice had stood in the photograph – and where Maude had rested her hand, as if to emphasize its presence.

Jack stood very still, struggling to fight back the overwhelming feeling that he had stepped into the past. But it's not my past, he thought, looking about him: it's Maude's past

– might it be a fragment of my father's past, as well? As he stood there, he had the sensation of something or someone wanting to take him by the hand and lead him back and back until he saw and knew and understood what had happened all those years ago.

He was pulled back into the present by the sound of the door behind him opening, and the realization that someone had come into the room. He took a deep breath, reminding himself that there was no reason why he should not be here – the audience had been invited to go anywhere on the ground floor – and also that Joseph Glennon was a scholarly gentleman, irresistibly drawn to libraries.

The man who had entered was perhaps in his middle or late forties. He had a thin face and soft dark brown hair that flopped over his forehead. His eyes were intelligent, and he had a sheaf of notes in one hand and a glass of wine in the other.

Jack, his mind still slightly off-balance, managed to smile and nod, and say, 'Good evening. I seem to have wandered in here without realizing it. I hope that's all right.'

'Perfectly all right. We like showing off all of Chauntry to visitors.'

He appeared to wait for Jack to say more, so Jack said, 'This has been an excellent evening's entertainment. I've greatly enjoyed it. That young pianist was especially gifted.'

'Yes, he's very talented. That Chopin piece is very complex, but we simplified it a bit and I was proud of his performance. He's what we call a scholarship boy – we have several such; Chauntry has an arrangement with St Botolph's Orphanage, which we're very keen on.' He closed the door and leaned against it, his eyes on Jack. 'I'm Declan Kendal,' he said, 'and I was more or less responsible for the concert, so I'm pleased to hear you enjoyed it.'

'Then I must congratulate you. It's good to meet you, Dr Kendal.'

Declan Kendal said, 'And to meet you, Mr . . .?'

'Glennon. Joseph Glennon.'

Somehow the name came out wrong. It struck a false note. Jack heard the falseness at once; it was as if a cracked bell had chimed. As a musician, Dr Kendal must have heard it, too. To cover the strangeness up, he said, 'From the programme notes it sounds as if you've spent most of your life with music.'

'I have. Chauntry has been my family – I can't imagine having had any other life. Although,' he said, carefully, 'I do have a few other interests beyond music.' A pause. His eyes had not left Jack's face. 'Photography is one of them,' he said, softly.

Photography. *He knows*, thought Jack at once. *He can't possibly know who I am, but he knows I'm here because of the chalice – he's realized I saw those photographs. How on earth does he know that, though? He's being cautious – he's giving me the opportunity to open up about my real purpose in being here. Hell's teeth, what do I do? Dare I trust him?*

After a moment, Dr Kendal said, 'Mr Glennon, forgive me if I'm mistaken, but I think there may be a link between us.'

'A link?'

'Yes.' A pause, then, 'I would rather be honest with you – I think the link may be Aiden Fitzglen.'

The quiet library blurred slightly, as if Jack was seeing it under water, then, from what felt like a long distance, he heard Declan Kendal say something about talking more privately.

'Have you time to come along to my study? It's only just beyond the hall. I needn't detain you longer than you can spare.'

Jack, his mind still tumbling, was grateful to be led, without fuss or awkwardness, across the hall. He saw Gus, who gave him a half nod, and found it reassuring. It reminded him that Gus was on hand, that life was not so very much out of kilter.

Dr Kendal took him into a room near the back of the building, closed the door, and gestured to him to sit down.

The room had a comfortable feel. There was a sense of it being a place of work and of music – the desk was strewn with sheet music, most with copious handwritten margin notes, and there were thick, bound music scores stacking the shelves. An upright piano, its lid open, stood against one wall, and two violins and a flute lay on a chair. On the walls were framed programmes, some of which looked like Chauntry's own events, but others that Jack saw were of performances at several well-known concert halls. He remembered that he had thought there was a professional feeling about the evening.

'It's all a bit untidy,' said Declan Kendal, taking the chair facing him, 'but it's where I work for a good part of the day – when I'm not teaching or rehearsing – and we won't be interrupted in here.' He paused, then said, 'You might not want to talk to me at all, of course, and if that's so, please say, and we'll end it now and be perfectly amicable about it. But if you are who I think you are—'

The decision seemed to have already been made. Jack said, 'I'm Jack Fitzglen. Aiden Fitzglen was my father.'

'Yes, I thought that must be it. You're astonishingly like him. For a moment, seeing you, I even thought . . . Well, for a moment it was as if Aiden had walked into that library. As if the past had suddenly broken into the present.'

'I felt something of that, as well,' Jack said at once. 'But it's a past I know hardly anything about.'

'Fifteen years,' said Declan, almost to himself. 'But I still remember it clearly. I remember Aiden and the Amaranth Theatre.'

It felt odd to hear this stranger talk about his father and about the theatre, but Jack was aware of a sense of kinship. He said, eagerly, 'The Amaranth is still going strong. It had to be restored after a fire, and I've done my best to keep up my father's tradition – and the tradition of his father and his father before him. The rest of the family do so, as well.'

'I knew about the fire. I'm glad it's all been restored. Aiden would have been pleased.' Declan frowned, then said, 'You recognized the library, didn't you?'

'Yes.'

'But – you've never been here before, have you? Stupid question – I know you haven't. Which means,' he said, slowly, 'that you could only have recognized it from a photograph.'

He waited, and at last, Jack said, 'I found two photographs recently, both showing that room.'

'And showing the Talisman Chalice,' said Declan.

If it had felt strange to hear him talk about Jack's father, it felt even stranger to hear the chalice mentioned with such familiarity.

But Jack said, 'Yes. It was a very clear photograph. I recognized the chalice – I half-remembered the stories of how it was said to have vanished – believed stolen, years ago, just before a display of royal items in London.'

'Part of Edward VII's fiftieth birthday celebrations,' said Declan, nodding. 'Prince of Wales he was then, of course. The loss of the chalice got a fair amount of publicity as a result.'

'Yes. I managed to turn up a bit of information about its history.' Jack paused, then said, 'Dr Kendal – the other photograph . . .'

'The other photograph showed Maude,' said Declan Kendal. 'Seated in the library here, by the window.' There was a trace of sadness in his voice, but he said, 'If you know about the chalice already, I may as well tell you how those photographs came into being. In any case you're Aiden's son . . .' This was said with a half-smile and Jack was aware again of the past reaching out. This man had known his father – he had liked him.

He said, carefully, 'I know nothing about Maude.'

'The chalice was a gift to her,' said Declan. 'From a member of the royal family. It was a mark of affection – perhaps it was also seen as an investment for her as well. Something she could even sell if ever the need arose.'

'When you say "a member of the royal family" . . .' said Jack. 'Was it the present king who gave it to her? Edward VII? Because it has to be said it would be in keeping with his early mode of life to be giving out valuable presents to ladies. Except that I don't think the dates and the ages fit. But one of Edward's sons, perhaps?'

'Yes, it was one of his sons. And that son is dead now,' said Declan Kendal, 'so it can't hurt him if I tell you what happened. It was the Duke of Clarence who gave Maude the chalice. Prince Albert Victor – known to his intimate friends as Eddy. He and Maude met, and for a very short time there was a closeness between them. Afterwards Eddy sent her the chalice.'

'So she was a royal prince's mistress,' said Jack, softly. His mind went back to the features of the lady in the photographs, and he said, 'That's something I hadn't expected.'

'She was innocent and she was dazzled by him, and I think she was very unhappily married,' said Dr Kendal, and the sadness was unmistakable now. 'The prince was very strongly attracted to her. He asked if it would be possible to have a photograph of her – with the chalice if it could be arranged – and photography had become something of a hobby of mine, so I was glad to be able to comply with the request. I had several images made from the plate – Maude asked to have a couple of them.'

'And she sent them to my father,' said Jack, thoughtfully.

'There was a note with the photographs. She thanked him for arranging a gift – clearly she meant the chalice. But she also warned him never to come to Vallow – to Vallow Hall.'

'I didn't know about that. But it explains why you're using a false name. So that no one here can connect you with Aiden?'

'Yes.' Jack frowned, then said, 'Dr Kendal – what happened to Maude? And why did she warn my father to stay away?'

'The answer to both those questions is that I don't know,' said Declan. 'All I can tell you is that Maude is – or was – Saul Vallow's wife.' He paused, as if looking back at some memory, then said, 'Shortly after she was given the chalice, Maude vanished. It was made known in a rather vague way that she was ill, although no details were ever given out. I went to the Hall twice, the first time hoping I would see her, the second time to leave a note – just sending her my very best wishes. I wasn't admitted to the house on either occasion and I don't know if my note ever reached her. Frankly, the reception I got was cold and unwelcoming.'

'Miss Grout,' said Jack, at once.

'You've met her?'

'I have.'

'Then you can imagine the meeting. After a while, a story got round that Maude had gone to stay with family on the coast – sea air for her health,' he said. 'But that she had died and was buried there. Saul was reported to be so devastated that he shut himself away. There were other rumours, though,' he said. 'Stories that the illness hadn't been physical – that she had had to be taken in secrecy to an asylum. I never believed that. I didn't know her very well – I only met her a handful of times – but the Maude Vallow I knew was entirely sane and normal. Sensitive and intelligent. I thought we had a closeness. One of those instant meetings of minds, if that doesn't sound fanciful.' He made a rueful gesture. 'I could have been wrong, though. I am not,' he said, 'very experienced when it comes to the ladies.'

Jack smiled. 'Which of us is when it comes down to it?'

'Saul Vallow is seldom seen abroad now,' said Declan Kendal. 'He never took much part in the immediate life of the village, although he attended church every Sunday. But he was quite active in the county – a Justice of the Peace in Alnwick and he sat on one or two charity committees. But for years now he's been the next thing to a recluse. As to whether Maude is alive or dead – I have no idea. No one seems to have seen her actually leave Vallow, and there's no grave in the local church.' He got up and took a decanter from a built-in cupboard, and poured two glasses of brandy.

'Restorative,' he said. 'Even medicinal. Although if any of the teachers knew I kept brandy in my study – not to mention the boys—'

'I'll never tell,' said Jack solemnly, accepting the glass of brandy handed to him.

'Shortly after Maude vanished,' said Declan, sitting down again, 'I wrote to several of the asylums in the county, asking if they had anyone by the name of Vallow, but none of them had – or if they had, they didn't admit to it.'

'She could have been there under a different name.' Jack put the suggestion tentatively.

'I suppose so. But – you'll think this is ridiculous, but even now when we have a concert here – even just a major rehearsal, I always make sure that the windows on that side of Chauntry are open.'

'In case she's still at the Hall and she can hear?'

'I told you it was ridiculous. But she was so fond of music – it was something we shared, very briefly. I like to pretend she might hear the music and enjoy it.'

'I understand that,' said Jack, and he was aware of a wrench of pity for this quiet, scholarly man who clearly had harboured a romantic dream about a young woman.

'The last time I saw Maude was in the library here,' said Declan. 'On the day the chalice was placed in her hands.'

But if the chalice falls into the hands of someone who has no right to it, then that person is dragged into a darkness from which he or she can never emerge . . . Byron's words brushed Jack's mind. Had Maude been a wrongful owner of the chalice, and dragged into a darkness because of it? Shut away in an asylum? Had she died far from home, and did she now inhabit a lonely grave . . .?

To quell these thoughts, he asked, 'Did Maude ever meet my father?'

'I don't believe so.'

'But you met him? You must have done, to recognize me.'

'I met him a few times. I seldom went to London – I rarely go now – but I was asked to help with a memorial concert for the prince, shortly after his death. I had a cousin . . .' He paused, then went on, 'A cousin who had a slight connection with Eddy. He wasn't a member of the royal household or anything as grand as that, but he was sometimes called in if the prince had to attend a musical event, or chair a meeting – he was patron of one or two musical organizations or charities. Your father had met my cousin a few times through their various theatrical activities, and he asked him to help with the Amaranth's memorial concert. Aiden wanted to confirm points of royal protocol – what music and which composers would be acceptable. I got involved with it, and I met Aiden at a couple of the rehearsals.'

Jack said, softly, 'It was in 1892, wasn't it?'

'Yes.'

Declan looked at him, and Jack knew they were both aware it had been in 1892 when the fire had almost destroyed the Amaranth Theatre, killing Aiden Fitzglen. The memory he had forced himself to suppress for so many years flickered into life for a moment, but he pushed it down, and said, 'Dr Kendal – what happened to the chalice?'

'Maude took it back to Vallow Hall that day.'

'Could it still be there? It's never come to light since the discovery that it vanished, I do know that.'

'Actually,' said Declan, 'I doubt anyone would have known it was missing at all if it hadn't been for that exhibition. I imagine it occurred to someone at the time – some curator at the V&A or one of the palace custodians – that it would be a nice item to include in the display. An illustration of how long the monarchy went back, or something of the kind.'

'But when they came to look for it, it couldn't be found,' said Jack. 'Was the prince suspected at the time? Eddy, I mean?'

'I don't know. He might have been. There were often rumours about him – about his way of life. He might have told one or two of his family what he had done, though – he might have needed help in actually getting the chalice out. It was his bad luck that somebody decided to use it in the exhibition, of course, but then he never did have much luck, poor Eddy.'

'And so the newspapers got to know the chalice had vanished, and they dug up the old legends, and made the most of it,' said Jack.

'Oh, yes. And as to where it is now, I have no idea,' said Declan. 'It might still be at the Hall. Or Saul Vallow might have sold it years ago. I scarcely know him, but he's spoken of as a miserly person – always looking to get his hands on whatever money he can. I wouldn't have thought he'd overlook something so potentially valuable, although he might not have known what it really was. It might simply have been placed in a glass cabinet, and forgotten. But it wouldn't be easy to sell. It's a famous piece, and most reputable dealers would probably recognize it.'

By now Jack's instinct was to trust Declan Kendal, but he dared not trust him to the extent of disclosing the filch and the plan for the extravagant play. Instead, he said, 'My cousin – Byron Fitzglen – has found some details about the chalice's history – not very much so far, although he's still working on it. But he's found enough to intrigue us.'

'It's supposed to have been passed down within the royal family over goodness knows how many centuries,' said Declan.

'And, of course, over several royal houses.' He frowned, then said, 'But there is one thing that I don't think was ever very widely known. When the chalice came here – to be handed to Maude – certain papers came with it. There were one or two legal documents that called for her signature . . .' He broke off, frowning.

Jack said, tentatively, 'There was a parchment document in one of the photographs. I couldn't make out what it was.'

'That wasn't relevant to the chalice,' said Declan at once, and there was a note in his voice that stopped Jack asking questions.

'There was another document,' said Declan. 'It wasn't given to Maude – she never knew about it. But it had been placed in the box with the chalice, and I assumed the prince believed it to be part of its provenance.'

'And is it?' Don't hope for too much, thought Jack. At best it'll be a workman's inventory from when the chalice was made. At worst it'll be somebody's lost laundry list.

'I trusted Maude,' Declan said, 'but I didn't feel justified in letting the document out of my hands. At the time there was a feeling that if the chalice were ever to be lost, the document would be the only proof of its existence.'

'What exactly—?'

'I don't know. I've never been able to decipher it, and I've never felt I could trust anyone with it. I think it's something like Blackletter or Gothic or one of those elaborate medieval scripts. It's written in Latin – didn't most scholars use Latin for anything they recorded in those days? I've made out the odd word here and there, but nothing that provides any real clues. I'm many things, Jack, but I'm no linguist and I'm certainly no medievalist.'

'No more am I.' Jack paused, and then said, 'Would you trust me to look at it?'

'Could you read it?'

'No. But my cousin, Byron, might. He's quite learned and completely trustworthy and he knows about the chalice.'

There was a moment when Declan Kendal hesitated again. He's not sure of my motives, thought Jack, and I can't blame him, because my motives are very dubious indeed.

Then Declan said, 'Yes, you could at least look at it.'

He got up and, as he went to the door leading to the main hall, Jack said, 'You keep it locked away?'

A smile that contained a glint of mischief showed suddenly, making Declan look much younger. 'It's hidden in plain sight,' he said. 'Where would you hide a leaf, other than in a forest? And on that premise, where would you hide a manuscript document, other than—'

'Other than on shelves stacked with other manuscript documents. Of course. It's in the library,' said Jack, following his host across the hall.

Once inside the library Declan Kendal locked the door.

'The audience is still milling around,' he said, going over to the shelves nearest the bay window, and pulling out a set of wheeled library steps. 'And I don't want anyone coming in.'

'It's up there?' said Jack, as Declan ascended the steps.

'It's been up there all the time. No one's ever moved it, though – I'm as sure as I can be of that. The cleaners flick a feather duster along the shelves at erratic intervals, but that's about all. The staff wouldn't have any reason to look along these high shelves. The books are almost all privately printed sermons by long-ago vicars, or essays on forgotten poets, and turgid accounts of people's rambles through Northumberland.'

'What about the pupils?'

The smile came again. 'We do have a few wild spirits at Chauntry,' said Declan, 'but it's not the kind of wildness that would send them swarming to the top of a ladder to investigate out-of-reach shelves.' He glanced down. 'That pianist who played the Chopin piece tonight, and the trio who gave us the Schubert *Lieder* – those artless little grubs certainly break a few rules, even though they do sing and perform like the celestial choirs. But it's nothing we can't cope with.'

Jack did not like to ask what rules there might be to break in this serious seat of musical learning, but Declan went on, 'They sometimes go down to the village after supper to get drunk on the local cider and to meet up with a few of the livelier local girls. High spirits and curiosity, and all entirely natural. None of them are likely to be interested in the possibilities of a dog-eared fifteenth-century manuscript – even if they could read it, which they certainly couldn't.' He moved his hands along the shelves, then said, 'Could you push the ladder about a foot farther along? I can see the manuscript, but I can't reach it. Thank you – I've got it now.' His hands had closed around what looked like a large flat cardboard folder, inconspicuous among the other books and documents alongside it. Jack saw what he had meant about hiding a leaf in a forest. He withdrew it from its place on the shelf with extreme care, and came back down the stepladder. 'We'll take it back to my study to look at it,' he said.

'Lead the way.'

TWELVE

As Declan Kendal spread the yellowing pages on his desk, Jack felt the past reach out to him all over again. The document was more substantial than he had expected – there were a fair number of thick parchment sheets, of varying sizes. It was impossible to know how old they were; the edges of most of the pages were deeply split, and there were cracks in the paper, some very small, but others obliterating entire sections.

He could not make so much as a guess at any of the content. Even without the elaborate script, whole lines had been scored out, and alterations re-written immediately above them. What looked like additional sentences had been written vertically in some of the margins – it was impossible to know where they were meant to fit in. In addition, almost all of the pages were badly foxed and damp-spotted and the whole document had such a sense of age and of fragility that Jack thought it would not take much for it to crumble away before their eyes. But even at first look, he was afraid that deciphering it might be beyond Byron's capabilities.

'I've only ever been able to make out one or two words,' said Declan. 'There – and there. D'you see?'

'That looks like London,' said Jack, after a few moments. 'And there, lower down, that word could be Ludlow.'

'Yes. Does that tie in with anything you found out?'

Jack hesitated, then said carefully, 'It's possible that the chalice was taken to Ludlow Castle for a time.'

'Was it? Do you know when that was?' Suddenly it was the schoolmaster speaking.

'Byron thought it could have been in the 1400s.'

'That's interesting. Because look at this.' He indicated four numbers written at the head of one of the early pages. Whatever language had been used for the rest of the document

– and whoever had written these pages – the numbers were clear: 1483.

After a moment, Jack said, 'It could be anything. A library reference, perhaps, for some long-vanished library. But it could also be—'

'The equivalent of writing a date at the start of a diary entry? A year?'

'Yes.'

1483, thought Jack, Byron's tentative findings in his mind. The year two young boys had been taken to the Tower of London by men who wanted to keep them away from England's throne. And those two boys had vanished without any explanation ever being given. He became aware that Declan had turned to the final pages, doing so with extreme care, but also with a kind of familiarity. He's studied this document several times, thought Jack. But he's never been able to understand it. I'm not surprised.

Declan said, 'Near what I think are the final pages is another date. Here, d'you see? The figures are set down in the same way as on that first page.'

'1526,' said Jack.

'Yes. If this is a second date, then taken with that first one, it suggests this was written across forty years.'

'The writing changes,' said Jack, studying the parchment more closely. 'Nearer the end it looks weaker. Shakier.'

'Yes. Almost as if it's an elderly person's writing.' Declan sat back. 'Although for all I can tell, these pages could have been written by half a dozen different people. This first page certainly looks more . . . vigorous is probably the right word. But if it's the same writer throughout, that could account for the shakier hand later on. He – or she, of course – would have been some forty years older: 1483 to 1526.'

'But if this is a journal,' said Jack, 'and I hardly dare to even frame the thought – there surely aren't forty years' worth of it here?'

'Parts could be missing. Damaged. Lost.'

'Or,' said Jack, still staring at the parchment, 'the writer was selective. Only setting down the important events.'

'Leaving out what wasn't important? Yes, that's a good

theory. Or even leaving out what would have been too dangerous to commit to paper. I know that's a sinister suggestion, but those were turbulent times.'

'Dr Kendal, how would you feel about letting Byron look at this? He might be persuaded to come up here – although that would attract attention, which I don't want.'

'Because of Maude's warning?'

'Yes. I'd like to preserve anonymity as long as I can. Also,' said Jack, 'Byron might need to consult various sources – references – to decipher this. The British Museum – the Reading Room. For that he'd need to be in London.'

'How could the manuscript be got to him, though? I wouldn't even consider posting it – it's much too fragile – and there's the risk of it being lost or stolen. Or were you thinking you'd take it yourself?'

Jack did not say that he had no intention of leaving Vallow yet, or that since Declan had told him how Maude had taken the chalice back to Vallow Hall – and had vanished soon afterwards herself – Vallow Hall had been sending out the equivalent of a siren's beckoning song to him.

'My manservant could take it,' he said. 'He's entirely trustworthy, and he knows about the chalice. We could parcel the document up, and Gus could get the earliest train available in the morning – even tonight if there's a late one that links up with the London main service. Either way, Byron would have the pages by tomorrow evening. If it would help you to make a decision, I could let you see Byron's research so far.'

'That almost sounds as if you're trying to bribe me with details about the chalice's history.'

'Are you bribe-able?' asked Jack, meeting the straight stare levelly.

Declan looked back at the faded pages. 'I could be,' he said, at last. 'Your man came with you tonight, didn't he?'

'Yes.'

The moment hung in the balance, then Declan Kendal said, 'All right. Consider me bribed. Let's have him in and we'll see if we can work something out. And while you fetch him, I'll pour us another drop of brandy.'

'You'd better pour one for Gus, too,' said Jack. 'He doesn't like long train journeys.'

Gus listened to the plan outlined to him in Dr Kendal's study, and expressed his willingness to set off for London as soon as might be possible.

'Good man,' said Jack, pleased. 'Dr Kendal thinks there's a train that leaves Vallow Halt just before midnight, and links up with the London train. You can get some breakfast on that train, I should think – I'll make sure you've got enough money, of course. We'll wrap this document up, and then we'll go back to the pub so you can collect a few things – it isn't too late for that, is it? No, it's only just on eleven, they'll still be up. When you get to King's Cross, send Byron a telegram letting him know you're in London and you need to see him as soon as possible. I'd send the telegram myself from here in the morning, but—'

'But Mrs Nithercott takes an inordinate interest in the contents of any telegrams sent from Vallow,' said Declan. 'And no matter how discreetly you worded it, she'd have the information all round the village by lunchtime – and it would probably be a lavishly embroidered version.'

They wrapped the battered parchment pages in silk and then in several layers of soft cotton, placing the whole in a box that appeared to have originally contained school textbooks.

'Don't let it out of your sight,' said Jack to Gus. 'And make sure Byron doesn't, either. I'll write to him – if I post it first thing tomorrow it might reach him by the evening post. But I'll write a short note now for you to take as well.'

'While I'm in London, I might go along to Todworthy Inkling's shop,' said Gus. 'There could still be a few fragments of that "Lament" lying around. Finding a bit more of it'd be worth the train journey and getting my insides jolted to a jelly all over again.'

Gus was very flattered that Mr Jack was entrusting this important task to him. He thought it was quite possible that Mr Byron, who was so clever and scholarly, might be able to make some sense of the old manuscript.

He told Mr Jack and Dr Kendal that he would guard the package with his life, but as he boarded the train at Vallow Halt he was already visualizing the various catastrophes that might strike him, any one of which would result in damaging the manuscript beyond repair, or even in its complete loss. He whiled away the journey before the connection by thinking what he would do if either of his trains met with a crash, or if desperate criminals stormed into the carriage and wrested the package from his hands, or if lightning struck the train, or . . . But of course none of these things would happen, although he thought he would feel safer when he got on to the London-bound train.

He did not feel safer at all, though. The London train was a busy one, and he could not help thinking that any one of the people who came and went might realize that he had with him something of immense value. That being so, he remained in his seat for the entire journey, certainly not venturing into the restaurant car when the call came along that breakfast was being served. He did, however, accept a cup of tea from a chatty lady who wheeled a large urn along the corridors, and declared it was a shame and a disgrace when a person travelling at this hour of a morning did not feel able to go along to the restaurant car.

'Supposing I bring along a bite for you to eat here, sir? Against regulations, of course, but the guards know me, and I daresay there'll be no questions asked.'

Gus, whose innards were behaving fairly well so far on this journey, thought he might manage a dry biscuit or two, or – yes, perhaps a small sandwich if such a thing was to be had. He was slightly taken aback when the chatty lady reappeared with a plate of bacon sandwiches, the grease soaking into the bread, the whole decorated with tomato and rich-looking chutney. He politely waited for her to leave, so he could dispose of the sandwiches through the window, but she perched on the edge of a seat, asking if he was bound for London, and did he live or work there? Ah, he worked for a gentleman of means, how very interesting. And what part of London would that be? She got around a fair bit, and it was always nice to know of a friend who might be visited . . .

By this time Gus suspected that the tea-dispensing lady had observed him guarding the package with such care and had some form of filch in mind. You did not work for a family with generations of high-class burglary behind them without picking up a few clues. So he said it was quite near to Belgravia – indeed, yes, a very nice part of the city.

'Of course, my wife and I don't live in the house – we're in the mews at the back,' he said. 'But very nice it is, although there's really only just enough room for the children. Still, since Algernon went for a soldier and Esmeralda went into service – a merchant banker's household and very well-placed they are – well, there's only four of them left at home.' He would have expanded on how smart Algernon looked in his uniform, and how little Araminta, the youngest, was learning her letters, but the lady got up quite hastily and said she could not sit here gossiping all day, there were folk waiting for their breakfasts.

Gus smiled, thought he had learned a good deal from the Fitzglens' tradition of spinning stories, and managed to throw the sandwiches out as they slowed down on the approach to Crewe. After this, he happily contemplated the fortunes of the mythical Algernon in his smart uniform, and the equally myth-ical Esmeralda serving afternoon tea to the merchant banker and his wife. As journeys went, it was unusually comfortable. He had not felt even a tremor of sickness, although it was probably as well he had disposed of the bacon sandwiches.

He sent the telegram to Mr Byron from King's Cross as instructed. He was not very used to the process, but he had watched Mr Jack enough times to know what you had to do, and Mr Jack had written out what should be said. He had made it sound exciting and intriguing, as well.

'Interesting evidence of Cup's origins found – Gus bringing to London today for you to decipher. Suggest meet him my rooms as soon as possible.'

Gus thought if that did not bring Mr Byron hotfoot, nothing would.

And in fact when finally he reached Mr Jack's rooms, the porter had a message for him, to say that Mr Byron Fitzglen had called earlier and would return later.

'Around four o'clock, he thought. That will be all right, will it, Mr Pocket?'

'Quite all right, thank you.'

Mr Byron was on time, in fact he was early. Gus had set out tea things, because this was what Mr Jack would have wanted. While the tea was brewing and Mr Byron was unwrapping the manuscript, he found himself describing the encounter with the lady of the tea urn, and how he had diverted her from possible suspicion of the wrapped manuscript. Mr Byron greatly enjoyed the story, and was delighted by the characters of Algernon, Esmeralda and Araminta.

'And, you know, Gus, I'm not sure you shouldn't have accepted what that good lady was clearly offering by way of a diversion of her own.'

'On a train?' said Gus, rather startled.

'I don't see why not. Especially if there were blinds to draw down over the corridor window. In fact I believe my cousin Jack once . . . But perhaps I'd better not relate that, and it's very likely an exaggeration anyway. Now, let's see what we've got in this old manuscript.'

Silence fell for what seemed to Gus to be a very long time. Eventually, Mr Byron sat back, thrust his fingers irritably through his hair, and said, 'Damn and blast this – it's as unfathomable as – as the depths of Shakespeare's oceanic mind. I can't make head or tail of it.'

'Nothing at all?' Gus had not realized how much he had been expecting Mr Byron, who was so extremely learned, to be able to read the battered manuscript there and then. He tried not to think how bitterly disappointed Mr Jack would be – and Dr Kendal, too.

'I can get the odd word here and there,' Mr Byron was saying, 'but I should think that Chauntry man could do that anyway. Here – and here . . .' He indicated one or two places on the manuscript's surface. 'Those numbers would be the year those pages were written, I'd think. And that word halfway down this page is certainly London. So we can assume this is something written in 1483 in London and – oh, and continued all the way up to 1526 – see there? And on the last page I think there's a reference to Norfolk, although how Norfolk's got itself into the story I have no idea.' He sat back, his dark brows drawn down, and relapsed into silence.

Gus waited, and eventually Mr Byron said, 'I can't really go hawking the thing around the British Library or the British Museum. It'd be giving too much away, and it might take weeks to find the right person. Although . . .'

'Yes?'

He sat up straighter. 'Gus, there might be someone on hand who could decipher this.'

'Might there?' Gus did not dare to sound too hopeful.

'There's a certain gentleman who owns a bookshop,' began Byron, and looked at Gus. 'A gentleman we both know very well indeed.'

Gus stared at him. 'Todworthy Inkling?' he said, at last.

'Don't look so startled. My Uncle Rudraige has often said old Inkling is a treasure house of knowledge when it comes to medieval history. He read history at Cambridge, so I believe, and he was regarded as one of the ablest scholars of his day.'

'He almost lives in the past anyway,' said Gus, thoughtfully. 'In that shop, it's as if he's called the past up, and surrounded himself with it.'

'That's astute of you, Gus. That's just what he has done. I wonder if we can risk showing him this,' said Mr Byron, frowning slightly. 'He's a shocking old rogue, of course – he's got all kinds of sidelines as well as selling old books, although it's probably as well not to delve too deeply into them.'

'He'll charge for reading this document,' said Gus.

'Aye, there's the rub. We'll have to pay, but I shall threaten him with the might of the Metropolitan Police if he tries to sell any of this to his customers – oh, and I'll invoke the equivalent of the Ten Plagues of Egypt, as well, if I can remember them all.' Mr Byron smiled, clearly enjoying this prospect. 'We'll go along in the morning, shall we, Gus? I always enjoy that shop. You wouldn't think that such a disreputable emporium could be a treasure trove of secrets and of signposts pointing you on to ancient pathways, but it is. It's an absolute Aladdin's cave – although on that subject, I tell you, Gus, that if my cousin Jack ever decides to put on a pantomime, I shall leave the Amaranth for ever and become a Trappist monk or join the circus.'

Todworthy Inkling was charmed to see his old friend Gus Pocket, who he regarded as something of a protégé, and to welcome the distinguished Mr Byron Fitzglen, for whom he had a good deal of respect.

'A scholar, that's what you are, Mr Fitzglen,' he said, shaking hands with his two visitors, and ushering them into his small, crowded private quarters. 'The groves of Academe lost a valuable asset when you took to the boards. Of course, they were your family's boards, that has to be remembered, and highly distinguished boards they are, too. I tell everyone so.'

He sat back in his creaking leather chair, revolved his thumbs, and waited to hear what might be wanted of him.

Gus was amused, but not surprised to see that this typical Todworthy ploy did not discompose Mr Byron in the least. He was well able to deal with the likes of Tod Inkling, was Mr Byron – he had the Fitzglen gift for adapting, and for adopting whatever manner best suited the occasion. It was a gift Mr Jack had to perfection, of course, but Mr Byron ran him a close second. He was telling Tod how much he always enjoyed visiting the bookshop.

'For I've found several very nice old volumes here from time to time – a treasure house of learning is what you have here, Mr Inkling. And that being so, we wondered, my cousin Jack and I – Gus, too, I should add – whether you might bend your considerable intellect and knowledge to the deciphering of a page or two of an old document.'

There was a short silence, then Mr Byron, who could judge a pause as well as any Fitzglen, said, casually, 'There would be a modest fee involved, of course.'

It was as if a light had been lit behind the small shrewd eyes. Mr Inkling, re-settled his crimson smoking cap, leaned forward, and said, 'What kind of an old document?'

THIRTEEN

At first Maude was frightened that she would fall again into the dark insanity that Saul and Aunt Hilda said had taken over her mind inside Bastle House. It was strange to find you had suffered a bout of madness, and not be able to remember anything about it. But the facts had been clear – there she had been, with Agnes's body, and there Saul and Aunt Hilda had been, able to see everything. Able to see what must have happened.

But they had been kind – Maude kept reminding herself how kind they had been. They had got her back to Vallow Hall, and Aunt Hilda had sent Lily scurrying off for hot-water jars and blankets and strong tea, and Maude had been grateful.

After she had recovered a little, they had talked to her for a long time – in fact they talked to her several times over several days. They could not, they told her very sombrely, pretend nothing had happened. Between the three of them, what Maude had done must be acknowledged. They were, though, going to protect her. They had worked out a plan, and they were going to make sure no one ever found out what she had done.

'Because you see, my dear—'

Maude winced at the small endearment, because when had Saul ever called her his 'dear', or used any term of affection to her at all? It was because Aunt Hilda was here, she knew.

'Because,' he went on, 'your aunt and I do know that you were not in possession of your senses when you killed Agnes.'

Maude said, as if trying out the words, 'I killed Agnes.'

'You were victim of a mental aberration when you did it,' put in Aunt Hilda, her thin lips in the drawstring-purse line.

'But – I did kill her?'

'Oh, yes. There's no other explanation. Your earrings . . .'

'There was one near the open cellar,' said Maude.

'Yes. But the other was down in the cellar itself,' he said. 'Your aunt and I saw it.'

'It's still down there,' Aunt Hilda added.

'Yes. So you do see, Maude, there's absolutely no doubt.'

'Yes, I see that. Does it mean I'm mad?'

'Perhaps for a little while, you were,' said Saul. 'Not now, though. And there's no reason to think that the madness will ever come to you again. No reason in the world.'

'Of course not,' said Aunt Hilda, a bit too quickly.

'One bout of insanity does not mean there must be more in the future,' said Saul. 'And your aunt and I will do everything possible to make sure the truth never comes out. But you see, if the truth *were* to come out, it would mean you having to stand trial for murder.'

Murder. It was as if the word had been scrawled on the air with the thick nib of a blood-laden pen. *But it's what I did*, thought Maude. *I murdered Agnes Scroop in that dark old house – my house that Eddy gave me. I imprisoned her in the dark underground room, the trapdoor slammed down so that she could not get out. It could only have been me. No one else could have got into the house. No one knew about the keys or where I had hidden them – and there aren't any other keys. And my earrings were there – one of them is still down in the cellar itself – Aunt Hilda said so. I don't know why I did this, but I see that I must have done.*

Saul said, 'If a trial took place, I'm afraid the evidence would be damning. My own years on the magistrates' bench have given me some insight into the law, and I believe it's inevitable that you would be found guilty.'

'They might decide you had been mad when you committed the crime,' said Aunt Hilda. 'But that would mean they would take you to a special institution.'

'An asylum,' said Maude, her mind flinching. Mr Dickens had written about asylums – she had read one of the accounts. He had described brutal physicians who often chained and even flogged those in their care . . . And dark, loathsome cells that never saw the light. How would it feel to be flung into one of those cells, knowing you would never again see the light . . .?

'They're dreadful places,' Saul was saying, with a gesture of distaste. 'No husband worth his salt would see his wife consigned to one.'

Maude said, 'No husband worth his salt would believe his wife could commit murder,' and was pleased to hear a note of sharpness in her tone.

But Saul only said, 'The alternative would be far worse. If you were found sane, I'm very much afraid you would be hanged. There would be nothing I or anyone else could do to prevent it.'

Hanged. Marched out to a squalid prison yard at dawn – perhaps in the darkness of some winter morning – and a rope looped around her neck. Did people strangle to death when they were hanged? Were the public allowed to watch any longer?

'And so, we have made a plan,' said Saul. 'It won't last for ever, but for the foreseeable future, your aunt and I think you must remain inside this house. Not be seen by anyone. No one must know you are still at Vallow.' He looked at her. 'It really is the only way, Maude,' he said.

Neither of them had used the word imprisonment, but Maude thought they all knew that was what this was going to be. But she tried to look at it sensibly. She understood that she had committed murder, even though she did not remember doing it. And murder had to be punished. This would be her punishment. Saul had promised it would only be for the foreseeable future, though. Could she trust that? She would have to.

'There are rooms at the top of this house that could be made perfectly comfortable,' Aunt Hilda said, later the same day. 'Within reason you could have whatever you wanted. As Cousin Saul has said, it won't be for ever.'

Maude wondered when Saul had become a cousin to Aunt Hilda.

'Certainly it need not be for ever,' Saul said. 'One day it will be safe for you to return to the normal world.'

'When I've served my sentence,' said Maude, half to herself.

He ignored this, and said, 'When memories have died down – when people have forgotten about a maidservant called Agnes

Scroop – then you could come back to the world. We could
let it be thought there had been a long illness – that you had
been living with relatives, somewhere abroad, perhaps. We
aren't going to shut you away for ever,' said Saul, with a half-
laugh at the absurdity of such an idea. 'Of course we are not.
But for the foreseeable future . . .' He made a brief gesture
with his hands, indicative of reluctant acceptance. 'No one
beyond these walls must know you are here. That is why your
aunt is making those upstairs rooms comfortable for you. It's
the only way we can keep you safe.'

Safe. Maude clung to the word, because it helped to shut out
that other word – *murder* – although it did not shut it
out completely. She did not think anything ever would. She
still had no memory of anything other than going out to
Bastle House to hide the chalice – she had placed it on the
nice old oak dresser where it would catch the sunlight. And
then she had found Agnes's body. Clearly something had
happened to her mind, but she had no memory of anything
other than the chalice and finding Agnes's body. What was
really terrible was that she had no feeling of guilt, either.
Even though she did not remember killing Agnes, surely she
ought to be feeling remorse and trying to atone for what
she had done. How did you atone for murder, though? The
Bible's teaching was a life for a life. *But I'm safe from that*,
thought Maude. *Saul and Aunt Hilda won't let me be hanged
or thrown into an asylum.*

Aunt Hilda, helped by Lily, made the attics into what she
said was a very acceptable set of apartments. The rooms were
rather small and the ceilings were low because they were directly
under the roof, but the discarded furniture and rubbish that
had accumulated up there over the years was taken out and
heaped on to two large bonfires at the back of Vallow's grounds.
Lily even wielded a paintbrush, which she said smartened it
all up a treat, and made it really fresh and nice.

Other furniture was taken up – chairs, a bed, a small table
to eat off. Rugs were laid down to soften the bare floorboards
and one or two pictures put on the walls. There were bookshelves, so that Maude could have her books and sketching

materials. There were views over the countryside from almost every window.

'Pity you can't have your piano up here, ain't it, mum?' Lily said. 'You'd've liked that. I always enjoyed hearing you play. We had music at home – a harmonium in the parlour we had, and Pa played hymns on Sundays. Me, I'd rather have a good tune you can dance to, although Pa used to say dancing was one of the Devil's instruments for leading you into sin.' Lily hunched a shoulder and grinned. 'Good thing he ain't going to find out how far into sin it did lead me, isn't it? Village dance, a glass too many of cider, a bit of sweet talk, and there I was. What they call "in trouble".'

'What . . .?'

'I didn't mean to speak out of my place,' said Lily, 'but I thought it'd be all right, you and me being in the same condition.' Again the grin. 'I get a few bad days and the morning sickness, like you do, mum, but you got to expect that, don't you? And I'm that grateful to the master – ever so kind he was when I told him, and said as I could stay on here. Turned out without a character you'd be at most houses, and if that'd happened, I don't know what I'd have done, for Pa'd never let me back in the house.'

Maude stared at her. Her mind was whirling, but she managed to say, 'You – you're going to have a child, Lily? I hadn't realized.'

'Shocking, ain't it? Don't take much, do it?'

'No, it . . . I'm very sorry about what's happened to you, though, Lily. But I'm glad the master has been so generous.'

'He'll see about a place for the child at St Botolph's,' said Lily proudly. 'And I can even go and visit, he says, providing I don't talk about – well, about you having to stay up here for a time. Bit confused in your mind was what he said you were, but that me and Mrs Cheesely didn't need to know anything else, and the less said the better. But we got to be discreet and look after you for a while, that's how he put it. Me and Mrs Cheesely promised we would. She's going to have something that'll give her a bit of money when she retires. Anni— something the master called it.'

'Annuity?'

'That was the word. Always been worried about what she'll
do when she can't work no more, so she's ever so grateful.
And I'll look after you very particular, us both being in the
same condition at the same time. Bit of a turn-up, ain't it?'

Both of us at the same time . . . With the words Maude felt
as if the room had suddenly begun to spin, like a child's spinning top. Out of the dizzying mist, she heard her voice saying,
in a completely natural tone, 'Yes. Both of us at the same
time, Lily.'

The realization that she was to have a child altered Maude's
whole horizon. A child. Out of all the fears and worries, was
to come a child. And then she thought – Eddy's child? Was that
why he had arranged for her to have Bastle House and the
chalice – because he suspected what might have happened?

But couldn't the child be Saul's? 'It don't take much', Lily
had said. Could what Saul had done – had tried to do – on
all those awkward embarrassing Saturday nights have been
enough to conceive a child? Maude had no idea, and there
was no one she could ask.

But whatever the facts, of course Saul would think the child
was his. He had no idea what had happened with Eddy, and
Maude had scarcely been out of his company since their
marriage, so it would not occur to him that she might have
had such an encounter with another man. It would be all right.
And after the birth he and Aunt Hilda would end this semi-
imprisonment – of course they would. Maude would not allow
herself to think anything else would happen. Life could be
normal again – and it would be a life that would include a
child.

FOURTEEN

It was shortly after Hilda Grout was ensconced at the Hall, with the courtesy title of housekeeper-companion, that she sought out Saul to ask, 'Do you know that Maude is going to have a child?'

'I do.'

'It's some months ahead, I think, but we would need a physician – or a nurse. How exactly will that be contrived?'

'I am afraid,' said Saul, 'that the child's birth must be part of the secret. For its own sake it can never know the truth.' He made a rueful gesture, expressive of sorrow. 'For a boy or girl to know its mother committed murder . . . That is not a burden that should be placed on any child's shoulders.'

'Yes, I see that,' said Hilda Grout, slowly. 'But—'

'I have a plan in my mind, Miss Grout – can I say Cousin Hilda, perhaps? So much friendlier. Well then, Cousin Hilda, when the time comes you may leave it all to me.'

She looked at him, and for a moment Saul thought she was going to ask to know more – even that she was suspicious of him. But she only nodded and no more was said. Like Lily and Mrs Cheesely she was grateful for her place here, and she would be loyal. Saul had arranged everything with great skill, and it was all working out as he had planned.

He had burned the Bastle House Title Deed, of course, taking it from where that sly, deceitful Maude had hidden it. He did not risk using the fireplace in the music room – it was rare for a fire to be lit there, anyway – and he had taken the document down to the sculleries. The range was never allowed to go out, and Saul dropped the Deed straight on to the glowing redness, standing for a moment to watch the parchment curl at the edges. It turned brown, and then shrivelled and finally became black cinders. A curious thing, though, had been that he had dropped the document in face down, so that it was the final page with the signature that stared up at him. Aiden

Fitzglen. The name scratched itself into his mind, because although he had erased the document's existence, somewhere in the world was a man called Aiden Fitzglen, who had witnessed it. Who *knew* about it. It was the one thing Saul had not been able to plan for, but although it worried him, he could not see how to deal with it. He could not see how he would find Aiden.

And then in the first week of the new year – 1892 – came the announcement that Prince Albert Victor was seriously ill. He had fallen victim to the influenza epidemic and he was being cared for at Sandringham House.

When it was announced that he had developed pneumonia the news eclipsed almost everything else – or at least consigned the majority of other items to lesser pages and smaller newsprint. Even the story about the valuable artefact apparently stolen from the royal collection ahead of a birthday exhibition for the Prince of Wales was relegated to inside pages. This had been a favourite story until now, treated with particular gusto by the more sensational publications. Several of them continued to speculate as to the truth of the apparent theft, but it was the prince's illness that dominated. The reports varied wildly. He was recovering – no, he was declining. The doctors were at a loss – no, they were confident, saying they would pull him through.

But the prince was not recovering, and the doctors did not pull him through. In the second week of January, his family and physicians around him and his chaplain chanting prayers, less than a week after his twenty-eighth birthday, Prince Albert Victor died.

The nation was shocked. He had had a somewhat colourful reputation, Prince Eddy, and there had been murmurs of scandals – visits to houses of ill repute, unwise friends. But there had been more than one King of England who had been a bit wild, and everyone had thought that by the time the prince ascended the throne he would have sown his wild oats, and got the rioting and drinking and all the other things out of his system. Except that now he would not ascend the throne at all. It was a massive shock, because you did not expect a young and healthy man of twenty-eight to up and die without warning.

In the days that followed there were a great many reports about the country having gone into mourning – how people had sobbed openly in the streets, and closed their shops. The prince's younger brother, George, stepped into Eddy's place in the line of succession, of course. George V he would be one day, said the papers, but were careful to remind readers that of course this would not be until the present Queen had passed on – God bless Her Majesty and may she reign for ever – and then her son, the Prince of Wales, would succeed. Nobody actually came out and said that it mightn't be so very long before George became King George V, because Victoria was already 73, and although the Prince of Wales might only be fifty-one, he could hardly be said to live a life conducive to a healthy old age.

An elaborate funeral took place, with Eddy's body laid to rest in the Albert Memorial Chapel, near St George's Chapel at Windsor Castle. Commemorations were held the length and breadth of the land – concerts, solemn readings, performances of orchestral pieces. Chauntry School held its own tribute with a requiem in the school's concert hall, and although several people murmured that the word 'requiem' smacked of Catholicism, the vicar had been in the audience and had appeared to find it all very acceptable and appropriate. And the music was certainly beautiful.

Miss Grout was not particularly interested in the prince's death. She would be respectful towards the Queen's grandson, of course, but she did not approve of wild young men with propensities for drinking and womanizing, and scant regard for any of the proprieties. Why, there was said to have been one female who had drunk carbolic acid for love of him. Granted, the female had been a chorus girl and you did not know what excesses such creatures might practise, but it was still shocking.

Still, she knew what was due to royalty, and she would trim her Sunday bonnet with mauve pansies and look out her best black silk for church.

Saul continued to read the newspaper reports, and it turned out that it was a very good thing he did, otherwise he might never have seen the notice about one memorial concert in particular. But he did see it, and the words seemed almost to leap off the page.

A memorial concert is to be held at the Amaranth Theatre in London, on the 7th of next month, in tribute to His Royal Highness, Prince Albert Victor, Duke of Clarence and Avondale, who died in January.

The concert will be under the direction of Mr Aiden Fitzglen, whom theatre-goers will know as the theatre's owner and manager. The guest musical director for the evening will be Mr Connor O'Kane.

Saul stared at these words in disbelief. There it was, the name of the man he had wanted to find ever since he had seen the signature on the Bastle House Deed. Aiden Fitzglen. He read the rest of the article with fierce concentration.

Mr Fitzglen is the head of the prestigious theatrical family who have owned and managed the Amaranth Theatre for over a century. He has entertained the prince at major events in his theatre, including the famous ball held there to mark Queen Victoria's Golden Jubilee in 1887.

Mr O'Kane has been associated with His Royal Highness for several years – often accompanying the prince to events arranged by music societies and orchestras, especially those for which His Royal Highness was patron.

Saul felt as if his mind was being illuminated by searing flashes of light, in the way the sky was illuminated during a bad thunderstorm.

It all fitted. Aiden Fitzglen was staging a memorial concert for the prince – he had been linked to the prince, and it was how he had come to be a witness on that Title Deed. It must be that. Saul was being handed exactly the information he wanted. Not only did he now know who this man was, he knew where he would be on a specific date. He would be at the Amaranth Theatre in London on the 7th of next month. He glanced at the calendar on his desk. Two weeks away.

It was easy to tell Miss Grout that he would be away for a night, or possibly two nights, because he had to attend a business meeting in London.

She did not ask what the meeting was about. Ladies did not ask about a gentleman's business affairs, and in any case, Hilda Grout was a dependant, and knew her place. She merely nodded, noted the dates, and went away to tell Mrs Cheesely not to trouble about a dining-room luncheon or dinner for those two days – that she herself would have a tray in the morning room.

Saul considered saying he was going into Alnwick for two sets of meetings to be held on two consecutive days, but Alnwick was not really far enough to warrant staying away from the Hall for a night. Also, he would have to arrange for Ned Nithercott's cart to take him to Vallow Halt, and Ned, or some equally gossipy person, might talk about him having boarded the London train.

His journey to London began badly. He had to set off at an ungodly hour, and Ned Nithercott's cart was late in collecting him, which meant they had to go full pelt along Candle Lane, resulting in Saul having to be scrambled on to the train in a very unseemly fashion.

As if that were not enough, the guards on the train were surly, and then there was a wait of a whole half-hour on a draughty platform for his connection. He would be writing a very stiff letter to the train company when he got home, demanding a refund not only of the train fare, but also of the extortionate amount he had had to pay for the very indifferent breakfast served to him in the restaurant carriage.

Once at King's Cross, the noise and the bustle and the sheer volume of people was slightly daunting. He seldom had reason to visit London, and he had forgotten how loud and frantic it all was. He stood for a moment on the platform, trying to see his way to the exit, peering through the constant bursts of steam from the trains and the throng of scurrying people. Trains chugged and shunted all around him, and whistles were blown piercingly to herald an arrival or warn of a departure. Porters pushed luggage trolleys along the platforms at a great rate – twice Saul had to skip out of their path, which discomposed him even further.

He eventually found his way out to the street, where he hailed a hansom. It rattled along the streets, and deposited him at the modest hotel he had booked. The cost of a night's stay had shocked him, but on the street map it had looked quite near to the Amaranth Theatre, which was what he wanted.

Once in his room he unpacked his things himself – he was not giving a chambermaid anything to gossip over. This done, he set out on what he believed soldiers called a reconnoitre – a preliminary inspection of the terrain. It was already mid-afternoon, so he had none too much time before this evening's concert.

The Amaranth Theatre, when finally he reached it, was much more imposing than he had expected. There was a stone façade with ornate pillars and engravings. Marble steps led up to a wide entrance, which had brass fittings and gilt doors. To Saul's mind this display of gilt and brass was ostentatious and even rather vulgar, but he would acknowledge that this was a place of some importance, which meant that Aiden Fitzglen must be a person of some importance. Posters were displayed outside the main entrance advertising the evening's concert – the memorial for Prince Albert Victor Christian Edward, Duke of Clarence and Avondale. Saul studied them openly, because it would be a normal thing to do. The name of the orchestra who would be performing was in large letters, and beneath were the names of a pianist, described as the soloist, and the conductor. Saul had never heard of any of them.

After this, he walked along the street, doing so purposefully as if he had an aim. He did have an aim, of course; he was looking for a side street that might lead to the rear of the theatre. At first he thought he was not going to find one, but then a few yards along he saw the narrow street, with the name Sloat Alley high up on the brickwork.

Sloat Alley was narrow and rather squalid after the splendour of the Amaranth's façade. There were buildings on both sides, looking as if they had been squeezed in at the last minute, and as if they might be propping one another up. Some of them were tiny shops with crowded front windows. As he walked along, he passed three or four deep-set doors with signs on them proclaiming them to be cellar restaurants. Saul did not accord any of these places a second glance; he was not here to look at seedy underground restaurants or peer into dusty shop windows where all manner of disreputable articles might be on view for sale.

People jostled him in a very ill-mannered way, and twice almost caused him to lose his footing on the uneven cobbles. The alley was narrow and dismal; most of the buildings were at least three storeys high, and in places the upper sections overhung the street, shutting out the daylight. At the far end was a tavern, with a sign outside proclaiming it to be The Punchbowl. Bursts of laughter and erratic snatches of music from a jangly sounding piano came from it, and when a group of people opened the door and spilled out into the street, laughing and linking arms, a waft of warm ale-scented air reached Saul. He was surprised that the authorities permitted such places to be open in the daytime, but he was not here to make judgements on badly behaved, half-drunken people or raucous taverns. He turned up his coat collar and walked on, looking into partly open gates with storage yards beyond, hoping to see a side entrance to the Amaranth.

Halfway along he saw it. A small door in a recess, set so far back into the brickwork of the wall that it would be easy to walk past without noticing it. A sign above the door said: *Stage door. Amaranth Theatre. No unauthorized admittance.*

No unauthorized admittance. But the door was slightly ajar. He could walk straight in. He had intended to wait for the actual performance – he had even planned how he would wear evening clothes to blend in with the audience, although he had no idea if that was how people dressed for such an event. But he was going to put his long travelling cloak around his shoulders, which would hide the evening things if he had got it wrong.

But standing in Sloat Alley, staring at the half-open door, it was as if huge invisible hands seized his plan, shook it violently, then let it fall into a whole new pattern. Saul's mind began to work at a very rapid rate. Supposing Fitzglen was in there now? It seemed likely that with a performance in the theatre this evening he would be. Rehearsing? Presumably there would be speeches, a tribute to Prince Albert Victor, some kind of welcome for the audience.

He glanced about him, but no one was paying him any attention, and so he stepped into the recess and went through the door.

FIFTEEN

The street sounds receded at once, and Saul had the sense of having stepped into a different world. He had expected to be immediately confronted by some minion, demanding to know his business, but he was going to say he was here to write a newspaper article about tonight's performance. As proof he had with him a notebook and pencil, which he thought was sufficient disguise.

But no one came out, and he was able to take stock of his surroundings. He was in a dim, narrow passage, stone-floored and with whitewashed walls, none too clean. There were gas brackets on the walls, presumably lit in the evenings. Immediately ahead was a spiral iron stair; it did not seem to be fastened to the walls, and it swayed slightly when he stepped on it. It appeared safe enough, though, and it led up to a wide corridor, with what Saul supposed were pieces of scenery standing against the walls – huge wooden frames with canvas stretched across them, and views painted on representing gardens or skies or castle. There was a smell of paint and timber.

Several doors opened off the corridor. From behind one of them was the sound of hammering, and farther along, music came from another room. At the far end was a small, tucked-away staircase which probably led up to the roof. The hammering broke off, and a voice called out to Bill the Chip to for heaven's sake bang in a few more nails, or that dais would collapse halfway through the concert and send the violins and the tuba tumbling into the front row of the stalls.

'And a shocking lack of respect for poor old Prince Eddy that'd show, and Mr Fitzglen'd be shouting his head off in the wings, never mind Mr O'Kane threatening us all with the Tower.'

An answering voice – presumably Bill the Chip – said indignantly that the dais would be perfectly safe, and even if the entire stage fell in, nobody would be sent to the Tower tonight.

'And for why? Because none of the royal family won't be here, that's for why. Deep mourning they're in, which means no public appearances.' A pause, then, ''Course, there might be one or two of the Prince of Wales's lady friends come along, so they can report to the old so-and-so about the concert. But Mr Fitzglen won't give a tinker's toss if the entire chorus of the Gaiety is in the front row of the stalls, s'long as they've paid for their seats.'

'True enough,' responded the first voice, and the hammering resumed.

Above the music from the far end of the corridor, a voice was now shouting angrily that the bloody wind section was *still* not coming in on the note so they would go back to bar eighty-eight – and there was no need for the scowls, Mr Flute-Player – it did not matter that they had done it ten times already; they would do it a hundred times if necessary.

Rehearsing for tonight, thought Saul, then turned as a man and a boy of eleven or twelve appeared around the far corner, the man saying something about the stage being almost ready.

'I didn't think we'd manage to carry all those music stands on to the stage between us, Master Jack, and I daresay Mr O'Kane will want them all changing round, but I think we did a good job. We'll let your father take a look when he comes down from the wardrobe room. He's looking for a dress suit for your Uncle Rudraige. He spilled soup down his own last week, and Mr Aiden won't let him appear tonight in a soup-splashed jacket, so he's gone up to find a replacement.'

'Uncle Rudraige won't go up to the wardrobe room himself,' said the boy. 'He says the stairs are too steep, and it's shockingly damp up there anyway on account of the rain coming in through the roof.'

'He's right about the rain coming in, and high time that bit of roof was put right, but— Ah, afternoon to you, sir.'

It was not quite a question, but the man looked enquiringly at Saul, who had had the forethought to take out his notebook, and had been pretending to make notes. He looked up as if startled.

'Good afternoon. I'm just waiting until Mr O'Kane's free so I can confirm these details with him.' Saul thought using this name would pass muster – he did not want to confront Aiden Fitzglen yet, but it had sounded as if O'Kane had some authority here. He tapped the open page with the pencil tip. 'Bill the Chip said he's rehearsing, so I won't interrupt that.'

This was taking a bit of a chance, but the man only grinned, and said it was more than anybody's life was worth to interrupt Mr O'Kane during a concert rehearsal. 'Shouldn't think he'll be long, though.'

He nodded to Saul, clearly unsuspicious, and he and the boy continued along the corridor. Bill the Chip had started hammering again, and the music had recommenced, but Saul scarcely heard it, because his mind was working at a furious speed. Aiden Fitzglen was here – he was in a room at the top of the theatre looking for a dress suit for somebody called Rudraige.

It sounded as if the man and the boy called Jack – Aiden's son from the sound of it – had come from the main part of the theatre, so Saul went in that direction. Ahead were heavy double doors, and he glanced over his shoulder to make sure no one was watching, then pushed them. They swung open with a gentle swish.

And now he was in the heart and the core of the theatre – in the vast dimness of the auditorium. This was where make-believe worlds were conjured up and paraded across a lighted stage. Ahead of him were tiered seats on three separate levels – rows and rows of them, going all the way down to the stage far below, and behind him stretching up almost as far as the vaulted ceiling. The ceiling was an extravagant affair, with painted romping nymphs and scantily clad blow-cheeked cherubs, and giant bunches of grapes carved out of the plasterwork. Massive chandeliers hung from the ceiling at several points, each set with dozens of tiny candle holders, which would be for show, because nobody could possibly get up there to light so many candles, never mind snuffing them afterwards.

Gilt and mahogany railings separated the tiers of seats, and there were carved pillars, with, between them, sections of richly flocked walls, crimson and gold. Everything was vulgar and ostentatious, but Saul grudgingly acknowledged that it was impressive.

Amidst all this splendour, the stage itself might have appeared almost small and even insignificant, but it did not. Saul could see the music stands and chairs that the man and the boy, Jack, had talked about. There was a grand piano, and tubs of flowers at the sides of the stage. The stage itself was surrounded by what might almost be called a giant frame: a plaster and gilt structure with elaborate patterns and carvings in it. He had no idea how theatre stages were lit, but he knew they always were, and clearly when the Amaranth's stage was glowing with life it would be as if the audience was being vouchsafed a glimpse through an immense magical window into another world.

On each side of the stage were rows of boxes, which would be for the more exalted members of the audience. Several of them had looped-back crimson velvet curtains at the sides, and most had gilt chairs, covered in crimson and cream velvet. On the largest of these boxes – the nearest one to the stage – was the unmistakable outline of the royal crest. Saul looked at it for a long moment, and then, despite the gravity and the fact that he was aware he might be caught at any moment, he smiled. It would be so beautifully appropriate to use the royal box for what he was about to do.

It was easy to retrace his steps – still being careful to display the notebook and pencil – and to follow neatly worded signs. *Audience, Front Stalls*, and *Audience, Dress Circle*. He did not expect the royal box itself to be indicated – it would be too private, too exclusive for the *hoi polloi* to be able to find their way there, and also there would be the concern about some madman trying to assassinate one of the royal family. That had happened more than once to Saul's knowledge.

But by keeping to the plusher parts of the corridor he found doors leading to the rear of the boxes. And here, finally, was what must certainly be the royal box itself. There was an ante room with a gilt-topped table and matching chairs, where

perhaps a light supper might be served. Doors, embellished
with more golden scrollwork, opened on to the box itself. Saul
hesitated, then stepped through.

He could no longer hear the music or the hammering now,
and it was very quiet, although if Saul had been given to
fanciful imaginings – which he was not – he might almost
have thought the shadows were stirring and watching him. He
reached into the deep pocket of his coat for the matches and
candles he had brought. Listening for the sound of anyone
approaching the boxes, he lit two of the candles and set them
on the floor of the box, close to the swathe of curtain. As he
stepped back, the tiny flame licked tentatively at the edge of
the velvet. That was good. The fabric should smoulder for a
while, and it would take time before the curtain actually started
burning, but there would be a good deal of smoke. He went
into the adjoining box and lit a second candle, which he set
against the curtains in the same way.

Once out in the corridor, he took a deep breath, then walked
quickly along it, banging on each door in turn, calling out as
loudly as he could.

'Fire! Fire in the boxes! Everyone out of the building!'

Doors were flung open, and people came rushing out, bewil-
dered, not quite panicking, but wanting to know what was
happening. Was there really a fire somewhere?

The musicians came tumbling out of the rehearsal room,
pushing and jostling, heading for the iron stairs, and Saul
turned back to the twisty stairs at the end of the corridor, and
went up them. They were unlit and awkward to navigate, but
he eventually reached a tiny landing, with a door. Had he
understood that snatch of conversation correctly? Was this
where Fitzglen was? If so, would he still be here? He called
out, banging hard on the door.

'Mr Fitzglen? Sir – are you in there? There's a fire –
everyone's to get out of the building at once!'

The door was thrown open, and a man who strongly resembled the boy stood there. He was dishevelled and dusty, and
he was younger than Saul had expected. He was also very
good-looking, with hair of an unusual golden brown, and
startlingly dark eyes.

He said, 'A fire? God almighty – where?'

'I think it's in the auditorium – it's being dealt with, though – I don't think it's a massive danger. But I've been told to make sure everyone leaves the building while it's put out.'

'Yes, of course.' Fitzglen was already through the door, so intent on what was happening that he did not question who this stranger was. He was halfway down the narrow stairs, Saul behind him, when he suddenly said, 'Where's Jack? He was helping Bill the Chip—'

'They've already taken him out into the alley,' said Saul, at once. 'Everyone's gone – Master Jack went with them.'

But even as he spoke, there was a small commotion at the foot of the stairs, and Jack Fitzglen appeared, almost throwing himself at his father, his eyes wide and filled with panic.

'I came back for you – we were outside, but I couldn't see you . . . And then Uncle Rudraige said you were still here, so I came back . . . There's a fire—'

'I know, but it's not a big fire, and it's all perfectly safe.'

Fitzglen did not quite pick up his son, but he wrapped both arms around him, and began to lead him to the iron stairway. Saul, immediately behind, felt a surge of anger, because this would have been the ideal opportunity. With such confusion everywhere, no one would have questioned the fact that Mr Fitzglen had tripped and gone headlong down those treacherous stairs to his death. It would not have occurred to anyone that he had been pushed. But Saul could not deliver that push with so many people still around, and he was forced to go with them, down to the stage door and out to the street.

A thin rain was falling on Sloat Alley. Lights were flaring in the windows of The Punchbowl and also in several shop windows, but the streetlamps had not yet been lit and the rain was misting everything. Saul turned up his coat collar and wound his scarf over the lower part of his face, blending with the people milling around.

Shopkeepers had come out and a group of revellers had spilled out of The Punchbowl, demanding to know what was happening. People were pointing at the upper floors of the theatre, and someone was shouting to ask if the fire brigade had been called. A voice that Saul thought belonged to Bill the Chip said that 'course it had, he had sent someone along himself as soon as the alarm was raised that there was a fire in the royal box.

'Wouldn't you know it would be the royal box,' said a voice within the crowd.

'Wherever it is, we'll have to cancel tonight,' said an older-sounding voice. 'And we'll just have to hope we aren't ruined altogether – Aiden, how ruined are we likely to be, because . . . Dammit, where is Aiden? I saw him out here a minute ago, and no call for anyone to say I'm getting short-sighted, for I can see as well as the next man.'

'He's over there, Rudraige,' said the first voice. 'Is everyone out of the building? Where's Connor O'Kane, though? Has anyone seen him?'

'The musicians came out, so he's bound to be with them,' said a female voice. 'And Aiden's over there – no, wait, he's going back into the theatre . . .'

Saul turned to see Aiden Fitzglen running across the cobbled pavement and vanishing through the stage door.

'He's mad!' shouted the older voice. 'Somebody stop him.'

'Rudraige, calm down, or you'll have an apoplexy. Aiden'll be out in a couple of minutes – he'll have gone back to rescue something valuable.'

'Daphnis, there isn't anything so valuable in there it's worth risking a fire!'

'There's that script of Sheridan's, signed by him—'

'And there's the chair David Garrick sat in when he played *Lear*,' chimed in another voice. 'Guest appearance it was, and the house packed to the rafters.'

'Aiden wouldn't go into a burning building for a chair or a signed play script.'

Aiden Fitzglen had already vanished through the stage door, and Saul knew it was his last chance. People were craning their necks, trying to see if any flames were visible at the upper windows, or they were running to the end of the alley to watch for the arrival of the fire brigade, and no one was looking in his direction. The deepening twilight and the rain were blurring everything – if he was quick and watchful he could go back inside without anyone noticing. It would be quite safe, because the fire would not have got much of a hold yet.

He stepped back from the throng, and re-entered the theatre.

Once at the upper corridor, though, smoke was already everywhere, and he could hear the crackling of flames, as well. He had not, in fact, meant the fire to be so bad; he had only wanted to cause sufficient disruption to get at Aiden Fitzglen. But it could not be helped now.

Fitzglen was at the far end of the long corridor – half-running towards the narrow stairway that went up to the roof. Saul's heart began to thud almost painfully against his ribs, but he ran forward and grabbed Fitzglen's arm.

'Come back down the stairs and out into the street,' he said, his voice urgent. 'They're saying something might be about to collapse in here.'

'Oh, God, no . . .' Fitzglen jerked his arm free, then looked sharply at Saul. 'Who the devil are you?' he said. 'And is everyone safe?'

'Everyone's quite safe,' said Saul. 'I was sent in to fetch you. The fire people will be here any minute – we have to get out and leave the way clear for them.'

'Is Jack all right?' said Fitzglen, and before Saul could answer, they heard the boy's voice.

'It's Jack. He's followed me,' said Aiden, and began to run towards the double doors that led to the auditorium. 'Jack – where are you? Are you all right?'

The reply came faintly. 'In the theatre – I've been trying to find you—'

Saul followed him into the auditorium, which was thick with smoke. The curtains of the royal box and the one next to it were burning up, and as he looked, a small figure appeared, outlined against the flames.

'*Jack!* Jack, run out into the corridor at once. I'm coming up to get you.'

Saul thought Aiden murmured something like *Please God, let him be safe*, and then he was running again, round to the corridor with the doors on to the boxes. The boy came tumbling out, his hands reaching for his father, who seized them.

'Everything's all right, Jack. You're safe – we're both safe.'
He looked through the billowing smoke into the box. 'And it
isn't at all bad, is it? It's just the smoke. If I can stamp that
bit of fire out, it'll stop it spreading . . . But you run outside,
Jack. Quickly now. Go down into the alley, and find Uncle
Rudraige and Aunt Daphnis. They're all there, aren't they?'

'Yes . . .'

'Everyone got out all right? Bill the Chip? And the musicians? Connor – Mr O'Kane?'

'I think they're all outside.' The boy looked from his father
to Saul, who was standing in the corner, then gave a half nod,
and went back out towards the main corridor.

Saul knew that Aiden's words had been intended for reassurance, because the flames had a firm hold of one entire side
of the curtains. Fitzglen flinched, coughing slightly, flinging
up a hand to shield his face, then squared his shoulders and
went into the box, reaching for the curtains hanging on the
other side, flinging them over the flames that were licking up
in the other corner, and stamping on them.

'Can you help me?' he shouted to Saul. 'It really isn't much
of a blaze, and if we can smother these flames—'

Saul said at once, 'Yes, I will. And the fire brigade will be
here any minute.'

It was easier than he had thought to rip from its hangings
the unscathed swathe of curtain, and seem to be helping Aiden
to smother the flames. It was very easy indeed to suddenly
shout to him that the fire was catching on the edges of the box.

'Over there – look . . .'

Fitzglen was at the edge of the box, and the smoke was
swirling everywhere, here and there shot with flames. As he
turned to look where Saul was pointing, Saul went forward,
his hands outstretched, and pushed with all his strength.

There was a moment when Aiden Fitzglen fought – when
he resisted and tried to save himself – but it was too late. He
was already toppling backwards, over the balcony, down, down
into the auditorium below. He cried out, and the cry spun and
echoed all around the theatre. It broke off abruptly and there
was a crunching, thudding sound. Saul reached the balcony's
edge, and peered over the rail. Supposing Fitzglen had

survived? But of course he had not. He was sprawled across
the seats below, his head at an unnatural angle. Broken neck?
Yes, for sure. Quick and clean and easily done. And no one
had seen what had happened.

Saul went out, coughing and shielding his face as much as
possible from the smoke. All he had to do now was reach the
iron stair and be down it and out into the alley.

He was halfway along when on the rim of his vision he
caught a movement – as if something small had darted through
the smoke and huddled into a corner. Saul's heart lurched with
fear, and despite the danger he stood where he was, trying to
see if anyone was here, the smoke half-blinding him and
making it difficult to make out shapes. He took a few steps
towards where the movement had seemed to be, but he could
not see anything, and if he did not get out now he might be
trapped.

He went quickly to the iron stair, and down into the alley.
The Amaranth people were still there, and it looked as if a
great many passers-by had joined them. They were huddled
in doorways, collars turned up, umbrellas open. A huge,
cumbersome contraption, drawn by two horses, had arrived at
the opening of the alley, and everyone's attention was on it.
No one saw Saul slip out of the stage door.

Men were already running along the alley, brandishing
pipes and uncoiling hoses, and bringing ladders, and Saul
was able to go unobtrusively along Sloat Alley – ostensibly
a solitary passer-by who had taken only the most rudimentary
interest in what was going on. He paused at the intersection
and glanced back, but no one was watching him. He walked
for a considerable distance through the streets before he felt
sufficiently distanced from the theatre to hail a hansom and
return to his hotel.

That night, in the hotel bedroom, he thought he could be
pleased with how he had handled everything. There was
nothing to be concerned about, and he was safe. Wasn't he?
What about that movement he had seen through the smoke?
It had almost certainly been the swirling smoke, but it might
just possibly have been the boy Jack. Had he been hiding –
watching Saul?

But even if Jack Fitzglen had remained in the theatre, and even if he had seen what Saul had done, he could only have seen a shadowy figure – a figure whose face would not have been visible because of the turned-up collar. Even then, he would have had no idea who Saul was or where he came from. He would know nothing about Vallow Hall.

It was two days later, back at Vallow Hall, that Miss Grout read the newspaper reports about the fire to Saul over breakfast.

'A shocking thing. I am not, generally, favourably disposed towards the theatrical profession. My father used to say it was full of rascals and profligates and loose livers. But it's terrible to hear of such an historic building being partly destroyed. They list some of the famous men and women of the theatre who have appeared on its stage – not that I have heard of any of them.' She rustled the pages, and peered more closely at the article over her rimless spectacles. 'It says it happened only a few hours before a memorial concert for the Duke of Clarence. To my mind there have been more than enough memorials to that young man.'

'It's very sad,' said Saul from behind *The Times*, willing the wretched woman to shut up, because he did not want to hear how tragic it was that an old theatre had been so severely damaged, or how venerable the Fitzglen dynasty was thought to be. He dared say it would not take much for the newspapers to start asking whether the fire might have been started deliberately – perhaps with some anti-royalist malice behind it. Nor did he need to know if the newspaper mentioned Aiden's son.

'They even go so far as to speculate whether it was a deliberate attempt to ruin the concert,' said Miss Grout, 'and ask if there might have been any anti-monarchist intention.' She crackled the page, reading down the column. 'Oh, and they say the theatre will be inherited by a boy of twelve – but that trustees within the family will administer it until he's of age.'

SIXTEEN

Gus thought you would not expect fragments of the past to reach you accompanied by the scents of paraffin lamps and the lingering aroma of the Turkish cigarettes which Todworthy Inkling smoked almost incessantly.

It did not matter, though, because in this shop the past was everywhere. Mr Byron said softly, 'Hands from the long ago are reaching out to us, aren't they?' Gus at once nodded in agreement. Mr Byron often used flowery language, but this time he was right – it felt exactly as if invisible hands were trying to pull all three of them – the room and even the entire shop, as well – back into the time when someone had written those yellowing pages.

It was clear that Mr Byron had no intention of leaving Tod alone with the Chauntry document, and Gus did not blame him, because he would not have left Tod alone with it, either. Flog it as soon as look at it, old Inkling would.

As the two of them leaned over the desk, Todworthy setting a horn inkstand and old-fashioned goose-quill pen to hand and a sheaf of notepaper on which to set down his findings, Gus got up.

'Tod, I'll take a look round your shelves while you work on this, if you don't mind.'

'What? Oh, certainly, dear boy.' Tod waved a vague hand, indicating that Gus was to make himself free of the entire premises, and Mr Byron dived forward to rescue the inkpot which was in danger of being swept off the edge of the desk by Tod's gesture.

Gus was thankful to be out of the fug of paraffin and cigarettes, although he would have liked to hear what Tod made of the strange manuscript. Probably, though, it would take a long time to decipher it – always supposing it could be deciphered – and then there would be a haggling session as to what Mr Byron was going to pay him. The entire day might go by before Gus knew anything.

It was a very good opportunity to look for more copies of old theatre magazines – in particular, ones that might contain more of that strange old song, 'The Lament of the Luck-filled Vessel'.

> Fortune's gone a-begging, and the luck's gone out
>   the door
> And the fences are a-cheering and the King ain't
>   safe no more
> For rum-dubbers picked the locks when no one
>   was around
> And they'll all be at the Tuck-up Fair/If the
>   Talisman don't return.

Mr Rudraige and Miss Daphnis had said the chalice was supposed to have been stolen in the early 1890s, and the scrap of playbill Gus had found in this shop had been dated 1893, which fitted.

Even though he had known Inkling's shop since he was quite small – since those days when he would come here in the hope of earning a penny or two which would buy a meat pie for the family's supper – it still held surprises. He might stumble across a room he did not recall seeing before – a room that had shelves or tables piled high with books and maps and old engravings. Or there might be a flight of steps going down to a room below street level where you had to fumble to light a candle to see your way.

It always looked as if the things in the shop had been crammed on to the shelves at random, but Gus knew it was really quite orderly. Rooms had their own particular subjects – the room he was in now was almost entirely given over to theatrical books and papers. Memorabilia it was called – Gus had heard both Mr Jack and Mr Byron use the word.

Here were the shelves where he had found the playbill, and he thought there might be a few new acquisitions since his last visit. People brought things in to sell – perhaps somebody had died and they were clearing out rooms, or perhaps they had found things in attics that they thought might be worth some money. Tod took almost everything that was offered him.

As Gus worked through the faded pages, the sense that he was touching a wholly different part of the past folded around him. It was not the past Mr Byron and Tod were trying to reach through the old manuscript; this was the past of a very particular section of London theatres. Rickety stages in underground clubs that had been called cellar clubs – the old lime cones that once had lit up stages. Bill the Chip and Mr Rudraige sometimes talked reminiscently about limelight – how it had given a bright but somehow mellow light of its own, and how a performer could move in and out of it as the character or the play or the song required.

In these pages, some of them with blurred sketch illustrations, was the very essence of those days. Gus turned pages carefully. From beyond the shop he could hear, very faintly, the ordinary, familiar street sounds. Voices, the rumble of cabs and omnibuses. But those sounds seemed to belong to another world, and he was scarcely aware of the shop and the clutter and the gas jets burning gradually lower.

It was a shock to suddenly hear Mr Byron saying, 'I should have known you'd be in here, Gus. Come back into Tod's room. We've deciphered most of the manuscript – which is to say Tod has – although there are a few pages left. Come and hear it all.'

Gus thrust the magazine he had been reading in the deep pocket of his coat, and followed Mr Byron. The manuscript was on Tod's desk, and next to it were several pages covered with Mr Byron's writing.

'What I'd like to do,' began Mr Byron, 'is to . . . Angels and ministers of grace defend me!'

'What is it?' said Gus, as Mr Byron went to stand at the door and peered through the small glass pane.

'Over there. Standing by those bookshelves.'

'I can't see . . .' And then Gus did see. A slender figure, wrapped in a stylish coat with a high turned-up fur collar, the whole outfit finished with a small hat that had a saucy little veil partly covering the face.

Mr Byron said, softly, 'As I live and die – Viola Gilfillan.' He glanced at Tod. 'Do Gilfillans often come in here, Tod?'

'It has been known,' said Tod, inspecting the figure over the top of his spectacles. 'But it's something of a coincidence to see the lady here on the same day that you've brought that manuscript. Is she keeping an eye on you, do you suppose – at least, not on you personally, but on the family in general?'

Mr Byron said, 'They do try to find out what we're doing. But I'd have to admit that we do the same with them.' A bit unwillingly, he said, 'Viola was in The Punchbowl the other night, and my Uncle Rudraige was talking at full pelt after the third glass. She might have heard something – you can't stop Rudraige once he gets going.' He watched Viola as she bent to examine some of the magazines Gus had left on a chair.

'I don't think the Gilfillans actually know for sure what we do off-stage,' he said, after a moment. 'Well, I don't think anyone outside the family does, or we'd all have been in the clink long since. But it's always been thought that they know more than we'd like. Uncle Rudraige was very chummy with old Furnival Gilfillan in their giddy youth. And if they've heard whispers that we've got a filch planned, and that it's a very big filch indeed, they might be trying to catch us out.'

Viola Gilfillan had taken two magazines from the pile, and was walking across to the small untidy desk where one of Tod's underlings sat. She handed over some coins, put the magazines in her bag, and strolled across to the street door. It might have been pure coincidence that she looked into Tod's room as she did so, but Gus did not think it was coincidence that caused her to wink at Byron very saucily, and put up a hand in a kind of mock-salute, before stepping out into the street.

'She's up to something,' said Byron, watching her make an unhurried way along the street. 'But it's no use me going after her and trying to find out what she's plotting – if she's plotting anything. She's clever, that one. She doesn't give away her family's secrets.'

Tod, his eyes on the manuscript on the desk, said in an absent voice, 'Of course, she might give them away to Mr

Jack.' He looked up, regarding Gus and Byron over the tops of his spectacles.

Mr Byron glanced at Gus, and then said, noncommittally, 'So she might.'

Todworthy smiled, then with an air of a man addressing a serious matter, said, 'I suggest you read out your notes, Mr Byron, and I'll compare it to the manuscript as you go along.'

'That way we can make sure I've understood it,' agreed Mr Byron. 'Gus, we've had to make a number of guesses at a great many of the words and expressions, and I've tried to put it in reasonably modern language. But I think between us we've got a fair sense of what was originally written. We both think you should hear the findings so far. You're as much a part of this as any of us.'

This pleased Gus so much he could only mumble something about finding it all very interesting and being glad to help.

'I'll be writing to Jack later today,' said Mr Byron. 'Sending the transcript.'

'Make a copy of whatever you send,' advised Tod. 'A tedious task, copying, I know, so if you should want me to undertake it for you—'

'I expect I can manage,' said Mr Byron, and half-winked at Gus, who knew, of course, that old Inkling made a charge for copying anything and everything if he could.

'And do warn him about Miss Viola, won't you? He'll want to know about that, I daresay.'

'Oh yes,' said Mr Byron, softly, 'he'll want to know.'

'Good. Now, Gus, you'll take a drop of malmsey, won't you?' said Tod. 'Nonsense, good wine can be drunk at any time of the day, and it's mid-afternoon already.'

Gus noticed Mr Byron had the slightly flushed, bright-eyed look of someone who has already had several glasses. Whatever else you might say about old Inkling, he was always generous when it came to dispensing wine; the trouble was that you did not always want quite that much generosity, not in the middle of the afternoon, and especially not when you were preparing to listen to the writings of someone who had lived hundreds of years ago. The date on the top of the first page had read

1483. That meant someone had sat at a table or a desk, and had written these words in the year 1483 . . .

But when Mr Byron began to read, it was not in the least what Gus had been expecting.

Tonight my brother and I are going to become thieves. It was Richard who had the idea – he says it will be an adventure. He has not had many adventures in his nine years, so I think he can be forgiven. I have not had many adventures either, so I hope I can be forgiven, as well. I do not count coming to this place, Ludlow Castle, as an adventure, because it is a vast gloomy place, full of echoes and darknesses.

Since we came here, we have both had nightmares, but we have not told anyone for fear of seeming weak. The nightmares we have are almost exactly the same, though: they are about being shut away in dark stone rooms far below the ground. Sometimes there are sounds of people moaning and of chains clanking within them.

Richard has confessed to me that he often tries to stay awake, because of the nightmares waiting for him. The adventure we are going to have will show him he is brave and able to fight nightmares off, though, so I think it is a good idea.

We are at Ludlow Castle to study and learn. I am doing my best, but Richard says books and learning are boring, and none of it will be of any use when we are grown up. He gives poor Master Godfric a terrible time – he often hides when it is the lesson hour, and Master Godfric has to go scurrying back and forth in search of him. It can take hours, even though I help and often some of the servants join the search, but by the time Richard is found it is usually past the hour, which is what he intends, of course.

We do not like this place, although Richard makes up stories and rude songs about the King who built it – William of Normandy. William the Conqueror people call him now. He made dungeons here – we have not been into them, but we know they are there. William did not call them dungeons; he called them *donjon* on account of him being French. Richard says it would have been better if William had stayed at home in France anyway, and not come marauding over here with his armies.

When I am King, which I think might be quite soon, I shall not maraud into other countries and turn them upside down, and pillage and rape. I am not entirely sure what rape means. I am not really sure what pillage means, either, so I shall ask Master Godfric, because he knows about words and language and history, which he learned when he was a monk. He is clever and kind and he knows interesting things. We like him very much.

Tonight is the night of our stealing adventure. It will be after everyone is in bed. If we can steal something and hide it without anyone catching us or finding out what we have done, we shall have proved that we are brave, and do not need to be frightened of the nightmares. If I have got to be the King I do not think I ought to have nightmares.

Later, we shall light a candle each, then creep out of our rooms. Richard thinks, and I agree, that we should go to the tapestry room. It has wall hangings all around, showing battles and people storming castles and galloping to wars on horseback waving swords. Our ancestors fought in some of those pictures in the tapestries. They fought against the French quite a lot – at Agincourt and Harfleur, when Henry V led his men into battle. Master Godfric has told us about the battles, and about Henry V and people like Harry Hotspur who fought the Scots, and has shown us the tapestries, and it is all quite exciting.

There are a great many small objects in that room, so we can choose something to steal.

It is not quite dawn, but it is nearly so, and there is light coming through the window of my room.

We are not in our beds, because Richard says we should write down what we have done. By this, he means I should write it down. When I have done so I will hide the pages. It will be a good thing to have an account of tonight. When we are much older, perhaps as much as thirty years of age, we can read it and remember that it was the night we became brave.

There were huge shadows as we tiptoed out of our rooms and went through the castle. I kept looking over my shoulder, because I could easily believe that one of the shadows would suddenly rear up and reach out long arms or clawed hands, and scoop us up and carry us off. I know of course that shadows are not real people, but that was how it felt.

There were whisperings, too.

'The wind in the chimneys,' I said at one point, but Richard said, very softly, 'Are you sure?'

I was not sure, really, and I am not sure now, but it was better to believe that than to believe the shadows were whispering and watching – even to think they were saying we were going to do a bad thing – stealing was a sin – and we would be thrown into prison.

There were no whisperings in the tapestry room, though. We set down our candles and went cautiously around. There were cupboards and shelves, with carved figures and bowls. Some were beautiful and some looked very old and some were too big for us to take.

Except for one thing.

It was on the end of a ledge, almost as if it had been given a place of its own. I think it is what is called a chalice – it might have been used as a communion cup for Mass. It is quite big, and made of coloured glass like the windows in some churches.

'And so,' said Byron Fitzglen, setting down his notes for a moment, 'there it is – the second theft of the chalice. And this time it was stolen by two princes who were already doomed.' He glanced at Gus. 'You understand who those two boys were?'

'The Princes in the Tower. The murdered boys.'

'Yes. The writer was the boy who would have been Edward V. And so,' said Byron, 'for the second time in its history the chalice had fallen into the wrong hands as the result of a theft.'

He frowned at his notes, then said, 'It doesn't sound as if this theft at Ludlow Castle was ever discovered – although there was so much unrest and threats of rebellion and usurping of the throne going on at that time, I should think half the contents of the place could have been loaded on to carts in broad daylight and nobody would have bothered. A missing communion chalice certainly wouldn't have been noticed. But two things are grabbing me by the throat.'

Gus said, 'Edward writing down his plans for when he's king – how he won't go off to war, but his brother will?'

'Yes. And,' said Mr Byron, 'the nightmares he describes. Darkness – images they had of being shut away in a dank cell. It's horribly prophetic, isn't it?'

Tod said, 'It's never been known what happened to those princes, of course, but they were certainly taken to the Tower of London by scheming, ambitious men who wanted to keep young Edward off the throne. It's generally accepted that he and Richard never came out of the Tower alive.'

Gus found it immeasurably tragic that the boy who had written about being king and describing the tapestries showing battles, and who had clearly been trying to protect his younger brother, was destined to die. But he said, 'What's the rest of the document, Mr Byron? Is it still written by the boys?'

'No. It's written by the man Edward refers to as a former monk and who tutored them.'

'And who had to search for Richard when he ran away to avoid lessons,' said Gus eagerly. Then, slightly defensively, he said, 'It makes them somehow real to hear that, doesn't it? Those boys. Children still run away to escape school today.'

'That monk,' said Mr Byron, 'is almost certainly the scholarly gentleman referred to in some of the sources I explored about the princes. They all referred to him just as some kind of librarian or under chaplain, who was "much given to recording his work". They all say his name was never discovered. Except that we've discovered it now. Godfric.'

'And,' said Tod, 'it's Godfric who wrote the main part of this document.'

'The one who set down the year he began writing,' added Byron. 'In 1483.'

SEVENTEEN

It is the year of 1483, by the grace of God, although I have to record that it is also by the grace of the usurper, Richard III.

Having read that sentence, I see it is something that would have been better left unwritten – I should likely be put to death for treason were anyone to read it. But I shall not scratch it out, for I cannot see him as anything other than an outright usurper. It is all very well for people to say the throne was offered to Richard by the citizens of London. So it was. But Richard accepted it very eagerly indeed. He did so within days – *days!* – and he was crowned at Westminster Abbey before a further ten days had passed.

As for the two boys I have in my care, perhaps I could be persuaded Richard did not play a major part in their imprisonment. I will never believe, though, that he did not know they were brought here.

So I shall let that first sentence stay, although I shall not put my name to this document. I know this could be classed as cowardly – I should be prepared to speak out for my beliefs, but I dare not. They say Richard Plantagenet is a temperate man with many good qualities, but I do not think his temperance or good qualities are likely to extend to a former monk calling him a usurper and questioning his right to the throne. I would rather be a coward than face being convicted of treason, and end in being hanged, drawn and quartered on Tower Green.

While I am in this place, I am going to set down events as they unfold around me. Even if the Tower guards should chance on these pages it will not matter, for of course I am writing in Latin, as we all did at the monastery. I cannot think any of the guards would be able to read and

understand Latin script. I cannot think that most of them
are able to read at all, in fact. No one is likely to find this
document until after my death, when I shall long since
have gone to my just reward (or punishment), and by then
it will not matter what I said about Richard Plantagenet.

I shall keep these pages behind my small stack of
books in this room. I was allowed to bring the books
with me, because it makes it look as if I am continuing
to tutor the two boys. Indeed, I shall endeavour to do so.
It may help to distract their minds from the fear I see in
their eyes. They are right to be fearful; I cannot believe
Richard Plantagenet's supporters will allow them to live.
Their claim on the throne is too close.

This morning I went along to the boys' rooms, as usual.
I should be accustomed to this place by now – we have
been here since the month of May – but I am not. I am
increasingly aware of a sensation of dread – almost as
if I am moving (or even being dragged) closer to some
vast tragedy. Several times while walking through the
passages I have felt actually sick, so much so I have had
to pause and take deep breaths before going on. The air
in here does not help quell sickness, in fact it feels like
breathing in the stench of death itself. Thankfully the
stink has not actually made me sick yet, which would
be undignified and humiliating, especially if the guards
were around – as well as the splattering mess it would
make on the floor, although the floors of these passages
bear evidence to the spillage of just about every bodily
fluid known to man, so I should not think a few drops
more would be noticed.

I constantly try to believe that the boys will not be
here for long. At the start, the men in power said it was,
'A ceremonial stay, in preparation for King Edward's
coronation. An old tradition.' They smiled when they said
this, in the smooth oily way of all liars.

It is a story only a fool would believe. There will never
be a coronation for young Edward. But I cannot believe
that any of the people who pushed the boys' uncle into

power would kill two innocent children. I cannot believe that the recent group of conspirators rumoured to be plotting to replace Richard of York with the greedily ambitious Welshman, Henry Tudor, would do so either. And yet today's Plantagenet monarch may well be tomorrow's Pretender, and little as I trust Richard, I trust that upstart Henry Tudor even less.

There are torch flares in places along the stone passages, but they often flicker out because of the damp, so that you have to feel your way along the walls. The stench of the River is ever present – it's a murky slimy old waterway, the Thames. My footsteps echo and I sometimes wonder if they are my own footsteps, or whether they might be the steps of the murdered souls who have perished in here. However, this morning I had donned light, very soft shoes – velvet, and embroidered with my initials by a lady. It would be ungallant to set down her name, but wearing the shoes recalls to me the memories of her – especially the memory of a long-ago afternoon beneath a willow tree, watching the sunlight reflect on the surface of a river . . .

This morning Edward seemed preoccupied, and presently he said, 'Master Godfric – am I allowed to make confession to you?'

I thought for a moment, then I said, 'It's an interesting point, sire.'

(I have always been careful to call both these boys 'sire', for to me they still command that form of address.)

'Once,' I said, 'I was a man of God – not empowered to give absolution, but perhaps able to guide and advise.'

Edward looked at his brother, then said, 'There is something we want to tell you – something we did just before we were brought here.'

Young Richard, seated quietly in his usual place, nodded with a solemnity he does not often display. 'We were bad,' he said. 'We committed a bad act.'

I waited, then Edward said, 'It was when we were at Ludlow Castle. We wanted to have an adventure.'

'We wanted to show the nightmares we were not feared

of them,' said Richard, and my heart constricted, for they are so young, so vulnerable.

'We stole something,' said Edward, his face white and set. 'We crept through the castle when everyone was asleep, and we took something from the tapestry room.'

'It was an act of bravery,' said Richard, hopefully. 'Because it was frightening to walk through those rooms in the middle of the night.'

'I am sure it was.' My mind was starting to churn with apprehension. The tapestry room, I thought. Dear God, what was it they took?

'We brought it here with us,' Edward was saying. 'We had hidden it in a chest in our rooms at the castle – and they let us bring the chest in here with us. It had clothes and some books.'

'And the story we wrote about what we did that night,' added Richard.

Edward had gone to the small box in a corner of the room, in which reposed their few belongings, and was kneeling down to open it.

'This is the confession,' he said, handing me a single sheet of parchment with his writing on it. 'This tells what we did. We wrote it in Latin, as you taught us, Master Godfric.'

'We don't know if the Latin is as good as you would like, but we did our best,' put in Richard, hopefully.

This last remark affected me more than I dared let them see, so I only nodded, took the paper, and slid it inside one of my own books, where it would not be noticed by the guards. I would read it later, but already I knew that whatever the level of the Latin they had managed, this would be one more keepsake, one more memory to cherish of these boys. Please God I won't need keepsakes, though.

'This is what we brought out of the castle with us,' said Edward, unfolding a velvet cloak.

And there it was. Vivid and glowing and beautiful beyond imagining. The communion chalice stolen by Richard II from an Essex monastery, almost a century earlier. A theft that few people knew of – but a theft that I, and every monk who entered that monastery, vowed to keep secret.

I am one of the monks who took the vow and I shall keep it, save for in the privacy of these pages. But I believe I can write here how the pitifully few possessions salvaged after Richard's death were taken to Ludlow Castle – that symbol of Yorkist authority – for safekeeping.

And how I, lured by the rumours that the chalice was within those ancient stone walls, intrigued to get the post of tutor to Edward and his young brother.

I will be honest. My motives were not entirely pure. I wanted to be the monk who restored the stolen Plantagenet chalice to the Essex monastery. I would still like to be.

However, I am huddled in a dank stone chamber in a vast Norman stronghold that was built over four centuries ago. I am writing by the light of a single candle, which drips sour-smelling grease on the floor, and wrapped in a blanket to keep out the seeping cold.

I cannot possibly take the chalice back to that monastery where once I lived a devout, studious life. I could no more take from those doomed princes the one beautiful object they have – the one thing that represents to them their small act of bravery and defiance – than I could sign a pact with the Devil to practise the Dark Arts.

There is a sense of furtive excitement within this part of the Tower.

Earlier, I went along to break my fast with my charges, as usual. I could not help seeing how the guards were gathering in little groups, their eyes watchful. Furtive is not a word I ever expected I would use to describe those men – they are hulking brutes with not the smallest shred of compassion or humanity in them. Today, though, they are furtive. I gave them good morning, and went on my way.

But I believe something is about to happen.

I am writing by the light of a single candle, and night has fallen. All around me this grim prison house is filling up with murmurings and echoes and stealthy footsteps. Shadowy figures whisk past my door.

I am waiting for the Watch to come along as he does every night, for I believe I have conceived a plan. It is very simple – perhaps the best plans are. It may fail. I may be caught and then I really will end in facing that grisly death on Tower Hill. I shall risk it, though.

As I wait, I am thinking that Time is a trickster, a cheat. First it drags with limping slowness so that I think the night will never pass, then it gallops apace, and panic overwhelms me because the hour is almost here and I am not ready.

But at last I hear him coming, the Watch, his slow, deliberate footsteps ringing out on the stone floors. He takes his time about his rounds – he likes to imbue his task with importance. It is probably all he has to do anyway.

Now he has gone past, snuffling and wheezing – he has walked those shadowy passages for so many years that the cold and the damp have affected his breathing.

I shall fold these pages into their hiding place with the boys' sad, brave confession, and then I shall go out into the darkness. I do not know if I shall return to write any more. That is in God's hands.

A thin dawn light is trickling into my room, and my hand is shaking so badly that I do not know how I am writing this. But somehow I must chronicle what I have done, even if the discovery of this document eventually results in my execution.

After the Watch had gone past my door I peered out, and saw his thick, squat figure illuminated by the flame of his candle going away. I waited until he had turned the corner then I went out.

There was no real need for me to keep out of sight – I am not a captive and there was no reason why I should not take a midnight walk. But if I were seen it might be remembered later. I had put on the embroidered slippers – once more there came the faint far-off comfort in remembering the lady who had fashioned them for me. I even tried to pretend that I could feel her hand taking mine, as if she was walking alongside me. I do not think that was an absurd thought to have; she would have understood, and she would have urged me to take all the risks if there was a chance of saving the princes. I had the thought that there would come a day when I would tell her about this, and she would listen with that absorbed attention that is so much part of her. There was strength and reassurance in that.

I had no candle, but threads of moonlight came from the narrow windows. They look out on to a small courtyard, where no one ever goes – one more of the many strange and lonely places in here.

I was grateful for the moonlight, but at the foot of the two short flights of stone steps leading to the boys' rooms, darkness came at me like a thick, stifling cloak. Even though I knew the way, several times I half stumbled on the uneven flagstones and had to put out a hand to the wall to keep my balance. The walls are cold and moisture lies on them – moisture that you hope is only where rain has trickled in or damp has soaked through the ancient walls, but that you are afraid might be human exudences. People sweat from fear in this place. They bleed from the injuries inflicted on them by the guards – they lose control of other body fluids in their terror.

The snatches of conversation I had heard earlier – the fragmented phrases that initially I had tried to ignore – were clawing their way to the surface of my mind.

'*It is to be at once . . . The order has come, as we knew it must . . .*'

'*How will it be done?*'

'*Best not to know . . . But they will not be seen or heard of again . . .*'

'*And then they will be wiped from history . . .*'

Oh, no they will not, I thought. They shall have their place in history, these boys.

I went quickly to their rooms. They share sleeping quarters, which I have always been glad of, for it gives them companionship and comfort. The key to the rooms hangs on a massive iron hook outside – it is not overly trustful of the guards to leave it there, because it makes it easy for them – also myself – to go in and out. In any case there are a great many locked doors and guarded gates between these rooms and the outer walls.

As I reached up to the key I had the sense of reaching for something far more massive than just a key – of carrying out an act that could have immense consequences.

They were clearly alarmed to see me at such a late hour, although I did not think they had been asleep. If the sounds and furtive footsteps had not kept them awake, their own fears would certainly have done so.

They sat up in their beds, tousled and wide-eyed, heart-breakingly young and vulnerable.

I said, in as down-to-earth a voice as I could manage, 'Sires – we must leave these rooms at once – your safety is at stake. But I think there might be a way of enabling you to escape. It will be dangerous and it may not be successful, though.'

I waited, and saw them exchange questioning looks. Then Edward gave a half nod, and they both reached for their robes.

With relief, I said, 'Thank you for trusting me. Can you look on this as another adventure – as something that will have a good ending?'

'Yes,' said Edward, without hesitation.

'Good. We must be soft and silent and watchful, and you must do everything I tell you.'

Once out of their rooms, both boys looked nervously about them, and my heart constricted with pity at seeing how fearful their captivity had made them. But I locked the door and hung the key on its hook, then I took their hands and, with them on each side of me, I led them along the dim passages. It called for more courage than I can describe; it felt as if the stored-up terrors of this place were gathering their strengths to use against us.

There are a great many complicated corners and little

flights of steps and unexpected corners and ramparts in William of Normandy's Tower. To some extent the layout has been sketched on maps, of course, and I had been fortunate enough to find two very detailed maps within the store of books I had brought with me. I had studied them, although I had had the eerie feeling that there would always be sections of this place that would never yield their secrets to map-makers – that there would always be hidden stairways or enclosed courtyards that the Tower would keep to itself.

I had committed to memory the way we must go, and we descended several flights of stone steps where the walls closed around us and the ceiling was so low I had to bend my head. But it was not as dark as I feared, for there were arrow slits in the thick walls, allowing light in.

We were within sight of our destination now. It was delineated on the maps as one of the oldest parts – the wing built more than two hundred years earlier by Edward I. Perhaps in later years it will come to be known by a different name, but my map calls it the Well Tower. A margin note stated it had been created to protect the then-new river frontage and how its architect had caused it to have four water shafts running down to an underground well from which fresh water could be drawn.

But if I had understood correctly – and if that map could be trusted – two of those water shafts had fallen into disuse. They had been allowed to dry out. And one, if not both of them, had a tunnel at the very bottom for workmen. Those tunnels came out beyond the Tower walls.

But as we went towards the door leading to the Well Tower there was a flurry of sound and shouts nearby – shouts of anger, mingled with rapped-out commands.

'Call out the Tower Watch! The boys have vanished!'

And then came the sound that struck terror and panic into me. The clang of a single bell, deep and discordant. It reverberated through those ancient walls, and I knew

what it was at once. The bell normally used to signal the
curfew – the time of day when prisoners permitted the
liberty of the Tower must return to their quarters. But it
was chiming with a thudding urgency – a rhythm that
signalled to the guards to turn out with no delay, because
something was wrong.

We began to run towards the Well Tower, but already
there were the sounds of guards ahead of us. I pulled the
boys back along the passage, but again there were the
heavy footsteps and the shouts.

'Dear God,' I said. 'We are trapped.'

Then Edward said, 'No – along here – this narrow
opening . . .'

'Where does it lead?' I said, but I was already following
him, and it did not matter where it led if it meant we
could hide.

It would have been easy to miss the narrow opening,
but Edward had not missed it, and he and Richard went
through it at once. I followed, glancing frantically over
my shoulder, praying the guards did not appear.

The narrow passage turned sharply to the left, and in
front of us was a low, wide door, pointed at the top, and
with a stone surround.

Edward grasped the thick iron handle – I expected the
door to be locked, but it was not. It opened on to a series
of rooms linked by low stone archways. Memories and
echoes clustered in the rooms, but they were not echoes
of terror or pain, as in so many of the other parts of the
Tower; these were lingering memories of hope – of plans
for battles that would surely lead to victory – of riding
out to war behind a trusted leader, brandishing swords
and bows, each man wearing splendid armour, tabours
beating the call to arms, pennants bearing the colours of
the king fluttering in the breeze.

It did not need Edward's soft whisper to tell me we
were in the outer armoury of the Tower of London. I
knew it already. Thick shadows lay everywhere, but we
could see the ghost outlines of armour and weaponry
and bows, all stacked against the walls. There were other

things that I could not put name to, let alone guess what their purpose might be. But they were the engines of war, that was clear.

The boys knew what all the objects were, though. As they stared around them, despite the danger threatening them, their eyes shone with excitement. Edward reached out to trace the outline of some fearsome-looking piece of iron and wood, as if it was something he understood, and not for the first time I was aware of these children's ancestry. They had grown up knowing the battles of their forbears – listening to the stories of war and violence and fighting that were their inheritance.

Then Richard turned sharply round. 'The guards,' he said. 'Outside the door.'

Fear sliced through me, for I had heard them as well, and they were so close they must be in the narrow passage beyond the main armoury. We could not go out there – we must remain in here, but we must do so in hiding. But where?

That was when I saw it. The arrow chest. The wide, deep chest with the domed lid. It was fashioned from solid oak, the surface scarred with age, the whole bound with thick iron strips. It was very large – more than large enough to conceal, for a short time, two children, so that they would be safe from the murderers hunting them down.

I pointed to it, but the boys had already seen it, and they were already opening the lid.

'Quickly,' I said, but they were already climbing inside the chest, and their instinctive understanding tore at my heart all over again. They knew their lives were in danger – they knew they represented a threat to the man who presently occupied England's throne, and they knew there were people who were going to kill them. They did not know the names of those people – I did not know the names either, and I still do not. Perhaps I never will, and perhaps no one ever will.

'I must close the lid,' I said. 'But stay quiet and still, and I promise to come back for you.'

As they crouched inside, and as I reached for the lid,

I said, 'This is another part of the adventure. Hold on to
that thought. Will you do that – Edward – Richard?'

That was the first time I had ever addressed them by
their given names, and it created a closeness.

Edward said, 'Whatever happens, we shall always be
grateful to you.'

I did something then that I had not thought I would
ever do. I knelt and took his hand and kissed it, and then
I did the same with his brother. It was an acknowledge-
ment of who I believed them to be – an admission that
I regarded Edward as the rightful king.

I glanced over my shoulder, expecting the door to be
flung open at any moment, and the guards to pour in.
But the door was still closed, although the men were
stamping around out there. Then I looked back at the
two small figures, and I reached down into my years
inside the monastery and the teachings I had absorbed.
I said, 'Try to keep in your minds an image of the purest
light you can think of. Something bright and glowing –
something that beckons to you and that represents safety.
And then hold on to that light.'

They looked at one another and, as clearly as if it had
been spoken aloud, I heard their shared thought.

It was Edward who spoke. 'The adventure in Ludlow
Castle,' he said.

'The night we took the chalice,' nodded Richard.

'We can keep the chalice in our minds,' said Edward.

I nodded, then when I was sure they were as comfortable
as was possible in the arrow chest, I closed the lid on them.
It made only the faintest creak, and there was a small hinged
catch on the outside. I hesitated, unable to decide if putting
the catch down would attract more attention or less. Then
I thought it would not make any difference either way, and
I left it loose.

It was easier than I had dared hope to slip outside,
and appear to be part of the group of guards in the
passageway. They did not question my presence – they
would think I had heard the bell sounding and had come
out to help.

They entered the armoury – of course they did – and I went in with them. They walked through all of the rooms, shining their lanterns into the corners, and peering into the crevices in the low roof. I prayed silently that they would not open the arrow chest. My prayers were answered – they did not open it, and at last they went out.

But – and this is the thing that is tearing at me as I write – they left three of their number on sentry duty outside the armoury. I went with the main group and again pretended to help with the search.

Four times now I have walked back to the armoury, but each time guards have been there. There is nothing I can do until they leave their posts. At the third visit – with a thin grey dawn breaking outside – I saw the guards were different, so clearly they are being replaced at intervals. It looks as if various places have been designated as permanent guard points, because the men are everywhere, watching and waiting.

As I write this I dare not count the hours that Edward and Richard have been inside that arrow chest.

My years in the monastery have come to my aid a little; I am not ashamed to set down here that I have been on my knees praying that the princes will be safe – that I can get them out of this dreadful place. I must have wearied Heaven with my pleas tonight.

I should not be committing any of this to paper, but I have a compulsion to do so – it is as if I must purge my mind – I will not say my soul – of what has happened, and as if setting it down might do so.

Twilight is again darkening the sky, and still the guards have not left their posts. I have tried several times to distract them, to lure them away from the armoury door, but they are not for distracting, nor are they for luring.

I do not know if the arrow chest can be opened from within, but even if it can, if the boys go outside the armoury, the guards will seize them.

I have to accept that I have failed – that my plan was impossibly hopeful and trustingly simple. I am wracked with guilt, and with the growing conviction that I shall not be able to reach Edward and Richard – that I have sent them to their deaths. In the monastery we were taught that despair – the sin of *accidie* – was one of the greatest of all the sins. That is because it is the abandoning of hope – almost a denial of God's existence. During these hours, though, that sin has claimed me, and I do not think I shall ever be free from the bitter, gnawing remorse.

As I write this, two pictures are vividly with me. One is of the princes themselves, shut away in their dark, cramped arrow chest.

The other picture is of the light-filled image they promised to keep in their minds in the darkness.

The image of the Plantagenet chalice.

Even though several weeks have passed, I still cling to the hope that Edward and Richard could have found a way to escape. I know this is illogical, but I weave stories of how they might have got out – dodging the sentries, and then making their unseen way through the dim passages, until they reached one of the water gates. If they did that there is a chance they might have slipped out.

The pain and the guilt have stayed with me – I see that they are making even the forming of these words erratic and nearly illegible, although that matters nothing, for no one will ever read these pages. There are nights when I wake, drenched in sweat, the images of the lid of the arrow chest closing down over them, the two small trustful faces blotted out of my sight. Perhaps if I knew what had finally befallen them – even if it was the worst fate of all – I might find some kind of peace.

When I was allowed to leave the Tower – my duties there were, after all, at an end – it seemed no one was interested in the few possessions the princes had brought with them. So I took them myself, and no one questioned it. There is very little – a few books, a sketch Edward made of their rooms. A velvet cap studded with seed pearls that Richard used to wear . . .

And the Plantagenet chalice.

It is with me now, standing on a ledge in these modest rooms I have taken in the City. I have placed it where it will catch the morning light, and when darkness begins to descend, I move it as close to the candlelight and the light from my fire as I can. I find I cannot bear it to be shrouded in darkness.

In bringing it out, I had intended to return it to the monastery in Essex. I have not done so, though. I have the absurd idea that by keeping it safe, there might come a day when I will be able to return it to Edward and Richard.

EIGHTEEN

B yron Fitzglen stopped reading, and drank from the wine
glass placed at his hand by Tod Inkling.
Gus was aware of a curious atmosphere in the room.
The oil lamps still burned, and from beyond the shop came the
ordinary, familiar street sounds. Voices, the rumble of cabs
and omnibus. But those sounds seemed to belong to another
world. It was as if the words on these dim pages really had
pulled them into the past.

Finally, Mr Byron said, 'There's a little more of Godfric's
account, Gus. But this is as far as we've got. And Tod, I see
that it's getting late, and I know you keep erratic hours,
but—'

'But,' said Todworthy, 'I am expected at a gathering of
booksellers and antiquarians in an hour's time.' He spread
his hands apologetically. 'A modest assembly,' he said, 'but
it will be convivial, and possibly good for business as well.'
He looked at the manuscript again. 'You could come back
tomorrow,' he said, 'and we could return to the fray. I would
like to know the outcome of this. I should think, in fact,
that a great many people would like to know the outcome.
If it solves the question of what happened to those two
boys . . .'

Mr Byron was reaching for his cloak. He placed the manuscript carefully in the packaging Gus had brought, and put it
and his own notes in the deep side pocket.

'I'll take everything back to my rooms and study it on my
own account,' he said. 'I can come along again in the morning,
though, if that would suit. Gus, too.'

'Indeed, yes.'

'I'm immensely grateful for your help, Tod. Jack and the rest
of the family will be, as well.'

Gus could see from the gleam in Tod Inkling's eye that he
was planning that the gratitude would take the form of some

kind of payment, but neither he nor Mr Byron would mention anything as vulgar as money at this stage.

'Gus,' said Mr Byron, once they were in the street, 'I can't think properly after the deciphering of that manuscript. I'm still more than half in the fifteenth century – in the Tower of London, with Godfric and those two boys. But the half of me that isn't there suspects I'm as drunk as an owl on old Inkling's malmsey, so you'd better keep hold of my arm. While we were working away, the old villain kept refilling the glasses. I didn't dare refuse in case he took umbrage and stopped deciphering. But I began to think I'd have to be wheeled home in a barrow boy's cart, which would have meant I'd be the laughing stock of the entire theatrical profession, and been dubbed Byron the Barrow or something equally revolting, which would have been extremely depressing to one who possesses a poet's soul, and I should have had to go off to the Trappist monastery after all.' He grinned. 'So I'm extremely glad that you're here, and . . . Yes, a hansom is a very good idea, if only we can see one and flag it down . . . Oh, good man.'

Finally at his rooms, he insisted on Gus coming in with him, and he threw his cloak on to a chair, placed the manuscript on a littered desk, then collapsed in the nearest chair.

Gus asked carefully if he might make a pot of black coffee, and Mr Byron said at once that it was a very good idea.

'I always said Jack had a treasure in you.'

When the coffee came, he drank it gratefully, praised its flavour, then sat up a little straighter and thrust his fingers through his already tousled hair.

'I am not yet altogether sober, but I'm already wondering . . .' He frowned, and said, 'Gus, I know this was all intended for the Amaranth's stage, but it's a grim old story we're uncovering. Chalice or no chalice, I'm not sure if it's something you'd want to display on a stage. It's the starkest kind of tragedy, and the Fitzglens don't go in for tragedy as a rule. Well, not unless it's Shakespeare or Webster or Marlowe – or outright melodrama. And whatever the ending of this story turns out to be – assuming we do reach an ending – it certainly doesn't deserve to be treated as melodrama.'

Gus said, fervently, 'I'm very glad indeed to hear you say that, Mr Byron. Those two boys . . .'

Byron glanced at him. 'They got to you, didn't they?' he said. 'Well, I can see they did. They got to me, as well, although how I'll tell Jack and the others that we think the project should be jettisoned . . .' He leaned back in his chair, staring up at the ceiling, then suddenly sat up, and said, 'You brought a magazine out of Inkling's, didn't you? And it's no good trying to look innocent, because I saw it in your hand and you kept a firm hold on it all the time we were in that shop. In fact you put it inside your jacket when Viola Gilfillan was wandering around. What have you found, Augustus Pocket?'

'I did find something,' began Gus. 'I did pay for it,' he added, a bit defensively. 'At the little desk by the door.'

'I'm sure you paid for it. But what is it? Is it something to do with The Quest? Something worth calling up a flourish and a fanfare of trumpets from the orchestra pit, and making an announcement in ringing tones?'

Gus said, 'It's about "The Lament of the Luck-filled Vessel".'

Gus had regretted that Mr Jack had not been at Tod Inkling's shop to hear the astonishing account written by Godfric. Now, preparing to tell Mr Byron about his discovery of more of the 'Lament', he regretted Mr Jack's absence even more.

However, Mr Byron was gratifyingly enthusiastic. He said, 'That sounds excellent, Gus. Pronounce, man. Read it out to me. Speak the speech trippingly.'

Gus hesitated, then said, 'Mr Byron, would you read it out?'

'I'm as soused as a herring,' said Mr Byron, at once. 'I'm likely to lose the place altogether – always supposing I don't fall off this chair halfway through.'

'You sound entirely sober,' said Gus, not altogether truthfully. 'And I'm not much of a hand at reading things out. And you do it beautifully, you really do. Like Mr Jack.'

'Flatterer,' said Mr Byron, but he sounded pleased. 'All

right, then, pour me another cup of coffee, and I'll do my best.'

Gus complied, then opened the magazine at the right page and handed it over.

'It's an account of a performance in one of the old cellar clubs,' he said. 'It was called Clinkers, and this was written in 1892 by somebody called Arthur Withering.'

'It sounds as if Mr Withering was a bit of a dilettante journalist and man-about-supper-clubs,' said Mr Byron, eyeing the pages. He drank some of his coffee, then began to read.

'A very convivial night was spent last evening at the newly opened Clinkers Cellars off Maiden Lane,' Arthur Withering had written.

'Having been sent a cordial invitation to the opening, and knowing how my readers enjoy my accounts of such places and my recommendations for the more congenial of them, I and a few friends repaired there.

'We were promised music, including some newly composed songs, good company and a generous supper. The supper was perhaps not quite as lavish as we were led to expect, but I can recommend the jugged hare.

'The stage was rather small and inclined to creak, and during an act involving some enthusiastic dancing, its supporting joists sagged visibly and quite alarmingly.

'However, the performances were spirited, and after supper a new ballad was announced – "For the first time on any stage" – and was proclaimed with much pride and also a degree of sly jokery. It turned out to be a rather curious and even slightly disconcerting song, clearly referring to the recent rumours of the disappearance of the famous royal Talisman Chalice – whose vanishment, readers will remember, was startlingly discovered around the time of the Victoria & Albert's exhibition plans for the Prince of Wales' birthday celebrations.

'The Chalice has supposedly been in the possession of our royal family for several centuries, and there are so many strange legends and near-myths about it that it's probable no one knows the truth about its origins. One of my companions said, robustly, that he questioned whether such an object even existed, but whoever had written the song performed for us believed it did – and also seemed to have researched quite thoroughly into its history. Either that, or the composer has a very fertile and possibly slightly treasonous imagination.

'I should like to set down the entire lyrics of the song for my readers, but my estimable editor advises me against it.'

'Why would that be?' asked Gus, as Byron turned the page.

'Possibly in case of infringement of copyright. Or it might even be that the editor thought the song was a bit anti-monarchist, and didn't want to offend the throne. This was written in the 1890s, and the King was still a mere Prince of Wales, roistering his way around theatres and supper clubs, getting into all the gossip columns. Victoria didn't like that.'

'Or,' said Gus, dryly, 'Mr Withering was too drunk to write down the entire song.'

'What a realist you are. You could be right, though.'

However, Mr Withering had not only set down a portion of the song, he had given a lively description of the singer as well.

'A gentleman of robust manner and jovial countenance,' he had written. 'There was a whisper in the audience that he had been a crony of the Prince of Wales – during the years when His Majesty had consorted with the ladies and gentlemen of the theatre. But it seems he fell from favour, and could now only get engagements performing in cellar clubs and taverns.'

'That would have been a bit of a come-down for the old boy, whoever he was,' observed Byron. 'Still, Uncle Rudraige sometimes says he was a crony of the Prince of Wales himself in his youth.'

'Mr Rudraige didn't end up singing questionable songs in dubious cellars,' pointed out Gus.

'True, O King.'

'I have set down the first verse and two lines of the second of the song,' went on Mr Withering, 'but those of my readers who go along to Clinkers themselves can hear it in its entirety. The song's title is "The Lament of the Luck-filled Vessel".

> Fortune's gone a-begging, and the luck's gone out
>   the door
> And the fences are a-cheering and the King ain't
>   safe no more
> For rum-dubbers picked the locks when no one
>   was around
> And they'll all be at the Tuck-up Fair/If the
>   Talisman don't return.
> For Yorkist Dick, the first of thieves, did die a
>   dungeon death;
> And after that, in Tower depths,
> Two boys gasped final breaths.

Mr Byron paused, frowning. 'Yorkist Dick,' he said. 'That's got to mean Richard II. And it echoes what we know from the legend. Richard was the first of the thieves and he died a dungeon death. And those next lines about "After that, in Tower depths/Two boys gasped final breaths." You know, without Godfric's journal, I'd have said this whole thing was just a romantic legend, created by people in the Nineties – songs spun from rumours and gossip. But in light of the Chauntry manuscript, I'm not so sure. Whoever wrote that ballad knew quite a bit about the chalice. I wish we knew who that composer was.' He looked at the printed verses of the 'Lament'. 'And those final two lines—'

'I couldn't make any sense of them,' said Gus.

'I don't know that I can.' Mr Byron read them out.

> A concubine then stole the Luck, but met
>   deserv'd fate.
> For Coppernose took grim revenge, and
>   summoned up the blade.

He put down the magazine, and sat in silence for a moment. '"Coppernose took grim revenge." I have a feeling I should know what's meant by that, but I don't. Probably Tod's malmsey's still fogging my brain. But we're making progress, Gus. We're unrolling the chalice's legend, a bit at a time, and when we go back to Tod's tomorrow we'll unroll what's in those final pages.' He frowned. 'But we still haven't found the chalice itself.'

'If anyone can find it, Mr Jack will.'

'Yes, he will. And he'll do it quietly and politely, and with the least upset to anyone. He really is the best there is, you know.'

'I do know.'

'I can't stop wondering how he's getting on at Vallow.'

'Nor can I,' said Gus.

NINETEEN

Saul Vallow felt as if his mind was being torn into jagged fragments. He felt as if he was being smothered by fear. It was all because of Aiden Fitzglen's son. When Saul had seen the young man framed in the wide doorway of Vallow Hall, it had been as if the years had dissolved, and it was Aiden who stood there. It was not, of course – he had quickly come to his senses about that. But it was certainly Aiden's son – there was the tawny hair, the colour of a roe deer's hide – and the dark eyes. This was the boy who would have inherited the theatre from his dead father.

But with the realization of this, anger and resentment welled up in Saul, because had the impudent arrogant creature truly not expected to be recognized? Had he really not thought Saul would see through the disguise – 'Mr Joseph Glennon with his spectacles and that false air of scholarly unworldliness'? Even with his hair combed back and spectacles partly obscuring his eyes, he was unmistakable.

Why had he asked about Bastle House? He could not know anything about it – or could he? His father had known about it – he had witnessed the conveyance – but Aiden had not known what happened in Bastle's grisly underground room. The only two people who were still able to speak about that were Saul himself and Hilda Grout, and Miss Grout liked her comfortable position at Vallow Hall far too much to risk talking about what had happened that night. In any case, if she were to do so, she could be regarded as complicit in a crime – of covering up a murder.

Saul got rid of 'Joseph Glennon' and the manservant who accompanied him as quickly as possible. He was polite but distant – very much the squire of the manor – but once Miss Grout had returned to whatever household duties she was engaged in, he shut himself in his study and watched through the window as the two men walked back down the drive. In his mind was the memory of the boy who had been in the royal box that night – the boy who had looked through the billowing smoke, and heard Saul's voice. And seen Saul himself? He had believed Jack had not seen him – he had kept his hat pulled well down and a scarf over the lower part of his face, but even so it had been a nightmare that had sometimes stalked his dreams.

But the boy had been very young on that day, and even if he had remembered anything he would have sought Saul out long since. But could he have found something that harked back to Bastle House? An old letter – a diary? A solicitor's memorandum referring to the Title Deed? People did find such things – perhaps when clearing out a family house or an attic. If Aiden's son had found something and was curious about the house and his father's part in a royal gift to a lady . . . Supposing he investigated further – even tried to get into Bastle House? And found out what lay down there in the cellar . . . New waves of fear washed chokingly over Saul, but he fought them back, and shut himself in his study to consider how to deal with this threat – for threat it undoubtedly was.

Then it came to him that Fitzglen's interest in Bastle House might be used. Supposing a letter were to be sent, suggesting the place might be available to buy? It seemed likely that Fitzglen would accept such an invitation – he would want to keep up the story he had spun about being here to purchase a house.

A carefully composed letter sent today to 'Joseph Glennon', discreetly posted in the postbox at the end of Candle Lane, should reach him at the Mercian Arms early tomorrow morning. The post service was reliable, and there would be sufficient time for an appointment for the same afternoon to be kept. Saul smiled, and reached for his writing things.

After Jack had seen Gus on to the train, he had found it difficult to concentrate on anything. He ought to be searching for the chalice. Trying to get into Vallow Hall, said his mind. Or even Bastle House?

He did not expect to hear anything for at least two days, but as he was finishing breakfast the following morning, Mrs

Gurning presented him with a letter. The envelope was addressed in an unfamiliar hand – Jack could only think of Dr Kendal who might use the Glennon name and who knew where he was staying, and he opened it eagerly.

But it was not from Dr Kendal.

My dear Mr Glennon,

Your name has been passed to me by a business acquaintance in Vallow as someone interested in properties that might be for sale in the area.

I have owned a house in Vallow for many years, but have not lived in it for a long time, and I only visit it very infrequently. It is known as Bastle House, and although it is not in a good state of repair, it may be of interest to you to view it.

Fortuitously, I will be in Vallow for a day or so this week to see to various business matters – largely related to the forthcoming Quarter Day – and I could be at Bastle House on Thursday afternoon if you should care to call. I am hopeful that this letter will reach you in time for this to be possible, although I am aware that it may be somewhat short notice.

I presume you are not very familiar with the area, so I should mention that it is difficult to reach the house by any form of transport. However, it can easily be reached on foot from Candle Lane. A short way beyond Vallow Hall is a farm track branching off to the left. I believe it is known as the meadow path, and it leads to an old stile. From there, Bastle House is visible, and it is a short and very pleasant walk past a small copse.

Trusting that this information will be of some interest, I am, sir, very sincerely yours . . .

The signature at the foot was scrawled, but Jack thought it was A.V. Athlone. A Scottish name? It could be; this place was near enough to the border, and Bastle House had been described to him as a former border fortification.

It was fortunate that the letter had arrived early on Thursday morning; it allowed plenty of time for Jack to go out there this afternoon, as Mr Athlone had suggested. It was intriguing, though, to speculate how the gentleman had come to hear of Mr Joseph Glennon's search for a property, but Jack had spoken to a number of people since coming here. His mind went to Saul Vallow, but Vallow had been distant and disinterested – and clearly bent on discouraging any interest in Bastle House.

That left people such as Mrs Gurning, together with the garrulous Ned and Nora Nithercott. There was also Mr Meazle in his Dickensian solicitor's office. Jack could easily see Mr Meazle spotting a possible pecuniary advantage, and sending a suitable message to a client.

It did not matter. What mattered was that he was going to get inside Bastle House – that strange, empty, mysterious old place. Saul Vallow had been dismissive of it, but the place intrigued Jack. Empty houses held secrets. Mr A.V. Athlone might know something about Vallow's history. It could be more grist to the mill, although Jack would admit that the grist he had collected so far was not yet amounting to anything very useful.

It was still only ten o'clock, so he collected his overcoat, and went out into the market square. One or two people nodded to him in friendly recognition, and two of them called out that they hoped he had enjoyed last evening's concert at Chauntry. Jack smiled and said he had enjoyed it very much. It was all very friendly and relaxing, and it was almost a pity he was not really here to seek out properties to buy.

He explored several of the little shops, exchanging a few words with the shopkeepers, picking up various snippets of local gossip, but nothing about Vallow Hall or Saul Vallow. Certainly nothing about Maude.

There was one attractive establishment advertising itself as 'Clockmakers, Repairers of Time-pieces, and Purveyors of Good Silverware since 1825' that Jack spent some time studying. Its window display included some very nice silver candlesticks and an epergne. He considered these with professional interest, but the shop looked like a family concern, and the Fitzglens had standards from which they seldom diverged. Filching from modest, hard-working establishments was considered unkind and unmannerly. Apart from that, it would be mad in the extreme to confuse the present situation by staging a secondary filch while he was here.

Saul found himself constantly watching the clock, counting the hours until he could set off for Bastle House this afternoon. He needed to be there well ahead of Jack Fitzglen, so he partook of an early luncheon, then from the small safe in his study he took the Bastle House keys. It felt curious to hold them – had Maude had the same feeling when the keys were given to her by that profligate young man all those years ago? Had Aiden Fitzglen been with them when that happened? The angry fear welled up again, and with it a burning jealousy. Maude ought not to have had all those things in her life, with Saul not knowing any of them. A lover – moreover a lover who had been heir to the throne – a house conveyed to her – and all of it done in that sly secrecy. Had she enjoyed having those secrets? Had she shared them with Aiden Fitzglen, perhaps?

Waiting until Lily and Miss Grout were out of the way, Saul took candles and matches from a store cupboard and stowed them in a small bag. There would be no lights in Bastle House, and for part of the plan at least he needed to be able to see.

The fifteen years seemed to dissolve as he went along the meadow path, and he could almost have been back in that afternoon when he had lured that grasping bitch Agnes Scroop out here, and had brought Hilda Grout to discover Maude with her body. So damning a sight it had been. Since that day, he had had to make some difficult decisions – decisions from which he dared say many men would have flinched, but he had held firm. He was holding firm to the decision he had made about Jack Fitzglen now, but he was aware of a tremor of apprehension when finally he stood before the old house. He walked around it, mindful of the need to make sure the low-set door from the bastle itself was secure. There was a key on the iron keyring that looked as if it fitted, and the door must certainly be locked.

It was all right, though. The door was locked, and it was as firm and strong a door as Saul could wish. He went back

to the short flight of steps that led up to the door at the house's
front, glanced about him, then unlocked the door and pushed
it open. The scent of age – of old timbers and of dust and
damp – came out.

The room immediately beyond the door was exactly as he
remembered – it was remarkable how vividly that memory
had stayed with him. There were the pieces of furniture, thickly
covered with dust, and the surfaces dull in the shadows. It was
very dark, and Saul managed to open one of the shutters across
the larger of the windows, and then light a couple of the
candles. There were, in fact, candle holders on the big dresser
standing against the wall, which he would use. Jack Fitzglen,
when he arrived – if he did arrive, which Saul thought he
would – would expect to see some slight signs of occupation.
He might be suspicious if Bastle House's owner did not appear
to have provided himself with some light.

Saul lit and set out the candles, listening intently for the
sounds that would herald Fitzglen's arrival. He positioned
the candles in all the downstairs rooms with care, making
sure that they could not be seen by a casual walker through
the meadow, but so that anyone entering the house would
see lights burning in the inner room, and investigate. He
wanted Aiden's son to explore – to follow the candlelight,
and to end in the cellar room itself.

He picked up the heavy, brass-handled poker from the deep
hearth, and went back to the cellar. The candle on the stone
ledge was burning up, casting its light across the floor and
showing up the trapdoor. Saul looked at it. He knew what he
must do, but it did not stop him from remembering what was
still down there.

He wedged the cellar door open, and placed the brass poker
just behind it. Then he knelt at the edge of the trapdoor – the
lid of the bastle itself – and grasped the thick black bar to lift
it. At first it resisted, but finally it gave a creaking shudder
and moved slightly. Saul recoiled – it had almost felt as if
something under the trapdoor was trying to push it open from
beneath. The memory of Agnes Scroop as he had seen her
that day – her hands imploringly thrust upwards, her lips
stretched in that silent scream – came to him, and he had to

take several deep breaths before he could take hold of the iron bar again.

But he had definitely succeeded in moving it – he could feel that it was lifting, and a dark rim was showing around the edges. A sour, dank stench breathed up from the darkness – as if a tomb had been unsealed. Saul wished he had not thought about tombs, but he reminded himself that he had been prepared for the stench. It was not as bad as he had feared, anyway.

The trapdoor suddenly came up all the way, and crashed down on to the floor with a sound that reverberated through the house. Saul recoiled, his hands instinctively clapped over his ears, but looking towards the open door leading back up to the main rooms. If Jack Fitzglen arrived now, the entire plan might go awry.

But the echoes were already dying away, and there were no footsteps and no enquiring voice calling out. Saul forced himself to look into the yawning blackness. No need to hold up the light, no need to look for what he knew to be lying down there. It was the rungs in the wall he needed to deal with – the iron rungs that he had not known existed last time, and that Agnes Scroop had tried to use to get out. There they were, rusting away from the wall, several of them broken away altogether. Saul reached for the heavy poker, and by dint of wedging it between the rungs and the wall was able to lever off the four topmost rungs. They fell clattering into the darkness. Good. No one could climb up now and reach the underside of the trap.

He went back into the main room. The main door was as he had left it – partly ajar, so that he would see anyone approaching the house. He did not think he would have to wait long – if Fitzglen was coming, he would be here quite soon. Saul was glad about that, because he was disliking this room – this entire house – very much. Despite the candles and the partly open door, a darkness clung everywhere. He was not a man to be made uneasy by a few shadows, but he began to feel as if he was being watched. This was ridiculous. And there was a glint of brightness in here after all – a patch of brilliance that owed nothing to the candles. For a moment he could not see where it came from, then he realized it was an engraved glass bowl – or was it a chalice? It stood on the oak settle, and although a film of dust lay over it, its brightness showed through.

Saul, briefly curious, went across to examine it, taking it between his hands, turning it around slowly to study it. He supposed most people would regard it as a beautiful object, and he would admit that the engravings were finely and delicately worked. He had no idea what they were intended to portray, although he suspected that several were Eastern and probably outright pagan. He stared at the bowl. It was absurd to imagine it stared back – that the flickering light from the candles turned its brilliance into a single eye that watched and that *knew* . . .

Wherever it had come from, it was an odd thing to find in a deserted border fortification. That ridiculous Title Deed had not referred to Bastle's contents or any furniture, and it had certainly not referred to an engraved glass bowl, glowingly coloured rather in the manner of a stained-glass window in a church. That being so, there was no reason why Saul could not take it back to Vallow Hall with him. If it remained here, it would simply collect even more dust, and spiders would spin webs around it. Also, it might be quite valuable. He could get it valued in Alnwick; there were several good jewellers' establishments, and he could let it be thought he was the rightful owner – perhaps say it had come to light while an attic was being cleared out. With this in mind he placed it in the small bag in which he had carried the candles and the tinder box, and set the bag by the door.

TWENTY

After an early lunch at the Mercian Arms, Jack spent half an hour reading the local paper. He was annoyed to realize he kept glancing at the time – that he was counting the hours until he could set off for Bastle House. Probably it would not contain anything at all, and Mr A.V. Athlone would not know anything in the least helpful.

At a quarter to two o'clock he felt it would be a reasonable time to set off. He thought it would allow about twenty minutes to reach the house, and to get there shortly after two o'clock ought to fit with Mr Athlone's idea of 'afternoon'.

He enjoyed the walk along Candle Lane. He slowed his steps as he went past Vallow Hall, looking through the iron gates. He could just see the house beyond the trees surrounding it. The afternoon sunlight lay across it, lending it a faint radiance it had not possessed on his earlier visit. Then, under a lowering grey sky, it had been the sombre near-gothic mansion of the darker kind of fiction, but today it might almost be the remote fairytale house at the heart of one of the old legends. *With a captured heroine inside, held fast by some spell?* asked Jack's mind sarcastically, and he went on to the farm track.

The stile was there as described, and the meadow path. It would be absurd to imagine Bastle House was watching his approach – it was simply the narrow windows, like vertical eyes, that gave that impression.

The door at the centre was partly open, so clearly Mr Athlone was here, and had left the door open for his visitor.

He went up the steps, glancing up at the old walls, wondering briefly what stories they might be able to tell of battles and border raids, and reached for the heavy door knocker. It fell dully on the weather-beaten oak, and died away. Jack waited, but there was no response. Still, the door was open, which seemed welcoming, so after a moment, he pushed it a little wider, and stepped inside.

A candle was burning on an oak dresser, and he called out. 'Hello? Mr Athlone? I'm Joseph Glennon. I had your letter – I hope this is a convenient time.'

His voice echoed hollowly, and Jack began to feel very slightly apprehensive. But perhaps Mr Athlone was upstairs – or in one of the rooms at the rear of the house. Perhaps he was elderly and a bit deaf. But the feeling of apprehension was increasing. *There's something wrong about all this*, he thought.

But he glanced into a room on the left of the huge old chimney breast, and found it empty. What about the door on the right? He pushed it cautiously open, and saw that a light was burning at the farthest end. He called out again, and this time thought there was a scrape of sound. He looked about him. *For a weapon in case you have to defend yourself?* his mind asked a bit jeeringly. No, of course he was not looking for a weapon. He was not liking this, though. He would look into this room, and if no one was around, he would leave, and Bastle House – Mr Athlone, too – could keep whatever secrets might be in here. Yes, but supposing there was something here that would lead him to the chalice?

At the far end of the room was a short flight of steps, leading down. The light seemed to be coming from the foot of the steps. Jack considered whether to go down there. Just down the steps, perhaps. He walked warily down into what looked like a kind of lower scullery, cobwebs dripping from the ceiling, everywhere thick with the grime and the dust of years. An old-fashioned bullseye lantern stood near the steps, its flickering light showing up the old stones of the floor. And in the far corner . . .

Jack stopped dead. The light showed up a yawning black square in the floor, with a trapdoor propped up against the wall behind it. An open cellar. He frowned, because this was becoming sinister, if it was not starting to be downright menacing. He turned to go back up the steps, but just then a shadow seemed to step out of a dim corner, and dealt him a hefty blow. Jack cried out, threw up his hands, partly in defence, partly to fight the shadow, then fell dizzily back on to the ground.

He did not quite lose consciousness, but the room spun sickeningly around him for several moments. He fought the dizziness off and looked up to see someone standing over him, a heavy brass candlestick in one hand, raising it, clearly with the intention of dealing a second blow.

Jack rolled out of the way, and managed to half sit up. He said, 'Mr Saul Vallow. Or should I say Mr A.V. Athlone? What the devil is this about?'

Saul was still holding the candlestick, and Jack eyed it warily. Vallow must be a good twenty-five years his senior, and he was quite slightly built. Normally Jack would have felt perfectly confident in dealing with him if a second physical assault came. But that first blow had rendered him dizzy and he was by no means sure if he could overcome Saul if it came to it.

Playing for time, willing the dizziness to recede, he said, 'You're the one who sent me that letter?'

'I am. I posted it very discreetly, making sure no one saw.'

'It was a trap,' said Jack.

'Of course it was. You were just too stupid to realize it. You didn't even recognize the name I used. Athlone. One of the minor titles of the Duke of Clarence. And A for Albert, V for Victor.'

Jack said slowly, 'But what has the Duke of Clarence got to do with this house?'

'He owned it,' said Saul.

'But didn't he die years ago?' Keep him talking, said Jack's mind. Get him off guard, and you can probably spring at him, and get away. But the conversation with Declan Kendal was vividly with him. Declan had said the Duke of Clarence had given the Talisman Chalice to Maude. And on one of the photographs Jack had found of her, she had been holding a legal-looking document. The Deeds to this house? Had the Duke not just given Maude the chalice, but also this house?

He moved cautiously, hoping he could bound forward and knock Vallow off balance, but the man was still gripping the candlestick. Jack eyed it uneasily.

'You really have been very trusting and naïve, Mr Glennon,'

he was saying. 'Or shall we dispense with the childish tricks
and disguises, and shall I simply call you Mr Fitzglen?'

'You know who I am?' said Jack, staring at him.

'Of course I do. You're Aiden's son.'

Jack started to say something, then stopped, because the
old childhood memory was starting to force its way upwards
– the memory that had lain in the darkest recesses of his
mind, and that he had never allowed into the light. But now
it was scalding its way into his mind, gradually taking dreadful
shape.

Saul said softly, 'You're remembering, aren't you? Or did
you know all along?'

'Know . . .?'

'That day in the theatre.'

With the words, it was as if the memory finally thrust its
way into a bright spotlight, and Jack said, in a half-whisper,
'You're the man who murdered my father fifteen years ago. I
saw you do it. But I've never dared to remember. Until now.'

Saul said, 'Do you know, I thought it was why you were
here. That you were hunting me down, because you'd found
out the part your father played in the conveyancing of this
house? It doesn't matter, though, because I can't let you go
now – not now you've recognized me. You do realize that?'

He said this as if it was all perfectly reasonable, and Jack
stared at him, still not entirely understanding, but trying to
decide if he dare leap upwards. But he was still unsure of
himself after the blow to his head, and he saw it was too late,
because Vallow had already crossed the short space between
them, the hand that held the candlestick raised. Jack recoiled
instinctively, and the blow, when it came, fell short, missing
his head but crunching down on his shoulder. Pain ripped
through him, and he cried out, then felt Saul thrusting his
hands out and pushing him straight at the open cellar. Jack,
reeling from the second blow, still dizzy from the first, strug-
gled to fight back, but felt himself fall into a deep whirling
blackness.

There was a sickening thud, and pain everywhere. Above
him he saw Saul Vallow's face framed in the opening, and
then he heard the man speaking.

'I had to get rid of you, Jack Fitzglen,' he was saying in a
dreadful whispering gloating tone. 'I couldn't risk you prying
and snooping – finding out about the past. I couldn't risk you
asking questions about this house, either – finding out about
the meddlesome bitch I killed to shut her up. She's down there
with you – where no one will find either of you. You're both
down there in the dark for ever.'

As if from a massive distance, Jack heard a scraping,
clanging sound, then the faint light from above shut off.
Darkness, complete and smothering, closed down.

Saul had been shocked to hear his own voice whispering like
that into the darkness of the cellar. It was almost as if something had seized his mind, and spoken through him, without
his control. But he thought he was entitled to feel triumphant
at the way his plan had worked – at the way all of his plans
had worked over the years.

When finally he slammed the bastle lid into place, the sound
reverberated through the whole house, and he stood there for
some minutes, looking down at the outline of the trapdoor.
There was no sound from below, of course. Jack Fitzglen could
not have survived that fall, but if by some remote chance he
had, he would not last very long. He would certainly not be
able to get out. The cellar had been designed to trap and hold
enemies who had come rampaging over the border; once they
were in there they could not get out – not through the trapdoor
into the house and not through the outer door that opened on
to the fields. There had not been a key to that door on the
heavy iron ring, but Saul had tried it himself earlier, and it
was locked as firmly as anyone could wish. It was a thick,
heavy door, and it would take an army to batter it down. As
for the trapdoor in this room, it was heavy and solid, and
certainly immoveable from beneath. But to make sure, he
dragged the scrubbed-top table across the ground, setting it
immediately on top of the trapdoor. It took considerable effort,
and he was out of breath when he had finished, but it was
worth it.

He picked up the candle from the low shelf and the bullseye
lantern, and went back up to the main room. There, he snuffed

all the other candles, and closed the shutter of the window that he had left slightly open. If anyone did make a cursory search for the missing Joseph Glennon, the longer it was before attention focused on Bastle House, the better. But people often stayed in pubs and hotels and vanished without paying their reckoning. Mr Glennon would be put down as being one more of these deceiving gentlemen, and people would tell one another they would not have thought it of him, but you could never tell.

There was the manservant who had been with him, of course – Saul considered this, but could not believe the servant would have been very much in Fitzglen's confidence. And even if the man started prying or asking questions, Saul would easily deal with him. In any case, nobody would take much notice of a servant prying around or asking questions.

Last of all, he picked up the small bag in which he had placed the engraved glass chalice earlier. He was rather pleased at having made the decision to take it back to Vallow Hall.

Walking back along the meadow path and on to Candle Lane, he was feeling safer than he had felt for a very long time.

There was no reason why anyone would connect the vanished Joseph Glennon with Saul Vallow of Vallow Hall. It was a pity he had not been able to look in Fitzglen's pockets for the letter he had so carefully composed and so secretly posted, but it would have meant climbing down into the bastle, and Saul was certainly not going to do that. The letter might have been left behind at the Mercian Arms, anyway, but even if it did come to light there was nothing to link it to Saul.

But he wished he had not let that strange whispering voice take him over.

'*I had to kill you, Jack Fitzglen,*' the voice had said. '*I couldn't risk you prying and snooping – finding out about the meddlesome bitch I killed to shut her up. She's down there with you – where no one will find either of you. You're both down there in the dark for ever.*'

It had been as if something in his mind had slipped, and as

if he had been taken over by some entity he had not known existed and that he could not control.

It could not matter, though. Jack Fitzglen was dead, and even if he were not yet, he could not escape to tell anyone. Saul was perfectly safe.

TWENTY-ONE

G us had hardly slept, and even when he did manage to sink into brief sleep, his dreams were peopled with the two young boys who were in the old manuscript – one who should have been crowned as King of England, and both of whom had been shut away in the Tower of London. In the dreams, their faces were dreadfully clear – Gus felt he would have known them if he had met them in the street, and that he would have gone up to speak to them. Towards dawn he dreamed that he was able to lift the lid of the old arrow chest – the lid that had been slammed down – and get them out.

How must Godfric have felt knowing what he had done? How would it feel to know you had left two young boys shut away in the dark, helpless, and at the mercy of men who were intent on murdering them? It was a dark and tragic story, and even though Pedlar's Yard had not taken much notice of history, Gus thought the tale of the Princes in the Tower was known to most people. It was woven into England's history, like a dark bloodied strand in the weft, and it was a piece of history that had come down to the present. Like the way that Henry VIII and his habit of chopping off people's heads – including those of a couple of his wives – had come down to the present.

He hoped Mr Byron would still say it was not a story that could be staged, and he tried to think whether Mr Jack would agree with him. Surely he would. He might seem frivolous and flippant, but he felt things very deeply. Not many people understood that. The unexpected thought that Viola Gilfillan might understand flickered across his mind. He would tell Mr Jack about her being at Inkling's yesterday, of course; Mr Jack would pretend not to find it interesting, but Gus knew he would not miss a single detail.

It felt strange to be returning to Inkling's, and to enter Tod's private room and see Mr Byron already there, the manuscript set out on the table, several sheets of notepaper covered with his writing. Last night they had laid aside the threads of this story, he thought, but this morning they were picking them up again.

Mr Byron was leafing through his notes, and saying something about having been able to read parts of the final pages.

'Have you indeed?'

'Yes, but only small sections.' Mr Byron spread his hands. 'After all that malmsey, sleep refused to help knit up the ravelled sleeve of care, so in the end I arose from my bed and sat down at my desk and plunged into the past. I kept in mind the principles you used yesterday, Tod, and applied them. As a result, I think I've found out a little more about what became of Godfric.' He looked at Tod and then at Gus. 'If I've understood correctly,' he said, 'Godfric was recommended to a post in a Norfolk household – a household whose members were to become very well known indeed to history.' He paused, as if waiting for a comment, and when none came, said, 'Godfric received a letter from a lady – he writes how she told him that although she had heard what she calls "many strange stories", she will only ever "believe the best" of him. Then there's mention of her having heard that a librarian is needed – she knows of it from a young relative. And,' said Byron, 'she asks him if he still wears the embroidered slippers.' He grinned. 'You may call me a shocking romantic—'

'I shouldn't dream of being so disagreeable.'

'—but I was rather pleased to find the lady was still in his life,' finished Byron. 'And I do think I've understood those sections more or less accurately. Can you see these lines here, Tod – and those just beneath . . .?'

Gus, seeing them both leaning over the desk, already absorbed in the document, asked, a bit hesitantly, whether he should go along to the nearby coffee shop to fetch a jug of coffee.

'What a very good idea,' said Mr Byron, immediately handing over some coins. That was like Mr Byron – he was extravagant and careless, but he was also thoughtful. As he went out, Mr Byron said, 'Tod, I think this post of librarian was at Blickling Hall.'

The name meant nothing to Gus, but there was no doubt about old Inkling's reaction. He said, very sharply, 'Blickling? But that was . . . My God, are you sure?'

'No, I'm not. That's why I want you to go through this with me.'

The coffee house was busy, and it was some while before Gus returned. When he did so, Mr Byron was writing at a furious rate and Tod was still studying the manuscript. He looked up, and said, 'Gus, you're timely come. We think we've reached the end, and a remarkable end it is.'

'Godfric wrote this over a number of years,' said Mr Byron, leaning back in his chair and easing his neck and shoulder muscles. 'We knew that already, of course, because of the dates – 1483 to 1526. But there are long gaps – often probably of several years – when he must have set the journal aside. We're calling it a journal for want of a better word, by the way,' he said, accepting the coffee Gus handed him. 'Whatever we call it, none of it is at all what I expected.'

'I don't think anyone could have expected any of it,' said Tod. 'But you read it all out as we've set it down, and I'll check the manuscript as we go. As we did before. Gus, you sit by the door, will you, so you can keep an eye on the shop?'

'In case of any more lurking Gilfillans,' said Mr Byron, with a grin, then began to read what Godfric had written.

I had not thought to find other work easily. Gossip and rumour were rife, and I thought anyone associated with the two princes would be a pariah – certainly not someone to employ or take into a private household.

But I am in Norfolk, and it is quiet and pleasant after the turmoil of the last months. The nightmares and the guilt will always be with me, but perhaps in this new place among new people, they will be easier to bear.

There is, too, pleasure for me in the presence of my lady's young relative – Esther – who recommended me for this post. I do not see her very often, but through her I send and receive messages to and from my love. That is the first time I have written that down, and I shall write it again, for the pleasure of seeing the words. My love.

The family here are relative newcomers to wealth and position, and there are whispers amongst the servants that they have their eye on court appointments. This is not my concern, though. Most of my day is spent in the library – cataloguing neglected books, and discovering old papers and arranging for them to be properly bound.

I have a bedchamber on the second floor. I had intended to keep my mementos of the princes locked away – this is a staunchly Tudor household, so I must be wary – but recently I took the chalice out, and set it in the bay window in my room. My room overlooks rolling lawns, and the chalice catches the late-afternoon light. Sometimes I think it glows with an inner life of its own as the sun sets.

I do not think it will attract any particular attention. None of the Boleyn family are likely to be interested in such an object.

'Boleyn,' said Byron, glancing up, and Gus thought that just as that earlier reference to Blickling had dropped into the room, so, now, did this name. But Mr Byron only said, 'There's another of the breaks at this point. Godfric was probably immersed in his work, and lived quietly and uneventfully for a number of years, with little or nothing worth recording. Or other pages might have existed, but have since been lost. Tod has consulted reference books, and although these entries aren't dated, he thinks the manuscript skips about fifteen years, and that this next part would have been written around 1500.'

'How old would Godfric have been by then?' asked Gus.

'That's an interesting question,' said Tod. 'Godfric sounds fairly young in the Tower pages. He mentions being in a monastery for ten years, so if we assume he was fifteen or sixteen when he entered, that could make him twenty-six or -seven when he was with the princes.'

'Born around the late 1450s,' suggested Byron.

'Yes. So he'd be – let me think – maybe in his late forties in 1500 when he wrote this next entry.' He beamed at Gus.

'A nice point to raise,' he said. 'It gives us a better idea of Godfric,' and he continued to read.

I had not thought to take up this journal again. These past years at Blickling Hall have been quiet and I have enjoyed my work and been left to pursue it.

But today was the marriage ceremony and feast to mark the wedding of young Thomas Boleyn to the Lady Elizabeth Howard. It was a splendid occasion, with much merriment and entertainment – worthy of chronicling.

They say Thomas and his new lady are already eyeing what will soon be their inheritance – old Sir William is not thought likely to last much longer. Then it will be Hever Castle for Thomas and his Elizabeth. It sounds very imposing and grand. I hope to be taken with them, for there will certainly be a library or book rooms at such a splendid place.

Tonight, there was ribaldry among the servants, and the health of the newlywed couple was drunk several times – along with a toast wishing vigour and upstanding passion to the bridegroom, although Thomas is considered a lusty enough young gentleman who will have no difficulty in standing-to. As for the Lady Elizabeth, the general view is that she has the look of one who will shake the sheets with enthusiasm.

The talk in the kitchens is that Elizabeth Howard – Elizabeth Boleyn as she now is – will have a fearsome ambition for any children that might be born – even aiming as high as the royal princes for any daughters she may have. For a Boleyn to join with a Tudor prince would be looking very high indeed. I doubt it is likely to ever happen.

In case anyone ever does read these pages, I will set down that I do not listen to kitchen gossip myself. Not often, anyway.

I found these pages earlier today – I had secreted them at the bottom of my box, which contains my few possessions. They came with me from Blickling Hall all those years

ago, and have resided in my room at Hever Castle ever
since. It is a beautiful place, and I have lived quietly, and
worked contentedly in its library. I realize with some
surprise that I have been with the Boleyn family for a
great many years – thirty-five is it? It must be.

When Sir Thomas Boleyn's servants travel to London
for any reason, I do not fail to engage their services to
deliver letters to my lady in her city house. It has been
a very quiet love between us, and we have rarely been
able to meet, but it is abiding and no less deep for that,
and our exchanges of letters are a source of great pleasure
to us both.

But always with me is the guilt and the knowledge of
betrayal left by that long-ago night inside the Tower of
London armoury. I no longer hope that one day I will
find out the truth about Edward and Richard, just as I no
longer pretend to myself that I shall one day be able to
return the Plantagenet chalice to them.

The Plantagenet chalice . . .

And now I come to the real reason for taking up my
pen again . . .

It is a remarkable thing how an object can remain in the
same place for a very long time, and then suddenly catch
the eye of an acquisitive young lady.

I have watched the two daughters and the son of this
household grow up. They have not been part of my life
very much, of course, for they have all spent time
abroad. But it's clear even from the gentle confines of
Hever's book rooms that Mary Boleyn is a frivolous
young thing, much drawn to the company of gentlemen.
Young George is a good deal at the Court, and known
to be very active with the ladies – 'Maidens I did
deflower, and my appetite was all women to devour',
as the satirical verse goes, and it might have been
written about him.

As for the younger girl . . . How can I describe Mistress
Anne Boleyn? She is not beautiful or even pretty, and yet
there is something about her – some quality – that makes

a man look at her a second time and then a third. I could write that she has a face to sack cities for, and perhaps it is. I know that is an astonishing statement for a former monk to make. But I would also have to write that it is not a face you would want to take into your bed. It is, though, a face that you might find you have taken into your dreams without realizing it – but then to find that those dreams are dark and disturbing . . .

On a practical note, she is strong-minded, with the avaricious streak of the Boleyns. If once she sees a thing that attracts her, she cannot rest until she gets it. And the first time she saw the chalice, she wanted it. I knew that at once.

'What a very beautiful piece,' she said, in that odd husky voice that most of the men seem to find so alluring (I am not among them). 'That is a bowl fit for emperors and kings.' She examined it, handling with care – also, I will admit, with respect.

'Clearly, it is very old. Is its history known?'

I considered how best to answer this. I did not want to remind her – or anyone – of my weeks in the Tower with the princes. This lady has already caught the King's eye, and it is said that he is laying siege to her virtue – if, indeed, virtue she still possesses. There is no knowing what use she might make of a chalice that has come down from the Plantagenet Richard and that accompanied his two nephews into the Tower of London. Even now, Henry VIII can be roused to jealous fury by the smallest hint that there might still be traces of the disgraced, deposed Plantagenets in his kingdom. He might have succeeded to his throne amidst cheers and approbation, and his coronation might have been marked by days of celebrations and banquets, but the suggestion of a Plantagenet lurking somewhere sparks in him a fire that all too often leads to the wielding of the axe.

Small wonder, then, that I hesitated to tell the history of the chalice to the lady who is the current object of his desires. While I was hesitating though, the decision was taken from me. She was still cupping the chalice in her hands, and she had taken it over to the latticed window of my room. The vagrant sunlight caught its brilliance, causing it to cast strange crimson and violet shadows across her face. She said, very softly, 'I have heard that Richard II took a very beautiful and very valuable chalice from an Essex monastery. It was described as, "In colour, of violet and magenta – of lapis lazuli blue and gentian and amaranthine purple so that the chalice should echo the Greek term for unfading or immortal".' She turned the chalice around, examining it. 'A description that might fit this.'

I said I suppose it might.

She had recognized the chalice, of course, and she wanted it. Not for herself, but as a gift for a king who was said to be deeply enamoured of her. And yet in that moment I saw something in Anne Boleyn's eyes that made me wonder who was laying siege to whom. I thought: she wants to give him the chalice as a symbol. As a Plantagenet possession that they lost and that can now be placed in the hands of the Tudors.

When, some little time after this conversation, I saw that the chalice had vanished from my room, I knew I was right. Mistress Anne stole the chalice. I do not like her, but I hope it will bring her better fortune than it has brought its owners so far.

'There's another of the breaks there,' said Tod as Byron paused, and reached for his coffee cup. 'And when Godfric resumes, his writing is noticeably different. Not actually weaker, but perhaps the hand of a man older and quieter.'

'Or,' said Mr Byron, 'the writing of a man who suffered a shock so immense that it damaged him for what was left of his life.'

I am deeply thankful, in light of recent events, that I am no longer part of the Boleyn household. I am glad that after so many years, my lady offered her home and her hearth, and that I accepted – and finally and at last we are together in the house overlooking All Hallows Church. Esther is often with us, for her duties in the Boleyn household are much reduced.

As for wider events – I believe it has been said that there is no fall so deep as the fall of those who have risen to high places. The truth of this is apparent now, like the unfurling of some dark pageant. It is known that the Queen – the girl who once was plain Mistress Boleyn, the girl who came to my room in the castle that day and eyed the Plantagenet chalice with avarice – has been taken to the Tower, there to await her execution. All of London – all of England – waits to hear if there will be a reprieve.

There has been no reprieve. I did not expect there to be. The King is vicious and brutal, and where once he loved so violently, now he hates with an even deeper violence. Damning evidence has been brought against the Queen – shocking accusations, some perhaps true, some perhaps with only a speck of truth – and some or perhaps all outright fabrications by her enemies. I do not think anyone can ever be sure of the truth. What is sure, though, is that the Queen will die. I think back to that girl at Hever, and I think she will face her enemies – and at the end her execution – with arrogance and scorn.

Esther is to be one of the ladies who will attend the Queen in the Tower during her final hours. She is reluctant, but she will do it, for she served the Boleyns for many years, and feels she must help perform this last service for them.

The candles are burning low and night has long since closed down on the City.

Esther came to the house earlier today to tell us of the execution. She is deeply distressed.

The execution was played out with all the macabre ceremony that attends such events – although I have never been at an execution, and pray God I never will be. The executioner was a swordsman, brought from France especially. It is said the Queen demanded it, which I find believable. She would be arrogant and imperious to the last, and I admit to an unwilling admiration.

Esther sat as close to the fire as she could, her hands cupped around a bowl of the mulled wine I had prepared, as if to draw its warmth into her hands and into the coldness of her heart.

'The blow was clean and swift and merciful enough,' she said, her eyes shadowed with the memory. 'Those of us who had been in the Boleyn household – some in the Queen's own service – thanked God for it. But afterwards—'

She shivered, and I knelt down to replenish the fire.

'It was afterwards that the horror came,' Esther went on. 'There she lay, the lady who had been England's Queen – who I had served at Hever Castle when she was a girl – her blood soaking into the sawdust, her hair tumbled about what was left of—' She broke off, but then drew a deep breath and continued.

'But we went forward, the other ladies and I, thinking to at least carry her coffin and to give some dignity to her death.'

My lady said, in her gentle voice, 'There is solace in the decent burying of the dead.' She glanced at me as she said this, and I nodded, and took her hand briefly.

'There was no solace,' said Esther. 'For there was no coffin – no arrangements for what should be done after the execution.' She gave an angry shrug. 'People simply walked away, and we were left with – with what lay on the ground in the blood and the mess . . . Not knowing what to do – not knowing what we were expected to do or were allowed to do . . .'

She broke off again, then said, "I did not dare put myself forward – I had been a lowly member of the household. But at last, two of our number went away to see what could be found to give her some kind of burial. The rest of us waited on Tower Green in the warm sunshine – that sunshine felt like a mockery. Presently, our people returned. They had found something within the Tower itself – I believe two of the guards helped them – and they carried it out between them. It was not a coffin, of course, but they said, shame-facedly, that it was the best they could find, and they believed it would suffice.'

A cold horror was starting to take hold of me. I said, 'What was it they carried out to use as a coffin? Esther, *what was it?*'

As if from a distance I heard her next words. 'An arrow chest,' she said. 'They had found it in the old armoury, and they thought it would be deep enough to take . . . what it had to take, and that there would be a dignity in using it.'

I knew what was coming, and I wanted to run from that warm safe room, and not hear any of it. But I had to stay, of course. I had to listen, and Esther's next words have burned into my mind, and I shall never be able to forget them.

'Between us we prised up the lid of the arrow chest,' said Esther. 'It was stiff and it resisted – clearly it had been closed for a very long time. And inside . . .' Again the shiver, and now tears were running down her face.

'They were nothing but small outlines that lay inside,' she said. 'The shapes of two children – just their bones and some scraps of hair and cloth.'

And so there it is. Finally I know what happened to my two ill-starred boys. I know now for certain that they died, and that I caused their deaths. I had no murderous or malicious intent, but there is no comfort in knowing that. I could not even restore the Plantagenet chalice to its rightful owners and I cannot do so now.

Or can I . . .?

Esther has told us that the few possessions the Queen still had are to be taken to Court – probably to Whitehall or perhaps Hampton Court.

'Is the chalice among them?' I asked.

'Yes. I have been asked to help place all the items in some chests and wrap the more fragile ones, and the chalice is there.'

It was then that I know the same thought passed between my lady and myself. That often happens for us – perhaps it happens for others, although I would not know. But we share thoughts, she and I, and we did so then. She spoke first, though.

'Godfric, if the chalice is to be returned to the royal household, could your chronicles of its history be placed with them in some way? Secrecy would be needed, but it would be a sad thing if the chalice's story were never to be known in the future.'

I said, slowly, 'There are parts of those pages I would not want to be read.'

'They could be removed.'

'Yes,' I said, staring at her. 'They could.' I thought for a moment. 'Esther – you said you and some of the other ladies would be wrapping up the Queen's possessions.'

'Yes.'

'Would it be thought strange if the chalice were found to have a box of its own – a box in which it had always been stored?'

She looked at me. 'It would not seem strange,' she said, slowly. 'It would be thought sensible for such a fragile object to be protected. But we do not have such a box.'

'We could have,' I said.

When I left the monastery all those years ago, I did so with a great many different emotions. There was resentment at the years I had wasted on God, but there was also gratitude at having found solace in prayer and music. That is something that has stayed with me.

But in most religious houses it is obligatory to learn a number of skills. I was always regarded as a scholar – the time spent tutoring the princes, and then the years in the Boleyn household bear witness to that. I had, though, acquired a number of more homely abilities during my monastic years. I could cook a reasonable meal; I could till a plot of land and sow seeds; I could even spin cloth (this last not very well). And I could turn my hand to simple carpentry – not to the extent of being able to make a piece of furniture, but I could fashion wooden bowls for the supper table, or shelves for household objects. I could make a small, lidded box . . .

The task had to be completed quickly, and I worked through two nights with very little sleep. I knew the precise size it had to be, for I had held the Plantagenet chalice in my hands many times. The lid was not hinged, for I had no knowledge of how to achieve that. But it was grooved and dovetailed, so that it clamped down on the base smoothly and firmly.

I sanded and polished it to a satin sheen. Then I fashioned, from softened beeswax and resin, a kind of oval plaque to be affixed to the side, and while it was still warm I carved into it the arms of the Essex monastery – the emblem of the prior who had founded the House, and who had come from a noble house. When it had cooled and hardened the outline was clear.

'And you see,' I said, showing the finished article with modest pride to my lady and to Esther, 'if you slide a fingernail into the base on the box's inside . . .'

'Oh! Oh, how clever of you.'

I was pleased at their reaction and I was pleased with my work. I had created a small, secret compartment in the box's base, and into it I shall place these pages. I shall include that sad, brave confession written by the princes, since it is as much part of the chalice's story – and of their own story – as the rest of this.

Esther will put the chalice inside the box, and it will be taken to Henry Tudor's Court, to be stored away with the rest of his valuable jewels and objects. She will do so quietly and unobtrusively, for she is clever and kind. Also, of course, she is a permanent and deeply happy reminder of that long-ago afternoon beneath a willow tree, watching the sunlight reflect on the surface of a river . . . It should have been a shameful act for the professed man of God I was at the time, but I only ever felt pride and love, and I still feel that for my lady – and for my daughter.

The Plantagenets are no longer on England's throne, but the chalice that, to a few of us, bears their name, will be owned by their successors, and for those who look, its story is with it.

I hope, though, that the chalice brings to future generations better fortune than it did to Richard II, to Prince Edward and his brother, and to Anne Boleyn.

TWENTY-TWO

For a long time no one in Todworthy Inkling's room spoke. Gus felt as if the memories were folding themselves back into their shadowy corners, a little regretful at having to retreat, but glad to have had their strange, sad stories brought into the present.

Eventually Tod said, 'That's a remarkable story.'

'How believable is it, Tod? That part about the arrow chest having to be used as a coffin for Anne Boleyn . . .'

'As a matter of fact I've come across that story,' said Tod. 'I think it was in the work of a writer of the last century called Agnes Strickland. She wrote a remarkable series of books called *The Lives of the Queens of England*. As far as I recall it runs to ten or even twelve volumes.' He took off his spectacles and polished them thoughtfully. 'She recounts that anecdote about Anne Boleyn,' he said, replacing the spectacles on his nose. 'I believe she says something about how King Henry showered Mistress Boleyn with riches – jewels, furs, houses – while she was his lady love, but that at the end he could not even bother to provide her with a coffin. But I don't know how much credence can be given to it. It might be one of those rather dark legends that's been passed down. But this . . .' He tapped the manuscript with a fingertip. 'This sounds to be almost a first-hand account. It's grisly and very sad.'

'Very,' said Mr Byron shortly, and Gus heard in his voice that he had banished all thoughts of mounting an Amaranth piece based on the chalice's history. But he suddenly said, 'Gus, that "Lament" you found,' and Gus jumped, because although he had not exactly forgotten about the 'Lament of the Luck-filled Vessel', he had been more taken up with Godfric. 'Have you got it with you?' asked Mr Byron.

'Yes.'

'Lament?' said Tod, looking up. 'What lament?'

'It's something Gus found in a magazine here a while

back. We didn't know if it would add anything to all this, but now that we've deciphered Godfric, one or two things might tie up.'

'You never know what might tie up,' said Tod rather dryly. 'Let's hear it, Gus.'

Gus glanced at Mr Byron, and, receiving a nod, took out the magazine and read the lines.

> Fortune's gone a-begging, and the luck's gone out
>   the door
> And the fences are a-cheering and the King ain't
>   safe no more
> For rum-dubbers picked the locks when no one
>   was around
> And they'll all be at the Tuck-up Fair/If the
>   Talisman don't return.
> For Yorkist Dick, the first of thieves, did die a
>   dungeon death;
> And after that, in Tower depths, two boys gasped
>   final breaths.
> A concubine then stole the Luck, but met
>   deserv'd fate.
> For Coppernose took grim revenge, and
>   summoned up the blade.

Tod said, 'Coppernose is Henry VIII – you did realize that?'

'Oh my goodness, yes of course it is. I knew I ought to recognize it,' said Byron. 'It was one of his nicknames – although not a very friendly one and not as well known as some of the other things he was dubbed.'

'Anne Boleyn was called the Concubine at various times, of course,' said Tod, nodding. 'And Henry's grim revenge was to decapitate her.'

'It looks as if whoever wrote the ballad must have known quite a bit about the story,' said Byron. He stood up and reached for the manuscript. 'Tod, I'm immensely grateful to you for all this,' he said. 'Jack will be, too. I'll write to him today and let him know what we've found.'

'You'll let me know the outcome?'

'Of course.'

Tod walked through the shop with them, which Gus knew to be a considerable compliment, because he did not often escort people to the street door. Not unless he thought they might filch a few choice items on the way out.

What Mr Byron called the Fitzglen elders were summoned to a small meeting that evening, and listened with fascination to the story of the Chauntry manuscript, and Godfric's tale, although Cecily had to reach in her bag for the hartshorn at the thought of the two boys so cruelly done to death.

They congratulated Gus on his findings over the 'Lament', Mr Rudraige saying he had always known Gus was one of the best things that had ever happened to the Fitzglens, Miss Daphnis saying crisply that Gus was entitled to feel very proud of himself, and Mr Ambrose shaking him by the hand. Cecily, recovering from the pathos of the two princes, bestowed an emotional kiss on his cheek.

'But you do see,' said Mr Byron, 'that this isn't going to be something on which we can base a play.'

They did see it, although they were disappointed. Ambrose said rather sadly that he had been researching Richard II in readiness for the dungeon scene, and had already discussed with Bill the Chip how they might construct stone walls.

'I'd have liked to take on Henry VIII for those scenes with Anne Boleyn,' said Rudraige, wistfully. 'I think I could have done it justice, as well.'

'You'd have had to dye your hair,' said Cecily. 'Or wear a wig.'

'I don't approve of wigs,' said Rudraige firmly. 'I remember the night old Furnival Gilfillan's wig fell off while he was playing Shylock. Smack in the middle of his best speech it was, and somebody accidentally kicked it off the edge of the stage and it landed in the lap of the president of the Thespis Club, who was in the front row. Furnival never got over it, although the Gilfillans put a story about that it had been deliberate sabotage.'

'But of course we can't do any kind of chalice piece,' said Ambrose, returning to the subject in hand. 'Even allowing for the current fashion for melodrama, this is – dammit, it's real. It all happened.'

'And,' said Daphnis thoughtfully, 'it happened to the ancestors of our present royal family, and whatever else we do, we don't want to upset anybody.'

'I should think not, indeed.'

'Those poor little boys . . .'

'I wonder who was the saucy old so-and-so who wrote that ballad,' asked Rudraige, as Cecily hunted for the hartshorn again. 'I've been to one or two of those cellar clubs—'

'Strange places you've frequented, Uncle Rudraige.'

'—and some of them had very good quality performers,' said Rudraige. 'Well, we'd better do that French Revolution thing next instead. *The Scarlet Pimpernel*. A lively piece, the *Pimpernel*.'

'If you're thinking of playing Sir Percy Blakeney, Rudraige, I'll tell you now you'd never manage it,' said Daphnis, at once. 'All that sword-fighting and leaping around outside the Bastille. That's Jack's part if it's anybody's. But we couldn't possibly afford to build the Bastille or a guillotine. Bill the Chip would have an apoplexy.'

'Not if we had a revolve he wouldn't.'

'Even with a revolve, how would we cope with all the crowd scenes? You can't stage the French Revolution with three or four extras.'

'We couldn't manage an entire army of revolutionaries, but I should think several of the regulars at The Punchbowl would come along,' said Rudraige, hopefully. 'They'd only need to stand around, shouting things like, "Liberty, Equality and Fraternity", and, "To the lamp-posts with the aristos".'

'Well, we'll wait for Jack's reactions, but for now I suggest we repair to The Punchbowl and drown our sorrows. Byron – Gus, too – deserve a glass or two after all their work.'

But as they walked along Sloat Alley, he suddenly said, 'If Jack manages to find and actually filch the chalice, what the devil are we going to do with it? We couldn't sell it.'

'We could not,' said Ambrose. 'It'd be like trying to sell the Koh-i-Noor.'

'We could keep to the original plan of Daphnis being

given it by an anonymous admirer from her past,' suggested
Byron.

'Yes, and present it to the King quite openly. We ought to
get some kudos out of that.'

'Never mind a reward.'

'I hope it'd be a generous reward,' remarked Rudraige.
'Don't let's forget the dry rot in the Amaranth.' He stood back
as Ambrose pushed the door of The Punchbowl open, surveyed
the room, and said, 'It looks as if there are some of their
mutton pies left. Nonsense, Cecily, they'll do your dyspepsia
a power of good. We'll drink to Jack's success in finding the
chalice.'

'Rudraige, keep your voice down. You don't want half of
London to hear you. I even spy one or two Gilfillans.'

'A fig for all your Gilfillans. May they be booed off every
stage in the land,' said Rudraige in ringing tones, and went
plunging off in the direction of the mutton pies.

TWENTY-THREE

J ack came out of the sick dizziness slowly and painfully.
The darkness was pressing down on him – it was like a
thick, stifling curtain. His head still throbbed, and his
shoulder was hurting furiously from that second vicious blow
Saul Vallow had aimed at him. He was aware of confusion,
but he knew quite well where he was and what had happened.
Saul Vallow had lured him to Bastle House, then had sprung
on him, knocked him half out with a brass candlestick, and
tipped him down into this place.

He thought I knew something about the Deeds of this house,
thought Jack, moving his hands and then his arms experimen-
tally, and wincing from the wrenches of pain. *Something about
my father's name being on them.* He frowned, but could not
make much sense of this. What he could make sense of, though,
was that Saul was the man who had killed Aiden all those
years ago. He had admitted it openly and calmly.

I saw him do it, thought Jack, still lying on the hard stones,
not yet daring to move, fearful of what injuries movement
might reveal. But his mind had gone back to that afternoon
inside the burning theatre, and he could remember the scorching
heat and feel the terror.

He had promised his father that he would go outside, but
he had stayed where he was, too afraid to move. He had seen
into the royal box, and he had seen the man who stepped
forward and pushed Aiden over the balcony's edge.

I was frozen with terror, thought Jack, lying in the dark
cellar of Bastle House, *and I never dared to look the memory
in the face afterwards.* But now he remembered huddling in
a corner, praying not to be found, and how it had only been
when the unknown man finally went down the iron stairway,
banging the stage door to Sloat Alley, that he had been able
to crawl out from his hiding place. He had been gasping and
shaking, half-blinded by tears and smoke, but he had managed

to get down the stairs, and he had never been so grateful to see his Uncle Rudraige and Aunt Daphnis in his life.

Everywhere was in confusion – there was still a search for people who could be trapped in the theatre – there were panic-stricken questions as to who was safe and who might not be. Had anyone seen Bill the Chip? No, it was all right, Bill was just over there. But what about Mr O'Kane? Could the firemen search the upper rooms to be sure? If he was still in there, he might have fallen – knocked himself out – could the firemen look in the main rehearsal room? Jack thought it was curious that out of those tumbling memories – in the midst of this grim situation he had been flung into by Saul Vallow – Connor O'Kane's name should have materialized. He could not remember what had happened – if O'Kane had been found or not. He did not recall any of the family ever mentioning him again.

There was another image within that panic-filled confusion, though. There had been a moment when he had looked towards the alley's opening and seen, framed against the pouring rain and the thickening twilight, the outline of a man walking away – a man whose coat collar was turned up, and who had a scarf wound around his neck, pulled up so that it covered most of his face . . .

He pushed the memories away, and tried to concentrate on getting out of the cellar. It was vital to think that he would get out.

He was aware of the heavy old house above him, and he supposed that deep down he was frightened, and that the fear would soon tip over into outright panic, but it had not done so yet. Was that arrogance, because he could not believe he would not escape? Was it because he could not believe someone would not come to rescue him? But who would do that? Saul Vallow was not likely to succumb to remorse, and in any case he believed Jack to be dead. As for Gus, it could be two or three days before Gus came back to Vallow. The Mercian Arms people might wonder where he was, although they were just as likely to assume he had sneaked off leaving the bill unpaid. Declan Kendal might miss him, though – but again it could be two or three days before Dr Kendal made any enquiries.

Hell's teeth, thought Jack, *I'm not going to die down here. I'm going to get out – I'm going to step on to the Amaranth's stage again – I'm going to find that bloody Talisman Chalice, and there's going to be the most extravagant piece of theatre pageantry London's ever seen! Royalty will be there – Edward himself, and the Queen – and as much of London society as we can pull in. We might even invite the Gilfillans.* This last idea pleased him so much that he at once began to visualize it – the Gilfillans en masse, seated in the stalls, envious but determined not to show it. *Viola?* said his mind. Yes, for sure Viola would be there, her eyes brilliant with curiosity and interest.

On this uplifting image, Jack managed to sit up. The darkness swung dizzily around him, and the pain of his shoulder tore into him, making him gasp. He felt as if every part of his body was bruised and probably bleeding. But as far as he could tell he did not have any broken bones. He thought he had still been dizzy and confused when Saul pushed him into the cellar, and that because of it he had, as was sometimes said of drunken men, 'fallen soft'. Vallow would not care how he had fallen, of course; he would not have cared if the fall had broken Jack's neck, or whether he would lie in the dark until the cold and hunger and thirst finished him off. This thought sent a jab of such anger through Jack that he forced himself to sit up, and then to get, very slowly and cautiously, to his feet. It was difficult to do this in the pitch dark, and he all but fell over, but instinctively threw out a hand to grab something to steady his balance.

His hand sank into soft layers of something he could not identify, and then on a hard cold shape beneath. He let out a cry that echoed through the darkness, and recoiled at once, snatching back his hand and half falling against a section of wall, jarring his damaged shoulder. He scarcely noticed the pain, though, because his mind was reeling. What he had touched – what his fingers had closed around – was dreadfully and unmistakably a human hand.

And then Saul Vallow's words came back to him.

'*I couldn't risk you prying and snooping – finding out about the past. I couldn't risk you asking questions about this house, either – finding out about the meddlesome bitch I killed to shut her up. She's down there with you – where no one will find either of you. You're both down there in the dark for ever.*'

This was a nightmare – it could not be real. Jack could not be trapped in this cellar, with someone whose dead hand he had just clasped.

But it could only be that. Because whoever he had touched had not moved – the fingers had not closed around his or responded in any way. He had not realized he was going to speak, but he heard his voice saying, 'Who's there? Can you hear me? Who are you?'

The blackness seemed to absorb his words, and absolute silence followed. And there was no feeling of any other living presence in here. Jack had stolen into enough darkened rooms to be able to tell if anyone was nearby. His eyes had adjusted slightly by now, and he could just make out blurred outlines, patches where the darkness was denser or where it was not quite so smothering. Was a trickle of light coming in from cracks in the floorboards above? He thought it might be. Whatever it was, it was enough to show him the huddled shape that lay on the ground.

Maude? Was this who Saul had meant when he had referred to a meddlesome bitch? 'I killed her to shut her up,' he had said.

'Please don't be Maude,' said Jack softly, to the dark outline. 'Please let Maude be safe and well – alive, somewhere. But whoever you were, I'm sorry I can't help you now, and I wish you could help me – I know that's selfish, but I do wish it. In any case, there's no way in which you could help me.'

But hope dies hard, and even though it made him feel sick to do it, he bent down, and forced himself to search the dark form, feeling through the folds of cloth, able to identify the remains of long skirts. A woman's body, then. Not Maude, though – please not Maude. He flinched as his hands encountered the hard shapes of bones, and he was aware that it was the maddest thing in the world to be doing this, because there would not be anything that would help him, he knew that . . .

But there *was* something. Within the remnants of the cloth were two items that had not disintegrated. Something the woman must have had in the pocket of her gown.

A tin of old-fashioned matches. And two candles.

It took a good deal of resolve to lift them clear, but Jack managed it. When finally he straightened up he felt remarkably heartened. The matches and candles themselves would not provide an escape route, but they would provide light, and he might see a way out. And the matches were in a tin, so they should have been preserved, which might not have been the case with a card box. The tin probably meant they would not be safety matches, so they ought to ignite on almost any surface. Such as a stone wall inside a cellar?

Moving cautiously, because it would be disastrous to spill the matches over the floor, and probably not be able to find them, Jack felt around until he found a couple of crevices into which a candle could be wedged – one in a section of wall, the other in the floor near to it. Then, taking a deep breath, he struck one of the matches sharply against the stone wall. His first attempt failed, and so did his second, and he was aware of panic, because it was possible the matches were too old or too damp to work.

But at the third attempt the match flared up. Please don't let it die, thought Jack. Please don't let this dank coldness douse it, and let me be able to light the candle.

There was another of the bad moments when he thought the candle was not going to light, but then it caught. Thank you, God. He lit the second candle from it, and wedged both in the crevices. As the candles burned up a little more strongly he turned to look back at what lay on the ground, seeing that it was dried and shrivelled, bones showing through the withered skin, the whole shape very nearly mummified. There were shreds of cloth that clearly had once been a gown, and fragments of leather from shoes or a belt. Wisps of hair, dried and coarse, clung to the skull. The head had fallen forward, and the jaw had dropped in a travesty of a grin.

'Whoever you were,' he said, softly, 'I'll always be grateful to you for providing me with the means to make a light.'

He lifted up one of the candles and held it up to see the

trapdoor. Was there any means of reaching it? It was a fair
way over his head, because the cellar was a deep one, and
there were iron rungs driven into the wall, presumably to
allow people in the house to get down here. Or to allow
anyone already down here to get up? But even by the flickering candlelight he could see that the rungs no longer
extended all the way up to the trapdoor. The top part had
either rusted away or been torn away, so that there was a gap
of perhaps six or seven feet from the final top rung to the
trapdoor. A circus acrobat could not reach it. Not even an
accomplished burglar, used to throwing a silken ladder over
walls and hooking it on windowsills in order to swarm up
sheer surfaces, could reach it.

Jack sat down and considered. Saul Vallow would not have
imprisoned him down here unless he was sure there was no
way of escape, but he could not have allowed for Jack
being able to make a light and examine his prison so thoroughly. The light was uncertain, but it showed up the cellar's
confines. The high ceiling with the rafters and the trapdoor,
and the useless iron rungs. The stone walls and floor, all
ingrained with the grime of many years. But in one section
of those stone walls . . .

In one section was the outline of a low-set door that could
only lead outside.

The shadowy outline of an idea began to form.

It was vital not to hope too much, because the idea was
tenuous, and it was also extremely risky.

Jack was not going to wonder if the low-set door might
only lead to another cellar – it was too substantial for that.
He wedged one of the candles in a fissure nearer the door,
and examined it carefully. On the left was a square of wood,
nailed on to the door's surface, which was very likely a wooden
lock plate. Locks could be picked if they could be reached,
and he had with him the leather wallet containing the lock-
picking tools. 'You never know when you might encounter a
house whose locks it would be useful to open,' his father used
to say, and Jack had always heeded this advice. If a lock was
indeed behind this square of oak, it would be a heavy, very

old-fashioned lock. But Jack had picked heavy, old-fashioned locks with complete success before.

He investigated the miscellaneous debris in the cellar, hoping to find something that could be used as a chisel, but there was nothing. He tilted the candle closer to the door to examine it more closely, scorching a fingertip from the candle in the process, and swearing. His cry echoed eerily in the dim cellar, but the small pain gave him an idea. It would be impossible to burn down the whole of the door – even if he could do so with a couple of candles and a tin of matches it would take a very long time, and he could well set light to the entire cellar, and still be trapped in it. But could he burn off the wooden lock plate? He searched again, this time looking for rags or cloth that would burn fairly easily. He sent a quick look to the shape in the corner, still partly wrapped in the remnants of its clothes. Would they burn? But he could not and would not take the tattered remains of the dead woman's clothes.

That left his own clothes, and his overcoat was thick cashmere. Jack took it off, along with his scarf, and rolled them into a tight bundle. He removed the wallet with the lock-picking tools and set it down near the door. There were leather gloves he could put on to protect his hands – they would probably catch fire, but not as quickly as the woollen coat and the scarf. He pulled the gloves on, grasped the folded coat with one hand, and held the top section of it against the candle. The flame licked at the cloth at once, and as it began to burn, Jack held it against the wooden square. The wood blistered almost immediately, and he moved the flame slowly around the edges. Smoke curled out, and the heat began to work down to the leather gloves, but the wood was blistering more with every minute.

The gloves were starting to become uncomfortable when one side of the wooden square sagged. Jack at once flung the makeshift torch down behind him, and seized the edge, wrenching it free. Please let there be a lock behind it, because if there was not . . .

But there was. It was a massive and very old lock, but he had expected that. He opened the wallet and began to slide the metal hooks into the keyhole, trying several different ones, quickly realizing that the slender, smaller ones were no use, and using instead the larger ones. Twice he glanced behind him to where the wadded overcoat still smouldered in a corner, but although it was creating a good deal of smoke, it was not an actual fire. The thought flickered across his mind that smoke issuing from the house would be a good thing anyway; if it were seen, people would come to douse it. He would let it burn quietly and slowly away, and with any degree of luck the smoke would trickle up through the cellar roof, into the house above, and from there outside. If it looked like by staying within the confines of the cellar and getting out of control, he could stamp it out.

At the fourth attempt there was a click and he felt the hook latch into the mechanism inside the door. *Slowly now*, thought Jack. *Don't rush it. Don't let me lose the connection. Don't let the lock be rusted beyond use.* He applied more pressure, and felt the mechanism spring back.

The door sagged, but it did not move. Jack pushed it as hard as he could, and there was a slow creaking sound, then slowly and reluctantly it gave way and swung a little way open. Jack pushed it wider, and fell thankfully out into the cool fresh air.

He lay for a little while in the field behind Bastle House, aware of his bruises and the pain of his injured shoulder more than he had been while he was opening the door. He realized, as well, that his hands were burned more than he had noticed.

He did not care about any of it. Presently he was able to sit up and then stand. The cold air was already clearing his head. He brushed some of the dust and grime away, and then saw that smoke was still curling upwards as he had hoped; it did not look like the beginnings of a real blaze, but he would have to go in search of someone and get help to quench it. He would have to do something about Saul Vallow as well, although he was not yet sure how he would deal with that.

But with the idea of at least containing the fire to some extent, he pushed the cellar door shut, and then went around the side of the house towards the narrow track that led to the meadow path and Candle Lane. He had only taken a few steps when he saw in the distance a figure climbing over the stile. Even from here he recognized it. Saul Vallow. Returning to Bastle House? To make sure Jack was dead after all? Or to deal with the fire before anyone saw it and came running out? Jack stepped back into the lee of the house's wall, and watched. As he stood there, Saul went up the stone steps at the front of the house, and unlocked the main door. Jack waited for a moment, then followed him.

Saul had returned to Vallow Hall with a sense of having dealt very satisfactorily with Jack Fitzglen.

He threw his overcoat on to the hall table for somebody to deal with, and carried his bag with the candles and the glass chalice into his study.

Seen in the better light of the room the chalice was a remarkable object. Saul had thought he might place it in full view of people here at the Hall – not that people came here these days, but situations could change. But now that he had it here he had a really curious feeling of wanting to keep it away from everyone – of secreting it in a place where no one but Saul himself could see it. For the moment he placed it in a wall cupboard, and closed the door on it. He would decide what to do with it later. He put the Bastle House keys in there with it.

It was a shock when the study door opened abruptly, and Hilda Grout's voice said, 'Have you seen?'

'Seen what?'

'Across the meadows. Bastle House. Look through the windows, for pity's sake. Smoke. The place is on fire.'

Saul turned and looked, and for a moment thought Hilda Grout must be seeing things, for there was nothing out there. And then he did see it. Miss Grout was quite right. Smoke was rising from Bastle House, and that could only mean one thing. There was a fire in the house.

He did not stop to reason or reach for logic. He only thought that Jack Fitzglen had not been dead after all, and that he had somehow started a fire. To escape? To attract attention so that people would go running out there, and get him out? People certainly would go running out there – not especially because anyone would want to save the strange, lonely old place, but because it was instinctive to stop any fire.

And if Fitzglen were rescued – brought out alive – he would tell people that Saul had tried to kill him. The memory of his own voice came to him – that strange voice that had welled up from the depths of his mind – the voice that had whispered and hissed about killing – about having killed a meddlesome bitch – about killing Jack . . .

He had convinced himself that it had not mattered – there had been no one to hear him. But if Jack Fitzglen had got out . . .

Saul snatched the Bastle House keys from the wall cupboard, and, almost pushing Miss Grout out of the way, went plunging across the hall and out of the house. Within minutes he was through the gates, and going along Candle Lane. When he reached the stile, as he clambered over it he could see the smoke spiralling up very clearly indeed. He paused to look about him. He did not think any houses or farms had a direct view of the house, and no one seemed to be around. *It will be all right*, thought Saul. *I can get there and douse the fire before anyone knows. I can make sure that if Fitzglen is still in there, he doesn't get out.*

There was a moment when he hesitated, wondering if it mightn't be better to let the place burn. To let the fire take hold, and destroy what lay inside it? But he could not take the risk. At any moment people might appear. At any moment Jack Fitzglen might be rescued and if he was, he would talk. Of course he would.

The smoke was coming from the rear of the house, but without a key to the door of the bastle Saul could not get in that way. He would have to go through the house. What then? Hadn't there been a half-rusted pump in the scullery? Water probably came from a well somewhere under the house, or even from the town well which served most of Vallow. If the pump still worked, he would be able to douse the fire. The situation might still be retrieved.

He went through to the old scullery, and there, sure enough, was smoke coming up through the trapdoor. It was an eerie sight to see it trickling up and laying across the old stones of the floor, but the pump was there as he had remembered, and providing it still worked, he could douse the fire.

He grasped the handle of the pump and forced it down. It resisted – heaven only knew how long it was since it had been operated – but he exerted all the pressure he could, and at last there was an ominous clanking deep within the bowels of the house. The pump juddered, then water began to spew out – erratically at first, brackish and evil-smelling and streaked with greenish slime – but then in a steadier stream. Saul left the handle open, so that the water would continue to run over the stone floor and down into the cellar. It would soak its way down, but it would be quicker if he opened the trapdoor.

The water was sopping around his shoes, leaving a slick of grease everywhere, but he dragged the table away, and got the door up easily enough. Smoke billowed into his face and he recoiled slightly. As he did so there was a footstep behind him. He spun round at once. Framed in the doorway was the unmistakable figure of the man he had tried to kill. Jack Fitzglen.

Saul gasped, and went to move forward, intending to strike Fitzglen again. His foot skidded on the slimy surface of the stones, and he slipped, losing his balance. There was the sensation of toppling backwards, of striking his head against the edge of the open cellar, and then of falling into a deep blackness.

Jack went towards the open cellar at once. He thought afterwards – when he could think clearly again – that it would be instinctive for almost everyone to go to help a fellow human being. *Even your father's murderer?* asked a small cynical voice in his head. Yes, even then.

He trod cautiously across the wet floor, and peered into the open cellar. The smoke was still billowing out, although the gushing water was quenching it, and through it all he could see Saul Vallow, lying like a broken puppet, his eyes wide and staring. Jack looked at him for several moments, then stepped back from the cellar. After a slight struggle he managed to close the pump. The smoke was dying down, and he thought there was no danger of fire, but he looked in all the rooms to make sure everything was secure. The house had an odd feel to it, although if anyone ever wanted to live in it, it probably could be made comfortable. Providing the dark memory of what lay in the cellar could be erased. Providing the two dead bodies could be quietly brought out and given a dignified burial.

At last he made his way along the meadow path and on to Candle Lane. Reaching the gates of Vallow Hall, he hesitated, unsure whether to go up to the door to tell them what had happened – wondering if it would be the forbidding Miss Grout he would have to speak to – or whether it would be better to do it all through official channels. The village presumably had some kind of police presence or could call someone in. But he was aching and bruised, and even walking the extra distance into the village was going to be a struggle.

He went down the drive and into the deep porch. It was unexpected to see that the door was slightly open, but it was likely that Saul had seen the smoke from Bastle House, and had gone immediately out to it, not troubling about closing doors. Probably not even letting any of his household know.

Jack stepped through the door into the big shadowy hall that he remembered from his earlier visit. No one was around, and he was about to call out to someone – Miss Grout? – when he became aware of sounds far above him. Music – but music so light and fragile he was not sure whether he really was hearing it . . . He stood there, listening, wondering if the experience in Bastle House had affected his mind. Or even – mundane possibility – his hearing. He remembered he had several times thought of Vallow Hall as sending out a siren call to him. Was it that siren call he was now hearing?

And then the common sense side of his mind reasserted itself, because of course this was not spirit music or beckoning sirens. Someone was playing a piano – there was nothing so very curious about that, but the music was coming from the very top of the house. How likely – how practical – was it to have a piano at the very top of a house, three – or would it even be four? – storeys from the ground? Would anyone – especially Saul Vallow or Miss Grout – have a piano dragged up all those stairs when there must be more than enough rooms on the ground floor?

It was at this point that he recognized the music. It was the music he had heard in Chauntry School's Hall – Frédéric Chopin's beautiful and evocative *Fantaisie-Impromptu.* With the recognition came the memory of Declan Kendal's words. '*When we have a concert here I always make sure that the windows on one side of Chauntry are open,*' he had said. And he had added, almost as an aside, something about the slight chance of Maude still being inside this house. '*I have an image of her being able to hear the music and enjoying it . . .*' he had said.

Jack hesitated, then started up the stairs towards the music. It was like following a silver thread to the land of heart's desire. Like picking up Ariadne's ball of twine that would take you safely to wherever you wanted to be.

The main stairs came out on to a wide L-shaped landing, and he paused, looking about him. The music was still overhead, and there must be another flight of stairs . . . He walked into the other part of the *L*, and at once the music was closer. At the far end was a small, second stair, and the music was coming from it. Jack went up the narrow stairs, moving slowly, partly because his bruised muscles were protesting, but also because he did not want to alarm whoever was up here.

He had just reached a small square landing, and he thought he must be immediately under the Hall's roof now, when the music stopped abruptly. In front of him was a door, with a key hanging on a hook to one side. Jack looked at it. He thought: *I don't know what's in there. That door is locked, and a door up here wouldn't be locked except for some very good reason. If I unlock it what might I find?*

But the memory of the gentle beautiful music was still with him, and whoever had been playing it could surely not pose any kind of threat. He realized his hand was already reaching for the key, and then sliding it into the lock. He lifted the latch and opened the door.

There was a movement from within the room – then a slight gasp of surprise. Jack stood in the doorway, his eyes adjusting to the different light up here, seeing the outline of furniture – chairs, tables, curtains at the tiny attic windows . . . And a small piano with music propped up on its stand, with a woman with dark hair seated at it.

She stood up and came towards him. Her eyes were wide and enquiring, and very slightly fearful, and Jack stood absolutely still looking at her. He felt as if the room – this entire house – everything – was blurring and dissolving into a day that had happened fifteen years earlier.

Because it was fifteen years since this woman had sat in the library at Chauntry School, the Talisman Chalice given to her by a royal prince in front of her. Fifteen years since Declan Kendal had taken photographs of her, and at the same time had taken into his mind the image of a gentle sensitive young woman for whom he always left windows open when his pupils performed their music in case she could hear it.

And it was fifteen years since this woman had sent a letter to a man she would never meet and had warned him away from Vallow Hall.

Jack heard his voice say, 'Maude,' and he moved forward into the room and took her hand.

TWENTY-FOUR

Maude had often thought that if it had not been for the music she would very soon have succumbed to the darkness that had surrounded her ever since that day in Bastle House. But the music had been something to cling to – it had almost become a companion.

Aunt Hilda had thought the attic rooms, when finally finished, were very nice indeed.

'And within reason, Maude, you can have other things, of course.'

'A piano?' Maude thought if she could ever lose the haunting memory of Agnes Scroop's dead face – if she could ever come to terms with being a murderess – she might manage to do so through music.

'Oh, that's impossible,' said Aunt Hilda at once. 'And impractical. How could a piano be got all the way up these narrow stairs? You must put that idea out of your mind.'

'I don't mean anything like the one downstairs,' said Maude. 'But a cottage piano could be got up the stairs, couldn't it? You could order it from Alnwick without anyone asking questions. The men from the shop could bring it up here and I'd stay in the bedroom while they do so.' The farthest of the three rooms had been made into a bedroom. Aunt Hilda had even found some chintz curtains that very nearly fitted the windows. 'You wouldn't even hear me playing it,' Maude said. 'Not down in the main part of the house.'

A few days later she said she thought she would write to the Alnwick shop herself, to ask what they had in the way of small cottage pianos. 'Lily could bring writing things up here, and I'm sure she would post the letter for me, too.'

Saul and Aunt Hilda did not like this. Maude knew they had not told Lily and Mrs Cheesely the truth; they had ensured their help – and discretion – with the promise of an annuity for Mrs Cheesely, and arrangements for Lily's child to be placed in St Botolph's, and for Lily to visit regularly. Saul had told them that the mistress had a confusion of the mind – it was very sad, and she must have complete quiet and care until it was all right again. In the meantime no one must know about it, because people could be very unkind about anything to do with the mind.

Lily and Mrs Cheesely had both accepted this without question; they had been sympathetic – Lily especially – and Maude thought they would see a request for a piano as innocent and ordinary. They would wonder why it could not be allowed, and why the master or Miss Grout could not write to Alnwick.

Shortly after Maude's suggestion that she would write to the Alnwick shop herself, a small cottage piano with a green silk front was installed in the largest of the three attic rooms. It had a quiet, gentle tone, and Maude loved the way it seemed to want to become part of the life in the secret rooms.

She did not dare ask Saul or Aunt Hilda to bring the music from the tapestry-lidded box, because she could not risk them finding the Deeds to Bastle House. But after the piano arrived Lily asked if the mistress might like those pieces of paper from the music room – the ones she made her music from. They were all stored away in the tapestry-lidded chest and Lily could easily look them out.

'Yes, I would like them,' said Maude at once. 'But only bring the music, Lily. There might be one or two old papers in the chest, and I don't want them cluttering up these rooms. Leave those where they are, with the lid closed on them.'

'I'll do it now, mum.' Lily hesitated, then said, 'We think, me and Mrs Cheesely, that it's ever so sad that you've got to be up here for a while, but the master explained it all, and Mrs Cheesely, she had a niece who had a time of being a bit strange. But she come through it, and she's right as rain now.'

'Ah,' said Maude. 'Yes, I see.'

'And it'll be nice if you can have your music, won't it?'

It was not just her own music, though – the music she played on the piano with the green silk front – it was the music she heard from Chauntry School that wove strands of light into the bleak darkness of the attics. After a while Maude came to know the times and the patterns of rehearsals, and they became something to look forward to. She could make sure she had her windows open to the widest possible point on those days. It was not always possible to hear – the wind might be in the wrong direction, or it might be pouring with rain, drowning all sounds – but often she was able to hear the boys singing, or the school orchestra. It was easy to visualize Dr Kendal conducting the musicians or playing one of the instruments himself.

Sometimes Lily brought a poster or a handbill from the village about a forthcoming concert at the school, and then Maude would try to find some of the pieces from the bundle of scores Lily had carried up from the music room. If the music was there, which often it was, she would attempt to master it, and she would imagine Declan Kendal standing at her side, explaining how Mozart or Beethoven would have wanted their music to sound. It was remarkable how she could remember his voice so clearly even now. She could remember the voice of his cousin, as well – Connor O'Kane. She often wondered what had happened to Mr O'Kane, but probably he had gone back to his life in the theatre, and was busy and happy and did not give Vallow or Chauntry School or Maude herself a backward glance.

Quite soon after she had moved into the attic rooms, Lily brought a handbill with details of a concert the school would be giving in the forthcoming autumn term.

'To celebrate St Crispin's Day on twenty-fifth October,' said Maude, reading it and nodding. 'I remember Dr Kendal saying they like to mark a religious festival each term.' She studied the handbill. '"Pupils will be performing the St Crispin hymn." I haven't heard of that, but this says it was composed thirty years ago by a choirmaster at St George's Chapel in Windsor.'

'Crispin,' said Lily, reading the handbill with her mistress. 'I never heard that name before. It's nice, ain't it?'

'Yes,' said Maude, softly. 'Yes, it's very nice.'

After Lily had gone, she looked at the handbill about the concert and the St Crispin hymn for a long time.

*　*　*

But if music – her own and Chauntry's – helped Maude to endure the attic rooms, the other thing that helped her do so was entirely different.

Maude had not known, until it began, that giving birth was so painful, and she had clung to Lily, gasping and trying not to panic, because Lily said it was perfectly normal.

'An' at the end of it, mum, you'll have your own little boy or girl.'

'Will I? Are you sure I'm not about to die?'

'Not in a hundred years, you ain't. Most natural thing in the world, childbirth. Just done it myself, remember? You'll be right as rain.'

'Shouldn't I have a doctor . . .?'

'Never no doctors when any of us were born, there weren't,' said Lily. 'Eleven of us there were – my mum gave birth like shelling peas. An' I'm the eldest, so I was there for most of them, and I know what's needed. I told you – you'll be all right. Anyway, time a doctor gets here, it'll all be over anyway, that's right, ain't it, Miss Grout?'

'Quite right,' said Aunt Hilda, who was in the room with them, rather as one who knows it to be her duty, but has no idea what to do.

Lily's small, workworn hand closed around Maude's, and Maude managed to say, 'I'm glad you're here, Lily. I'm sorry your baby had to be taken to St Botolph's, though.'

'Master says I can visit him at Botolph's – once a week I can go, on my day off. He'll give me the money for the train and everything, as well. Ever so good to me he's been.'

Maude managed to say, 'I'm glad you'll be going to see him, Lily.'

'Me, too. He was a bit small, on account of him being earlier than he should have been. What they call a bit pingling. Master says they'll look after him, though.'

Maude started to say something, but the pain wrenched at her again and there was nothing in the world except the need to get through it. But she would do it, because at the end of it there would be something good and real – something to hold on to and something that would give meaning to this half-world she must inhabit. Even if it were Saul's child – she was still not clear about that – she did not care.

The pain reached an unbelievable peak, and a cup of something warm and syrupy and strangely scented was held to her lips.

'To help with the pain,' she heard Aunt Hilda say, and then Lily's voice protesting.

'Ain't right – ain't natural – she's got to stay awake for the birth—'

'The master was most insistent she be given it,' Aunt Hilda interrupted. 'Laudanum is frequently used in childbirth, Lily. Do as you're told. Maude, drink it.'

Maude drank obediently, and it began to pull her back from the pain, into a vague drifting world where nothing mattered any longer. From a distance she was aware of Lily's voice saying not to give way, not to let the laudanum take her.

'Fight it off, mum, the filthy unnatural stuff that it is. Stay with us – it'll soon be over, and you got me here for you when it is.'

Maude was vaguely aware of Aunt Hilda telling Lily to fetch something – towels, was it? Hot water? And of Lily going to the door, but pausing by it, and calling out to her.

'Soon be over, it will. And you'll have the child. You'll have the child, remember.'

She thought Aunt Hilda shut the door after Lily, and as Lily's steps went down the stairs, Maude heard her own voice saying, very faintly, 'Yes, I'll have the child . . .'

But she did not have the child, at all.

When, some immeasurable time later, she came up out of the strange drifting world, Aunt Hilda was sitting on the side of her bed, and saying something about being sorry and sad.

'Deeply sad, my dear Maude, to have to tell you . . .'

She broke off, and Maude, exhausted and still seeing the world through a confused, half-drugged blur, understood dimly that her aunt was at a loss for words, which was strange and unlike Aunt Hilda. Even stranger was that she took Maude's hand.

She said, 'Maude, everything was done that could be done,

but I'm afraid the child didn't . . . It wasn't strong enough to live.'

Maude tried to make sense of these words, then said, 'The baby died? You're telling me it died? But didn't you send for a doctor, or . . .' She stopped, trying to remember, but only able to recall the pain and then the strange, unreal world after she drank the laudanum.

'We did everything possible,' said Aunt Hilda, but by this time Maude was coming sufficiently back to the world to see that her aunt's eyes slid away when she said this. *She's lying*, Maude thought. *She can't look me in the face and say everything possible was done, because it wasn't. They didn't try to get a doctor – I would have remembered it. They let it die – my child – the one thing I was going to live for and see as hope for a return to an ordinary life. And then – was that because it was easy for them to hide a murderer, but it would have been very difficult indeed to hide a child? And if they saw it as a murderer's child . . .*

In a sharper voice, she said, 'Was it a boy or a girl?'

'Maude, it can't matter now. It never lived . . .'

'Was it a boy or a girl?' Maude said again. 'Tell me!'

She waited, and at last, with what seemed to be extreme reluctance, her aunt said, 'It was a boy.'

Saul thought he could be justifiably pleased at the way his plan was working out.

Maude had surprised him once or twice over these months, he would acknowledge that. That insistence on the provision of a piano, for instance – that had indicated a streak of defiance for which he had not bargained. It was a small price to pay, though, and he had agreed to it.

She was secure in those rooms and, even if she did get out, once beyond Vallow's grounds she would be helpless. Indeed, if she were to be found wandering around the lanes it would confirm any rumours about her mental state. Saul could put such rumours out himself, of course, but the timing would have to be prudently judged.

But Maude was unlikely to try to get out. Apart from anything else, Saul had been very careful to plant in her mind the belief that her sojourn in the attic rooms was not indefinite. She would go on believing that one day she could come back to a normal life, and she could be made to believe that for a very long time.

Everything had been neatly dealt with. Lily, the light-minded little slut, had played straight into Saul's hands by getting herself with child. He had been stern with her, but forgiving. He would not ask Miss Grout to dismiss her without a character, he said, although it was what almost any other employer would have done. The child would be placed in a respectable children's home – it would have a good and useful life and be taught a trade. Lily could remain at Vallow Hall – although in return he would ask that she help look after the mistress. But there must be no gossip beyond these walls; that must be understood.

Lily was vociferous in her gratitude and her promises of loyalty, and Saul was satisfied. The brat could go to St Botolph's. He knew one or two of the governing board through his JP work, in fact he had recently been invited to take a seat on the governing board himself. He was not going to accept, though. For one thing it was too far to travel with any regularity, particularly since he needed to be here at the Hall to keep an eye on Maude and to make sure Hilda Grout did not overstep her place. But, more importantly, he did not care for the path that Botolph's seemed to be taking. Some nonsense about an education programme for the children – even the awarding of scholarships where it was thought they might be beneficial. The governors were appointing a new chairman, and it seemed he was very enthusiastic about the idea. The trustees were enthusiastic, too. They said it was the way of the future, and you had to move with the times.

They could move with the times as quickly as they wanted; Saul did not want any part of such new-fangled schemes. Still, the place would do for Lily's brat and it would mean she would feel obligated to Saul. Accordingly, he wrote a careful letter to St Botolph's. A sad case, he explained. A young girl in his household, innocent and trusting, had been taken cruel advantage of without Saul's knowledge until it was too late.

'The girl is local and her family most respectable,' he wrote.

'I should therefore wish to give her the reassurance that the child will have a fair start in life. I would, of course, make some suitable donation to the home, since I appreciate that your means are slender.'

They agreed to take the child. Of course they did. Saul read, with some cynicism the reply sent by the new chairman of the governors.

> . . . most grateful for your kind offer of financial endow-
> ment, which we should receive very gladly. As I believe
> you know, we are committed to providing education,
> and possibly apprenticeships, for as many of our children
> as we can. I have only recently been appointed to my
> post here, so I am not yet familiar with local people. I
> was sorry to hear that you are unable to be a part of St
> Botolph's managing board; your experience as a justice
> of the peace and also your local knowledge would have
> been very valuable. I should like to have met you to
> see if you could not be persuaded to change your deci-
> sion, and also, of course, to thank you for your generous
> donation. Sadly, though, I am unable to travel much
> nowadays.

Saul folded the letter away in his desk. He was relieved that the new chairman did not travel, since Vallow Hall must remain in its own isolation. But at least he had been able to give the man the impression that Saul Vallow of Vallow Hall was kindly and philanthropic. He wondered, vaguely, if the man was elderly, although an elderly person did not somehow match the reports of an enthusiastic educationist. Not that it mattered.

Maude thought of all the difficult and painful things she had had to do in her life, letting Lily talk to her about her fort-nightly visits to St Botolph's home to see her little boy were the most difficult and the most painful so far.

But Lily had no one else to whom she could talk, and Maude was grateful to Lily who had been kindness itself to her, so she always listened.

'Ever so bright they say he is, mum – even at this age. I talked to one of the ladies there about him. They think he can be moved into the school when he's old enough – they've got a classroom all set up these days. It's the new head one there that's done it all. My boy'll be taught reading and writing, and figures and everything.' A pause, then, 'Mum – am I a bad girl to feel he ain't really a part of me now?'

'You're not bad at all, Lily. It will be because he was taken away from you straight after he was born.'

'I'm making up for it, though,' said Lily, determinedly. 'I'll go to see him regular, and I'll talk to the teachers and everyone there about him.' She sent Maude a look from the corners of her eyes. 'Don't upset you, do it, mum, me talking about him? You not having . . . I mean your baby not . . .'

'It doesn't upset me now,' said Maude. 'Not in that way.'

'I wish I'd been there when the birth happened,' said Lily, her eyes wide and sad. 'But Miss Grout, she'd sent me out for towels and hot water. You was getting fuzzy like from the laudanum, so you wouldn't have been much aware of anything by then.' She paused, then said, in a rush, 'I didn't want you having that stuff, mum – I wanted you knowing what was happening, but Miss Grout insisted on giving it you.'

'Laudanum,' said Maude, remembering the strange dream-like state where the pain had receded, and the world had seemed to float out of her grasp.

'I keep thinking that if I'd been with you – still in the room – I might have thought of something to do that might've saved your baby. But I don't think there was anything that could've been done, not from what Miss Grout said.'

'I don't think there was, either. But I'd like you to tell me about your little boy,' said Maude, firmly. 'That way I'd feel I had a small share in him.' Then, as Lily still looked unhappy, she said, 'What's the matter? Is there something still wrong?'

'No, but . . . I don't know how you'll feel about it, mum.' Lily looked as worried as one with her cheerful disposition could look. She said, in a rush, 'I took that name you liked. I liked it, as well, see. I called him after that hymn they did at the school.'

'Crispin,' said Maude, very softly.
'Yes.'

Maude had expected Lily's visits to the St Botolph's institution to gradually cease, but rather surprisingly they did not.
Lily went off to Alnwick without fail every two weeks,
dressed in her Sunday best, catching a train from Vallow
Halt at midday, and getting on an omnibus at Alnwick to
reach the home itself.

She returned to Vallow by a six o'clock train, which Hilda
Grout said verged on taking advantage of the master's generosity, but which Mrs Cheesely did not mind, since it gave her
the entire afternoon to put her feet up and read one of the
gossipy magazines to which she subscribed. Anyway, the master
did not dine until eight.

Maude was glad that Saul was allowing Lily to visit St
Botolph's, even though she knew it was one of his ways of
ensuring Lily's loyalty. She thought Lily was feeling guilty at
having had the child at all – that strict, religious father who
played hymns every Sunday and thought music was the instrument of the Devil – and that she was trying to atone by her
visits.

What did surprise her, though, was that she found herself
looking forward to the visits herself. Lily always came running
up to the attics when she returned from Alnwick, full of her
afternoon's exploits. Maude liked hearing about it all – she
was glad to hear that the home was friendly and clean, and
that little Crispin was growing up to be sharp and bright.
'Although a bit naughty at times, so they say,' added Lily,
with a grin. 'Mr Mischief, that's what he is.'

Maude could share Lily's delight when, later on, Crispin
was given a place in St Botolph's small school, and when, at
Christmas the following year, he was chosen to be one of the
shepherds in the Nativity play.

'Although I don't know how he'll behave on the afternoon,
mum, for he's likely to play some trick on the others, and it
ain't my day to go to Alnwick so I won't know. They'll tell
me all about it next time, though. Got really friendly with a
couple of those teachers, I have. Nothing wrong, though –

wouldn't want you to think that. Learned my lesson with the poulterer's boy. But they let me help with the work while I'm there – only bits of cleaning, it is, and tidying up, but . . .'

'But it makes you feel part of Crispin's life,' said Maude.

'Thought you'd understand,' said Lily, pleased. 'One of the teachers says how Crispin might be given what they call a scholarship, and it'd mean going to a proper school with the scholarship paying for it. Somewhere like the one we got here.'

'Chauntry?'

'Yes. Somewhere like that.'

It was after the Christmas of the Nativity play – halfway through a snowy January – that Lily brought more news. She sat down facing Maude's chair – they had long since got past the servant-standing, mistress-seated arrangement – and said she had something to show her.

'Something about Crispin?'

'It's because of the one they call the governor at Botolph's, mum. A real gentleman he is, but he don't walk very well – he ain't in a wheelchair, but he has to use a stick and he only moves about very slow. I only seen him once or twice, but he smiled at me once, and said good afternoon. Well, he got someone to take photographs of the Christmas play. All the children on the stage, and pictures showing the crib and the manger and all. It weren't somebody from a shop as took the photographs, it was someone the governor knew who likes taking photographs.'

Maude felt as if a hand had suddenly closed around her heart. She said, 'Lily – who was it who took the photographs?'

'Nobody said. But quite a lot was took, and I asked to have one, and – well, mum, I brought it for you to see. It's of the children who were in the play, and Crispin is in it. I thought I'd like you to see him.'

Maude said, 'Of course I'd like to see him.'

'But it give me a bit of a start,' said Lily. 'Seeing him on that photo. He looks different somehow. Made me feel a bit odd seeing him like that.'

She brought out the photograph, which was wrapped in

paper to protect it, and placed it on the small table in front of
Maude's chair. It was late afternoon, and the oil lamps had
been lit. The glow fell across the table's surface and across
the photograph.

Maude sat very still. The small room seemed to be closing
around her – she thought if she had not been sitting down she
would have fallen. It did not need Lily's voice saying that
Crispin was at the centre of the little cluster of children on
the left-hand side; to explain that he had lost the shepherd's
head covering and no one had been able to find it, which was
why he was bareheaded.

'And can you see why I never felt like he's mine? Not like
me at all, is he?'

The boy was looking straight into the photographer's
camera. His eyes were dark and there was somehow a dreamy
look to them. The word that leapt to Maude's mind was
slumbrous. His hair was dark, as well, slightly rumpled, and
it would probably be glossy under a light. It would feel silky
if you touched it . . . The lines of his face, even in the black
and white of the photograph, were clear and definite. Rather
wide cheekbones, and quite full lips, and a jaw that was a
little too heavy for conventional good looks.

She could not take her eyes from him. She had never seen
him before, but she knew his features at once. These were the
features, in childish mode, of the man who had smiled at her
at a dinner table, who had given her champagne, who had lain
with her in a bed . . .

The boy in the photograph was not Lily's son. It was Maude's
son, conceived with the man she had known as Eddy. Taken
away while she was barely conscious from the laudanum.
Placed in St Botolph's as Lily's child while Maude herself
was told her baby had died.

Did that mean Lily's child had died? That Saul and Cousin
Hilda had switched the babies? Maude's mind was spinning
with horror, but also with hope. Surely it would have been too
outrageous, too bizarre, too cruel an act, even for those two.
But she looked at the photograph again, and she knew it was
what had happened.

She could not let anyone know, though – certainly not Lily.

But as she tried to think what to say, Lily said suddenly, 'He ain't mine, is he?'

'Lily, just because he doesn't look like you—'

''Tisn't that,' Lily put in. 'I dunno how to put it, mum, but it's – it's something you know that don't have anything to do with looks or hair or a voice. I think I've known it for a long time now. It's . . .'

'Something at a deeper level than his appearance?' said Maude, still not knowing how far she dared go.

'Yes.' Lily stared at the photograph. 'Know what I think? I think it was your little boy they took to Botolph's that night. They didn't want you to keep him – couldn't keep a child up here, could you? Soon as he was old enough, it'd have got out that you'd been shut away up here. So what I think, is that it was my boy that died. I said he was what we call pingling, didn't I?'

'Oh, Lily . . .'

'Don't matter, not that much. I got a share in this one, haven't I? Crispin. I'm glad I called him that – that name you liked.'

'So am I.'

'And, see, I can keep going to visit him, and telling you about him. That way you'll know a bit about him, and one day . . . Well, things got an odd way of working out sometimes.'

Maude could not speak. She was aware that Lily had taken her hand – Saul and Cousin Hilda would be appalled at such behaviour from a servant, but Maude did not care. Tears were streaming down her cheeks, but she did not care about that, either, because her mind was alight and alive with the knowledge that her boy had not died. He was alive – he was learning and seemingly proving to be clever – occasionally he was naughty. He was at St Botolph's Orphanage and, if Lily had the facts correctly, he might be going to Chauntry School.

Despite the confines of the attic – despite the knowledge that she had committed a murder and she might never be able to go out into the world again – Maude was aware of hope unfolding within her mind. *One day I might meet you*, she said to the small figure looking out of the photograph.

It was something to live for. Something to hope for. It made for patches of light in the dark confines of the attic rooms. Maude was able to think: *One day . . . One day I will be away from these rooms . . . One day I will meet Crispin . . .*

She refused to let herself think it was a daydream, a castle in the air. She held on to the belief that Lily had been right to say things had an odd way of working out. She had no idea how that could happen, though.

And then, years later, a completely strange young man came up the attic stairs, unlocked the door, and came into Maude's room.

TWENTY-FIVE

Jack would always remember how, after he had led her out of the attic rooms, Maude entered the big drawing-room uncertainly, holding on to his hand. He would always remember how warily she looked round, almost as if she was not sure whether she had the right to be in the room at all. She walked around for a few moments, touching the edges of furniture and looking at the view from the window, then a woman who was clearly a servant came almost running in, beaming. She seized Maude's arm, and led her to one of the chairs nearest the fire.

'You're back where you belong, mum,' she said. 'An' I don't apologize for saying it. Now then, we don't know where the master is, but that Miss Grout has up and gone, Mrs Cheesely and me do know that, for we saw her go.'

'Lily, where did she go?'

'No idea, but she put her things in a suitcase, and walked down to the village not an hour since, and to my mind folks with suitcases only go to one place.'

'The railway station?' said Jack.

'Yes, sir. And good riddance to bad rubbish, not that it's for me to say that.' Lily cast an approving eye over Jack and, receiving a nod from Maude, she went out.

'Lily,' said Maude to Jack, by way of explanation. 'Without her I'm not sure if I would have survived all these years.' She leaned back in the chair, then, as if trying out words that were unfamiliar, she said, 'Will you have a cup of tea? I can ask Lily to bring it.' She sat up straighter, and said, with a kind of realization, 'Yes – I can ask her to do that.' But then, as he glanced at the decanters on a sideboard, she smiled. 'Would you rather have a glass of brandy? Please pour whatever you want.'

'And for you, as well? Because I think you've been enduring a much longer ordeal than I have.'

She said, 'I haven't drunk anything stronger than tea or coffee for fifteen years. I should love a glass of brandy.'

As they drank the brandy, Jack told her as carefully as he could all that had happened, not wanting to distress her, but aware it would all come out anyway.

'There will have to be an inquest on Saul,' he said finally. 'Presumably on the woman whose body I found, as well. I hope it's been easier for you to hear the story like this from me, rather than at a public hearing.'

'You've been very considerate,' she said. 'I'm very grateful. I knew a few of those details, but only a very few.' She frowned. 'Have I understood what happened? Saul saw the smoke from Bastle House and he thought a fire had started? He thought you were still alive – that you had got out – that you would tell people what he had done?'

'You've understood exactly,' said Jack. 'And even if I hadn't survived, the smoke would soon have attracted attention. People would have found two bodies in the cellar, and they would have started asking questions. Saul couldn't risk that. He wanted that woman's body – mine too, of course – to remain undiscovered down in that cellar.'

'I'm glad you haven't got his death on your conscience,' said Maude. 'That he fell into the cellar accidentally. But I'm not sorry he's dead. Is that wicked of me?'

'No,' said Jack quickly. Then he paused, unsure how far to take this, then said, 'I'm not sorry either. He killed my father fifteen years ago.'

'Aiden.'

'Yes. I saw him do it,' said Jack, and, as she looked at him, he said, 'I pushed it out of my mind for years – I think I couldn't bear to remember it or acknowledge it. But today I did. And you know, Maude, even if I hadn't realized what Saul did all those years ago, he said something while we were in Bastle House that . . .'

'Yes? Tell me what he said.' She leaned forward, her eyes fixed on him. 'Please. I must know everything.'

'It was a kind of triumphant whisper,' said Jack, hearing again Saul Vallow's voice as he lay in the darkness of the bastle. 'I was down there in the cellar, and he was leaning over, staring down at me. It was almost as if something was speaking through him – as if he had no control over the words. He said that he had had to kill me – that he couldn't risk me prying – finding out about what he called "the meddlesome bitch".'

'Agnes,' said Maude, almost in a whisper.

'He didn't name her, but he said, "The meddlesome bitch I killed to shut her up. She's down there with you – where no one will find either of you. You're both down there in the dark for ever."'

'Oh!' she said, in a voice of such shock that Jack reached for her hand, afraid she might be about to faint. But she asked, 'That's what he said? That he had killed the meddlesome bitch to shut her up?'

'He did.'

Half to herself, as if staring at some inner image, she said, 'Then I was right – I didn't kill Agnes – I wasn't mad. I haven't been mad at all. And all these years . . .' She sat in silence for a few moments.

At last, Jack said, 'There's a great deal for you to take in. Including the fact that you're out of those loathsome attics and there aren't any locked doors.'

'I always knew that one day something would happen,' she said. 'I had to believe it would. I didn't know it would happen like this, though. I didn't allow for you, Mr Fitzglen.'

'Maude,' said Jack, 'in the past hour I've addressed you by your first name at least twice, which certainly isn't correct etiquette. But I feel as if I've lived alongside you and certain parts of your past for the last three weeks. And all that seems to make a nonsense of etiquette, so if you could manage to call me Jack . . .?'

'Someone said something like that to me – oh, fifteen years ago,' she said. 'About sharing secrets sweeping etiquette aside. I've never forgotten it.'

'Was it Declan Kendal who said it?' asked Jack, aware that he was feeling his way along another person's memories.

'It was a man called Connor O'Kane, and . . . That name means something to you, doesn't it?'

'Yes. I knew Connor O'Kane when I was a child,' said Jack,

sipping his brandy. 'My father occasionally worked with him. But, Maude, I'm sorry to say this, especially on top of Saul's death, and even more so if you knew O'Kane well, but – I'm afraid he's dead, too. He died in a fire at my family's theatre fifteen years ago.'

Maude said at once, 'But he didn't. I've only ever known there was some kind of accident, and that it took a long time for him to recover – although I don't think he ever did, not completely. I didn't know it was the result of the fire, though, but I do know he was able to make a new life.'

Jack sat back in his chair, staring at her. 'Maude, I can't tell you how glad I am to hear that,' he said. 'I never knew what happened to him – I was very young at the time of the fire, and afterwards my family concentrated on rebuilding our lives. Restoring the Amaranth, regaining their place in the theatre world – looking ahead rather than back. But I remember Connor. He was a musician. Gifted, and quite distinguished, I think. And I certainly remember that he was passionate about his music.'

'He still is. He took a post on the governing board at a children's home just outside Alnwick. He set up scholarships for the pupils – campaigned for funding, and persuaded various government departments and arts authorities to provide money . . .'

She paused, and Jack said, 'Maude, I don't know all of your story – although I hope I can know it in time. But I know a little, and I know you've been kept away from the world for many years. That being so, how do you know all that about Connor O'Kane?'

'Lily – you met her just now – used to visit the children's home in Alnwick,' said Maude. 'She . . . there was a boy she had a great interest in. He was awarded one of the scholarships, and she managed to keep in touch with him when he went to Chauntry. A number of the scholarships Mr O'Kane set up were in conjunction with Chauntry School. The precentor there – Dr Kendal – is Connor O'Kane's cousin.'

'I didn't know that, either. But it's all falling into place,' said Jack, thoughtfully. 'Except for one thing.'

'Yes?'

'The chalice. The prince gave you the Talisman Chalice, didn't he?'

She looked at him, then said, 'Yes.'

'What happened to it?'

Maude hesitated, then said, 'After I brought it back here, I began to have nightmares about it. I felt as if a darkness clung to it. I know that sounds strange . . .'

'When I tell you its history it won't sound strange to you at all,' said Jack.

'I took it to Bastle House,' she said. 'It was the only place I could think of to keep it safe.' She glanced at him. 'Bastle is my house. It was given to me many years ago.'

'By the prince?'

'Yes. And Aiden's name was on the Deeds. As a witness to the . . . transfer of ownership to me.'

Jack had the sensation of a final piece falling into place in a puzzle. He said, 'I didn't know that. But that's why you wrote to him, wasn't it? Warning him never to come to Vallow?'

'I couldn't risk Saul finding out about Eddy – about the house. I couldn't risk anyone involved in any of it coming here, and the truth becoming known. I left the chalice on a big oak dresser just inside Bastle House. Where it would catch sunlight each day.'

'I saw the dresser, but the chalice wasn't there,' said Jack. He thought for a moment, then said, 'You'd have had keys to the house, of course? And Saul must have taken them. He couldn't have got in otherwise. And if he saw the chalice—'

'He'd have taken it,' she said at once. 'He'd have seen it as valuable. He was acquisitive.'

She's trying not to say he was mean, thought Jack. *Even though he was a murderer – and even though he kept her locked away all those years she's trying not to speak against him.*

He said, 'If Saul brought the chalice here, where would he have hidden it?'

'I don't know. But we can search.' She stood up. 'Will you help me to look for it?'

'Oh, yes,' said Jack.

*   *   *

Seated at a trestle table on the bare stage of the Amaranth
Theatre three days later, Jack looked round his family, and
said, 'So there you have it. The various thefts of the chalice
– some given provenance by the Chauntry manuscript, others
by the scrap of the old song Gus found . . .' He sketched a
mock salute to Gus who was sitting at one end of the table,
listening. 'Maude Vallow being pulled into the story after
she met the Duke of Clarence,' said Jack, 'and my father's
involvement and why Maude sent that warning to him. It all
ties up.'

Rudraige said, 'It's an extraordinary tale, Jack.'

'Truly a "tale to harrow up the soul",' murmured Byron.

'You can certainly consider me harrowed,' said Daphnis.
'Cecily, if you must have the vapours—'

'I'm not having the vapours, Daphnis. Nobody's had vapours
since Victoria was on the throne.'

'But the chalice?' said Ambrose. 'You're stretching out the
suspense, Jack. Did you find it?'

'I did,' said Jack softly. 'Maude and I searched the Hall.
Saul had stowed it in a cupboard in his study – pushed at the
back of a cupboard behind some old books.'

'Where is it now?'

'Maude didn't want it in the house – I can't say I blame
her. I took it to the one person in Vallow I knew I could trust.'

'Dr Kendal?'

'Who else?'

'But it still belongs to Maude Vallow,' said Byron. 'It was
given to her, and it's for her to say what happens to it.'

'Does she want it, though?'

'No,' said Jack. 'She's asked me to find a . . . a diplomatic
way of returning it to – well, to its rightful owners.'

'Along with the luck,' murmured Byron.

'And,' said Jack, 'although we've agreed we can't stage the
piece we originally planned, I don't see why we can't openly
give the chalice back to the royal family.'

'Openly? You don't mean telling them about Maude, and
Connor O'Kane, and how the prince gave Maude the chalice?'

'No, of course not. I thought we could use our original idea
about Daphnis's anonymous admirer,' said Jack.

There was a short silence while they considered this, then Ambrose said, 'I believe we could. How would we actually reach the royal family, though? You can't just write a note to the King and drop it in a post box.'

'Connor O'Kane might know one or two useful names,' suggested Rudraige.

Cecily said, slowly, 'Could we perhaps . . .? No, that's a bad idea.'

'Tell it anyway.' Jack was pleased to hear Cecily offering a suggestion.

Cecily said, 'I wondered about the school – Chauntry. If the chalice is there, could there be a reason for the King to visit the school? Something to do with the endowments, perhaps? We could hand over the chalice during his visit – just a small ceremony, quite private, although we'd include Dr Kendal, of course – oh, and Mr O'Kane if he's able to travel. Especially if he manages to put us in touch with the right person at the Palace.'

'I'd like to see O'Kane again,' said Rudraige, and Daphnis nodded her agreement.

'I think it's a very good idea,' she said.

'I do, too,' said Jack. 'Thank you, Cecily.'

'I think it would be nice if it could happen at that school,' said Cecily, encouraged at these positive reactions. 'What with Godfric's manuscript being kept there.'

'Maude could be part of it, too,' said Jack, thoughtfully. 'I think she ought to be, and it could be made to seem perfectly natural – a local lady with an interest in the school.'

'And it could be given out that the royal party stopped at Vallow overnight as part of an existing schedule,' said Byron. 'Are they likely to be going to Balmoral, does anyone know? Is it the shooting season?'

Rudraige murmured vaguely about the Glorious Twelfth, which Daphnis said was in August. 'But it goes on for – well, about three or four months, so it might fit.'

Jack looked across at Byron. 'And Daphnis's anonymous admirer?' he said.

Byron said, elaborately casually, 'Well, I did happen to jot down a few notes.'

'Then let's hear them,' said Rudraige, banging the table enthusiastically. 'Pronounce, dear boy, pronounce.'

Byron produced a sheaf of notes, and pronounced.

'"My very dear Daphnis, I venture to hope you still remember me, and that our summer of madness has remained a cherished memory for you all these years – as it has for me . . ."'

'Why summer?' demanded Daphnis. 'I could as well have had a romance in winter or spring.'

'Summer is poetic,' said Byron, firmly.

'"And it is with that in mind, dear Daphnis, that I send you something I acquired many years ago – an acquisition that you, my dearest love, inspired. You will remember, I hope, the night of the Midsummer Ball? It was after we parted that night that I conceived the idea of possessing myself of something unique and precious that I might one day bestow on you. I must not write how I did so, but I will say that while my actions were reprehensible, my intentions were of the purest.

'"I never had the courage to make the gift, but all these years later I find I have the courage now – for I am about to embark on a great and perilous journey. I cannot bring myself to write more than that. It would, though, make me very happy if you would accept what I took in your name all those years ago, and allow me to think that you will treasure it as a symbol of one who loved you well if not perhaps wisely."'

'I wondered,' said Byron, looking up, 'whether to make it an actual deathbed legacy, but I didn't want it to be too doom-filled.'

'No, don't let's have a deathbed,' said Daphnis. 'I like the "great and perilous journey" touch. It's nicely vague and mysterious. It might be interpreted as a deathbed legacy, of course, but it might as easily mean some dangerous expedition – the Amazon jungle or the remote Tibet mountains, or—'

'How far back is this mad summer?' demanded Rudraige. 'Because if this wild interlude is from your giddy youth, Daphnis, the gentleman would be a bit advanced in years by now to be romping off to the jungle or climbing mountains.'

'I think he may have been a little younger than me,' said Daphnis, in a dignified tone. 'We would not have let that matter, of course.'

'Why didn't you marry?' Cecily wanted to know.

'He was pledged to another,' said Daphnis, very grandly.

'Or he could have taken a vow to – to give his life to God, or to his country, or mission work in Africa,' said Byron.

'Let's leave vows out of it,' suggested Jack. 'We've got enough of those with Godfric. But I like the perilous journey touch. I like the bit about his actions being reprehensible, but his intentions pure, too.'

'Hints at a filch, without actually saying so,' nodded Rudraige.

'How will he have signed it?' Ambrose asked.

'I thought just his initials,' said Byron. 'He didn't dare put his name to it, you see, not even after so many years.'

'And I swore never to disclose his name,' said Daphnis.

Ambrose said, thoughtfully, 'You do realize that if the King reads this letter – which is what I suppose you intend – he might link the whole thing to the Duke of Clarence?'

'Would that matter? The royal family could have suspected Eddy of filching the chalice at the time anyway. They wouldn't have let any such detail get out, of course – they're good at keeping secrets.'

'Centuries of practice,' murmured Byron. 'And if they did know, I think they'd have let the general rumours and speculation about a theft stand. They'd probably have welcomed them, in fact, so as not to blacken Eddy's reputation.'

'The rumours certainly didn't leave much doubt about it being an outright theft,' said Rudraige. 'Although I don't recall any mention of Prince Eddy ever being suspected. Those verses Gus found – there was nothing in them about him.'

'But there was,' said a voice from the shadows at the back of the auditorium. A slender figure walked down the wide aisle between the stalls seats, unhurried and with complete self-possession.

Jack said, very softly, 'Viola Gilfillan.'

'I suppose,' said Miss Gilfillan, standing just below the stage and looking at them, 'that I can come up there, can I? Ah,

thank you.' This was to Ambrose, who had got up to help her
mount the steps which Gus had placed against the apron.

Once on the stage, she turned to survey the auditorium.

'I expect this is an historic moment, isn't it?' she said. 'A
Gilfillan on the stage of the Amaranth.'

'What do you want?' said Jack, in what was very nearly a
growl.

Ambrose, who would probably be polite on his way to his
own execution, indicated to her to sit down.

'It's only one of the carpenter's chairs, but perfectly
serviceable.'

The chair she took was directly beneath a flaring gas jet; it
lit her hair to a copper glow. Jack thought crossly that she
would deliberately have chosen it for that reason.

'How did you get in?' demanded Rudraige. 'Not that we
aren't always pleased to welcome a lady, but . . .'

'I walked through the stage door and along the corridors.
No one challenged me.'

She looked round the table, as if waiting for more
questions.

Jack said, 'How do you know about the song – the "Lament"
– and the chalice?'

'Don't most people know about the chalice in a general
way?' said Viola. 'My family certainly do. As for the song
– the Gilfillans have known about that for a great many years.'

'How?'

'Because,' said Viola, 'it was my Uncle Furnival who
composed it and who sang it in that cellar club.'

'Good God,' said Rudraige, staring at her, and Gus
murmured, '"A gentleman of robust manner and jovial countenance". That was how that old magazine described him,' he
said.

'It's a good description,' nodded Rudraige. 'Furnival to the
life.' He looked at Viola. 'I knew him in his youth.'

'So I believe.'

'He was a real old rogue, but such good company,' said
Rudraige, reminiscing. 'He used to drink with the King – when
he was Prince of Wales, that was. His Majesty liked the
company of actors – well, actresses too, of course.'

'I believe Furnival used to tell some marvellous stories about those years,' said Viola. 'Probably most of them actionable, of course.'

'What happened to him?' asked Byron.

'I'm afraid he got a bit too fond of a drink, and fell by the wayside.'

'Into cellar clubs and taverns,' said Rudraige, nodding. 'I heard about that. I was very sorry. He was an accomplished player, you know.'

'Thank you,' said Viola. 'I never saw him perform, but there are some good memories of him in my family, and I'm glad you remember him.' She paused, and then said, 'I've been trying to find the song he wrote for a long time – that was why I was in Todworthy Inkling's shop that day. But Gus got there before me.' She gave a sudden street-urchin grin to Gus. 'Only you didn't find the entire song, Gus. You didn't find the last two lines.'

'How do you know?' demanded Jack.

'The final lines were never allowed into print after that performance my uncle gave at that old cellar club,' said Viola. 'No one ever saw or heard them again.'

'Then how do you know they even exist?'

'Because I've got them,' said Viola.

TWENTY-SIX

A s Viola handed Jack a single sheet of paper with two lines written on it in a slanting hand, an immense silence seemed to descend on the stage, and the shadows at the back of the auditorium seemed almost to uncoil and steal forward to listen.

Jack became aware that Gus had reached across the table and placed in front of him the eight lines found in Tod Inkling's shop. As he did so, Viola said, 'I think you take centre stage for this, Jack.'

Their eyes met, and she said softly, 'Read it to us. The whole thing. Put the two parts of the song together.'

Jack hesitated, then nodded, and began to read.

> Fortune's gone a-begging, and the luck's gone out
> the door
> And the fences are a-cheering and the King ain't
> safe no more
> For rum-dubbers picked the locks when no one
> was around
> And they'll all be at the Tuck-up Fair/If the
> Talisman don't return.

He paused, glanced at Viola, then went on.

> For Yorkist Dick, the first of thieves, did die a
> dungeon death;
> And after that, in Tower depths, two boys gasped
> final breaths.

Jack paused, and Viola said, 'Yorkist Dick? Oh, wait – Richard Plantagenet. It must be. The whole legend dates to the fourteen hundreds, doesn't it? And the two boys are the Princes in the Tower – yes?'

'Yes.' Jack supposed he had always known she would possess this quick instinctive comprehension.

> A concubine then stole the Luck, but met deserv'd
> fate.
> For Coppernose took grim revenge, and
> summoned up the blade.

'That meaning does elude me,' said Viola, after a moment.

'Coppernose was Henry VIII,' said Byron. 'And the concubine was Anne Boleyn.'

'Oh. Yes, of course.'

Then Rudraige said, 'The final two lines, Jack?' and Jack picked up the second sheet of paper.

> But legends never wholly die and Crowns still slip
> away.
> Cleveland Clarence stole the Luck and died before
> his day.

'*Cleveland* Clarence?' said Byron. 'Presumably that means the Duke of Clarence – Prince Eddy. But I don't understand the Cleveland reference.'

'Nor do I. But if it's implying Eddy stole it, I think it's stretching the truth,' said Ambrose. 'His family owned it.'

'Eddy died young, though,' said Daphnis. 'That part's right.'

'Yes, but it was a natural death. Pneumonia. He wasn't – what were the words, Byron?'

'Dragged into a darkness from which he would never emerge.'

'Exactly.'

Rudraige frowned, then said, slowly, 'But you know, there were one or two scandals about Eddy.' He glanced at the three ladies, then said, 'There was a certain house he was said to frequent – and that house was in Cleveland Street. A house of – hum – ill repute.'

'Rudraige, if you mean a brothel, for goodness' sake say so. We aren't going to swoon like Victorian schoolgirls.'

'All I know,' said Rudraige, 'and all I suspect most people

know, is the gossip that circulated at the time. Very spiteful, it was. The Cleveland Street house had a very colourful reputation. But enough said. And if there was anything to cover up about the prince, it was covered up very thoroughly. He was heir to the throne, after all.'

'And the last two lines of that song were covered up as well,' said Jack thoughtfully.

'Yes. I wonder, Miss Gilfillan, if it was the "Lament" that started your Uncle Furnival's descent,' said Rudraige, thoughtfully.

'Almost certainly, I'd imagine. You don't offend royalty and emerge unscathed.'

'It was very sad for him if so,' put in Cecily. 'I am sorry, Viola.'

'Angels and ministers of grace defend me – Cecily, are you offering sympathy to a Gilfillan?'

'Well, if she is, I accept it in the spirit it's offered,' said Viola, promptly.

'Personally,' said Rudraige, 'I wouldn't like to go bail that a few of the stories about Prince Eddy won't re-surface here and there in the years ahead.'

'Sadly, people love a scandal,' agreed Daphnis. 'And the more unsavoury the better.'

'So I think that even if the darkness of the legend didn't drag him down, it certainly brushed him,' said Rudraige. 'Not that I believe in the legend, of course.'

'Of course not.'

When the discussion finally ended, Jack, seeing the lateness of the hour, accompanied Viola out to Sloat Alley and walked with her towards the main thoroughfare to hail a cab for her.

'Were you surprised to see me tonight?' she said. 'Or did you think it might be a case of "I'll follow thee my lord throughout the world—"?'

'So that all my fortunes at your feet I can lay? It's not very likely I'd do that. I haven't got a fortune of any kind to lay anywhere,' said Jack tersely.

'You know,' she said, unexpectedly, 'you really should be my Romeo one day. Wouldn't we light a spark?' She looked up at him. It was ridiculous to think that in the faint spill of light from the streetlamps her eyes were lambent green like a cat's.

'It'd more likely be a damp squib.'

'And if we ever appeared on the same stage, our families would never have got over it, anyway.'

'I shouldn't think so.'

'But our families know a good deal about one another anyway,' said Viola, thoughtfully. 'They have done for two or three generations. All the secrets and the scandals. My aunts used to tell some very colourful tales about your Aunt Daphnis – and about Rudraige.'

To keep pace with this, Jack said, 'I heard a bit about your Uncle Furnival. Apparently he and Rudraige held bets involving opera dancers. Of course, I have no idea of what those bets might have involved,' he said, deadpan.

'Of course you haven't,' she said, and grinned at him. 'We do spring from colourful stock, don't we? I like having lively ancestors, though.'

'I do, too.'

There was a moment when he was aware of a sudden closeness – of sharing something with her that very few other people would be able to share or comprehend – but he pushed it away, and said, 'There's a cab – stay here – I'll flag it down.'

'Thank you,' she said, as the cab drew up. 'We're still sworn rivals, of course – even with the chalice and that old song.' A hand reached out to touch his cheek lightly.

'I'm not likely to forget it,' said Jack. He watched her get into the cab, putting up a hand in a farewell gesture as she did so.

Going back along Sloat Alley, he was very glad that when she had touched his cheek he had had no desire whatsoever to reach up to enclose her hand in his own.

Maude was trying not to be nervous about the evening ahead of her at Chauntry School, but she thought no one could be exactly calm at the prospect of meeting the King and Queen.

But Dr Kendal – Declan – would be there, and that was a very good thought indeed.

He had come to the Hall after Saul's funeral, and they had talked for a long time. He had listened, absorbed, in exactly the way Maude remembered, and he had looked at her and seemed to be deeply moved that she had returned to the world. Maude thought this was probably a melodramatic term to use, but she liked thinking of it in such a way.

The remarkable thing was that while they talked, she had not felt in the least awkward. She said, 'I heard the music you played all these years – the concerts and even just the rehearsals.'

'I used to hope you would. I didn't dare hope too much, though.'

'I always heard it,' said Maude. 'I tried to play some of it, as well.'

'I wish I'd known that.' He paused, then said, 'You're coming to this presentation evening, aren't you? It's supposed to be very informal – although I shouldn't think any event with the sovereign present is ever really informal. There'll be a brief concert – just a handful of some of our pupils. It's not exactly to disguise the real purpose of the evening, but it's meant to distract attention from it. It's meant to seem to be about the scholarships and St Botolph's work.'

'I'm looking forward to it,' said Maude.

'So am I.'

Lily helped Maude choose a gown for the Chauntry evening from the many that hung in her wardrobe, most of which she had never worn. They decided on a green velvet gown, Lily insisting that it did not look in the least old-fashioned.

'It could be a bit shorter on the hem, and narrower in the skirt,' she said. 'I can alter it for you, though. It'll be ever so smart.'

Maude knew she ought to wear mourning really. She had worn it for Saul's funeral and for about three weeks afterwards. She was not, however, going to be so false as to wear it for the customary twelve months.

Lily said, 'Mr Fitzglen's manservant brought along the notes about the evening, mum. Very splendid, it sounds – I've left them on the desk for you. We had a bit of a chat, him and

me. I gave him a cup of tea in the kitchen. I didn't think you'd
mind. Nice man, ain't he?'

'Lily, you don't change.'

'No fear of that,' said Lily, with a grin.

She helped Maude to get ready for the evening, as excited
as if she were going herself.

'You'll look as good as any of them,' she said. 'And better
than most. And the King's still got an eye for the ladies, so I
hear.'

Maude said, 'It's not the King I'm nervous of meeting, Lily.'

They looked at one another, then Lily said, 'I know it isn't.
But it'll be all right.'

Chauntry School, when Maude got there a little ahead of the
concert, was almost exactly as she had remembered it.

'Like coming home?' said Declan, taking her into the library.

'Yes. Oh, yes.' She looked round the library, aware that he
was watching her.

'Are the memories in here good ones?' he said. 'If they're
bad ones, we'll go straight into the concert hall.'

'They're good,' said Maude, at once, and smiled. 'They're
very good.'

'I'm glad. Come over to this window – you can just see the
old schoolhouse from here.' He drew back the edge of a curtain.
'It's on the edge of Chauntry's grounds – a lovely old place,
and we're restoring it. It hasn't been used for years, but it's
in surprisingly good condition.'

'It's nice,' said Maude, studying it.

'It'll be a nice place to live quite soon.' He let the curtain
fall back into place. 'Perhaps you could come over one day
and see what's being done.'

'I could, couldn't I?' Again came the realization that she
could go anywhere and do anything.

'We'll arrange a day,' he said, smiling at her.

She sat in the concert hall between Declan and Connor O'Kane.
It was very good indeed to see Connor again. Part of returning
to the world, Maude thought again.

Connor was thinner and somehow gentler than she remembered, and he walked with a stick. But his smile was just the same.

'It's quite an event for me to travel so far,' he said. 'So this is a very special night.'

Maude did not, of course, ask about his injuries, but he suddenly indicated the walking stick, and said, 'Wretched nuisance to have to use that. But I fell down a flight of stairs – treacherous things they were, and there was a fire raging through the building at the time, so everything was in confusion and panic. I lost a good friend that day, but I was lucky to survive. And time heals, even if bones don't, or don't heal completely. I'd have hated to miss all this. I'd have hated to miss meeting you again.' He paused and looked at her. 'You've had some bad years, too, haven't you?'

'Yes. But, as you said, time heals.'

'It will,' he said, gravely. 'It's a good maxim. Keep hold of it, Maude.'

Jack, seated in the front row, looked about him. A very small audience, but the people who mattered were all here. Byron and Rudraige and Daphnis. Ambrose and Cecily. Viola Gilfillan was sitting with Daphnis; she was wearing a sleek plain gown of dark blue silk, understated but probably extremely expensive. She caught Jack's eye, and for once her smile contained none of the usual slight mockery. She gave him a small nod, as if to say *isn't this marvellous?* Jack nodded in response, because there was no reason not to be friendly, and again came the sense of a sharing. *She understands how I feel*, he thought. He remembered that Chauntry, hospitable as ever, had arranged a buffet supper in the dining hall later. There was no reason why he could not take Viola in on his arm.

A little farther along, he could see Maude sitting between Declan Kendal and Connor O'Kane. On Jack's other side, Gus said softly, 'Which of them will she end up with, do you suppose, Mr Jack?'

Jack said, 'Don't you know?'

'I think so. Do you?'

'I think so, too,' he said, and smiled.

* * *

When the concert started, Maude sat very still, her eyes never leaving the performers on the small stage. It was a good concert, with polished performances and gifted young musicians. There was a really beautiful rendering of some Debussy. She liked Debussy.

As the applause died away, she was aware of Declan touching her arm, and asking if she would like to meet some of the pupils prior to the royal presentation.

'Perhaps the boy who played the Debussy piece?'

The boy who played the Debussy piece . . . The boy who had dark eyes and a mischievous smile . . .

Maude met Declan's steady look. 'I would like that,' she said.

'I thought so.'

The boy seemed to be expecting the introduction. He looked at Maude with curiosity, and then smiled, and it was the smile Maude had seen across a dinner table fifteen years earlier. She wanted to go on seeing it for ever. But it was vital to behave as if this was an ordinary meeting, so she put out her hand, and said, 'Good evening. I'm very glad to meet you, Crispin.' There was more delight in saying his name and taking his hand than she could have believed existed in the entire world.

He said. 'I'm glad, as well. Did you enjoy the concert?'

'Very much. Do you often play at Chauntry concerts?'

'Quite often. There's one next week – for half-term.' He considered her, then said, a bit hesitantly, 'Might you come to that?'

'I could. Would you like me to?'

'Yes,' he said, at once. 'Yes, I would like that very much.'

This is it, thought Jack, standing on the side of the platform, seeing the King, with Queen Alexandra at his side, ushered into place. Two discreet-looking aides were with them, and Declan Kendal stood on their left. *This is going to be the most memorable stage appearance I will ever make*, thought Jack.

He waited for Declan's signal, then, holding the chalice carefully, walked on to the stage. The applause was polite and muted, but Jack felt the emotion filling up the hall.

They had agreed there should be no speeches, and so, after a small bow, he said, 'It's my honour to return this to you, Your Majesty.'

'And my honour to accept it, Mr Fitzglen. An object with a remarkable history, or so I believe.'

'I believe so, Sire.'

Jack held the chalice up for a few seconds, wanting the audience to see it more clearly. For an incredible moment he thought it pulled slightly away from him, as if trying to reach up to the light from the stage lamps. He thought he had never been more aware of the chalice's history than in this moment – of the dark radiance that had beckoned to a Plantagenet King inside a long-ago monastery . . . That had accompanied two doomed boys to a grim prison fortress . . . That had taken a lady who had been loved by a Tudor monarch to the scaffold . . . And that, in living memory, had caused a girl who had been admired by a royal prince to be shut away in a dark attic for fifteen years . . .

Violence and murder and old tragedies, thought Jack. Then he placed the Plantagenet chalice in the hands of England's King, and as the King's hands closed around it, he stepped back.

AUTHOR'S NOTE

English history is threaded with legends, many of which have a pleasing touch of eeriness. There are spectral coaches that rattle across ancient courtyards to herald a death – ghostly music that issues from empty rooms – disgruntled apparitions demanding the righting of wrongs . . . And there are gifts allegedly bestowed by grateful monarchs – bowls or cups or religious vessels, beautiful and valuable, but carrying strange pledges or disquieting warnings.

For me, searching for a plot on which to base the exploits of the newly created Fitzglen family, one legend in particular stood out.

The Muncaster Luck.

The story goes that in the mid-1400s no less a person than Henry VI gave to a Cumbrian family a Venetian glass bowl, in gratitude to them for sheltering him after he lost his throne to Edward IV.

The family were the Penningtons of Muncaster Castle, and Henry's gift to Sir John Pennington carried a vow that the bowl held good fortune, and that as long as it was unbroken the Penningtons would prosper. That belief has survived from that century to this – and so, remarkably, has the bowl itself.

A fragment of an old verse apparently promises:

> It shall bless thy bed, it shall bless thy board,
> They shall prosper by this token,
> In Muncaster Castle good luck shall be
> Till the charmèd cup is broken.

To use the Muncaster legend in a novel – especially as the bowl can still be viewed in the castle – seemed fraught with potential problems. Historical facts often have an annoying way of tripping up fictional events. But there seemed no reason why a whole new legend could not be created – that of a bowl, or better still a chalice, in similar vein to the Muncaster bowl, but with a dark back story that would be all its own.

And so the Talisman Chalice came into being.

Rather than assign its origins to the hapless Henry VI, I arranged for it to make its first appearance in the company of Richard II, who already had a few robust tales in his armoury, and whose reputation could probably take one more. The chalice itself had collected a few robust tales of its own, as well – most notably a belief that anyone who possessed it 'wrongfully' would be dragged into a darkness 'from which he or she would never emerge'. A medieval way of warning enterprising thieves that if the chalice were to be stolen, a very bad fate would befall those who stole it.

I'm immensely grateful to Henry VI for giving the Pennington family the Muncaster bowl, and in the process providing me with the inspiration for *Chalice of Darkness*. And I'm delighted that the bowl itself is still at Muncaster Castle – still intact – and hopefully still containing the luck handed down by a long-ago King of England.

Sarah Rayne

Milton Keynes UK
Ingram Content Group UK Ltd.
UKHW011814200923
429068UK00006B/220